Praise for
THIS BURNING HARVEST

"Imagine an exciting history teacher who owns a special lantern that can light up, with vivid clarity and color, the most intense moments of the recent past. Imagine an adroit storyteller who can penetrate into the meaning of the most crucial scenes of Jewish sensibility and landscape. Imagine the storyteller's mastery of headlong narrative and the poignant look of a flower combined with the teacher's authority over real events and their shapers. All this is Gloria Goldreich."

—*Cynthia Ozick, author of*
LEVITATION: FIVE FICTIONS

"THIS BURNING HARVEST is a work of epic grandeur, ingeniously weaving high romance and historical detail into a narrative that throbs with passion and truth. It is the story of a family; it is the story of a people. It is a story laced with power and poetry, and humanity."

—*Francine Klagsbrun, author of*
VOICES OF WISDOM

Also by Gloria Goldreich

THIS BURNING HARVEST

GLORIA GOLDREICH

BERKLEY BOOKS, NEW YORK

For Ilse and Henry Weingartner

THIS BURNING HARVEST

A Berkley Book/published by·arrangement with the author

PRINTING HISTORY
Berkley edition/September 1983

ISBN: 0-425-06078-0

A BERKLEY BOOK ® TM 757,375

Berkley Books are published by The Berkley Publishing Group,
200 Madison Avenue, New York, New York 10016. The name
"BERKLEY" and the stylized "B" with design are trademarks
belonging to Berkley Publishing Corporation.

PRINTED IN THE UNITED STATES OF AMERICA

PART ONE

Achmed and Elana:
The Approaching Storm

1929–1931

Chapter 1

ELANA MAIMON SAT at her bedroom window wearing only a
sheer white chemise, beneath which her skin glowed like burnished amber. The untamed branch of a plum tree stretched
toward the sun-streaked pane, and two nightingales, perched
upon it, sang a mournful duet. She listened, half smiling, as
she spread a cream smelling of jasmine and lilac across her
shoulders and into the narrow cleft at her throat. Rhythmically,
her long fingers caressed thigh and arm, and she smoothed her
neck with a lingering stroke, as though bemused by its slender
curve, then rubbed the cream gently into the rose-gold nipples
of newly rounded breasts, pleased and surprised again at their
fullness, their tenderness. Abruptly she stood, shook her dark
hair loose about her shoulders, and hummed, moving her feet
in an intricate dance step. She bent and swayed and lifted her
arms above her head; she placed her hands on her hips and
whirled about in a brief and wild dervish. Her shadow drifted
across the whitewashed wall, and the startled birds rustled the
fragile silver-green leaves as they flew away.

"Elana!"

Small Balfouria's voice, vibrant with excitement, pierced
the melancholy silence of the summer morning. Elana did not
answer, although she watched from the window as her younger
sister dashed into the house. She fingered the blue satin ribbons
of her chemise and wondered if she could be seen at the window from the orchard. Could the young men her father hired to
help with the harvest catch glimpses of her brushing her hair
while they plucked the newly ripened fruit? Could Achmed
ibn-Saleem see her as he made his way from the Sadot Shalom

farmhouse back to his parents' homestead? When the gauzy white curtains were drawn, was her body visible in teasing silhouette?

"Elana! There's a letter for you. A letter!"

Elana shrugged. Whatever the letter was, it could not be important. It could not be from her brother Amos, because she had received a postcard from him only a week ago with a photograph of the Grand Canyon. "The American desert is as beautiful and mysterious as our Negev," Amos had written, and Elana had wondered why he did not return home if he missed Palestine so much. The letter was probably another missive from her Jerusalem cousin, Nadav Langerfeld, giving her a list of books to read. The thought of the closely written pages in Nadav's neat script bored Elana. Often, she left his letters sealed for days at a time.

Balfouria burst into the room, her plump pink face damp with perspiration and her dark cluster of curls moist and tangled. She held a long envelope in her outstretched hand.

"Why didn't you answer me?" she scolded with the petulant impatience of the petted and coddled younger sister. "You have a letter from Imma. From Switzerland."

"From Mazal? For me?"

Color flooded Elana's cheeks as she took the envelope from Balfouria and stared with pleasure at the pastel-colored postage stamps that danced across the envelope. Blue gentians sparkled on an alpine slope. The red and white *Croix de Suisse* was framed against a background of gold. So much prettier than the dull British stamps used in Mandate Palestine. A frowning Queen Victoria. A corpulent Edward.

"Open it. Open it now," Balfouria pleaded.

The family had received only one letter from Ezra and Mazal Maimon since they had sailed from Jaffa to attend the sixteenth Zionist Congress in Zurich, earlier in the summer. And that single letter had disappointed his daughters. Ezra had filled several pages with a discussion of the congress' agenda and a description of the various motions being considered. He himself was scheduled to address a plenary session on the formation of an official political unit. The Jewish Agency would, in effect, become a temporary government. Mazal, in turn, had filled her portion of the letter with instructions about the management of the household, the care of the children. Baby Rivka needed a medical checkup, and the twins, Nachum and Tamar, needed new sandals. ("She told me all that before she left," grumbled her sister-in-law, Chania Maimon, who had come to stay with the children during their parents' absence.) Mazal had worried, too, about Amnon running barefoot in the wheat-field and whether Balfouria was practicing the flute. And she had hoped that Elana was not working too hard and was not too lonely.

"But I *am* working too hard, and I *am* lonely," Elana had thought when she read her stepmother's words. Self-pity had engulfed her luxuriously, and her eyes had filled with tears. Chania had made no move to stop her when she ran to her room, where she wept with swift and violent passion at her window. Achmed had passed through the orchard just then, playing a reed pipe. Briefly, he had paused beneath her window and played a wistful shepherd's song. The airborne music had calmed her, and she had leaned her forehead against the cool glass until he walked slowly on, the music trailing behind him.

Somehow, Elana thought now, Mazal must have sensed her mood. This letter would contain words of comfort and ap-peasement, perhaps even a promise to take Elana to the next congress. There were those who said that Elana and Mazal were more like sisters than stepmother and stepdaughter. Al-ways, Mazal had been able to discern Elana's feelings, to guess her wishes, to resolve her uncertainties. And Elana, from the beginning, had loved her father's second wife, the young Yemenite woman whose gaiety had shattered the sorrowing silence of the Galilean farm house. Mazal had brought laughter and children into the empty rooms, filling them with excite-ment and color. Elana had been her constant companion as she awaited the birth of each child—first Balfouria and then dreamy-eyed Amnon, followed by the twins, Tamar and Nachum. The baby, Rivka, had been born that winter and named for Ezra's mother. The elderly mistress of the Rishon homestead had drifted into death only a few months before her namesake's birth. Her body had grown frailer and her voice fainter with each passing day until, at last, she lay still and

silent, her wasted face turned toward the orange groves where
the trees were in full blossom.

It was cruel to die during the season of blooming, Elana had
thought at her grandmother's funeral. She was conscious suddenly of her young breasts straining against her blouse, and she
turned her eyes away from the grave of her uncle, the golden-
haired doctor, Avremel Schoenbaum, who had died so young.
She shivered then with unarticulated fear. But Mazal, who
stood beside her, had taken her hand and pressed it against her
own life-filled abdomen. The child within her stirred, and
Elana felt the fetal movement and knew that her stepmother
was comforting her, reminding her of the miracle of birth even
as they stood on the sacred ground that belonged to the dead.

Now, too, Mazal's letter would comfort and soothe the loneliness of the long summer months of her absence. Carefully
Elana slit open the cream-colored envelope that bore the seal of
the Tolle Hotel in Zurich, and removed the closely written
pages it contained. Her full lips curved into a smile, and a
laugh burgeoned at the back of her throat. The letter slipped to
the floor, and Elana grasped Balfouria's hands and whirled
about the bedroom with her.

"Oh, Balfouria, it's wonderful! You'll never guess what
Imma wants me to do. You'll never guess."

"She wants you to go to them in Switzerland and to bring
me, too," Balfouria shouted.

"Oh no. Not quite that wonderful. But she wants me to go
to Hebron."

"To Hebron?" Balfouria's voice dropped in disappointment, and she sat down forlornly on the bed. She had been to
Hebron, that sleepy city on the West Bank where Mazal often
journeyed to purchase hand-blown glassware from the skilled
artisans. Mazal traveled the length and breadth of Palestine,
searching out hand-crafted objects for her expanding enterprise, and often Balfouria and Elana accompanied her. But
Hebron was her least favorite place, Balfouria had decided on
their last visit. It was so dusty, closed in by the crouching dun-
colored hills of Judea. Balfouria was a child of the Galilee, and
she missed the verdant meadowlands, the green hillocks and
graceful slopes of the mountains.

"I don't want to go to Hebron," she said. "I hate Hebron."

"Well, you're not supposed to go. I'm going alone. I have to place orders for glassware and then make sure that they are properly shipped. Mazal writes that she sold everything she brought with her! A physicist named Albert Einstein bought those beautiful olive wood bookends, and Madame Léon Blum bought up all the Hebron glass. Now the American delegates, Mrs. Warburg and Mrs. Brandeis, want some, and I'm to order and arrange everything. Oh, Balfouria, I'm so excited."

"Where will you stay?"

"With my mother's family—the Langerfelds, in Jerusalem." Elana glanced guiltily at Nadav's letter. Oh well, she would read it before she saw him.

Now she danced about the room, plucking up items of clothing. She slipped on a bright pink blouse and a dark blue traveling skirt, fumbling with buttons and snaps. Barefoot still, she placed small piles of clothing in the purple, embroidered portmanteau her grandmother Rivka had brought from Russia. Minutes ago she had been oppressed by solitude, weighted down by an inexplicable melancholy. Now, suddenly, she was spurred by a sense of urgency, fired by pride that Mazal, her stepmother, thought her capable of so much responsibility. If she hurried, she could just catch the afternoon jitney that traveled the coastal road southward to Jerusalem.

"What will Aunt Chania say?" Balfouria asked. She was pouting still, but she moved about the room, helping her sister find her handkerchiefs and placing Elana's best shoes in the portmanteau.

"Oh, she won't mind if it's what Imma wants. And besides, a new Polish girl is coming this afternoon to help her."

"I hope she'll be nicer than the last one," Balfouria said.

Balfouria and Elana were secretly contemptuous of the Polish girls who arrived periodically to work at the Sadot Shalom farmhouse.

"They're so silly, these new immigrants," Elana had said once after a spat with one of them.

"I, too, was an immigrant," her father had replied gently. "And your mother, Nechama, was an immigrant. And so was Mazal. Immigration is the lifeblood of the country."

"But you were different," Elana had protested. "You were Zionists."

It was true that survival rather than ideology motivated the young women who were now sent to Palestine by their families in Warsaw and Vilna, Lublin and Oswiecim. Their families' small businesses had been nationalized by Grabski, the Polish finance minister, and the golden door to the United States had slammed shut with the passage of the restrictive McCarran immigration laws. They did not come to Palestine because they dreamed of a Jewish homeland but because it was the last refuge for those who sensed imminent danger. Many of the new arrivals thought of it as temporary haven until visas could be arranged for New York or London, Melbourne or Johannesburg. Dozens of Polish families lived in tents on the beaches of Tel Aviv and Jaffa. There was no housing and few jobs. The hard-pressed Labor Exchange was grateful that help was so often needed on the Jewish farm at Sadot Shalom, where young Mrs. Maimon seemed always to be having another baby or have need of a bright girl to help her with her handicraft projects.

Elana had never liked the Polish girls whose cheeks were daubed with rouge and whose eyes were wistful for the Saski Gardens of Warsaw, the perfumed darkness of the Lublin theater. And they, in turn, were bewildered by the Jewish farm in the Galilee. They walked awkwardly in their city pumps across the soft tumuli of newly plowed earth. They had never known anyone like Ezra Maimon, the tall, golden-skinned farmer who worked the fields all day and read French novels and volumes of political theory at night. Mazal, his tiny wife, so many years his junior ("his second wife," they whispered breathlessly and wondered what had happened to his first wife, stuck-up Elana's mother), mystified them—a joyous mother, a talented businesswoman, a skillful artist. They cast uneasy glances at tall, handsome Achmed, so gentle and well spoken, who often spent an evening with the family. He did not conform to their image of an Arab. But they all loved the five young children of the marriage, and they agreed that Elana Maimon was very beautiful.

They marveled at the fragrance of the plums and peaches, the apricots and lady apples, that weighted down the thick-branched trees. They discarded their pumps for work shoes and their georgette dresses for *rubashka*i and muslin skirts. Slowly, they learned Hebrew. Some of them rode through the fields during the season of the *revia*, the night grazing, and danced horas by firelight. But often, they wept softly into their pillows during the long, silent nights.

Elana was moved by the sounds of their sorrow. She understood loneliness and longing. She had never known her mother, tall, pale Nechama, who had died bringing her into life. Throughout Elana's childhood her father had been a soldier in distant lands, and she had lived on the fringes of her uncles' families, on Kibbutz Gan Noar. Her brother Amos had deserted her and had been in America for many years, ever since her father's marriage to Mazal. Sadness tinged their voices when they spoke of him. In mist-bound dreams Elana repeated endless farewells and searched through barren orchards for a vanished father, an absent brother, an unknown mother.

"Things will get better," she advised the Polish girls. Things had, after all, gotten better for her. Ezra had returned from the war and married Mazal. Now she had her stepmother for a friend and small brothers and sisters for company. Amos would return, and meanwhile Achmed spent time with her, giving her Arabic lessons, sharing the letters he received from Amos. She never felt alone when she was with Achmed.

"I must tell Achmed I'm going to Hebron," Elana said.

"You won't have time. You've just got a few minutes for Aunt Chania if you're going to catch the jitney. I'll find her for you." Balfouria dashed to the door.

"Balfouria. Wait." There was an unsettling tremor in Elana's voice, and her younger sister turned and looked at her.

Elana stood before the mirror. She had swept her long, dark hair upward into two braids that formed a gleaming silken coronet, and now she turned slowly, studying herself in the mirror, her lips curled into an odd smile, her eyes opened too wide.

"Balfouria—do you think I'm pretty?" Her voice was soft and fragile.

"Oh, Elana. You're not just pretty. You're beautiful."

The small girl rushed to her sister and clung to her, offering comfort and protection with the force and heat of her sturdy body because, quite suddenly, tall, exquisite Elana, who had been entrusted with an adult assignment, who would travel alone through the country, who comforted Balfouria in the night and knew how to fashion dolls from corn husks—wonderful, strong Elana had begun to cry. She wept silently, like a frightened child who cannot comprehend the source of a mysterious and nameless fear.

Chapter 2

ACHMED IBN-SALEEM removed his white keffiyah and felt the full impact of the summer heat. There was an almost corporeal heaviness to the sunlight, but he welcomed the golden weight that seared his body and sent rivulets of sweat down his limbs. The overwhelming heat meant that a *sharav* wind would blow within the next few days, breathing its way northward from the desert plain, and then the rains would come. Brief, fretful showers would tease the leaves into luminescent verdancy and dampen the newly dug earth of the irrigation ditches. There would be just enough moisture to be absorbed by the roots of the young plum trees and to guarantee the survival of the second planting of maize and alfalfa. Ezra Maimon had been dubious about the success of such a crop, but as always he had taken Achmed's advice.

"You, after all, are the graduate agronomist," he had said. "And God knows we will need as much fodder as we can store this winter." A frown had creased his forehead. He worried that perhaps he had moved too swiftly to replace the livestock lost during the war. Still, it was a risk he had to take, and he was a farmer whose livelihood depended on risk and gamble. The rains might come or they might not. Locusts might decimate the crop. The animals might fall victim to a parasite. The vagaries of nature were as unpredictable as the toss of the dice.

"We will manage," Achmed had assured him.

"But I will not be here to oversee the planting. Can you arrange for a leave from the agricultural station? It's a damn nuisance—holding the Zionist Congress in August, just when a farmer is busiest. Shows how much those Diaspora Jews with

11

all their statistics actually understand about the land they're
supposed to be reclaiming.''

"I will arrange to be here," Achmed said. "The second
planting is part of an experiment I am working on. It fits in
well with the work of the station.''

"Elana will be glad to have you here. It is lonely for her
with only the smaller children about. How are her Arabic
lessons progressing?''

"Well," Achmed replied, "she has a gift for the language.
Like Amos," he added and felt in his pocket for the bulk of the
long letter he had received from his friend that week. Amos
was en route to New York, where he would be a visiting
professor at Columbia University. Then he would return to
Palestine.

That would be good, Achmed thought. Too much time had
passed since Amos had left the country—seven long years
during which he had earned a doctoral degree with honors at
Oxford and published a volume on archaeology which had won
him an international reputation. But they had been lonely years
for Amos. His letters hinted of homesickness and longing. "I
think often of the skies of the Galilee," he wrote to Achmed.
"I miss the seasons of Sadot Shalom.''

The seven years had been busy ones for Sadot Shalom. Once
again the fields glowed golden with full-headed grain, and the
branches of the fruit trees drooped beneath their bright burdens
of silken plums and thin-skinned peaches that glowed like fairy
lights in the darkness. Rooms had been added to the small
house for the children born to Ezra Maimon's new wife. Their
laughter rilled through open windows. Bright woven fabrics
covered the floors and furniture, and dried meadow grasses and
lucent flowers filled the copper pots that Mazal Maimon collected on her many journeys through the countryside.

She was like a firefly, Ezra Maimon's tiny wife, Achmed
thought. She never stopped moving but flitted from project to
project, from child to child, settling down just long enough to
accomplish a prescribed task—to gather up a new load of
woven placemats to be shipped to Paris or Vienna—to dry a
child's tears—to shape Amnon's golden aureole of hair or to
dress Balfouria in a clever pinafore embroidered with the
Bukharian designs that would be snapped up by tourists in the

shops of Tel Aviv and Jerusalem. Even in the last stages of her pregnancies, her fingers deftly handled gleaming needles, laden paintbrushes. Her babies were born swiftly, even the twins, as though they knew that their busy mother did not have the time to spare for a long labor and recovery.

But Mazal did not have the time or the patience for growing things. It was Elana who tended the kitchen garden which her mother, Nechama, had cultivated, and Elana who patiently pruned the flowering almond trees and arranged the cyclamen and mint in orderly beds. Occasionally Achmed would see her sitting on the terrace in the same chair in which pale Nechama had sat as she watched the boys he and Amos had been play the games of their childhood. They had been David and Jonathan, fierce Bedouin warriors, Jacob and Esau.

"I had hoped to see Amos at the congress," Ezra had said, "but he arranged to leave Europe just as we are scheduled to arrive. A startling coincidence. But perhaps it's just as well." His voice, as always, was toneless when he spoke of Amos, as though his oldest son was a drifting shadow that darkened his bright new life.

"Perhaps he could not arrange it otherwise." Achmed had been cautious. He loved his childhood friend but felt loyal to Ezra Maimon. He had never understood the terrible chasm of silence and anger that had stretched between Amos and Ezra since Mazal had come into their lives, but he knew that he could not bridge it. Deftly, he changed the subject.

"I will remain at Sadot Shalom as long as necessary. I must attend a meeting in Jerusalem late in August, but by that time the grain will be sown and the orchard harvest completed."

"I depend on you," Ezra had said. His large hand briefly grasped the young Arab's shoulder, and then his arms came around Achmed's back and they embraced in brief and open affection.

"You are like a son to me," Ezra said.

"I honor and love you as I honor and love my father."

Days later, Ezra and Mazal had left for Zurich, and the summer had passed as predicted. The grain crops had been duly sown and the young fruit trees had been planted on terraced slopes. The cattle grew fat on sweet dried grass. A herd of goats frolicked in the clover, teasing stolid, indifferent sheep that wove their way lazily through patches of sunlight.

Achmed turned his gaze to the huge corral where a fierce bull chomped clusters of wild sorrel; clouds of foam dripped at his jaws. In an adjacent field fecund cows bleated, and the bull arched his back and snorted at them. The animals would be kept apart until time came for them to mate, and then they would rush together in heated passion. The great, clumsy creatures coupled without skill. Their bodies heaved with raw desire. The breath of the beasts, redolent with the fragrance of sweet grass, emerged in misty clouds of urgent panting, and their hoofs clawed the air in desperate agony. Ezra Maimon, who supervised the breeding of the cattle, understood the mystery of lust, Achmed thought. A long, enforced separation was necessary, and then sudden freedom and the violent release of desire.

He replaced his keffiyah, adjusting the black band that held it in place, and realized with a start that he had been staring at the swollen organ of the bull and that his own penis stood in mild erection. In the distance, he saw Elana and Balfouria emerge from the farmhouse hand in hand. Elana's dark hair was gathered into braids and piled high on her head, but as he watched she unpinned and loosed it, allowing it to fall in waves of darkness about her face.

"When do you leave for Jerusalem, Achmed?" Saleem, his father, had come up silently beside him, and he stood now so that his son could no longer see Ezra Maimon's first-born daughter—an unlucky child whose birth had caused her mother's death.

"Soon. Within the hour," Achmed answered.

"I ask you to visit my cousin Mahmoud in the village of Silwan near Jerusalem. He has many children, and it is said that his eldest daughter is wonderfully beautiful. She is a nurse now, in Jerusalem."

"I am too busy for beautiful cousins, Father," Achmed replied.

"Your two younger brothers are married. It is time for you to take a wife."

"When the time is right I will take a wife," Achmed replied shortly. Perhaps this was the time, he thought, to tell his father that he had been offered a scholarship to the School of Agriculture at Cornell University in the United States. No. He would wait until he was sure he wished to go. "My friend Amos is not yet married," he added.

"We are different from the Jews," Saleem replied sharply. "You have your people and your customs. Amos has his own."

"You and I do not think alike about life, Father," Achmed said mildly.

"There is only one life and only one way to live it—for us. Look to the word of the Prophet," Saleem persisted.

"Even the Prophet would grant us choices," Achmed countered mildly, but there was no defiance in his voice. Saleem was his father, and an Arab son did not argue openly with his father. He pointed to a distant field.

"Next year we must plant the barley in the southern field. The fruit trees cast a shadow and rob the grain of the sunlight."

It was safer to discuss the situation of the grain than his cousin Mahmoud's beautiful daughter.

"I will tell Adon Maimon," Saleem said.

Achmed frowned in annoyance. His father had been a field laborer on Yehuda Maimon's Rishon farm when Ezra was a boy. He had helped to break the land of Sadot Shalom, and during the war, when Ezra himself was away, it had been Saleem who protected the farm from looters and vagrants. He was as devoted to Sadot Shalom as he was to his own small farm, which Ezra Maimon had deeded to him years ago. Ezra Maimon called him Saleem, but Saleem used only the formal address: *Adon*. Master. Ezra did not claim mastery, but Saleem assigned it to him. But it was unimportant, really, Achmed assured himself, struggling against his irritation. The next generation, the children born to himself and to his friend Amos, would address each other by first name, easily, just as he and Amos did. Such things required time, patience.

But he could not explain the need for patience to other young Arabs, like his cousin Hassan and Hassan's friends. Too often he spent long hours with them in the coffeehouses, in futile arguments.

"Do not talk to me of patience," Hassan had said bitterly.

"Allah has given me just this one life, and because of the Jews I have no way to live it."

Hassan saw only the aimless pattern of his days and despaired of altering it. Jews lived on the land his father had farmed. It did not matter that they had bought it, for an exorbitant price, from an absentee Arab landowner who counted his profits in a Beirut villa. He, Hassan, had been irrevocably dispossessed. Did Achmed not see that the Jewish children wore shoes while the children of the fellahin went barefoot?

"Yet the children of the effendis wear shoes," Achmed pointed out, "You are wasting your anger on the Jews. The land policy of the Arabs must be reformed."

But Hassan and his friends were indifferent to logic. They fingered the tassels of their belts, tossed the dice across their *shesh-besh* boards, and sipped thick, sweet coffee from tiny white cups. Between plays they sat back and read from *Al-Karmel*, the weekly newspaper published in Haifa.

Achmed occasionally glanced at the flimsy journal, whose masthead carried the motto of the mufti of Jerusalem—"Death to the Infidel!" He laughed mirthlessly when he read an article which charged that the Jews were distributing poisoned sweets and figs in the Arab markets. Still, he had mailed the paper to Amos Maimon, who had expressed a particular interest in being kept abreast of such propaganda.

"What the Jews ought to do," Achmed wrote his friend, "is publish a newspaper in Arabic so that my people will know what Jews are like and what Jewish settlers truly want."

Amos had replied from London, enclosing a German newspaper clipping which he had translated for Achmed. Astoundingly, it was the same story, with two slight differences. The Jews were purportedly distributing the poisoned sweets to German children, and the allegation had originated with a minor political functionary named Adolf Hitler. A particularly ugly little man, Achmed thought, studying the news photo.

"The voice of hatred says the same thing in many different languages," Amos had written to his boyhood friend. In the same letter he informed Achmed that an association of Arab and Jewish intellectuals had formed in Jerusalem to discuss ways to build bridges of cooperation between the two communities. Like Achmed, they had thought of issuing a newspaper.

They would welcome his insights, Amos said, and he enclosed their address. Brith Shalom they called themselves—Covenant of Peace. Hesitantly, Achmed had written to them and had received an immediate reply and an invitation to a meeting in Jerusalem.

Still hesitant, he had gone to Jerusalem and sat in a book-filled room with an Arab poet, with Musa Alami and other leaders of the moderate Istaqlal party. The bearded American, Judah Magnes, was there, as well as two German professors, Hugo Bergmann and Martin Buber, who put too much sugar in their tea. Achmed told them of the frustration experienced by Hassan and his friends. Judah Magnes remained standing and shifted his weight from one leg to another. He was the tallest man Achmed had ever seen. Were all Americans so tall? he wondered, and he saw himself lost among the giant students of Cornell. But the American's voice was soft and tinged with sorrow when he reacted to Achmed's narrative.

"These are serious things which our young Arab friend has told us—more serious than all the other problems which confront us. More important than the draining of the Huleh swamps or the settlement of Polish Jews. We have a moral obligation to the Arab community, and before we can proceed with Jewish settlements we must determine what is to be done about that obligation."

"We are in agreement," Martin Buber said in his strangely accented Hebrew. He had made copious notes as Achmed spoke, and his shoulders drooped as though weighted down by the magnitude of unending problems. "We must breach our differences and establish a *modus vivendi*. We Jews can do much to aid you in your own struggle for unity. Our goals are not in opposition to each other. Perhaps we can devise a method of land transfer so that no one will be without land. It is not impossible, no, not impossible." He sighed, and the heaviness of that outpouring of breath denied the fragile optimism of his words. "A dialogue must be established. Yes. A dialogue." The term seemed to lift his spirits, and he looked encouragingly at Achmed.

Musa Alami fingered the scarlet tassel of his satin belt. He sat erect in his white *jabaliyah*, his large stomach straining across the fine linen. He was known among the Arabs as a moderate—a realistic man who did not deny his own personal ambitions.

"If it is possible that the aims of both our national movements can be coordinated," he said in mellifluous tones, "Then surely we would encourage our Jewish cousins to share the land with us. I think I can speak for the entire Istaqlal party."

He looked at the other Arabs, who nodded their agreement.

Judah Magnes's wife served coffee yet again, and they spoke quietly as they sipped from the fragile teacups which the Magneses had brought from their New York home to this sitting room in a southland city carved of stone.

Hugo Bergmann spoke of how sorely Lord Plumer was missed.

"This new high commissioner, Chancellor, does not understand our region," he said.

"How can one trust a man who wears a top hat and a frock coat in a *hamsin?*" Abdul Hadi asked, and they laughed together, Jew and Arab alike linked in their contempt for the British functionary who could understand neither their climate nor their separate aspirations for the country they each would call their own.

Achmed had been cheered when he left the meeting. Clearly there was hope and willingness on both sides. He was impressed that the Jews had taken time out for this meeting during the holiest time of their year—the interval between the New Year and the Day of Atonement. That surely meant that they cared deeply. He had walked east in the direction of the Al Aksa Mosque, wondering how he could communicate the sense of the meeting to Hassan and other embittered young Arabs.

It had been a long time since he had intoned his evening prayers in Jerusalem. As he walked he took note of the huge stone houses which were being built in the section of the city the Jews called Rehavia. He was pleased that the Jews were using Jerusalem stone to build their homes and adhering to a pattern of architecture that emulated the arched doorways and corniced windows of old Jerusalem dwellings. The terraces were bathed in the dull gold light of late afternoon, and women clustered on them, their faces turned toward the waning sun.

As he walked through the Talpiyot section, Achmed noticed a new Jewish home that had been built so close to an Arab villa that the Jewish woman who stood on her balcony could pass a handful of lemons to her Arab neighbor. The Jewish woman wore a short-sleeved blouse that exposed arms bronzed by the sun, while her Arab friend was dressed in a long peacock-blue *abayah* and a veil that concealed the lower portion of her face. Yet they chatted easily as the golden fruit was passed from hand to hand, while their small sons tossed a red ball from one balcony to the other. Achmed paused to watch the small tableau. Boys who played ball with each other would not grow up to be armed adversaries.

He entered Old Jerusalem through the Damascus Gate and hurried down the Street of the Chain, stopping to buy a bag of cactus pears from a barefoot Arab boy who wore only the discarded khaki undershirt of a British military policeman. Mounds of white crust caked the child's long, dark lashes, and Achmed knew that within the year he would not be selling fruit. He would be sitting with the row of blind beggars, his hands outstretched, jangling a tin plate and moaning softly.

"You must go to the Hadassah clinic in the new city," Achmed told the boy. "They will take care of your eyes."

"*YaMustafa*. The Jewish doctors poison Arab children. The mufti has told us. The mufti knows." The boy ran off, clutching his coins with one hand and rubbing his trachoma-infested eyes with the other.

Achmed shrugged. His country was a maze of contradictions. Hope and disappointment danced side by side on the sun-flecked streets. On El-Wad Street he stepped aside to allow a group of black-frocked Jews to enter the Torat Chaim synagogue. One of them spoke to the Arab caretaker, who took up a bright leather drum and stationed himself in front of the synagogue, pounding it.

"*Maariv* prayers," he called. "One more Jew needed to form a *minyan*."

The Arab waited until another Jew scurried up the stairwell that led to the synagogue, and then took up his prayer rug and hurried to the small mosque on Bab el-Hadid Street.

Achmed continued on his way. The voice of the muezzin had not yet been raised, so there was time enough for him to reach the Mosque of Omar. He had a particular affection for the crenellated building, and he retained the sense of awe he had felt when he'd first walked up its collonaded steps. He had been a young boy then, and Ezra Maimon had brought him there while the Maimon family went to the adjacent Western Wall. Achmed looked across the open courtyard bordered with ashlars and noticed that there was unusual activity at the usually peaceful Wall. Groups of Arabs had assembled, blocking the pathway of frock-coated Jews who carried a large green baize screen. The air shrilled with the muttering of angry voices. An Arab lifted a threatening fist. A Jew lurched forward, but before the two men could meet, a British gendarme stepped between them, thrusting each backward several steps. Now the angry voices rose in a thunder of a protest. Curses were shrieked in Hebrew and Arabic.

"Down with the infidel!" an Arab screamed.

"The temple is ours," was the fierce reply in Hebrew.

"What is happening?" Achmed asked a stallkeeper who stood surrounded by sacks of nuts. The man offered him a slender green branch to which pistachio nuts still clung by fragile stems.

"The Jews want to put up a screen to separate the men and the women for their Yom Kippur services."

"But they have always had such a screen," Achmed said.

"Always is not forever. This year the muezzins do not want it. They say it is a violation of the mosque."

"And what do you think?" Achmed asked.

"Ask me about nuts. I have many answers about nuts. The pistachios are sweet this year. The almonds are too small. The *hamsin* parched the sunflower seeds. I know nothing about mosques and temples and screens."

"Nor do most of those who are arguing," Achmed said. "They know only what was said in last Friday's political sermon."

Pensively he removed his sandals and washed his hands and feet at the El-Kas fountain. In the mosque he spread his prayer rug and performed the rites of prayer. But his mood had been shattered. He saw, as he left the area, that the screen had been erected after all and that a redheaded officer wearing the uniform of the Royal Irish Constabulary stood guard, clutching his billy club. Jews approached the wall, but the Arabs still clustered about, their anger controlled, though not abated.

Achmed had left Jerusalem, but throughout the months that followed, the incident continued to percolate, and reports of developments were recorded in both the Hebrew and the Arabic press. The British had ordered the removal of the screen. The Zionist organization filed complaints against the decision in both Geneva and London. The Arabs countered by instituting a schedule of building operations in the area so that the sound of hammers and drills against wood and steel drowned out the chanting of Jewish prayers. The Jews countered by strewing refuse on the steps of the mosque.

Achmed's cousin Hassan and his friends muttered bitterly as they read the editorials in *Al-Karmel* and the daily *Miraat al-Shar*. The mufti was much quoted, and new vows were sworn to the Black Hand, the Jaffa-based terrorist organization which would celebrate its tenth anniversary that year. The Arab newspapers spoke of a "Communist and atheist peril." The Jewish press inveighed against Arab intransigence.

There was subdued rage in the coffeehouse conversations.

"They have taken our land, and now they will take our places of prayer," Hassan said darkly.

Achmed knew that his cousin was quoting a Black Hand propaganda pamphlet financed by a group of effendis who were angered because the Jewish farmers paid the fellahin higher wages than they received from Arab landowners. But he did not answer Hassan. He wrote instead to the committee members of Brith Shalom. They had all agreed that danger was imminent, and a meeting had been scheduled for August in Jerusalem. It was to that meeting that Achmed now prepared to travel as small clouds drifted through the skies above Sadot Shalom, tossed by the beginning sharav wind.

"You will be careful in Jerusalem?" Saleem asked his son. He had not asked Achmed why it was necessary to journey to the capital. Saleem believed in the protection of ignorance. A man could not divulge information he did not possess. The lesson of the Turks had been well learned.

"I will be careful, my father," Achmed said.

He bent to kiss his father's hand and then turned to his mother to take the parcel of food she shyly held out to him.

Hulda stood in awe of her eldest son, who could read and write and was addressed with respect by Ezra Maimon's important friends. She was bemused by the beauty of this man, grown so swiftly to maturity from the infant who had slipped with such ease from her womb—the easiest of all her many labors. He had come so quickly that there had been no need to cry out and summon Saleem from the fields, and she had severed the cord with the garden knife she kept always at her waist. He was the tallest of their family, and his thick black mustache glittered against his skin, which was the color of the almond shell at the time of ripening. He wore Western dress—a blue work shirt and khaki trousers—but a snowy-white keffiyah of finest linen covered his head, and a jeweled dagger dangled at his belt. He belonged to a new generation, and she marveled that she had birthed him.

"Salaam, Imum," he said, and her heart melted at his smile.

He left Sadot Shalom, taking the path that cut through to the new main road where a jitney would carry him southward. He did not hurry. A holiday mood had come upon him, and he walked slowly, ambling through the fields as he and Amos had when they were boys and time had seemed an endless gift. They had strolled then, with their heads bent low, searching out small treasures in the debris of nature. They had plucked up oddly shaped stones, heron's teeth, and once the gleaming skeleton of a young stork plucked clean by vultures. He stooped now, and his nostrils quivered with the scent of dried sweet grass, wild columbine, and clover. He bent low and loosed a cluster of marjoram which grew wild in this field, and when he straightened he was suddenly aware that he was not alone. Someone stood behind him, and instinctively he put his hand on the jeweled handle of his dagger.

"There is no need to protect yourself against me, Achmed ibn-Saleem," Elana Maimon said laughingly.

She stood in the shadow of an acacia tree, but sunlight stole between the leaves, splaying her skin with radiant waves and slatting her long, dark hair with brightness. A sprig of marjoram blossomed in her mouth. She carried the purple portmanteau that Achmed had so often carried into the Sadot

Shalom farmhouse when Elana's grandmother arrived for a visit.

"And where do you journey today, Elana?" he asked, taking the portmanteau from her.

"First to my uncle Langerfeld in Jerusalem. And then to Hebron. My mother wrote from Zurich that she has taken some important orders for Hebron glass, and I must arrange for them."

"Then we travel together," Achmed said. "I, too, am bound for Jerusalem."

She nodded, and they made their way through the fragrant field, casting long twin shadows as they walked. They did not speak but smiled shyly at each other, like children accustomed to meeting in one play area who suddenly find themselves in unfamiliar and intriguing surroundings.

Chapter 3

NARROW BANDS OF rose-colored light drifted through the bedroom shutters and teased Elana into fitful wakefulness. As
always, she resisted the day's beginning and squeezed her eyes
tightly shut. She raised her arm to shield her face from the
encroaching light, turned in her bed, and sniffed the acrid scent
of bleach on stiffly ironed linen. She frowned in puzzlement
and then remembered that she was not at home. The counter-
pane at Sadot Shalom smelled of the jasmine and wild lilac
which Mazal spread across the shelves of the linen cabinets.
And in the Galilee, dawn began with strips of soft green light
that cracked the shell of night darkness. She was in Jerusalem,
in her uncle Langerfeld's flat, and the narrow bed she slept on
had once belonged to the small cousin she hardly remembered,
the young girl who had been killed during the Nebi Musa riots
so many years ago.

Elana shivered, but she did not stir from the dead girl's bed.
She was familiar enough with death to be unafraid of it; she
had lived in its shadow from her birth. Despite everything, she
was alive and on holiday in Jerusalem, and the quiet of the
softly breaking morning was part of that holiday. There was no
morning quiet at Sadot Shalom. Ever since Balfouria's birth
Elana had awakened to the hungry wail of a baby. As other
children were born, Mazal hurried from crib to crib, her
footsteps swift, her voice reassuring. There would be the
morning babble of small voices, interjected with laughter and
weeping, tempered by Ezra's firm commands. "Amnon, eat
your egg. Balfouria, stop playing with your food."

At home Elana lay abed only briefly, until she heard the

impact of the large kettle on the iron primus. Then she dressed quickly and plunged into the cheerful cacophony of early morning. She helped Mazal and the Polish girls slice the breakfast vegetables, dicing the translucent cucumbers into tiny cubes, shredding carrots into an orange snowdrift. She sipped her own coffee as she helped to feed the younger children or tied Balfouria's hair ribbon.

She loved the noisy excitement of the morning—perhaps because she remembered so well the deathly quiet of the Sadot Shalom farmhouse during the years between the time Ezra had returned from the war and his marriage to Mazal. She and her father had been alone in the house then, except for a single brief and strained visit from blond Amos. Quiet had stretched between them, sometimes so tautly that Elana feared it would snap into sorrow. She had struggled against that silence and busied herself with such frenetic activity that her father called her his little bee and held her on his lap in the evening, stroking her into calmness. But still she had darted through each day, flitting about the fields and the house, trailing after him as he worked, busily amusing him so that he would love her and never go away again and leave her—as he had from the day of her birth until she was a small girl. She remembered still how the children at Gan Noar had thought her an orphan and how proud she had been to prove them wrong when Ezra returned from the war.

"Ha-abba sheli," she told them proudly. "My father." She sat perched on his shoulders while he carried her the length of the kibbutz.

"You will never leave me again, will you, Abba?" she asked him.

"Never," he promised her solemnly and kissed her fingers one by one while the kibbutz children laughed and kissed each other's fingers in imitative glee.

But he had left her again, to go to Egypt for a meeting with Winston Churchill.

"It is for the good of the country," her aunt Mirra told her.

"I don't care about the country," Elana had cried. "I care about me."

But in the end she had been glad to be back at Gan Noar, where there were other children and where every building was resonant with life and activity. Besides, this time she knew what her father looked like (how tall and handsome he was with his sea-green eyes and dark hair) and that he would be returning. And he had come home, and soon afterward had brought Mazal to join them—lovely, tiny Mazal, who laughed and sang as she cooked and worked, who drew Elana into the circle of her swift gaiety, releasing the small girl from the need to enchant her father. No one could leave Mazal, and Mazal would never leave them.

Elana had stayed close to Mazal during her pregnancies. Elana's own birth had meant her mother's death. Mazal understood. When she was pregnant with Balfouria, she held Elana's hand on her abdomen as the child within her stirred with life.

"See how strong the baby is," she told Elana. "It will be as strong as you are and I hope as beautiful as you. After all, you share one father."

Elana's fingers trembled as she felt the thrashing energy of the unborn infant.

"Won't it hurt you when it's born?" she asked.

"It will hurt me, but it will not kill me," Mazal promised.

Elana had held the newborn Balfouria and threaded her fingers through the new baby's thick, dark curls.

"How dark her hair is," visitors exclaimed. "Just like Mazal's."

"No. Just like mine," Elana replied. "We are sisters. We have the same father and we share Mazal."

Elana had not been frightened at all when the other children were born. And one of the twins, Nachum, had been named for her own mother, Nechama, although Grandma Rivka had wept and said that it was bad luck to name a child for someone who had died so young.

"That's nonsense," Mazal said firmly to Ezra. "We must humor your mother, but we don't have to submit to her."

In the end it had not mattered because Rivka mixed up the names of all the babies. She called Nachum, Shimon and Tamar, Sara, and she spoke to them softly, sometimes laughing and sometimes crying. Grandpa Yehuda would gently wipe away the tears carving small lanes in her pale, powdered face.

Mazal's sister-in-law Mirra, too, had questioned the wisdom of calling the child Nachum. Elana had heard them talking.

"Are you sure you want a child who carries the name of Ezra's first wife?" Mirra asked Mazal.

"But Ezra had another wife. She was Elana's mother. She planted the kitchen garden and sat beneath the avocado tree. We do not deny her. Life banishes death."

When the last child, the baby, Rivka, had been named for Ezra's mother—who had faded quietly into death as she slept—Ezra had said, "I hope her life will be happier than my mother's was."

"Perhaps your mother was as happy in Palestine as she would have been anywhere," Mazal had answered.

Mazal had helped Mirra and Chania go through Rivka's drawers, and she had brought back with her to Sadot Shalom a single white glove which she had found wrapped in tissue paper in a faded silken case. Ezra had explained that his mother had bought it the day of their arrival in Jaffa. He did not know why. He had never understood his mother, who had longed to be an artist, a poetess, to act as the *grande dame* of a salon where intellectuals gathered to exchange ideas as they sipped wine from crystal glasses. Ezra had loved her, but he had not understood her. He wept at her funeral and wept again when he wrote his sister Sara, in Oswiecim, to tell her that their mother was dead. She would never again sit beneath the citron tree and pour tea into fragile cups. Mazal watched him write and fingered the satin glove.

In the end she gave the glove to Elana, who looked at it with bewilderment.

"What shall I do with one glove?" she asked. "I have two hands."

Mazal smiled gently.

"Not all things are meant to be useful," she replied. "One day you will be glad to have it. It will remind you of your grandmother. Perhaps you will understand why she treasured it, how she yearned for such elegance. You will learn, Elana. As you grow, you will learn."

"But I am grown. I am bigger than you are." Elana had laughed delightedly and danced around her father's tiny wife, holding out the white glove so that small Balfouria took hold of a fabric finger and joined in the strange game, dancing and laughing with her mother and Elana until they all collapsed with laughter and the toddling twins climbed over them and chortled with glee.

That had happened months and months ago, and now, lying in the narrow Jerusalem bedroom, Elana suddenly believed the words she had uttered with playful laughter. She was grown-up—grown-up enough to take care of Balfouria while her father and Mazal were in Zurich—grown-up enough to be entrusted with the buying trip to Hebron.

Elana had often accompanied Mazal on visits to artisans. She had watched Mazal study carefully crafted objects—now running a finger across a ceramic bowl to test the glaze for evenness, now holding a glass goblet to the light to search for imperfections. She had listened as Mazal bargained, first asking the artisan for his price, then offering her own, and gradually, with gentle banter and skillful adjustment, arriving at a sum that suited them both.

Mazal had taught Elana how the merchandise had to be wrapped for shipment to shops and private purchasers abroad. And now, at last, she was allowing Elana to conduct an entire transaction alone. Her letter from Zurich had been specific only about the type of glassware needed and the amounts to be sent. Three dozen goblets of cerulean blue for Mrs. Weizmann's Manchester dining room. A large vase of rose-gold glass for Madame Léon Blum, who had a penchant for the long-stemmed roses sold on Paris street corners. Mrs. Warburg and Mrs. Justice Brandeis had each ordered a half-dozen large flat plates in Ibrahim ibn-Mahmoud's special golden glaze. It was a great responsibility, Mazal wrote, but she was sure Elana could manage. Ezra, however, suggested that one of Elana's Langerfeld cousins accompany her to Hebron. Nadav, perhaps. He was a capable boy and had always been fond of Elana.

But of course she could manage by herself, Elana decided, smiling into the half-light of the Jerusalem morning. She was responsible, grown-up.

Grown-up enough, too, to have traveled alone from Sadot Shalom to Jerusalem with Achmed—to have allowed him to lift her portmanteau and place it on the rack of the jitney and then to take her hand and help her enter the car. There had been such supple elegance in the gesture. Suddenly she thought of her grandmother's white glove and imagined her fingers encased in its silken purity—Achmed's slender hand dark against its whiteness. She acknowledged, as she smoothed her skirt, that a border had been crossed. Achmed was a man, and she herself was no longer the small girl who had scurried after her brother's Arab friend across the fields of her father's farm. Her height almost matched his own, and her eyes flickered with pleasure when he smiled. How handsome he was—his black mustache gleaming silkily against his almond-colored skin, its fine hairs matched by the winged curve of eyebrows above his blue eyes.

When she was a small girl, Elana had asked her uncle David why so many Arabs had blue eyes. His hand had flown to his black eye patch, and briefly she regretted the question. But he replied with easy humor.

"A legacy from the Crusaders. They came to Palestine and left fortresses, aqueducts, and hordes of blue-eyed children."

She had been rather pleased that Achmed had Crusader blood. It added intrigue and mystery to her friendship with him, and it linked them in odd ancestry. Somewhere in the vanished genealogy of Achmed's family there lurked a man of Europe, drawn from his northern clime to this desert land by fanatic dreams and religious fervor just as her own grandfathers had sailed across the Mediterranean pulled by a messianic magnet that her grandfather Langerfeld ascribed to religion and her grandfather Yehuda Maimon called Jewish liberation. The names they gave their dreams were irrelevant. Even as a child, listening to their arguments, she had recognized that nothing less than fierce, inexplicable zeal welded them to this land so distant and different from the steppe cities of their birth.

Elana and Achmed sat side by side through the long journey south to Jerusalem. They spoke softly, wearing the adult masks of polite indifference, because they shared the jitney with other travelers who glanced curiously at the Jewish girl and her Arab companion. But their eyes had flashed signals, and they had struggled together to restrain their laughter when a sudden gust of wind dislodged the *shetl*, the ceremonial wig, of a young Orthodox woman who sat primly next to Elana. The wig, ostensibly worn so that a married woman would not attract the

covetous glances of other men, was fashioned of luxuriant
chestnut hair, intricately braided, while the woman's own revealed hair was of a mousy brown that thinly covered her head.
Their eyes locked also when, just north of Jerusalem, at the
Arab village of Beth Liqya, where they stopped to replenish
their water, a large roe, its auburn hide flecked with white
petals, sailed across their path, followed by two yearlings who
lifted their slender feet daintily and focused their long-lashed
eyes on the shadowed ground before gliding into a grove of
cypresses. Elana held her breath and Achmed's clenched hands
were still. Briefly, they were paralyzed and linked by the
streaking beauty they had witnessed.

"How Amos would have loved to see them," Achmed said.

"You know my brother better than I do."

"I know him well. I love him dearly," Achmed replied in
elegant Arabic, and she was ashamed that she had begrudged
her brother and his friend an intimacy that excluded her. "He
will return to the country, to Sadot Shalom. You, too, will
come to know him," Achmed assured her, lapsing back into
Hebrew.

The other passengers averted their eyes. They stared out the
windows and hid their faces behind books and newspapers, as
though they were somehow threatened by the two young people who seesawed so gracefully from one language to another,
their talk flowing with the easy familiarity of those who have
known each other always.

It was late when they arrived in Jerusalem. The lights of the
gas lamps splayed across the cobbled streets and formed trembling luminous feathers on the stone buildings. Achmed
walked Elana to the corner of the street where her uncle Langerfeld lived and then handed the purple portmanteau to her.
He did not suggest that he come in, nor did she invite him to do
so. Their friendship was restricted by discreet, carefully defined boundaries which neither of them would cross.

"What will you do tomorrow?" he asked.

"Tomorrow is the Ninth of Av, the anniversary of the destruction of the Temple. I imagine that I will go to services at
the Western Wall with my uncle and his family."

"And after that?" Achmed asked.

He was startled by the intensity in his voice. Why should he be concerned with Elana Maimon's activities in Jerusalem? His own week was filled with meetings. He was to meet with members of the Brith Shalom, with leaders of the Istaqlal party, there were conferences scheduled with British officials of the Ministry of Agriculture to report on the rotation plantings on Sadot Shalom. And there were monographs on desert agriculture that he wanted to read. A young American soil conservation expert, Walter Lowdermilk, had published an interesting theory about utilizing subterranean water sources. He certainly had enough to occupy him during his stay in Jerusalem without involving himself in Elana's activities. But he did, after all, have a responsibility to her. He had known Elana from the moment of her birth. He had taught her how to handle her small pets, how to read Arabic, and he had gone with her to search out sweet herbs amid the wild grass.

And today, he had heard the sudden intake of her breath, felt the soft pressure of her arm, when the wild roe sailed past them. How beautiful she had looked, her eyes bright with wonder, her small mouth open like a thirsty flower as her tongue darted across soft lips, already moist and glowing.

"I must go to Hebron to order the glassware for Mazal and then wait for the orders to be completed. Then I will see to their packing and shipping."

"What day will that be?" he asked.

"I think all the glassware will be ready by August twenty-sixth."

"You will need help, then," he said. "I shall come with you to Hebron." She was, after all, only a young girl, still hovering at the edge of childhood. He could not leave her alone, unprotected, unaided. She was the daughter of his mentor, the sister of his friend. Ezra Maimon would not have it otherwise.

"I am grateful."

She had not hesitated. It had been right of him to offer his aid and right of her to accept it. He was fulfilling his role as Achmed, son of Saleem, who had always been available to assist the family of Ezra Maimon.

She extended her hand, and he held it gravely to his lips. Her fingers carried the scent of the sweet marjoram they had picked together that morning. His lips were feather-soft against

her skin, his mustache silken where it touched her wrist in the
darkness.

"We meet then at daybreak on the twenty-sixth in the small
café near the Lion's Gate. A jitney leaves there for Hebron.
L'hitraot."

"*L'hitraot.* Until we see each other again."

But that time was ten days away, Elana thought, and there
was much to do before then. Today she would join the Langerfeld family in worship services at the Wall. Spurred by a
sudden burst of energy, she jumped out of bed and dressed
quickly, selecting a long-sleeved frock fashioned of light-blue
georgette which Aunt Sara had sent her from Poland. She
would wear that dress again when she journeyed to Hebron
with Achmed. He liked the color blue, she remembered. He
had told her so once, and she had not forgotten it.

"What a pretty dress, Elana," her aunt Freya Langerfeld
said when Elana came into the dining room. "Let me fix the
bow."

Freya studied her niece as she tied the narrow strip of ribbon. How like Nechama she looked in that dress. She had
inherited her mother's ability to command attention while
maintaining a quiet presence. Yet she did not have Nechama's
pliant quiescence but seemed always possessed of a pulsing
energy, a determination to do things her own way. Even now
Elana untied her aunt's neat bow and formed a jaunty knot
instead, smiling at Freya, practicing both charm and defiance
with a single gesture.

"My aunt Sara sent the dress to me."

Freya Langerfeld did not reply. In this house, where
orthodox Judaism was practiced, Sara was considered dead.
She had abandoned her faith, and thus they had abandoned her.
But Sara had not abandoned her family. She wrote her brothers
often and sent gifts to their children.

"I have mourned our mother," she wrote Ezra, weeks after
learning of Rivka's death, and Elana envisioned her mysterious
unknown aunt, alone in a darkened corner of her Polish manor,
her dark dress rent with the mourning tear, a yellow candle of
grief weeping tallow tears in its tall glass container. She re-

membered a picture she had seen of a Marrano woman, a secret Jewess, lighting Sabbath candles in a windowless basement.

"Are you going to the Wall with us, Elana?" her cousin Naomi asked.

Naomi was Elana's age, but she wore her hair twisted into schoolgirl braids, and she dressed in the costume of the Beth Yaakov seminar where she had been enrolled since childhood—a white middy blouse and a dark skirt, her legs shrouded in thick dark stockings.

"I don't know if it is wise for the girls to go to the Wall," Daniel Langerfeld said.

A frown creased his forehead and he lowered the newspaper he had been reading. He read four newspapers each day—the Hebrew daily *Davar,* the revisionist newspaper *Doar HaYom,* the Arab *Miraat Al-Shar,* and the English Language daily, the *Palestine Post.* Later in the day he would receive the international editions of the *Herald Tribune* and the *Manchester Guardian.* Since the killing of his daughter, he read the newspapers with obsessive vigilance. Forewarned was forearmed. If he had been careful during the Nebi Musa riots, if he had read between the lines, he never would have allowed Chanele out that day, and she would be sitting with them now at the polished mahogany table, pleased and excited because her cousin Elana was visiting from Sadot Shalom.

"We always go to the Wall on the Ninth of Av," Freya Langerfeld said. She was a woman who always shopped at the same market, vacationed at the same hotel.

"This year it may be dangerous." He spread all his newspapers out on the table and studied them as though he were contemplating a jigsaw puzzle and could not find a missing piece.

"My uncle David says that if we are to live in this country, we must accept the fact that we live in constant danger. Once we begin to hide because we are frightened, we have no right to be here," Elana said. "I will go to the Wall."

"I am familiar with your uncle David's feelings," Daniel Langerfeld retorted dryly. Ezra's brother, David Maimon, wore that damn eye patch like a *croix de guerre.* And each year he rode the revia to the exact cove where he had been shot. A dramatic bit of heroics. But apparently he had influenced Elana. His niece was young, impressionable. And beautiful. As Nechama, her mother, his sister, had been. Fear and sorrow plucked at his heart.

"You must admit, Abba, that what the Arabs have been doing at the Wall throughout the year is not right. It violates an accepted code for maintaining the status quo."

Cleverly, Nadav, the eldest Langerfeld son, couched his argument in the academic language his father loved. He was a political science student at the Hebrew University, although he had wanted a career in medicine. At twenty-two, he was already beginning to lose his hair. A pale crescent crowned his head, and he covered it with sparse brown strands. His eyes, weak since boyhood, were covered by thick lenses encircled in horn-rimmed frames that elongated his oval face. The weak eyes were the legacy of Freya's first husband, a talmudic scholar turned farmer, who had died of malaria when Nadav was an infant. Daniel Langerfeld had adopted the child when he married Freya and always thought of him as his own son. He felt mysteriously betrayed because Nadav insisted on saying Kaddish for the father he had never known.

"There will be enough doctors," Daniel had told Nadav, "but a Jewish state will need trained administrators, legislators, ambassadors."

Daniel Langerfeld no longer saw the Jewish community in Palestine as a tentative settlement, dependent on British sufferance, British protection, content to build a city in the south, a settlement in the north. He envisioned a sovereign Jewish state and knew that the apparatus for self-government had to be made ready. Let David Maimon brandish his weapons and sing battle hymns around kibbutz campfires. Let Jabotinsky sound a call to arms. The Langerfelds had their own work cut out. His sons would represent their people in the councils of nations and work for government agencies. Already a beginning had been made. He himself sat on the Vaad LeUmi—the National Assembly—and even now in Zurich, Chaim Weizmann was arguing for the strengthening and expansion of the Jewish Agency. They would be ready when the time came. He smiled proudly at Nadav, who could so easily manipulate phrases like "the acceptable status quo." That was the sort of language the British understood and admired.

"I admit that there was no need for them to launch a building campaign and have their jackhammers in full operation just when Jews congregated for prayers," Daniel replied. "Of course, we know that they are simply being provocative. They want a confrontation, and we must deny them that. Do you remember what I used to tell you when you were a small boy returning from the yeshiva and that crowd of bullies used to tease you?"

"You told me to ignore them, but even there you were not always right. Ignoring them did not make them disappear. Sometimes they attacked me even more viciously. And the same thing may happen with the Arabs. They will not go away even if we pretend not to see them."

"I don't want them to disappear," Daniel Langerfeld said mildly. "But I don't want to use tactics that will only harm our cause and give our enemies ammunition against us. We are Jews. We must be doubly careful. Our defenses are seen as offenses. Our entreaties become ultimatums."

"If we do not pray at the Wall on the Ninth of Av, it will signify only that we are frightened, and a community of cowards will not build the third Jewish commonwealth," Nadav replied, and now there was impatience in his voice.

Daniel Langerfeld sighed and looked at the outstretched newspapers. Idly, he read an item on the New York stock market. It was dangerously inflated. He dismissed it. There had been sinister stories about the market for months now.

"You are right. I agree that you are right, Nadav. We will go to the Wall, all of us. But let us go as worshipers, not as warriors. Do you agree, Elana?"

He smiled at his sister's daughter, who nodded gravely. Strange. She was only a schoolgirl, yet she spoke and moved with the certainty of a mature woman, and she had the same determination that had given Nechama the courage to live on a lonely farm in the Galilee.

"Let us go together, then."

He rose from the table and took the red velvet case that contained his prayer shawl. His sons carried their own bags, and they hugged them close to their chests, in the manner of soldiers caressing their rifles. Elana paused to tie the ribbon of her hat, and her glance rested on the lead article in *Doar HaYom*. It was signed by her father's old friend Zev Jabotinsky, and its words were impassioned: "Wake up and unite! Move heaven and earth against this unprecedented and unspeakable injustice."

She smiled. Clearly, Zev Jabotinsky had not taken courses in government at the Hebrew University.

The family walked eastward through the city, trailing after throngs of Jerusalemites who threaded their way through the narrow paths of shadow cast by the stone buildings. Bearded Chassidim, their faces sleek with sweat beneath the fur-trimmed hats they wore despite the heat, chanted mournfully as they proceeded from street to street.

"How doth the city sit solitary," they intoned. "She weepeth sore into the night . . . the tears are on her cheeks."

They themselves wept and swayed dangerously, pounding their chests with feeble gesture. Two pale youths supported an aged rabbi who was perceptibly weakened by the fast. Each held him by an arm, and once they paused to wipe his rheumy eyes with a large white handkerchief. Drops of spittle glittered on his beard, but he urged his students on. "We must go to the Wall," he said, and it seemed to Elana that it was he who supported them. Their pallor repelled her, and she slipped into a doorway to allow them to pass.

Uniformed secondary school students marched in single file through the middle of the street, forcing horse-drawn carriages to the side. An impatient motorist in a British command car squeezed his horn. He wore the uniform of the Royal Irish Constabulary, and as he waited impatiently he studied the scene with a practiced eye. Grudgingly, he admired the uniform pace of the students, the neatness of their white shirts and navy blue trousers. They were followed by a group of kibbutzniks from Ramat Rachel who walked briskly, bareheaded, defying both the heat and their religion. The farmers were not keeping the fast day. They munched fruit and tossed nut shells to the ground as they marched. They did not read from Lamentations but sang songs that were vaguely familiar to the Irish officer. Songs about guarding the city and rebuilding the land.

Someone had explained the words to him once, and he wished he could remember them.

He stared at a group of orphans from the Diskin Home who twirled their earlocks with dirt-streaked fingers. Their white socks crawled about their ankles, and they were as pale as ghosts although it was high summer. Poor little beggars. His own children on the Derry farm would be as brown as berries now. Liam Halloran felt pangs of homesickness. He had been sure he would be demobilized after Gallipoli, but His Majesty's surgeons had one set of standards for Britishers and another for the Irish Constabulary.

The next group of children, from the Mizrachi and Hillsverein schools, were not pale, but as sturdy and golden as the oranges they had spent the summer picking. They laughed and jostled each other as they walked, while the Diskin children kept their heads down, their lips tightly pressed together. It was hard to believe they were all Jews, Liam thought. So many different types celebrating the same holy day in the same city. He'd gone to a couple of briefing sessions and strained to understand the difference between the orthodox, the religious moderates, the socialist atheists. Someday he'd look up that bloke who had saved his life on Gallipoli—Ezra Maimon— and get him to explain it. He had his address somewhere. Son of a bitch, would he ever get out of this intersection? Impatiently, he groped for the horn and gave it two powerful squeezes. The group of Chassidim just ahead of him glared but moved out of the road and allowed him to continue on. He caught the eye of a tall young girl in a light blue dress and doffed his cap to her. She smiled and demurely tied the ribbons of her broad-brimmed hat.

"Look. Isn't that Judah Magnes?" Freya Langerfeld asked as they crossed onto David Street in the Armenian quarter.

"Yes. I wonder who that young Arab with him is." Daniel squinted into the sunlight. "Why, it's Achmed—Saleem's son, Achmed. Did you know he was in Jerusalem, Elana?"

He did not wait for his niece to reply but watched the tall American and the Arab youth as they disappeared into the courtyard of the Church of Archangels. Daniel Langerfeld approved their selection of a meeting place. The Armenian quarter was neutral territory, and there was a wide-boughed olive

tree in the church garden which afforded both privacy and
shade. It was interesting that Achmed was involved with the
Brith Shalom movement. Daniel Langerfeld admired the organization, agreed with its principles. Jews and Arabs in dialogue
together to solve their problems. An admirable aim. More the
pity that it simply had no chance of working. Not with the
mufti's strident voice calling for a *jihad* against the Jews of
Jerusalem and the leaders of the Black Hand reprinting copies
of the *Protocols of the Elders of Israel* in Arabic translation.

"I didn't see Achmed," Elana answered, and it was not
until sometime later that her uncle realized she had never answered his question.

The courtyard in front of the Western Wall was crowded.
The Chassidim pressed forward and stood before the ancient
stones, their faces touching the huge earth-colored slabs.
Mournful wails filled the air as a chorus of voices, each differently accented, recited from Lamentations. One youth
struck his forehead against the Wall again and again until a
ribbon of blood streaked his brow and an older man restrained
him and led him away. Women approached the wall furtively
and pressed folded scraps of paper into the crevices. The Diskin orphans marched past, each cupping a memorial candle.
The tiny tongues of flame licked the brilliant light of the summer day. Then, suddenly, they heard the steady marching of
feet, and the worshipers turned. Mothers reached for the hands
of small children. Husbands moved closer to their wives.

Several hundred young Jews, wearing the light blue shirts
and navy blue bandannas of the Revisionist movement,
marched toward the Wall. A path was unprotestingly cleared
for them. Elana clutched her cousin Naomi's hand and felt her
heart beat faster. Her breath came in painful rasps.

"The Wall is ours! The Wall is ours! The Wall is ours!"
The slogan was repeated again and again in staccato bursts
until it resounded in a single deafening shout punctuated by the
waving of the blue-and-white flag emblazoned with the Star of
David, carried by an advance honor guard. Then, suddenly,
there was absolute silence as the young people stood at attention. The flag furled and unfurled in a gentle breeze. One
minute passed and then another. Elana watched as individual
Arabs gathered near Robinson's Arch. They formed a small

group which grew larger and larger, spreading out until they blocked the Gate of the Moors. Any moment now they would surge forward, their anger forming a huge wave that would soar and break against the neat Revisionist ranks.

Still the silence stretched until it was broken at last by the strong, sweet sound of a young girl's voice singing the opening strains of "HaTikva," the Jewish national anthem. Other voices joined hers in a huge and vibrant chorus rising strong from the disciplined Revisionists, the earlocked and bearded worshipers, kerchiefed women and sandaled kibbutzniks. The Revisionists turned then and marched out of the Temple courtyard, still keeping perfect order, their flag triumphantly scraping the air.

"The Wall is ours. The Wall is ours. The Wall is ours." They murmured the slogan now so that it rumbled forth like hushed thunder and the Arabs, assembled still in the shadow of Robinson's Arch, stared after them.

Daniel Langerfeld opened his velvet case and removed his prayer shawl.

"Let us pray now," he said.

"You see, Abba, we took a stand and nothing happened." Nadav's voice trembled with excitement and pride. His classmates at the Hebrew University had been among the group who stood at attention and sang the national anthem. His generation would not be content to sit by and allow injustice. These were new times and called for new measures. A convention in Zurich could not deal with the daily problems of Jerusalem.

"Do we know that?" Daniel asked.

He opened his prayer book and moved his lips in silent supplication. He had lived for many years in the Middle East, and he knew that desert storms often brew slowly over many days until at last they gather full momentum and their winds blow with wild abandon.

Chapter 4

ON THE ELEVENTH day of Av, Nadav Langerfeld, walking home from the library on Mount Scopus, paused to buy a glass of freshly squeezed grapefruit juice at a kiosk on El HaKiri Road. The juice was warm because it had been standing too long in the sun, but he drank it thirstily and ordered another. He was in no hurry to return to his father's house. His cousin Elana would not yet be back from the journey she had made to Hebron to place her orders. He had wanted to join her but had felt uneasy inviting himself along. He was annoyed with himself. She was, after all, only fifteen, seven years his junior, but still he felt awkward in her presence. And she was so beautiful. Nadav sipped his second glass of juice, colder than the first, and wondered how she managed to weave her dark hair into the intricate coronet of braids and curls she had worn the previous evening when the family had gone to see the Tower of David illuminated by moonlight. His father had not allowed them to linger there and watch the slender monument draped in silvery light. Daniel Langerfeld had been uneasy since the demonstration at the Wall. He had glanced nervously at passing Arabs who were seemingly indifferent to the small groups of strolling Jews.

"Let us go," Daniel had beseeched them. "Something will happen. I can feel it."

Nadav had struggled to conceal his impatience. His father still lived in the shadow of exile. The echoed shouts of raiding Cossacks rang in his ears, and the sour breath of fear filled his nostrils. When his young daughter had been killed during the Nebi Musa riots, Daniel Langerfeld had been desolated but unsurprised. He anticipated murder and bloodshed. Sometimes

40

it seemed to Nadav that his father might feel betrayed if his grim prophecies were not realized. Were messengers of doom disgraced when danger did not come?

Yet even Daniel Langerfeld had to admit that there had been no singular outbreak of violence over the past eight years. Jews and Arabs lived peacefully in Palestine, and the British did maintain order. Lord Plumer had brooked no nonsense, and he had transferred a competent and tranquil administration to Chancellor, the new high commissioner. This business at the Wall was simply mischief created by one man—the mufti, Haj Amin. Left to themselves, the Arab population of Palestine might be content to live side by side with their Jewish neighbors. Certainly they traveled the roads built with Jewish money and used the electricity generated by the Palestine Economic Corporation. More and more frequently, Arabs could be seen in the queues at the Hadassah clinics, and Ezra's wife, Mazal, had done business easily with Arab artisans. Relationships between the two communities might normalize if the mufti would stop stirring his people to religious fervor. He was helped, of course, by the effendis, who were afraid that Jewish labor policy would adversely influence the fellahin. They linked Zionism with communism and envisioned a socialist peril.

And the Jews themselves would have to make adjustments, Nadav thought. It was all very well for his father and others like him to have nurtured separate dreams of Zion and to have packed their bags and left their homes in Europe in search of those dreams. But damn it, the land to which they came, the mythical Zion of their dreams and prayers, was an occupied land. It would take more than lyric verses, horas danced about fires, and impassioned speeches to work their way around that. Nadav's courses at the university the past semester had included a study of nationalism. He had read Mazzini and Garibaldi with mounting excitement. Their concepts of nationhood and unification did not differ dramatically from those of Herzl.

But there was a difference between unifying an Italy already inhabited by Italians and coming into an unknown land after a long exile and blindly reclaiming it. There was a resident population in Palestine which could not be ignored. The Jews would have to accommodate themselves to the situation. Yitzchak

Epstein had been arguing sensibly for almost twenty years that
Jews had to recognize the national aspirations of the Arabs and
help them to find their own identity by opening their schools
and universities to Arab enrollment.

Certainly, such a step had been successful in the case of
Achmed ibn-Saleem. He had been educated at a Jewish agri-
cultural institute, and he remained a loyal friend to the Jewish
community. Nadav had just seen his name on a roster of Brith
Shalom supporters. And Nachum Sokolov had an idea for a
Palestinian Congress comprised of Arabs and Jews. Men like
Chaim Arlosoroff thought in terms of population transfers.
When Jews acquired property, they must make certain that no
Arabs were displaced. New homes must be found for them.
Certainly, there was no dearth of land in this region.

Nadav Langerfeld was not pessimistic. His father was training him for service in the diplomatic corps of a nonexistent
Jewish state, but before such service could be contemplated,
negotiations would have to be conducted within their own
territory.

Jews like himself and his cousin Amos would have to work
things out with Arabs like Achmed and moderate members of
the Istaqlal and Nashashibi parties. Extremists on both sides
would have to be defused. It was encouraging that things were
going so well in Zurich, where plans for an expanded Jewish
Agency had been approved. Such an organization would have
an Arab section to deal with ideas like Epstein's and Arlosoroff's. A new era was dawning. His father and Ezra
Maimon had sown the fields, but it was his generation that
would nurture the crops and reap a harvest of hope.

When his aunt and uncle returned from Europe, he would
travel to Sadot Shalom and listen to their account of the Zurich
proceedings. And then he would see Elana again. She was still
his family's guest in Jerusalem, but he anticipated her leavetaking and prepared himself for the lingering melancholy that
overtook him whenever she left. Abruptly, he felt annoyed
with himself. Why was he so preoccupied with his cousin?
Elana Maimon was a child still. She was, in fact, no older than
the group of boys who were kicking a soccer ball the length of
the El HaKiri Road.

Nadav turned his attention to their game. He had not been a
bad player as a student at the gymnasia, but boys who wore

spectacles were not often chosen for games. Still, he enjoyed watching the game, and these boys were skillful players. He watched as a tall youth, sweat streaking in rivulets down his sun-pinkened face, dashed after the black-and-white ball and aimed a kick at it. It soared skyward but not in the direction of the goal.

"Lousy peripheral vision," Nadav thought lazily and he watched the ball veer off the street and over a wrought-iron fence that girdled a small villa. The walls of the house were painted blue to ward off the evil eye. An Arab house. Nadav hoped that the ball had fallen clear and inflicted no damage, and he was relieved when he saw it fall, finally, in a bed of tomato plants. He could see the bright red fruit through the bars of the gate, crimson globules almost ready for picking.

"Get the ball, Yossi," a boy shouted. "It's just there, over the fence. Get it."

The tall boy hesitated.

"Scared?" an opposing team player taunted. "What are you afraid of? The tomato plant? The big, bad Arabs? Or maybe you're afraid we'll win if we keep on playing."

"I'll get the ball," the boy called Yossi said. He shook his hair out of his eyes, wiped his face with his sleeve, and strode up to the house. A bell dangled at the gate, and he pulled at it once and then again. Nadav thought he discerned movement in the shrubbery, but no one came to the gate. It had been the wind, after all.

"All right. So they're not home. Arabs who aren't home can't hurt you. What are you waiting for? Just go in and get the damn ball."

"Go on, Yossi."

The boys were growing impatient. The afternoon was waning, and they knew that soon enough they would have to be home to help their mothers fill the water barrels and the kerosene containers.

"All right. I'm going in."

Yossi flashed them a defiant smile and opened the gate. Nadav watched as he entered the garden. Through the iron bars, he saw the boy's hands reach for the ball, encircle it, and lift it out of the tomato patch. Good. He had the ball. The minor crisis was over. Nadav felt in his pocket for change to

pay the kiosk keeper who hovered near him, his eyes also fixed
on the small garden.

Nadav followed the man's gaze, suddenly apprehensive. He
saw the tomato plants rustle as though thrashed by a violent
wind, yet the air was still, weighted down by hamsin heat. A
tenuous silence cloaked the street. The soccer players stood in
an uneasy cluster, and in the neighboring Arab houses window
curtains were drawn, shutters slammed shut. And then a
scream pierced the air—a boy's voice shrill with pain and
terror. Nadav rose swiftly. Perhaps the boy, Yossi, had damaged a plant and the owner of the house had aimed a blow at
him, threatened him. Yes. That was it. Nadav could see the
rich dark earth of the tomato garden saturated with red juice.
The ripe fruit must have been harshly crushed, drained of its
liquid. But there was a strange thickness, a vivid brightness, to
the carmine rivulet that leaked through the gate and onto the
ocher paving stones of El HaKiri Road. Again the boy's voice
rose in a trembling octave and subsided into low moans.

The soccer players surged forward, and one boy touched a
finger to the ground and tentatively stared at its reddened tip.

"It's blood," he called. "Blood! Yossi! Yossi!"

There was no answer from within the courtyard. The moans
had ceased.

"Constable! Constable!"

The boys scattered wildly. They shouted for help. They
pounded at doors. Their running feet beat out a crescendo of
panic on the stone street. A woman wailed in fear and bewilderment.

Nadav dashed across the street and through the gate. He
caught a glimpse of two Arabs in white abayahs as they leaped
over a low stone wall at the rear of the house. Within the house
itself a shutter was drawn closed. He hurried into the garden
and followed the strip of blood to the tomato patch where the
slender soccer player named Yossi lay. The boy's face was
turned upward so that the sun shone brightly upon it, but his
eyes did not close in defense against the brilliant light. His
hands still clutched the soccer ball, its black-and-white surface
petaled scarlet by the blood that had gushed from the slashes
that ribboned his chest and legs.

"What happened?" A British gendarme knelt beside Nadav,
his ear pressed to the boy's chest, his fingers pulling at the skin

beneath the eyes. Nadav took up the wrist, passed his fingers across it, and felt the barely perceptible flicker of a pulse.

"He's alive!" he said. "I get a pulse. He's alive!"

"Ambulance!" the British officer bellowed. "He's alive. Ambulance!"

White-coated attendants sprinted into the garden. The boy was lifted onto a stretcher, and as he was propelled forward the black-and-white ball tumbled onto the ground.

"What happened?" The British officer had whipped out a notebook, and he waited expectantly for Nadav to reply. He kept his eyes riveted to the pad so that he would not see the blood that soaked the earth. He had a younger brother who played soccer for a team in Manchester.

Nadav lifted the ball. The blood that clung to it was sticky and warm against his fingers.

"A soccer ball, kicked by Jewish boys, fell into the garden of an Arab house. The boy who went to retrieve it was stabbed. That is what happened," he replied softly.

He smiled bitterly at the absurdity of his own words. A ball, a garden, a sun-streaked day shadowed by ancient hatreds, and suddenly a Jewish boy lay dying while his panicstricken Arab murderers fled for their lives.

He gave the officer his name and walked through the gate. Once outside it, he bent forward slightly and vomited. He clung to the stakes of the gate and felt the metal pierce his flesh. The boy named Yossi would die, he knew. He had been stabbed perhaps a dozen times while he, Nadav Langerfeld, sat at a kiosk table and pondered proposals for redistribution of land and the creation of an Arab Affairs section within the Jewish Agency. Another wave of nausea, of near-faintness washed over him, and to steady himself he thought of his cousin Elana, standing strong and straight in her blue georgette dress, her broad-brimmed hat balanced in her hand. Carefully, he skirted the pool of his own vomit and walked homeward. Halfway there, he realized that he still held the soccer ball. He allowed it to drop from his hand, and he watched as it rolled slowly into a nearby ditch.

Chapter 5

ELANA SHIVERED IN the cold air of early dawn and wondered if she should order a coffee. She had not stopped for breakfast before leaving, fearful that if the Langerfeld family heard her moving about the kitchen they would forbid her journey to Hebron.

"Surely you do not think of returning there now," her uncle had said matter-of-factly the previous evening.

Her reply neatly avoided a direct answer to his question. Elana never lied. She simply managed to avoid the truth—the lessons of her motherless childhood had been well learned. Always, she had created her own defenses so that others beat their wings helplessly against the protective mesh of her half-truths. ("Who spilled the jam?" "I was not in the kitchen today.")

"Hebron has been quiet," she told her uncle. Later he would remember that she had given him no answer just as the counsellor at the kibbutz always remembered later that the jam had not been spilled that day.

"As quiet as Jerusalem was until a soccer ball was tossed into the wrong garden," Nadav had interposed dryly.

· Elana had been disconcerted. Nadav was generally on her side, always prepared to argue for courage and fairness in dealing with the Arabs. Often during such arguments with his father and with other Zionist leaders who visited the Langerfeld flat, he would wearily remove his eyeglasses and pass his fingers across his eyes as though he might, by such casual gesture, banish stubborn prejudice, inherited fear. Yet the past week had changed him—it had changed them all, Elana ac-

46

knowledged. They had felt the storm of violence slowly gather, causing them to walk swiftly through familiar streets, like pedestrians who anticipate a sudden downpour. They glanced always from left to right, stepping swiftly into doorways at the sound of unfamiliar steps.

They had learned to live with undiminished fear. Elana had gone with her aunt and Naomi to the small neighborhood grocery where Freya Langerfeld stocked up on staples. She bought sacks of sugar and flour, shortening, oil for the paraffin lamps and candles, cured beef, onions and potatoes, as though readying herself for a siege.

The shelves of the small store were almost empty, and the storekeeper's wife implored them to complete their purchases quickly. The proprietor himself was already sawing boards and nailing them in place across the shop's entry.

Daniel Langerfeld arrived home with long metal cartridge cases. He and Nadav disappeared into his study, and when Elana carried the tea tray in, she was startled to see them surrounded by rifles. Uncle Daniel was carefully inserting bullets into the chamber of an ancient rifle—her uncle, the orthodox Zionist administrator who prayed thrice daily and once had not allowed her to kill a centipede but had lifted it gently and dropped it into a bush because, he explained to her, the Holy One, blessed be He, gave life to every living thing. Her cousin Nadav, the scholar, the advocate of Arab rights, held a pistol up to the light. Sweat gleamed on his balding head, forming an odd halo that made her smile fleetingly. The two men sat in the book-lined room and readied their weapons, concentrating fiercely on a bolt that would not slide properly, adjusting the sights of a rifle. Oil stains streaked their faces.

"You won't need guns," Elana had cried out, frightened.

"Don't be foolish, Elana. You saw the funeral. You saw what was happening in the streets when we walked home." Nadav's voice was flat, unemotional. He spoke in the bloodless, dazed tone of the newly bereaved. He had seen death— the death of the boy Yossi, who had lived for only a few hours after the assault, and the death of his own dreams. There would be no easy peace between Jew and Arab in this land. His hope for that had rolled away as swiftly as the bloodstained soccer ball which lay at the bottom of a ditch.

"Yes. I saw the funeral."

She had seen it quite by accident. She and Naomi had gone
to the open-air market at Machane Yehuda to buy summer fruit
for a cold compote. As they walked home, carrying their string
shopping bags filled to the brim with peaches and apricots that
matched the sultry golden light of the Jerusalem day, they
encountered the funeral procession. They waited to take their
turn at the rear of the cortege so that they might follow the
requisite four paces, according to the custom they had known
since childhood.

The plain pine coffin was a narrow one that shifted from side
to side on the horse-drawn hearse as though the corpse within it
were too light to weight the death box down. It was followed
by a thin woman and a short man whose blond Vandyke beard
was neatly combed. The two leaned against each other so that
they moved as one, although others hovered near them, prepared to help if they could no longer support each other. Their
pale, tired faces were masks of incomprehension. The woman
moaned softly, and the man whispered to her and glanced back
at the three youngsters who followed them, their school shirts
marked by the mourning tear, the rabbi's symbolic razoring of
cloth to mark the severing of a life.

"It must be the funeral of the boy, Yossi. The boy Nadav
told us about yesterday," Naomi whispered.

"Of course," Elana said.

Now she understood why the long cortege was flanked by
uniformed members of the Revisionist movement. They trailed
the mourners and the rabbi, carrying their blue-and-white banners and chanting over and over, "The land of Israel is ours.
Jewish death will be avenged. The land of Israel is ours. Let
the will of God be done."

Who was God and what was His will? Elana wondered. And
why was His name invoked so loudly by both the marching
Jews and the mufti who spewed hatred on the steps of the
mosque each Friday morning? Did men use God to justify their
own ends? Her uncle Langerfeld would think such a thought
blasphemous, but she suspected that it would not surprise either Nadav or Achmed.

"A funeral is no place for a demonstration," Naomi said
disapprovingly.

"Surely, that's the least of it, Naomi," Elana replied crisply, but she took Naomi's arm and urged her on. She had noticed groups of Arabs who gathered at the roadside to watch the solemn procession. Their eyes were hard, and those who wore daggers at their belts kept their hands on the hilts of their weapons. Many carried clubs and knives, and Elana noticed that many wore the abayahs of fellahin rather than the jackets and pantalooned trousers of city Arabs. Her fingers trembled and the handles of the string bag slipped dangerously, spilling the bright fruit onto the cobbled street.

"Elana, Naomi, come with me."

Miraculously, Nadav emerged from the crowd. He took their bags and steered them through narrow streets and alleys, following an obscure route until they at last reached the broader avenues of Rehavia. The blue steel of a revolver handle jutted from his pocket, and Elana knew that the bulk beneath his jacket was that of a cartridge belt.

She wondered if Nadav, the weak-eyed, balding scholar, knew how to shoot, and she suppressed a wild desire to laugh, to relieve her fear and convert it into merriment, to splinter the silence of death. But within seconds all thoughts of laughter vanished. There was sudden turmoil in the street. A woman rushed past them, clutching a small boy in her arms. Her dress was ripped at the bodice and sleeve, and the child wailed uncontrollably, tears streaking through a half-closed blackened eye.

"He hit me. The Arab hit me. Why did he hit me, Imma?"

They heard the sound of carts being overturned, the battening down of iron slats over the doorways of shops. In the distance they saw a cloud of smoke, and the air filled with the acrid scent of burning food, of raw vegetables scorching on unrestrained flame.

"So the heroes have burned a vegetable seller's stand," Nadav said bitterly.

They were running now, their breath rasping painfully, their hearts beating wildly, placing as much distance as they could between themselves and the cacophony of violence, the funereal threads of smoke.

They had recounted their story to Daniel Langerfeld when they reached home.

"Perhaps these are only sporadic disturbances. Action and reaction," he said. "Do not worry." But his eyes narrowed and his brow creased with worry.

It was then that Freya Langerfeld went to stock up on provisions and that Daniel himself put on his good black frock coat and his stiff white collar and silk cravat. A visit to the police chief of Jerusalem was in order.

Two hours later he and Nadav were home again, carrying the cartridge cases. The police chief had been extremely courteous. He regretted that Commissioner Chancellor was on leave, but he himself and his deputies had not been unaware of the large number of Arabs in the city. They had, of course, noticed that many were not from Jerusalem and were armed with clubs and knives. Even before Mr. Langerfeld's thoughtful visit, he himself had called on the mufti of Jerusalem. A charming man, the mufti, the British officer observed. Had Daniel Langerfeld ever met him?

"We have not met, but we are aware of each other."

On another occasion the Zionist leader might have been amused at the police chief's naïveté. Did this bureaucrat from Leeds think that a member of the Jewish Council and the mufti of Jerusalem took tea together? Now he shuddered with fear that the safety of the Jews of Jerusalem rested in the hands of this ingenuous Englishman who kept bits of a Wedgwood tea service in his office and smiled reassuringly throughout their conversation while shouts from the street below shrilled through the open windows: "Death to the Jews. Al Aksa is ours!"

"And what did the mufti say, Your Honor?" Daniel Langerfeld had asked.

"He assured me that the Arabs are armed only because recent events have made them afraid of the Jews—the demonstration at the Wall, the funeral today. And they are disturbed also by the meetings in Zurich. They are frightened by this Jewish Agency your people propose."

The police chief held his hands out helplessly. In England worship was conducted in an orderly manner in ancient cathedrals. He did not understand the Moslems and Jews of this rock-bound city who argued over remnants of a wall and came to blows over baize screens stretched across an open courtyard.

"Would it not be wise to at least disarm the Arabs?" Nadav asked.

"That would be a difficult and provocative operation," a lieutenant replied.

"I see." The Langerfelds knew that meant that the British had few men they could rely on. The entire force numbered only three hundred. The period of peace had made Lord Plumer unduly optimistic, and he had drastically reduced the force. And the Arab officers could not be relied on to deal with brother Arabs effectively.

"Would it perhaps be wise to use Jewish volunteers?" Daniel Langerfeld tossed the suggestion out without hope.

"That would certainly provoke the Arab population," the police chief said stiffly. "It is unfortunate that Commissioner Chancellor is in London, but I have consulted with his deputy and we have sent for reinforcements from the British garrison in Cairo."

"But it will take them at least three days to reach Jerusalem," Nadav interposed. "By then every Jew in Palestine could be dead."

"My boy, you are being dramatic, near-hysterical."

Nadav's outburst pleased the officer. A man who lost control was a man he could dominate, and inevitably these natives all lost control. He knew how to deal with the hysteria of a resident population. He had been with the Blacks and Tans in Ireland, and they had taught those damn Irish zealots a thing or two. He felt reassured. One religious conflict was, after all, pretty much like another. The British had dealt with Catholic intransigence in Ireland. They were managing to keep peace between Hindu and Moslem in India. They could certainly deal with conflict between Jew and Moslem in Palestine. It was their duty, their responsibility.

"A cup of tea?" He turned cordially to the Jewish leaders.

Daniel Langerfeld shook his head sadly. "I am afraid we have no time," he said.

There was time only to make sure they had ammunition for their weapons, provisions in their homes. The Langerfelds knew now what they had to do. A cable would be sent to Weizmann in Switzerland. Messages of caution would be relayed to every Jewish village and settlement in the country.

David Maimon, the unofficial commander of Jewish security forces, would be alerted.

Daniel Langerfeld worked on his journal that evening, carefully recording his conversation with the police chief. He looked up occasionally at his niece Elana, who sat opposite him, her head bent over her order books. It was clear that she would have to abandon her plans to go to Hebron. He had been informed that disturbing numbers of armed Arabs were gathering there. Odd that they should converge on such a small Jewish community. There were only seven hundred Jews in Hebron, and most of them were affiliated to the talmudic college there. But he could not worry about the Jews of Hebron. It was Jerusalem that concerned him. Elana would not go to the ancient hamlet. She knew the danger, and she had, that day, witnessed the letting of blood, the surge of hatred. Still, he glanced nervously at his niece. There was a quality in her that he did not comprehend—the odd fearlessness of one who has always lived close to death and so has ceased to be afraid of it. She reminded him, disturbingly, of her uncle David Maimon.

He had been asleep when Elana left that morning, sliding silently out of the flat while the Langerfeld family slept. Quietly, she had unlatched the bolts with which Daniel Langerfeld had girdled the front door shut, and slipped out into the gray dawn. She had to go. She had promised Mazal that the glassware would be delivered according to schedule, and she knew that Achmed would be waiting for her at the Lion's Gate.

Now she stood at the appointed meeting place and looked up and down the road for her Arab friend. Streaks of pale light lit the sky, and shopkeepers rolled up the corrugated tin shutters that sealed their doorways and methodically set their wares out for display. The Arab vendor of street maps and postcards unfurled a large framed photograph of the mufti. The tobacconist spread his small chamois pouches of Turkish tobacco and English cigarettes on a battered folding table and then carefully arranged his own narghile next to the old leather chair with its worn-out cushions. A pot of water was already boiling on the charcoal brazier, and he smiled toothlessly. But Elana noticed that the baker and the greengrocer had not opened their shops, nor had the cobbler, who usually did a brisk business in the early morning.

She entered the kiosk and ordered a coffee, which was served thick and sweet in a large glass.

"Why are so many shops closed?" she asked the proprietor.

"I, too, will close soon," he replied sourly. "There will be trouble in Jerusalem today. Worse than yesterday. Don't you see?"

He motioned to the street where groups of young Arabs paced, glancing from side to side without breaking step. They carried sticks and clubs, and occasionally one young man would pause to remove his dagger from its scabbard and study the glinting blade in the steadily brightening daylight.

"They are reading the shadows," the kiosk keeper said, and she remembered that her uncle David had told her that if an Arab sees a shadow fall across his weapon, he knows that death will darken his path that day.

"But whose death—his own or his enemy's?" she had asked with a child's insistence on logic.

Where was Achmed? Impatiently, she opened her purse and studied herself in her pocket mirror. Deftly, she thrust a vagrant strand of hair back into place, ran a finger across her thick, dark eyebrows to smooth them, and then, on sudden impulse, she held the glass up to the sunlight. A crescent of shadow trailed across it, and she felt a tremor of fear.

"Surely you are not reading the shadows, Elana Maimon," Achmed said. Laughter licked at his words, and he touched her arm lightly, pleased that he had taken her by surprise.

"Achmed, you are late. I did not think you would be coming," she said and quickly replaced the mirror. Circlets of heat burned her cheeks, and she licked her lips, which had grown suddenly dry.

"And why should I not come? Did you think I would be afraid?"

"No. Of course not. If I am not afraid, why should you be?" she replied, and they smiled at each other, proud of their shared recklessness, eager suddenly to be on their way. The denial of fear banished it. Adventure awaited them this summer morning. She dismissed all lingering worries about the groups of Arabs who prowled the narrow streets, their weapons at the ready; she did not think about her uncle and her cousin who sat in a book-lined room taking inventory of their ammunition. Death and danger came to others, and dancing shadows were accidents of fragmented light.

The sun had burst through at last, and the air shimmered with harsh gold light. A dry heat had replaced the chill of dawn, and the women shoppers who passed them removed their shawls and placed them in shopping baskets.

"Come, we must try to get you a seat near the window," Achmed said, and he slapped a few coins down on the wooden counter of the kiosk to pay for her coffee.

"Where do you journey today, effendi?" the kiosk keeper asked. Achmed had overpaid him, and he felt a fleeting kindness toward the tall, slender youth.

"We go to Hebron. The lady has business there," Achmed replied.

The kiosk keeper leaned across the counter and beckoned them closer. His breath smelled of tehina paste and garlic, and Elana felt her own mouth sour.

"Do not go to Hebron today. There will be trouble there as there is trouble here."

He pointed to the street, and they saw that the shops so recently opened were already being shut. Only the large photograph of the mufti remained on display—a talisman of protection.

"If we wait for trouble, then surely it will come," Achmed said. "What we must do is live our lives normally, proceed with our plans. Danger comes to those who seek it and those who fear it. Come, Elana."

As she entered the jitney she thought of the boy Yossi. He had been playing soccer on a sun-streaked street. He had neither anticipated danger nor tried to flee it, yet he had become its victim. But she said nothing to Achmed, who carefully wiped the leather seat for her and placed her basket beneath his feet. A leaflet in Arabic lay on the floor of the cab, and he picked it up and read it.

"What does it say?" Elana asked.

He scanned the sheet of newsprint impatiently.

"Nothing important," he replied. The poisonous words repelled him, but there was no need to frighten Elana by reading them to her. She sat beside him, holding her broad-brimmed hat, fingering the blue georgette fabric of her wide skirt.

"O Arab," the leaflet read, "Remember that the Jew is your strongest enemy and the enemy of your ancestors since olden times. Do not be misled by his tricks because it was he who tortured Christ (peace be unto him) and poisoned Mohammed (peace and worship be unto him). Save yourself and your fatherland from the grasp of the foreign intruder and greedy Jew."

The language did not surprise Achmed. Similar leaflets had been displayed at meetings of the Brith Shalom, which made it a point to keep abreast of all propaganda. Achmed's cousin Hassan had shown him other flyers and leaflets. The mufti, it seemed, was generous with the distribution of funds for printing.

"These pamphlets are a response to the meetings of the Zionist Congress in Zurich," Musa Alami, who was known as an Arab moderate, had insisted at the last Brith Shalom meeting. "One does not necessarily agree with them, but one knows what inspired them."

"But the creation of a Jewish Agency does not threaten the situation of the Arab population. We should, in fact, like to see an Arab agency emerge," Judah Magnes protested.

"One that will be similar to the Bureau of Indian Affairs in your native United States?" Alami asked, and he smiled when the American blushed.

In the end they had abandoned philosophy and settled for strategy. They agreed that the Arab members of the group would temporize with their people and that the Jewish leaders, too, would advocate moderation. It was essential that normal routines be maintained.

"We must not precipitate a state of war by acting as though we are at war," Judah Magnes said. "Remember, there has been relative peace for eight years—perhaps because Plumer anticipated peace." The philosophic balance of his argument had soothed Achmed.

It was for that reason that he had decided to proceed with the trip to Hebron. He and Elana Maimon, Jew and Arab, traveling together, were a symbol of peaceful coexistence, of friendship. But it was also his duty to protect Elana, his best friend's sister, his mentor's daughter. Now, seated beside her in the jitney, he touched the cold blue steel of a small German revolver tucked into a holster concealed at his belt.

As the vehicle rolled southward, they passed the new kibbutz of Ramat Rachel, where the settlers still lived in tents. Achmed had visited Ramat Rachel that week and taken soil samples. The ground was rocky and hill-bound, but it could sustain a date plantation and terraced fruit crops of the kind Ezra Maimon had cultivated at Sadot Shalom. Even now the soil was slowly, laboriously being turned. He waved to a young man and woman, perched together on the seat of a tractor. The woman wore a bright red sun hat, which she tossed suddenly into the air, and her companion leaped after it, laughing at her foolishness. They were lovers, then, Achmed thought with sudden melancholy, and he glanced down at Elana's beribboned blue hat, which rested half on her lap and half on his knee.

As they rode through Bethlehem he noticed that the streets were strangely empty and that most of the shops were closed. The jitney stopped, and the driver, a swarthy Arab who carried two revolvers in the holster that swung from his waist, alighted to fill his canvas water bag. When he returned, his face was creased in lines of worry.

"Riots have broken out all over Jerusalem," he told his passengers. "I am not sure it is safe to continue."

"Is it safe to return?" Achmed asked.

The driver shrugged. "For myself, I don't care." He patted his weapons and took a long drink of water, allowing it to dribble down the sides of his mouth. "But for the others . . . for the women . . ."

He turned to Achmed and spoke in an Arabic so rapid that Elana could not follow him.

"What did he say?" she asked.

Achmed hesitated.

"He is afraid that if there is trouble you will be raped—you and the other women. And that the old men will be robbed and killed."

Their fellow passengers in the cab were two old rabbis and their wives and a small girl who drifted between the elderly couples, first clutching the hand of one old woman and then that of the other. She was their grandchild. Her parents, they had explained to Elana, had been killed in an accident, and they were taking the small orphan back to Hebron. The women wore the wigs of the Orthodox, and their small faces, lined and shriveled by sun and age, resembled the juiceless globes of fruit that dangled from the trees of Sadot Shalom at summer's end. Their heavy bodies strained against the fabric of their dark, shapeless dresses and their legs bulged in ripples of flesh over tightly laced oxfords.

Together, Achmed and Elana looked at them.

"I really do not think they will be raped," she said gravely in Arabic, and suddenly they were both laughing. They bent over, grasped each other's hands, and laughed still more as though their wild glee might dispel their fear.

"If we return to Jerusalem, we add to the atmosphere of panic," he said soberly when their merriment was spent. "If shops remain open and people go about their business, then a spirit of normality remains and it would be difficult for violence to take hold." He struggled to paraphrase Magnes, to help her understand that fear itself begat violence.

"Besides, if there is violence already in Jerusalem, what is to be gained by driving back into it?" Elana added. "Still, we must tell these people the situation and let them decide for themselves."

She turned to the elderly couples and repeated the driver's admonitions. They looked sadly at each other, and one of the women lifted the small girl onto her lap. She sang softly in Yiddish—a protective song from another world.

> Don't fear my child—God is near.
> Sleep my child—life is dear.

The two men consulted briefly and then turned to Achmed.

"Let us go on to Hebron," he said. "Whatever God wills will happen. Blessed be the name of the Lord."

They continued on their way, but now the passengers did not lean back against the leather cushions. They sat on the edges of their seats, staring out of the window, as though they might perceive hidden dangers in the rolling desert hills, in the bright and cloudless skies, wary suddenly of the stripped acacias that lined the roadside. They did not avert their eyes, depending now on their own vigilance for protection. The heat of the day crowded them; the desert wind was as hot as the breath of a blazing oven. The small girl wept piteously and pulled at the black stockings that covered her legs. At the Arab village of Battis, they stopped to buy cactus fruit, which the child sucked thirstily. The streets of the small, prosperous hamlet were empty, and Achmed asked the fruit seller where everyone had gone.

"To Hebron," he said. "Much will happen in Hebron today." He laughed, revealing toothless gums, bloodied and puckered with sores, and bent to sip from the stream. He had rested his wagon beside the flowing waters just below the huge, brooding rock mound of Betar, where the Romans had at last defeated the Jews. He pointed up to the rock.

"Do you know what that rock is called?" he asked Elana.

His eyes glinted when he looked at this tall Jewish girl, but he had noticed how swiftly she withdrew her hand when she took the cactus fruit from him. Jewish bitch. She could not bear to be sullied by his touch. Perhaps, then, she would be frightened by his words.

"Betar," she replied.

"You call it Betar. But we call it Khirbat al-Yahud." He mouthed the words slowly, his face bent toward her own.

"What does that mean?" she asked Achmed.

"It means 'Ruin of the Jews,'" he said slowly, his eyes on the vendor's face.

"After today they will change the name of Hebron itself to Khirbat al-Yahud," the fruit seller said, and his lips curled with pleasure.

"What will happen in Hebron today?" Achmed asked, but the fruit seller busied himself suddenly with gathering up his wares, counting his money. He sang to himself as he worked and flashed Achmed a mocking glance. *Stupid boy,* he thought. *Son of Mohammed, traveling with an infidel slut.*

"Back to the car," the driver called.

Achmed hesitated, but Elana was already dashing across the road, holding the small girl's hand.

"Hurry, Achmed," she called. "We want to reach Hebron before the noon hour."

Achmed glanced back at the fruit seller, who pursed his lips and spat a wad of chewed fruit at the edge of the water outlet. The glob of masticated pink pulp clung to the barely legible Latin inscription that testified that the Legions of Rome—the Fifth Macedonians and the Eleventh Claudians—had encamped on that spot almost two thousand years past.

And what of it? Achmed thought bitterly and dismissed the fruit vendor and his grim prophecy.

He felt more confident as they rode on. All seemed normal in the tiny hamlets they passed. At Khirbat Tubeika the driver paused briefly to buy newly baked hot pita breads from two children who stood at the roadside. At Ein el-Dirweh, women in colorful gowns gathered at the well to fill their graceful long-necked pitchers with water. The women lingered at their task, speaking with each other, shielding their eyes from the sun as they stared at the passing car. One woman brushed the air with her hand—a hesitant gesture of acknowledgment. All was as it should be, Achmed thought, and he too waved, but the women had dispersed and walked single file to their homes hidden in the hillocks.

"Where are the men today?" the old rabbi asked him.

"Where they should be—in the fields," Achmed replied. He had indeed caught a glimpse of a single Arab farmer walking with a scythe, the sunlight bouncing off the exposed steel.

And when they reached Hebron, all seemed peaceful in the market town. The cab stopped in the main square, and Achmed and Elana said goodbye to their fellow passengers. Elana kissed the small girl's cheek, and the child reached up and touched the blue satin ribbon that rimmed the hat which Sara had sent from Oswiecem.

"How pretty," she said.

"Then you may have it."

Elana ripped the streamer loose and tied it through a thick curl of her young friend's hair. The child's fingers reached up to stroke the smooth, silky fabric. She smiled, reminding Elana of Balfouria, who at this hour would be feeding the chicks at Sadot Shalom.

"We must hurry, Achmed," she said and removed her order book from her basket.

They spent the next two hours hurrying from one small glass workshop to another, collecting the items that Elana had ordered the previous week. While the cases were packed, Achmed watched the orange flames of the blazing furnaces lick at the jewel-colored melting glass. The molten liquid was swiftly blown into a dish, a jug, a vase, and the tiny rooms were aglow with beautiful objects.

Elana examined each purchase carefully. She had often traveled with Mazal and had mastered the small intricacies of trade. She held a golden bowl up to the light, pointed out a tiny air bubble, and asked for a reduction in price. She lifted her hands in shocked surprise when an artisan demanded a fee she considered too high. They sparred gently, making offers and counteroffers, sipping cups of strong, sweet coffee, until at last a price was agreed upon. Each purchase was carefully wrapped for shipping, and she checked each parcel carefully before placing it in the large carton which Achmed carried.

Finally, she checked the last entry in her order book, and they went to the post office in the main square where the parcels would be mailed. She felt a sense of achievement and relief as she counted out the money for the postage. She had not failed Mazal. The orders had been shipped at the specified time.

"Come," she said to Achmed, "let us have some lunch."

Chapter 6

THEY SELECTED A CAFÉ in the marketplace from which they could easily see the Cave of the Machpelah and the Pool of Hebron. The proprietor approached their table, wiping his hands on his white apron.

"You will want to sit inside," he said.

"On a day like this?" She laughed. She had forgotten all the warnings of the previous evening and the apprehensions of the drive. Her business had been easily accomplished, and this was the hour to sit in the sun and scoop up tehina sauce and salad with crisp strips of newly baked pita and sip espresso from tiny cups. She smiled at Achmed, who tilted his face toward the sun. His skin was the color of honey, and his blue eyes matched the cerulean glass plates she had just sent to Boston for Mrs. Justice Brandeis.

He smiled back. The demeanor with which she had conducted her business had impressed him. She was no longer a child. When he returned from his studies in America she would be seventeen, almost eighteen. His own mother had married at fourteen.

"We will sit outside," he told the proprietor, who shrugged and brought them their order. But the man did not linger to ask if everything was satisfactory. They ate slowly, now for the first time exchanging news of the past week. She told Achmed of her uncle's fears and how even Nadav shared them.

"They are realistic fears," he acknowledged, "but it takes as much courage to seek out peace as to engage in war. That is what we did when we came to Hebron today. We sought out peace and normality."

She blushed, pleased that he thought her courageous. She had thought only of proving herself to Mazal, of sharing the day with him. Still, she did not protest but glanced about for the waiter because their coffee cups were empty.

"Elana—listen!"

Achmed's fingers were tight about her wrist. Her breath stopped. A strange silence had settled over the busy marketplace. Doors and windows were drawn shut. Across the road a lone bearded Jew huddled in a doorway. She sat perfectly still, struggling to atune herself to the sudden quiet—a quiet that reminded her of the stillness that fell across Sadot Shalom in the minutes before a sudden mountain storm. She remembered how that stillness was shattered by the muted roll of thunder, the jagged streak of lightning. She listened expectantly and heard the rumble then, low at first and growing louder, steadier. But it was not the rumble of thunder. It was the beat of many feet, a synchronistic march, leather against stone in steady tympanic onslaught. And then the measured steps broke into a brisk run, and the silence was pierced by curdling shrieks.

"Death to the infidels! Death to the Jews!"

They sped through the streets, all uniformity abandoned. They filled the market square and the great ridge road—men and boys in the white abayahs of the peasants, in the striped robes and Western jackets of city merchants, barefoot and booted, in fez and keffiyah. Steel-bladed daggers and intricately handled knives glinted in their hands. Axes and slaughterers' implements were proudly held aloft. They carried clubs fashioned from the legs of chairs, branches roughly wrested from terebinth and olive trees, scythes and pruning shears thrust forward like spears. Achmed realized then what had disturbed him about the Arab he had seen earlier, walking across the fields with a scythe in hand. It was not the season of harvest—the passing farmer had held death in his grasp.

"There's one!"

A tall young Arab in a ragged blue jabaliyah pointed to the young talmudic student who had flattened himself against the shadows of the entryway. The youth's slender body trembled within his dark caftan, and his chestnut earlocks fluttered. He clutched the large leatherbound tome he was carrying against his chest, as though it might shield him from a projected onslaught.

A small ax flew across the road, swerving so that its edge bit neatly into the young Jew's neck, severing the jugular vein. A gush of crimson stained the stone, and slowly, as though in languid dance, the black-coated figure swayed, slid to the ground, and was still, the ancient volume fallen to the ground, open to a closely columned page.

The crowd stared at its victim and shouted wildly. Achmed was reminded of the night he had surprised a pack of jackals in the fields of Sadot Shalom. They had killed an ewe lamb, and the sight and taste of her blood had excited them to a wild frenzy. They had bared their teeth, shrieked, and wailed—hungry for yet another kill, their tongues licking at blood as yet untasted. They had not dispersed until he shot two of them, and even then their golden eyes had blazed with fury as they fled. The assembled mob was not unlike the scavenger animals, and he felt again the fear and disgust that had swept over him in the moonlit field.

He took hold of Elana's hand. They had not yet noticed her. "Walk close to me," he whispered, and he pressed his body against hers so that they moved as one. All that the advancing Arab mob could see was the white drape of his keffiyah. They would not pursue another Arab, and he knew that there was a Jewish hotel only half a block away where they could find refuge. He all but carried Elana now. His hands were wrapped tightly about her quivering body, and her sweat mingled with his own. The shouts of the mob increased in intensity. He stepped up his pace and wished that he had thought to hold his small revolver instead of leaving it in his holster.

"Halt! Identify yourselves!"

A British officer stood before them, a revolver extended.

"I am Achmed ibn-Saleem, and this is Elana Maimon. I must get her to safety." His words rushed desperately.

"Hurry, then. The hotel is just up the street. I will cover here for you. I am Commander Raymond Cafferata. Good luck to you, Achmed ibn-Saleem."

"Are there other police in the town?" Achmed asked.

"Reinforcements have been sent for. From the garrison at Cairo. Hurry now!"

But it was too late. A group of Arabs hurtled toward them. They had glimpsed Elana's blue skirt.

"Jewish whore!"

"Daughter of infidels!"

The air bristled with their hatred. A shot winged by. A stone barely missed Achmed's head as he hurried forward. The sound of their pursuers' thunderous footsteps rang in his ears. But the young British commander knelt in the center of the road, placing himself between Achmed and the advancing crowd, his rifle poised. A shot rang out, then another.

Fool. They will kill you, Achmed thought, and he did not know whether Raymond Cafferata was the bravest man he had ever met or the most foolish.

But the mob did not kill the British officer. One and then another Arab fell to the ground, and the others dispersed, running in varied directions, away from the death-spewing rifle.

"All right—go now!" Cafferata shouted after Achmed, but he was already at his destination.

The door to the hotel was bolted, but he kicked at it mightily.

"Elana, tell them who you are so that they will open the door," he gasped. He held her still, but his strength was draining.

"Please," Elana shouted, "you must let us in. I am Elana Maimon, the daughter of Ezra Maimon of Sadot Shalom, the niece of Daniel Langerfeld." Desperately she offered any scrap of identification which might be recognized.

"What is the name of Daniel Langerfeld's eldest son?" a man's voice asked from within.

"Nadav."

The door slid open, and they hurried inside.

The half-dozen assembled Jews stared at Achmed in surprise.

"He is a friend, Achmed ibn-Saleem," Elana told them. "He saved my life."

The hotelkeeper, a bearded Jew, held out his hand to Achmed.

"We thank you," he said. "Have you weapons?"

He pointed to the broad table on which three carving knives, two knitting needles, and a long hatpin had been placed. Achmed placed his dagger and revolver beside them.

"A pathetic armory," the hotelkeeper acknowledged, "but we never considered Hebron to be in danger. What could they want with seven hundred Jews, all studying Talmud?" He shrugged and held his hands out as though puzzling out a legal problem in the Mishnah.

"Is there anyone else in the building?" Achmed asked.

"There are some twenty-five lodgers in the rooms above. We have advised them to stay inside their rooms and lock the doors."

"That is good advice," Achmed said.

He looked around the room, studying it carefully. There was a large reception desk of golden wood and small storage cabinets where travelers might leave their luggage. He cursed the absence of a closet or even an armoire.

"All right," he said finally. "All the women must get behind the reception table and kneel as low as they can. You must not be seen."

The three women scurried to follow his orders. Their faces were pale and their eyes glazed.

"Good."

He stood in the doorway and found that he could not discern their presence at all.

"Now the children must crawl into the storage cabinets."

The one small boy took his two sisters by their hands.

"Don't cry," he told them severely. "I am here to take care of you."

Obediently they crouched into the tiny enclosures, and Achmed closed the door, leaving them only a scarce inch for air.

"It won't be for long," he called to them.

There was one small utility closet. He removed mops and brooms and motioned the innkeeper and another man into it.

"Unbolt the door, Elana," he said, "and leave it slightly ajar."

"But why?"

"The mob will assume that an unlocked door means an empty room. They will be sure of it when they come in and see no one. Everyone—children—try not to make a sound, not to move at all. It is our only chance. Knitting needles and carving knives will not save us.''

He swept the weapons into a drawer but gave his revolver to Elana. He himself had taught her to shoot, and he remembered still the delicate feel of her finger as he held it over the trigger. He took his dagger himself. Its blade was newly sharpened, and the hilt was comfortable in his grasp. David Maimon had given it to him after the war—a gift of thanks for the journey through the desert that had brought David to safety. Fleetingly he thought of the curious irony that this weapon, given to him by a Jew who had fled the Turks, should now be used to defend himself, Achmed ibn-Saleem, against his own people. What strange alliances were welded in this complex land of his birth.

''Come.'' He took Elana's hand, and they concealed themselves behind the large red plush sofa that dominated the inn's small lobby.

They pressed their heads against the sofa's dusty back. There was no sound, no movement, within that room where ten human beings huddled and prayed silently that the day might end, that the terror might cease, that they might survive. A child sneezed, and Elana's breath came in shallow gasps. Her long black hair had fallen free of its pins and caped her shoulders in a velvet sweep. He longed to touch it, but although he had held her so closely that her body seemed to meld into his only moments ago, now he dared not reach a finger to a single dark strand. She brushed her hand across her eyes, and he saw the fear and tiredness etched into her face. She was only a child after all—a young girl who had been jolted too suddenly into womanhood.

''Don't be afraid, Elana,'' he whispered.

''If you are here, I am not afraid.'' Her trusting child's answer came in a woman's throaty whisper.

''Shh.''

He heard the rushing of feet. The outside door swung open. Somewhere in the room someone moaned softly, almost imperceptibly, and was instantly quiet. The door to the room was kicked open.

''It's not locked!'' a man shouted hoarsely. ''They must have run for it. The rotten Jew cowards.''

There were footsteps in the room now, the harsh ring of

boots on the tiled floor. How many, he wondered—two intruders, three, four? There were eight bullets in the revolver's chamber. He curled his fingers around the hilt of his dagger, felt the smoothness of the studded stones.

Someone advanced to the sofa, pulled a pillow loose, and plunged a knife through it. Feathers filled the air. One lit on Elana's hair, a misplaced snowflake on a darkened landscape.

"Where do the bastards keep their money?" the man muttered.

"Not in the sofa. And they'll have taken the cash box. But upstairs, in the bedrooms, where the lodgers stay, there'll be money there, and jewels. That's probably where they're hiding."

"Upstairs!"

They sounded the word like a battle cry that was echoed by other men who swarmed into the hotel.

"Upstairs!"

They left the reception room, reeling through the doorway, but suddenly one man began firing aimless shots. The first shot shattered a terra-cotta pitcher, the second splintered the glass in a painting. At the sound of the shots Achmed instinctively placed himself between Elana and the sofa. A third shot whizzed across the room. The bullet pierced the upholstery and grazed his shoulder. He felt it as a sharp sting. His fingers flew to the source of his pain and came away covered with blood. He bit his lips shut to stifle the scream that welled within him.

Elana pressed herself close against him, but still they dared not move. The second floor of the hotel was overrun now. Men ran from room to room, and they heard the shouts and screams of the lodgers as door after door was broken down. In the room just above them a woman screamed desperately, wildly. Achmed thought of his mother's screams in childbirth. Rape. Labor. A woman's body being forced, intruded upon, violated. Bodies rolled about in fierce combat. A man's voice shrilled the *Sh'ma*. "Hear O Israel, the Lord is God, the Lord is one. . . ." The shrillness became a moan, and he was silent. A body fell with a heavy thud, and then there came the terrible crying of children: "Abba, Abba!"

Achmed's cheeks were wet, and he felt Elana's tears burn through his shirt. Glass shattered. Wood crashed and was splintered by ax and hatchet. The screams were infrequent now, each rising to a crescendo and falling away into a silence more frightening than the curdling sound. Footsteps thundered down the stairwell. It was almost over, then.

He felt a warm spatter on his head. He touched the moisture that rained down upon him, warm and thick against his skin. His fingers came away sticky, reddened. Blood. He crouched behind the sofa, beneath a storm of blood. He had gone mad, then. The terror and pain had caused him to hallucinate. But he looked up and saw that the ceiling was soaked with blood that dripped steadily down. Cautiously, he moved Elana out of the way and saw, with relief, that she had fainted. The blood of his shoulder wound petaled her blue dress with oddly shaped flowers, and the revolver that she had not, after all, had to use, lay limp in her hand.

He took it and waited, listening as keenly to the silence as he had listened to the noise of the invaders. Minutes passed and the building remained quiet except for a dislodged shutter that swung open and shut in a steady dirge.

"It's all right, I think," he said at last.

The men emerged from the utility closet. The women crept out from behind the counter and hurried to the children. The small girls hugged each other, frozen into silence. The soft hills of their cheeks were swollen with tears. The boy stood rigid, his fists clenched.

"Take them away," Achmed told the women and pointed upward.

They stared at the ceiling, crimson-wet still, dripping the warm rain of death in tiny heart-shaped drops, and hurried the children into the kitchen. Achmed put a pillow beneath Elana's head and followed the men upstairs.

They did not speak as they went from room to room. Words were lost to them. The lifeless bodies of two small boys were sprawled next to their mother's corpse, each clinging to one of her hands. She had been pregnant, and her abdomen had been slit wide so that they saw the fetus, a homunculus in its shimmering coating, still linked to the umbilical cord, moving slightly—life trapped in death, struggling to be nurtured. Achmed gagged and the innkeeper vomited. Green pools of bilious phlegm floated on the scarlet rivulets of blood.

Men lay with their throats cut, limbs chopped off and tossed in a heap. The women had been killed with daggers thrust through breasts. The murderers could not wait to slide a bracelet off. They had severed hand from wrist for the simpler seizure of a circlet of gold. Fingers, too, had been hacked off and floated like fingerlings in the puddles of blood that filled every floor. In the last room he found the body of the small orphan girl who had traveled with them to Hebron. Elana's blue satin ribbon nestled still in her hair, and he untied it and slipped it into his pocket.

"There is nothing to be done," he told the innkeeper. "There is no one to help, no one to save."

The man covered his face with trembling hands, and his companion wept. Achmed felt hot tears streak his own face. His shoulders shook but no sound came from his mouth.

Silently then, they joined the women and the children in the kitchen, and it was not until Elana carefully cut his shirt away and cleansed the wound with warm water that Achmed remembered that a steel bullet had ripped through his flesh and splintered a tiny knob of shoulder bone. She had shown him the minuscule ivory fragment, and he studied it with great attention. Pain seethed, but it brought him an odd pleasure. He had saved her life.

"Elana," he whispered.

He lifted a sheaf of her dark hair and let the silken strands drift through his fingers.

"Elana."

He had saved her life.

Chapter 7

EZRA MAIMON STOOD before the small mirror framed in olive-wood that Mazal had hung in their bedroom and combed his beard. With great deliberation he pulled the comb through the thick mass of dark hair that grew luxuriantly about his chin. He had been dubious about the beard at first, strangely fearful that it made him look too old, but Mazal had insisted.

"It makes you look distinguished," she had said, thrusting a mirror playfully at him. *"Très distingué."* She was proud of the fragments of French she had acquired in Switzerland.

That had been in Zurich, more than two years past, during the Zionist Congress, but he remembered still the touch of Mazal's fingers as they curled teasingly about the newly grown beard, begun as a bit of vacation laziness during the Mediterranean crossing. He had discovered that he liked the feel of it and the sense of disguise it offered him. He wondered vaguely if all bearded men shared this sense of masquerade. Or was a beard a hirsute acknowledgment of manhood? Mostly he had kept it because Mazal liked it, and always, Mazal's whim became his command.

"Do you know," she had continued, "when I was in the lobby of the Tolle Hotel this afternoon, I saw you come in. You were wearing your new suit and carrying your attaché case. Your beard was so neat, ending in that nice square you just manage. You were with Dr. Einstein, and I remember thinking, 'Who is that fine-looking bearded man talking to Einstein? He must be very important.' It took me some moments to realize that it was you—my husband, Ezra Maimon, and when I did I was so proud, so very proud."

He smiled, remembering that as he entered he had glimpsed

her standing across the crowded lobby wearing a peacock-blue robe of her own design, her dark hair intricately entwined with woven ropes of gold. She stood beneath a glittering crystal chandelier, in earnest conversation with an elderly delegate from South Africa, and Ezra was not surprised when the man reached into his pocket for a memo pad on which he made some notes. All who met his petite, tawny-skinned wife were anxious to be of service to her. Within the next several months a letter would arrive from Durban or Capetown, reminding Mazal of their conversation and enclosing either an order for handiworks or a check to cover the purchase of new machinery for her workshops. She already had the promise of looms and kilns, of long work tables and properly backed stools for her artisans.

"That is my wife," he told Albert Einstein, and the physicist had nodded wisely and studied Mazal.

"She is most exquisite," he said in his courtly Old World way, and Ezra had glowed with pleasure and marveled anew that the diminutive beautiful woman who rushed across the room to his side was indeed his own. Always he felt renewed wonderment that they had somehow found each other, that they belonged together and that they were together.

He frowned now at the discovery of two gray hairs in his beard, and thought back to the congress. He remembered it so vividly, even the day they had so hurriedly left Switzerland, their hearts pounding with fear, barely speaking to each other during the long journey to London, because to exchange their thoughts would mean an articulation of what they both feared. Words made secret terror real. They had left when they learned of the Arab riots in Palestine, although the full facts would not be available until they reached London. Still, they knew that the Arabs had swept through Hebron on precisely the day that Elana had planned to be in the ancient city.

If she is dead, Ezra had thought, *I shall have nothing left of Nechama. Amos is lost to me in life and Elana will be lost to me in death.* He had looked away from Mazal, ashamed because his fear betrayed their love.

If she is dead, Ezra will blame me, Mazal had thought. *She went to Hebron because I asked her to. I will have lost both his children for him—both of Nechama's children. He will not forgive me.* And she, too, felt shamed because her first fear had been for herself and for Ezra's love for her, and not for sweet young Elana, whom she had loved since her arrival at Sadot Shalom.

And so they had remained silent, and they did not turn their heads as the westbound express train left Zurich. They had no wish to look back at the city where they had been so happy for the time of the congress. Those halcyon weeks of achievement and togetherness had been shadowed by the terrible news from Palestine. If the omens had not been so favorable, their disappointment would not have been so deep and piercing.

The congress had been a honeymoon for Ezra and Mazal—a honeymoon after seven years of marriage. Their courtship had been swift and complex, and they had not paused between the celebration of their marriage and the beginning of their shared life for even the briefest respite from care and duty. There was, after all, so much to do. There was Elana to be cared for and the farm itself to be revitalized after the long war years of neglect. Always, they were haunted by the feeling that they had lost a great deal of time and must somehow compensate for it. They seldom spoke of the difference in their ages, but they did not ignore it. Ezra was not a young man. They could not wait to commence the large family they both wanted. And so the children had been born, one after the other—Balfouria and Amnon, then the twins, and finally the baby, Rivka. And the house had been expanded to provide room for them and for the succession of Polish girls who arrived to help Mazal. And her network of craft workshops had also expanded—Chemed Handicrafts she called them, choosing the Hebrew word for beauty and grace.

The pace of their lives, the multitude of their blessings, occasionally startled Ezra. One afternoon shortly after Rivka's birth, he had carried in a basket of the first plums, a harvest from the young trees in his newly planted orchard. Their golden pulp glowed through thin purple skin, and he arranged them on the low olivewood table in the living room, in a pale blue ceramic bowl fashioned in a Chemed workshop. Through an open doorway, he saw Mazal nursing the new baby as Elana played with the twins. As he watched, Balfouria and Amnon flew through the room. Each plucked a fruit, their laughter trilling, their fingers deft. The combined beauty caused him to tremble suddenly, and tears burned his eyes. It seemed almost dangerous that so much loveliness was theirs and in their power. His wonder and fear puzzled him until he remembered that he was the son of a woman who had hung red ribbons above the cribs of sleeping children as a talisman against evil.

But there had been little time during those busy, joyous years for him and Mazal to celebrate their love alone, to enjoy sweet silence and tender solitude. The journey to the congress was indeed like a honeymoon voyage, made all the sweeter because now their love was neither tentative nor vulnerable. Their spacious bedroom in Zurich's Tolle Hotel was a luxurious nuptial chamber. On the large, soft bed, spread with embroidered linens, she became again his bride, his mistress, his tawny desert love. They looked through the wide window at the shimmering waters of the Limmat, and Mazal marveled at the Grossmünster, which shadowed the right bank of the narrow flowing river.

They walked hand in hand into the Civic Theater, where a huge Jewish flag hung over the stately entrance. Mazal allowed her feet to slide across the marble floors, as delighted as a child with their alabaster smoothness. Ezra smiled. Too often he forgot that his tiny wife was a daughter of the desert. This was her first visit to Europe, her first venture out of the Middle East. Never before had she seen a landscape that was not bounded by sand or felt winds that had traveled through snow-capped mountains and verdant valleys to caress her upturned face.

They visited the Roman Castellum and Customs House on the Lindenhof and were reminded of the ruins at Caesaria and of the military fortresses hidden deep in the hills of the Galilee. They marveled at the mysterious and resonant rhythms of history, so strangely miscible. Here, in this quiet Alpine country, where once Romans had ruled, Jews, once subdued by those same Romans, had gathered to discuss the re-creation of their state.

In the auditorium of the theater, they listened to the extravagant speeches of the delegates and to the bitter internecine arguments. Those who followed Weizmann could not abide Jabotinsky. The Zionists spoke of statehood, a national home, while others argued for the strengthening of the Jewish community in the Diaspora. Léon Blum, the French socialist, sat beside Max Warburg, the American banker. Ezra's turn to speak came, and he succinctly described the situation with regard to the Arabs. A spirit of cooperation had to be encouraged. There would have to be justice and equity.

"But aren't the Palestinian Arabs too intransigent—too set against Jewish immigration?" an American delegate asked.

"There is no single voice speaking for the so-called Palestinian Arabs," Ezra replied. "Just as we are of many different opinions, they, too, are splintered. There are many who are not afraid of Jewish immigration and the benefits it brings. My own closest adviser in the development of my farm is a young Arab, a graduate of a Jewish agricultural school who will go to Cornell for advanced training and then return to Palestine to help both Arab and Jewish farmers."

There was warmth in his voice as he spoke of Achmed, who had followed the path he would have chosen for his own son. Still, many delegates from England and the United States had approached him to offer congratulations on Amos's achievements. His monographs had won coveted prizes in English academic circles. Amos's new book had been a sensation in the archaeological world. *Amos's new book.* Ezra felt a heaviness of heart. He had not even known of Amos's book. His son had neither sent him a copy nor mentioned it in his perfunctory letters to Sadot Shalom. How long, he wondered, would Amos continue to punish him for the crime of loving and claiming Mazal?

The delegates congregated in the wainscoted corridors of the *Tonhalle* and exchanged impressions. Clearly, the Jewish Agency would be approved by the congress and become a central focus for Jewish life everywhere. It would unite both Zionists and non-Zionists and provide the world Jewish community with one voice. Chaim Weizmann, the voice of moderation, had triumphed, and even Jabotinsky did not begrudge him his victory.

The assemblage lit a memorial candle for Theodor Herzl and said Kaddish for him. It was the twenty-fifth anniversary of his death. Over three decades had passed, Ezra thought, since the Zionist leader had visited the Rishon farm, sat in Rivka's best chair, and told Ezra to fix his gaze on the north, to seek his future in the Galilee. Ezra had been a youth then, still reading French poetry and trailing after his sister Sara. And now the great man was twenty-five years dead, and he himself wore a beard through which strands of silver wandered.

Mazal's discussion of her work in Chemed Handicrafts was well attended. Her sample items were purchased, and she had cabled Elana for the additional glassware. Mrs. Louis Marshall fingered the woven fabrics, draped a scarf stiff with metallic embroidery about her shoulders.

"I will visit your boutiques when I am next in Palestine," she told Mazal. "I have a friend who might be interested in opening such a shop in New York."

"One day there will be Chemed boutiques in every important city," Mazal said. "We have only just begun."

She smiled to think that the glazed bowls she collected in her donkey cart from the mud huts of Arab women would be sold on Fifth Avenue and the Champs Elysées, in Harrod's and in the wide-windowed department stores of Johannesburg.

They attended the final dinner in the thickly carpeted ballroom of the Tolle Hotel. Ezra, the farmer from the Galilee, bowed from the waist and kissed the hand of Mrs. Cyrus Adler. David Ben Gurion waltzed with Vera Weizmann, whose lips were set in a grim line because his rather large feet collided too often with her delicately shod toes. Mazal told the novelist Shalom Asch about the beauty of sunsets in the Galilee.

"Perhaps I will visit Palestine one day," the novelist said. "I am planning a novel about the life of Christ."

"It is interesting that a Jewish novelist should choose to write about the life of Christ," she said carefully. Asch's eyes were dangerously brilliant, and he drank too much red wine.

"The Nazarene. I shall call it *The Nazarene*," he replied dreamily. "It is a natural topic for a Jewish novelist. Christ was such a typical Jew. Persecuted. Misunderstood. Betrayed and finally murdered. His life was Jewish history *in brevis*, don't you agree, dear madame?" He did not wait for her reply but sailed across the room to join a conversation with Léon Blum and Albert Einstein.

There was ebullience of spirit, unrestrained optimism, at that congress. The delegates were possessed of a sense of destiny. They were creating history. It seemed only natural, at the conclusion of the sessions, when the plans for the Jewish

Agency had been agreed upon and ratified, when budgets had been approved and committee reports heard, that the Maimons would decide to take a real vacation without plenaries and committees. Chania wrote from Sadot Shalom encouraging them to do so. The children did not miss them unduly, Elana was managing things in Jerusalem, and Achmed had done a splendid job organizing the harvest. "Do take a holiday," she wrote.

And so they accepted the Weizmanns' invitation to accompany them to Wengen, an Alpine hamlet which Vera Weizmann was certain would delight Mazal. Vera Weizmann, the sophisticated physician, was fascinated by Mazal Maimon. Like many intellectual women, she was intrigued by the accomplishments of those who are skilled with their hands, who demonstrate an instinct for beauty. She clapped her hands at Mazal's swift sketches, at the deftness with which she molded swathes of fabric into elegant stoles. Chaim Weizmann had always respected Ezra's firsthand views on Palestine. The improbable friends looked forward to a happy holiday.

But they had never reached Wengen. The cable, informing them in stark language of the massacres in Palestine, arrived. Safed. Jerusalem. Hebron. Cities become slaughtering grounds. Ezra stared at the place names with talons of terror clutching his chest. There was no mention of Rishon or of Gan Noar. But Ramat Rachel had been decimated. Ramat Rachel, a young kibbutz named for Jacob's favorite wife, whose tomb could be seen from its hills. He remembered the verses from Jeremiah: "A voice was heard in Ramah, lamentations and bitter weeping: Rachel weeping for her children because they were not. . . ." Now again, mothers would weep for their children, for the young kibbutzniks who had come to build new lives and collided with death instead. Achmed had visited Ramat Rachel not long ago and gathered soil samples. Almonds might grow there, the young agronomist had told Ezra. Terracing was possible. But now the fallow ground was soaked with blood. Was blood a good fertilizer for almond saplings? Ezra wondered briefly, bitterly, fixing his thoughts on Ramat Rachel so that he would not think about Elana, so that he would not face the unbearable possibility that Elana might be dead or maimed.

He stared at the figures with uncomprehending eyes. The

casualty reports differed each day. One hundred and fifty had been wounded and fifty killed. No. Two hundred had been wounded and seventy-five killed. How safe numbers were, Ezra thought. There was no grief in the recitation of statistics. Men did not mourn for ten dead or one hundred dead. Their sorrow was for boys named Moshe and Aaron, Zvi and David. They wept for the rapes of Miriam and Ruth. (But not Elana. Please, God. Not Elana.)

In the end they learned that one hundred and thirty-three Jews had been killed and over three hundred and thirty had been wounded. In haunted dreams, Ezra heard the wails of the mourners, saw the shredded clothing, the battered bodies. They had been deceived in Zurich. They had thought they were creating history with their resolutions and counterresolutions, while the future was being written in Hebron, in droplets of blood.

Their train sped through a Europe caught in the chill of an early autumn. In Palestine the air would be bright with golden heat, and his children would be toddling barefoot through fragrant meadows. But they had traveled to London with the Weizmanns because the scientist had prevailed upon him.

"You know the Arabs well, Ezra. You will be able to describe the situation to MacDonald and Passfield. And you know Churchill. He will have some influence. You must come."

Ezra had longed for Palestine, for his children and for the fields of Sadot Shalom. He yearned, above all, for the sound of Elana's voice. He dreamed that he saw her standing in the arched doorway of the farmhouse, her long, dark hair hanging loose, staring across the fields as though she could read a secret in the waving stalks of grain. But he went to London, just as he had gone to Cairo and to Gallipoli and to New York and Boston so many years ago. Always, it seemed, there were obligations to be met.

When will my life be my own? he thought, and briefly he envied those private men who cultivated their gardens and wrote their books and left their laboratories for a familiar hearthside when the day's work was done.

He was too old for historic missions that did not make history, for futile meetings with powerful men who denied him their power. But he could not refuse Weizmann.

In London, at the small hotel on Curzon Street, a cable had been waiting. Mazal ripped it open with trembling fingers.

"It's from Elana. She's all right. She's home—back at Sadot Shalom. She's all right, Ezra."

She went to him and he held her close, her tears hot against his chest. Relief weakened him, and he sank down on the bed, pulling her with him. How light she was, his tiny Mazal, how fragile the wings of her shoulders. They celebrated life then, as the bells of Saint Paul's tolled, coming together with the passion of those who know each other's secrets, who have seen heart and dream exposed and shared terror and its surcease.

It was cool in London where autumn came early, darkening the sun in the late afternoon and wafting winds from the Scottish highlands. They shivered in their light clothing, and Mazal lifted her head to the penumbral sky and yearned for sunlight and desert. She watched the children sailing their boats in Regent's Park and longed for Balfouria and Amnon, for the twins and Rivka, and for Elana. Still they waited. Churchill was at Chartwell. He wrote a courteous note. He would be pleased to see his old companion Ezra Maimon, but he did not know how he could be of service.

Ezra and Mazal journeyed there, and Mazal carried with her, as a gift for Clementine Churchill, a golden bowl of Hebron glass that caught the dying light of the late afternoon.

"It is the color of Jerusalem stone at daybreak, my dear," Churchill told his wife. "We must visit the holy city together one day."

"Yes, indeed," Lady Churchill agreed cordially. She was a handsome woman whose complexion matched the late-blooming pale roses in her wonderfully patterned gardens. "But it is so very hot in the Middle East. Perhaps your skin protects you from the sun, my dear?" She smiled graciously at Mazal.

Churchill was accommodating, understanding, and powerless.

"We're out of office," he said disconsolately. "Balfour, Amery, myself. There is not a word we can say, not a thing we can do."

The smoke of his cigar trailed in a thin gray ribbon, and his jowls hung in limp packets of florid flesh. He had grown older, more corpulent. His fingers swelled about his signet ring, and his small eyes were tired and red-rimmed. He had turned to scholarship when his party was turned out of office and was writing a history of the English language.

"If I cannot mold the future, I will protect the past," he said and neatly clipped another cigar. "But we will be back. One day they will call us back."

He looked out at the green meadowlands of Chartwell, as though anticipating the arrival of a courier who would summon him to Downing Street.

"But I'll tell you something, Maimon. It's not the Arabs who worry me. It's this Hitler in Germany."

"He's a rabble-rouser—a nonentity," Ezra said. "One day they will fish his body out of the Rhine, and that will be the end of him."

"I think not," Churchill said. "As for your situation, I assume Lord Passfield will appoint a commission of inquiry. He is extraordinarily fond of commissions. I will enlist the aid of Balfour and some others, and we will make a statement in the *London Times* urging the commission to be fair and to uphold the promises of the Balfour Declaration."

"That will be helpful," Ezra said politely.

He reported the results of his meeting to Weizmann, who still waited in London for a hearing with Lord Passfield. It was ironic that the Baldwin government had fallen even as the Zionist Congress convened in Zurich. Ramsay MacDonald, the new prime minister, was not sympathetic to the Russian-born chemist. He had appointed Sidney Webb as colonial secretary, and the crusading socialist had been given the title Lord Passfield.

"Surely Passfield will be sympathetic to us," Ezra said. He had read writings by both Sidney Webb and his wife, Beatrice, in various socialist journals. In Palestine, on *kibbutzim* and *moshavim*, Jews were translating socialist ideals into reality. Surely the Webbs would admire this.

"I doubt it," Weizmann said dryly. "The socialists stereotype Jews as capitalists. Their reasoning is impeccable. If Rothschild is a Jew and a banker, then all Jews must be bankers. It follows as the day the night. The Arabs make wonderful downtrodden victims. The international socialists turn to Comrade Stalin for guidance. Still, we must persevere."

Weizmann wrote letters and sent telegrams. Each day he

neatly knotted his cravat and left his card at the homes and offices of influential men. He was a supplicant on behalf of his people, an emissary for those murdered on the cobbled streets of Safed, Hebron, and Jerusalem.

At last he was invited to tea by Beatrice Webb, Lady Passfield, the colonial secretary's wife. Ezra accompanied him, wearing the new suit that he had acquired for his visit to Chartwell and the city shoes that blistered his feet.

Lady Passfield was an angular lady whose tallow white skin was stretched tightly across thin features. Her weak, pale eyes were cold, and her breasts were shrunken within a somber black dress, the rusted funereal fabric relieved only by a sparse white collar. The tea she poured them was tepid, and the crustless bread, covered by thin slices of cucumber and darkened watercress, was stale. She did not consider it proper to gorge on good food while most of the world starved, she told them sternly.

They agreed and dutifully declined sugar.

"Our mutual friend, Josiah Wedgwood, tells me that you are concerned about the incidents in Palestine," she said.

"They are not mere incidents, dear lady," Chaim Weizmann replied, and he bravely selected a watercress sandwich. "One hundred and thirty-three Jews have been killed. Three hundred and thirty-nine have been wounded."

She stared at them through narrowed eyes, the color of soiled winter ice. Her voice was brittle.

"I can't understand," she snapped, "why you Jews make such a fuss over a few dozen of your people killed in Palestine. As many are killed every week in London in traffic accidents, and no one pays any attention."

"I bid you good day, madame," Weizmann said, and his voice was heavy with sadness and defeat.

But Ezra Maimon offered no courteous farewell, and when he replaced his teacup, he tipped it and the residue of yellow liquid in his cup formed a neat puddle on the Oriental rug, for which he made no apology.

The next day he and Mazal left for Palestine.

"I learned something as I listened to that lady," he told Mazal. "That great socialist lady who eats stale bread on behalf of the downtrodden of the world and who writes learned papers on the Poor Law. I learned that her humanitarianism does not extend to the Jews. We must depend only on ourselves. The good will and evil intentions of others are not relevant to our survival. My brother David is right. We must govern ourselves and we must learn to protect ourselves.''

"And produce for ourselves," Mazal said. It was time to expand Chemed Handicrafts. Elana could work more closely with her. She was so mature for her age.

They were relieved to return to Palestine, happy to find all the children well and Elana unaffected by her terrible experiences in Hebron. Yet there was a new calmness about her, a steady patience that reminded Mazal of a young woman in Saana who had waited many years for her fiancé to return from a long journey to the Lebanon. Mazal tried to remember if the young man had ever come back, but she retained only a mental image of the waiting bride sewing an endless trousseau. No, Elana was not like that, but still, something about her triggered the memory.

Achmed visited them before he left for America, and sat alone with Ezra on the bench beneath the avocado tree. Mazal and Elana saw the twin glow of Achmed's cigarette and Ezra's cigar in the darkness.

Ezra came into the house holding the slip of paper on which Achmed had written his address in Ithaca, New York.

"He is a good and brave man, Achmed ibn-Saleem," Ezra said. "I shall miss him when he is in the United States."

"He saved my life," Elana replied. Her voice was very low. She heard again the bullet whistle across the room and felt Achmed's hands seize her shoulder, shove her behind him, as he became a shield for her trembling body.

"You know what the Arabs say," Ezra said teasingly. "He who saves a life cheats the shadows, and he must then be responsible for the one he has saved. Achmed will be responsible for you always."

"Yes. Always," Elana said, and a small, satisfied smile curled her lips. Mazal glanced at her curiously but said nothing.

The two years of Achmed's absence were busy ones. Ezra expanded his livestock holdings and planted additional fields of grain to feed his growing flocks. Visitors came to the farm. Nadav Langerfeld spent every vacation period at Sadot

Shalom. He brought Elana books and journals to read and went with her on errands for Chemed Handicrafts, which was exporting many items abroad. Liam Halloran, whose life Ezra had saved on Gallipoli, sought them out and became a frequent visitor. He, too, was a farmer, and he missed his fields in Derry and his wife and children. Balfouria and Amnon trailed after him, and he held the twins and Rivka on his knees and sang them songs of his country. Ezra welcomed him. Liam was an intelligent man, lonely in a land not his own. And besides, Ezra had saved his life and thus had a responsibility to him. *Like Achmed and Elana,* he thought, and poured his friend a shot of whiskey from the bottle he had brought home from London.

Achmed sent detailed letters from America. He suffered greatly from the cold, but his agricultural studies were engrossing. He often visited Amos in New York City. Amos was very respected in the academic community. When Professor Maimon lectured at Columbia or Cornell on biblical archaeology, every seat in the large auditoriums was occupied. The two men who had shared their childhoods on Sadot Shalom remained very close. They had toured the United States together, and today the S.S. *Patria* that docked in Haifa Harbor would bring them both home to Palestine, home to Sadot Shalom.

Ezra finished combing his beard. He curled it at the bottom, a rare vanity. No, the beard did not make him look too old, he decided.

"Ezra!" Mazal called impatiently.

"I'm coming," he replied and glanced once more in the mirror. So many years had passed since he had last seen his son. Would Amos find him changed? Would he find Amos changed? Vaguely troubled, he joined the rest of the family for the journey north to Haifa.

Chapter 8

"How STRANGE—to be sailing into Haifa Bay," Amos Maimon said. "It's like a dream, Achmed."

He stared out at the blue-green waters of the Mediterranean, which seemed to have magically changed color since the S.S. *Patria* had cruised into the territorial waters of Palestine. The gentle waves were shot through with silver streaks and delicately capped with lacy fringes of foam. Toward shore they could see the heavy dredging ships, their huge cranes plunging deep to the ocean floor to clear the harbor. The port area was nearing completion, and the army of construction workers, viewed from the distance, resembled the tiny mechanical soldiers with which Amos's young American cousin, Sammy Wade, played endlessly.

He would have to write the Wades, Amos reminded himself. Sonia, his cousin Alex's wife and mother of young Sammy, had pressed him to send her a photo of the Sadot Shalom family. She and his father had been friends, she told him, during Ezra's stay in New York. A strange friendship, Amos had thought. What could Ezra Maimon have had in common with the somewhat dowdy physician who spent so much of her time in a Lower East Side clinic? She had particularly pressed Amos for information about Mazal.

"Is she pretty?" she had asked.

"Beautiful," he had replied and felt again the piercing sense of loss.

He turned his attention back now to the approaching shoreline and saw how the seaside city rose in gentle ascendancy, from the port to the peak of Mount Carmel. Haifa had been a hamlet during his boyhood, a sleepy little Arab town which had been saved from total decline by the building of the Hejaz railways. But then the Jews had begun building there, erecting stone houses on streets carved into the belly of the mountain. Hadar HaCarmel, they called their new neighborhood, the Glory of the Carmel, and busily they named their streets with biblical extravagance. Their city would fulfill Herzl's dream, they said, and every Haifa home contained a copy of the Zionist leader's novel, *Old New Land,* set in the mythical city they had made their own. They pointed proudly to the buildings of the Hebrew Technical College that hugged the sloping green mountainside. Villas appeared on the mountain's peak, and igneous flames from the refineries for the oil of the Kirkuk fields blazed day and night. Grain storage silos and the squat, ugly buildings of Nesher cement dotted the newly built port area.

The city had come to life during the years of his absence, Amos realized. He was returning to a land much altered, and he felt strangely cheated. He had not experienced the metamorphosis of dream-draped Palestine into the active, vibrant land toward which the *Patria* sailed. This, too, his father had robbed him of. True, he had always intended to go abroad to study, but if circumstances had been different he would not have stayed away so long.

"Do you think your father will meet the ship?" Achmed asked.

He, too, was studying the port area, but not with Amos's wonderment. He had, after all, been away for only two years, and he had watched Haifa gradually emerge from its sleepy lethargy and become an exciting nascent city. In another year, or perhaps even less, great sailing ships would no longer have to anchor at bay but would be able to sail into the harbor. Wonderful things were happening, things which could not help benefiting the Arab community as well as the Jews.

"I would imagine so. I sent him a Marconigram from Bari."

"Will the family come with him?" Achmed asked.

He put his hand in his pocket and felt again the tissue-thin texture of the envelope in which Elana had enclosed her last letter. It was brief, as all her letters had been. She mentioned the weather. "We have had almost a week of hamsin," she wrote, and he remembered that her honey-colored skin glistened with beads of perspiration during hamsin heat and that she gathered her long hair up into a single coil that exposed the moist, graceful curve of her neck. "We harvest plums this week," she wrote, and he saw her lithe body entwined in a gnarled branch, her hands flying as she deftly tossed the new sweet fruit to Balfouria and Amnon. Later, the fruity fragrance would cling to her body. Once, on such a day, a twig had scratched her forehead. He had brushed away the slit of blood with his finger, and, when she had gone, he had sucked the sweetness of her blood that adhered to his flesh. "I am going to Haifa with Mazal on Chemed business," she wrote and he saw her oval face framed in the broad-brimmed hat. He kept the ribbon of that hat with him always, never forgetting that he had removed it, oh so gently, from the hair of the dead child in the Hebron hotel.

He had kept each letter, savoring the secrets concealed within her innocent observations on the weather and the season.

"I imagine Elana will come," Amos said. "And perhaps one of the children."

One of the children. His half brothers and sisters, the fruit of Mazal's womb, the children who might have been his own sons and daughters. His lips twisted bitterly. Balfouria, Amnon, Tamar and Nachum, Rivka. His mother's and his grandmother's names living on in the children of the petite Yemenite woman he had held so closely through long, cold Jerusalem nights. How stubborn Jews were. They would not relinquish their names. How stubborn he was. He could not relinquish his love.

"Yes. Perhaps Elana will come," Achmed said. It was a luxury to say her name aloud.

"I am glad you and she became friends," Amos said.

"Sadot Shalom is no longer a lonely place," Achmed replied.

He glanced curiously at his friend. He and Amos had shared a great deal in America, but always a constraint fell between them when they spoke of Sadot Shalom. They had talked about everything but the Galilee farm during Achmed's two years in

America. Achmed had visited Amos in New York, and he had been a welcome guest in the home of Amos's American uncle.

"I wish we could entertain you as we were able to entertain Ezra Maimon," Martin Wasser had said regretfully.

The stock market crash of 1929 had ruined the Wassers. They had moved to the Bronx from Park Avenue, and Martin Wasser no longer maintained a car and chauffeur but rode the subways to the loft on East Broadway where he had re-established his fur business. The tailor-made suits cut of heavy English wool which he had purchased in what he referred to still as "the good days" were threadbare, and the Wassers' ornate furniture, too large for the small rooms in their new apartment, was in need of reupholstering, but Martin Wasser was not discouraged.

"I came to this country with less, and I didn't know even a word of English. What I did then I can do now. What's wrong with starting over? I know how to be poor, how to be hungry. Poor I am. Hungry I'm not. I should jump from a rooftop because I'm poor? Let those who never knew poverty be frightened of it. I know how to begin again."

Achmed was reminded of Yehuda Maimon's return to the Rishon plantation after the war. Achmed had been sent to Rishon to help. The old man stared at the stripped and neglected trees. Angrily, he had snapped off a decaying branch and straightened his shoulders.

"Once there were oranges. There will be oranges again. I will begin from the beginning."

A special tenacity had been bred in the brothers. They were survivors who had never forgotten the stern lessons of the narrow streets of Kharkov. They had had the courage to build new lives in unfamiliar lands. They would rebuild those lives, so wantonly destroyed by war and economic disaster.

The Arabs could do as much, Achmed thought. He recalled a portion of the desert where the sand glowed red. Bedouin tribes avoided it because it was said that the son of a sheik had killed his father there and the sands were stained by his blood. The Jews would not accept such a curse. They would settle on such a land and defiantly wrest life from its legacy of death. The Arabs would have to learn to create their own destiny.

In New York City, the two Palestinians went for long walks,

often taking little Sammy Wade, Martin Wasser's grandson, with them. The child had sea-green eyes that matched Amos's own, and he walked with his shoulders thrown back as Ezra Maimon did. Often strangers stopped Amos to tell him how handsome his son was.

"He is not my son. He's my cousin," Amos corrected them, and always, after such an incident, he glanced curiously at small Sammy as though there were a secret to be discovered in the child's sweet, upturned face.

Amos had visited Achmed at Cornell. They had walked together across the narrow bridge above the wild water of the Cayuga River and, as harsh wintry winds bruised their faces, Achmed had told his friend of the events in Hebron. He described what he and Elana had witnessed in the small hotel and how they had returned to Jerusalem as though traversing the terrain of a nightmare. On the streets of Kiryat Arba, members of the burial society knelt in the roadways and wrapped corpses in wrinkled cerements. Whatever burial clothes were available were used. Small children were encased in billowing shrouds. No one had anticipated preparation for so many tiny corpses. They passed Ramat Rachel, where only the day before they had seen the two lovers in a newly plowed field. There were no young farmers in those fields now. Instead, black-robed rabbinical students shoveled the earth, placing the top layers in pine coffins. Elana understood then that the fields were bloodstained and that the students were adhering to the Jewish precept that all parts of a body, even spilled blood, be interred with the corpse. There would be no almond grove on Ramat Rachel. The kibbutz had been abandoned.

"But only temporarily," her uncle David Maimon had said later. "We will return to Ramat Rachel. We will return to all the lost settlements."

"My uncle has not changed, then," Amos said. He dropped a pebble into the Cayuga and strained to see the concentric whirls of water.

"Nor will he," Achmed replied.

The Arabs feared the one-eyed Jew. Bedouin children closed their eyes because it was said to be bad luck to see his eye patch. Women peered at him from behind their tent flaps. Some reported that an Arab woman's passionate fingers had plucked the eye from its socket. But there was peace between Achmed ibn-Saleem and David Maimon. They had crossed a desert together, shared sunsets and water jugs, slept together through long nights when stars flashed through the skies in silvery flood. Achmed had cheated the shadows, and because of him David Maimon lived.

"But there will have to be changes if we want to live in peace," Amos said impatiently. "Look, Achmed, it is not impossible. Here in the United States, people come from many lands and yet they all manage to share and help each other. I visited Sonia's clinic on the Lower East Side last week. In the waiting room there were people from Italy and Ireland, Polish Jews, Ukrainians, even Chinese. The doctor who is training with Sonia came from India. It is not impossible for people from many different cultures to share one land."

"It is not me you have to persuade, Amos," Achmed replied.

He, too, had been struck by the diverse backgrounds of his fellow students at Cornell. His laboratory partner was an American Indian, and his roommate, Sven, was a tall Swede from Minnesota. But there was a vast difference, of course. The United States was an enormous country, and immigration was an integral part of its history. Those who had flocked to its shores were all new immigrants, each beginning a new life in a new country. Their shared strangeness created an almost spontaneous democracy. Palestine was a sliver of a land, and it had been largely populated by Arabs for generations, while the Jews had only begun to settle there in significant number less than half a century past. There was a significant difference. Even Amos would have to acknowledge that. He himself did not believe that the difference was insurmountable. Despite Hebron, he still believed that somehow their people could coexist. A Jewish presence could only benefit the Arabs of Palestine.

"There are many options," Amos had mused. "The Arabs, too, speak of peoplehood. If there were to be a single united Arab nation in the region, then the Palestinians would be part of it—perhaps there could be an Arab federation based in Transjordan. And the Jews would cooperate with such an Arab nation."

"That would not be impossible," Achmed was thoughtful. His own family was scattered throughout the Middle East. There were cousins and aunts and uncles in Lebanon and Syria. His brother had taken a bride who lived in Transjordan. The Arabs were united by ties of family, religion, and language. A single Arab federation could lay claim to countless dunams of land, and a cooperative Jewish Palestine in a small defined area could be an asset, exporting its produce through modern ports, sharing technological advances and health services.

"And the Palestinian Arabs would not have to leave their lands if they chose to remain," Amos said. "Arrangements would be made. Didn't Jews live in Arab lands for generations? Don't they still?"

Had not Mazal's family lived for centuries in Yemen? A brief recurrent melancholy settled over him. She had told him of her life in Yemen during the long evenings they spent in his whitewashed student's room, his fingers traveling languidly across her body and now and again plucking up masses of her long, dark hair. He remembered still how quiescent she had been beneath his hands—his love, his mistress, become his stepmother and his father's wife.

"I agree with all you say," Achmed said. "But there must be an understanding, a coming together. Amos, I can never forget what I saw that day in Hebron. I could not believe that the murders were being committed by those who called themselves children of Allah. The Prophet preached peace. They are not evil men. It is only that they do not understand, that they are too often hungry and idle. My cousin Hassan is not evil, but he is bitter, and we know that malformed plants grow from bitter earth."

He had struggled mightily to sort out his reactions to that dread day in Hebron, thankful always that he had not had to press the trigger and kill an Arab brother. But he would have done so, he knew. He would have done anything to protect Elana.

Since that August day, he had been haunted by a dream that wakened him in the dead of night. It had pursued him during those last feverish days in Palestine as he readied himself for the journey to the United States, and he had dreamed it yet again as he crossed the Mediterranean, the plains and mountains of Europe, the great Atlantic Ocean. In his narrow dormitory room at Cornell, he had jerked into fearful wakefulness and sat bolt upright in bed, sweat streaming down his back although the campus of Cornell shimmered beneath a layer of ice.

"What's the matter, Achmed?" Sven, his lanky blond roommate had asked, but Achmed did not reply.

How could the tall Swede from the peaceful farmland of Minnesota comprehend the terrors of that sun-drenched day when he and Elana had run for their lives through the cobbled streets of an ancient Judean town? His nighttime terror was born of those death-filled hours.

In his dream, he and Elana were on opposite sides of a river. They each stood on a grassy promontory, and they waved joyously at each other. Elana wore her light blue dress, which exactly matched the sky and the pale blue water. He beckoned to her, and she waded into the river. He, too, plunged in and swam toward her. She laughed and also began to swim. Their bodies knifed through wavelets of blue, and the lucent drops of water fell from their fingers in shimmering shower. Then, suddenly, the sky darkened, and where clouds had drifted and birds had sung, there was shadowed, ominous stillness. The water became heavier, and although he lifted his arms and legs strenuously he could not move through it, and Elana drifted farther away. Now the sky was lashed with streaks of lightning, and the water was no longer blue but rose and fell in thick crimson waves that pulled at his body with fierce and contrary current. The river had turned to blood, fed by the darkening sky from which drops of blood fell in bullets of carmine liquid. He felt the blood warm against his face, as warm as the drops of blood that had rained down upon him from the hotel ceiling in Hebron.

"Elana," he shouted from the depths of sleep, and he saw that she was sinking beneath a frothing wave.

"Elana!"

Her golden hand fluttered briefly, helplessly, above the reddened waters and then she vanished beneath them, and he was left, sitting upright in his bed, because his love had drowned in a river of blood.

He no longer deceived himself that his interest in Elana was that of friendship. He acknowledged that he loved her and that despite the complications that love would bring, they belonged together. Allah Himself had given Achmed her life. He was responsible for her and always would be.

Often, he had thought of telling Amos that he loved his sister. He had few secrets from his boyhood friend. But some instinct had restrained him. Amos remembered Elana as a child, a buzzing, playful girl.

"What gift shall I bring the little bee, my sister, Elana, from America?" he had asked Achmed, and he had looked at Achmed curiously when his friend replied, too quietly, that Elana was no longer a child.

"She is a young woman—a beautiful young woman," he added. She would be almost eighteen when they returned to Palestine. At her age, Achmed's mother had already borne two children.

Then, too, he hesitated to tell Amos how thoughts of Elana filled his life, when Amos was clearly so alone and lonely. Achmed knew that young women were attracted to the handsome Palestinian archaeologist. They flocked to his lectures and sent him sweetly phrased invitations to dinner parties and concerts. Once Achmed had collided with a beautiful young blond woman just leaving Amos's New York apartment in the early hours of the morning.

"An actress," Amos said carelessly. "She stays over occasionally."

Her green robe and a pink frock hung in a corner of his closet. Achmed saw her a few more times, and then the robe and dress disappeared and he did not see her again. Amos's aunt and his cousin's wife, Sonia, arranged introductions for him, and always Amos was amenable. He made polite conversation through dinner and sat patiently in theaters and concert halls. Occasionally, he made arrangements for another meeting, but always his sea-green eyes remained cool and indifferent, his voice calm and dispassionate.

"Don't you get lonely, Amos?" he had asked his friend once.

"I have always been lonely," Amos said. "Always. Except for a brief time, and that was long ago."

Achmed did not question his friend further. He knew, instinctively, that that long ago "brief time" was somehow associated with Mazal Maimon and the terrible rift between father and son. But years had passed since Ezra Maimon had brought Mazal to Sadot Shalom—time enough to heal even the deepest wound. Things would be better. Amos would be seduced by the warmth and gaiety of Sadot Shalom, by the laughing children and the beauty of the home Mazal had created. Surely, by now, Amos could accept whatever had happened in the past.

Achmed glanced at his tall blond friend, who was leaning over the rail now, straining to catch a glimpse of the shore. Abruptly, he dismissed Amos's problems as he, too, looked toward the coastline, shadowed by the cliffs of the Carmel.

Now, as they drew closer, they could discern small figures on the dock, moving swiftly it seemed, and signaling the approaching ship. Women waved handkerchiefs and men fanned the air with their hats. Achmed spotted a group of children all dressed alike in short blue pants and white shirts. Kibbutz children, he guessed, welcoming a returning member home. An Arab family huddled together, the man holding a large sheet of netting into which he would gather the luggage of the returning traveler. Stylishly dressed Haifa matrons, carrying colorful parasols to ward off the brilliant sunlight, strolled down the wharf, studying the new arrivals for a hint of current European fashion. A platoon of British soldiers stood at attention. A ranking British officer was aboard the S.S. *Patria,* and the assembled soldiers were his escort to his new command. A group of nuns stood with their hands on their olivewood crosses, and a monk in brown soutane strode up and down the pier impatiently.

But where were the Maimons? Achmed wondered. The great horn of the ship honked importantly once and then twice. Sailors scurried about. The anchor was dropped with a mighty splash, and long boats were lowered. The British soldiers lifted shining instruments—cornets and trumpets, silver flutes and polished cymbals—and played a rousing song of welcome. The kibbutz children sang with boisterous enthusiasm. Passengers gathered their hand luggage and hurried to the side of the deck where rope ladders were being lowered.

Still, Achmed studied the shore, trepidation and disappointment subduing the exultation he had felt at the first sight of

land. Something had happened. Why weren't they there? Unbidden, fragments of his dream burst upon his mind, and he
looked down at the blue waters, half expecting them to be
tinged by crimson.

"They didn't come." Amos's voice was flat and unsurprised. He had prepared himself for disappointment. He
was girded for sorrow.

"They will come," Achmed replied irritably.

Cars and carriages were still arriving, speeding toward the
pier. They heard the impatient wheeze of military lorries, huge
vans awaiting cargo, the shouts of stevedores.

And then he saw them, hurrying across the planks. Saleem,
his father, grown newly gray, in a striped jabaliyah, his most
festive robe. Ezra Maimon with Mazal, Balfouria between
them. And Elana. She had come. She looked as he had envisioned her through the years of their separation. She stood
apart from the others on the sun-streaked pier, her hands
shielding her eyes as she gazed toward the ship, slender and
graceful in her pale blue dress. Her long, dark hair, hanging
loose, was riddled with light. His heart stirred with happiness.
No river of blood stretched between them, only the silver-
flecked, clear green waters of Haifa Bay. She spotted them at
last and lifted her arms in greeting. He took the blue satin
ribbon from his pocket and waved it in a gentle whip of declaration, a sky-colored symbol of affirmation.

"Amos!" Ezra's mighty voice rose above the cacophony
that filled the bay.

Amos searched the shore and found his father. When had
Ezra grown that beard, he wondered, and who was the woman
who stood beside him? With a start, he realized that it was
Mazal. Mazal grown older, with new lines on her face, her
slender body altered by successive births. He had not remembered that she wore her hair so severely. She was different
somehow, this woman who stood at his father's side, from the
Mazal with whom he had walked through quiet Jerusalem
streets.

"Amos!" His father's voice boomed with warmth and excitement.

"Abba!" He returned the call and waved frantically.

The father and son, one on ship and one on shore, stretched

their arms toward each other as the voices of the kibbutz children rose in happy chorus.

"*Haveinu shalom aleichem.* We welcome you unto the land."

"Did you think of me often?" she asked.

"Often. Always," he replied, and shifted position so that he could see her face in shadow.

They sat side by side beneath a date palm that dropped a tent of filtered shadow on the grassy mound where they rested briefly on their hike northward. Its fronds were laden with thick clumps of the golden fruit, hanging so low that he easily lifted a hand and plucked several free. They would eat them later with their lunch.

"How could you think of me when you were studying?" she retorted teasingly. "When your mind was so full of cross-fertilization and plant genetics?"

"Were my letters so boring, then?" he asked. She knew about his studies because he had written to her in great detail about his work, about his life on the sprawling Ithaca campus. Sometimes, writing to her, watching the cone of light from his student lamp spread across the paper, it seemed to him that his life was real only when he shared it with her. During the winter months he had walked the white-cloaked campus and wondered how he might best describe the thickly falling snow to her. "Small drops of magic, whiter than mountain cyclamen," he had written, and she read his words sitting on the low-hanging branch of an ancient olive tree, fretted with silver leaves.

She wept that he would share the beauty of his private landscape with her. In her next letter she had enclosed a single olive leaf, its delicate veins forming a mysterious map. He had it still, pressed between the pages of his Koran.

"Oh yes. So very boring. When one arrived I would say to Balfouria, 'Oh dear, now I shall have to read another boring letter from Achmed.' Oh, don't be foolish," she laughed. "Your letters were wonderful."

She did not tell him how often she had wandered down the road to await the postman's arrival, her heart beating faster as she watched impatiently for him to sort through the post and produce at last the pale yellow envelopes in which Achmed placed his long and detailed letters. She read each letter on the road and thrust the loose pages into her pocket so that they would not be visible amid the other mail—Ezra's correspondence with Zionist leaders all over the world, agricultural journals, Mazal's orders and requisitions, and her own frequent packets of reading material and notes from her cousin Nadav Langerfeld, who was troubled because she had left school to work with Mazal.

"Was that all the mail?" Mazal would ask. She searched always for a letter from Amos, a magical missive that would cancel out the hurt between them.

"Yes. That was all."

In the room she shared with Balfouria, she read Achmed's letters again and again, but she did not puzzle out why she had lied to Mazal. Often, she would seek out an excuse and wander down to Saleem's house, where she sipped coffee and chatted with Hulda, Achmed's mother.

Taking up a tomato, she would say, "Achmed loves tomatoes," and listen happily while Hulda chronicled other delicacies which her son enjoyed. Lamb and couscous. Grape leaves cured in lemon juice. Rice flecked with pepper. Hulda worried that he did not find food to his liking in America. She had worried, too, when he lived away from home at the agricultural training school and later at the experimental station.

"A man of Achmed's years should be married and have a wife to cook for him and care for him," she told Elana. "His brothers have taken wives."

"Oh, surely he will marry," Elana said and coaxed forth other stories in which Achmed figured—Achmed as a small boy, playing with Amos, Achmed as a diligent student, a devoted son.

She took long walks alone, scavenging days when Mazal could spare her from the intense activity of Chemed Handicrafts. The business was growing rapidly, and the newly arrived Jews from Eastern Europe and Germany had their own special crafts, challah cloths embroidered on fine linen, wonderfully wrought metal lamps that burned the length of a Sabbath, woodwork fashioned by those who had lived always in the heart of forestlands.

"Where are you going, Elana?" Ezra would ask. "Mazal needs your help."

"She needs a day to herself," Mazal always interceded. "Young people need time alone. You remember?"

Ezra remembered. He remembered his own youthful need for quiet, for the silence that blotted out the tumult of the Rishon farmhouse. And Nechama, even before she had met him, took long walks by herself through the hills of the Galilee to escape her crowded Jaffa household. Elana, their daughter, had inherited that need for solitude, and he was grateful to Mazal for understanding.

It was during one of those hikes that Elana had found an abandoned shepherd's lean-to, a tiny shack flimsily constructed of bamboo rods and loose branches, concealed amid hillock and tumulus. She had converted it into a private retreat, her own secret place, where she could be alone. She swept its dirt floor clean and covered it with a narrow strip of tent canvas so that she might lie down and stare up at the fragments of clouds and light that drifted above its bamboo roof.

Covertly, she furnished it, concealing small items in her basket—two brightly colored cushions, a long strip of woven blue fabric which she spread across a couch fashioned of wild ferns, dried to softness but smelling still of the summer fields where they had grown to thickness. She fashioned a tiny table from a slab of olivewood, which she rested on two small rocks. On its rough surface she placed a small copper bowl which she filled with dried flowers, and a small enamel candle holder. Once, too, she brought a candle and lit it so that she might see the tiny hut bathed in the gentle glow of candlelight. Beneath her small improvised table, she hid Achmed's letters, thus converting the rough shelter into a private refuge, a secret home for herself and her absent friend.

Now, at last, she would show Achmed the hut.

"Another walk?" Mazal had asked as she left.

"Yes." But she did not tell her father's wife that she was meeting Achmed, although it had been arranged the previous day.

"Where are you going?" Saleem had asked his son. It was incomprehensible to him that with so much work to be done both on his own land and on Sadot Shalom, Achmed was taking a holiday. Saleem himself abstained from work only on religious days, and he watched as Achmed packed his rucksack with his shepherd's flute, his whittling knife, and some newly baked pitas wrapped in cloth. Achmed was a man, yet he packed the toys of a boy. It was time he married. Again, Saleem's thoughts turned to his cousin's daughter. He would have to make plans.

"I have only a few more weeks home, and then I must begin work at the agricultural station and make my report to Jerusalem," Achmed said. He did not tell his father that he was walking with Elana Maimon.

Leisurely, they had made their way across the fields, Achmed carrying the straw basket in which Elana had packed their lunch. They paused now and again to pluck the flowers of fall, the last of the wild iris, dried stalks of long, sweet grass. He cut her a narrow wand of willow.

"A wishing stick," he told her. "You must make a wish."

Dutifully, she closed her eyes as they lay sheltered in the shade of the date palm, waved the sun bleached branch, and made her wish.

"What did you wish?" he asked teasingly.

"If you tell a wish, it does not come true," she said. "And now it is your turn."

"All right."

He, too, closed his eyes and was silent for a moment.

"And what did you wish?" she asked.

"Ah, that I cannot tell you. The same rules apply to both of us," he said and laughed, pulling her up. "Come. I'm hungry and I want to eat lunch at your hideaway. Is it far?"

"A few more meters," she said and felt a sudden shyness. Would he think her foolish when he saw it—a small girl playing house? He would think of her then as his friend's small sister who dreamed the dreams of a child and created a fantasy retreat in which she played out her childish games.

"You won't laugh?" she said softly.

"Elana."

He took her hand and his blue eyes stared at her, mingling sadness and concern.

"I could never laugh at you."

Almost involuntarily, he touched his shoulder, reminding

them both of the ivory fragment of bone that had splintered from his body to save her life. He wove her fingers through his own, and together they walked through the tall, fragrant grasses, sun-dried and wind-swept, and made their way through curving hills and gentle vales. Once they waved to a passing shepherd boy, who disappeared with chimeric swiftness. They were alone in the hills of the Galilee, and only the cries of the mountain birds and their own softly falling feet broke the silence. At last they reached the tiny hut she had turned into a secret home.

"It's wonderful," he said and watched her arrange the flowers they had gathered in the copper bowl and straighten the blue cloth—a diligent housewife neatening her pastoral hideaway.

They ate their lunch beneath the euphrat poplar that grew just outside the hut, and the shadows of the triangular leaves danced across her golden skin. They shared the food she had brought, tucking the roasted chicken from the Sadot Shalom kitchen into the circlets of pita his mother had baked that morning. They drank water from his canvas carrier, warm from the sun yet sweet and quenching. They fed each other the newly ripe dates. Eating the fruit from his hand, her tongue caressed his fingers. When she fed him, his small white teeth grazed the flesh of her thumb. He saved the pits and set them out on a flat stone to dry.

"A habit," he said, laughing apologetically. "When we were boys, Amos and I used to rub the pits of fruits and make rings and beads of them. Now I find myself forming designs. See, I have written your name." He had spelled out ELANA in Arabic letters.

"Then I shall write yours," she said and took up dried grass and the remaining pits to form the letters of his name in Hebrew.

"How alike the letters are," he said.

"And we—are we alike, Achmed?" she asked.

"Don't you know?"

He smiled at her and took up his shepherd's pipe, playing now the sweet, mournful songs she had heard all her life. How often, as a child, she had heard him playing, through the long evenings, the force of his breath creating the lovely, melancholy, airborne songs, hymns to star-fraught nights and the secrets of cloud-bound hills. She, the child Elana, had listened as she lay on her narrow bed, feeling herself alone yet protected. Now she watched his fingers dance across the wood, and she smiled sadly for the child she had been who had so often fallen asleep to the sound of his music. A sweet lassitude overcame her. Her limbs grew heavy, and she felt that she must close her eyes.

"Come." His voice was gentle, the softest whisper in her ear, and his arm was around her waist supporting her. "It is too hot to sleep outside. Come in. Come in, Elana."

And then they were in the hut, and she was lying down on the sweet-smelling bower of fern and dried grass. Her sudden fatigue had been replaced by a kindling of flesh, a strange soaring of blood. As he eased her down, she saw that his lips were the wine-red hue of the thin-skinned plums that blossomed in the early spring. She lifted her face toward him, toward the soft fullness of his plum-colored lips, and felt his mouth soft upon hers, his tongue a rushing hardness in her mouth. Her hands traveled over his body, beneath his shirt, across his almond-colored flesh, so smooth, so smooth. She pressed her lips against his arms, his chest. Sprigs of body hair tickled, made her smile, and she licked the shoulder where once she had washed exposed bone free of blood.

"No, Elana," he said. "No." But his body gave lie to his whispered protest. He held her so closely that she felt the beat of his heart, the pulse of his passion.

"Yes," she said. "Oh yes."

Their bodies held no secrets from each other. Her breasts were made to fit his hands; they formed small fruit in his harvesting palms.

She gazed up through the bamboo slits to the clear blue sky and felt his strength rise and stir within her, calling forth her own. A cloud drifted by and joy cracked her throat, sparked her limbs. She quivered and heard a voice she did not recognize shout his name.

"Achmed!"

She was calling to him in a woman's voice that rose from the depths of her body.

"Elana!"

He surged within her, riding hard, his breath coming in stertorous gasps. Her body rose to meet his own, rhythm finding rhythm. She was newly born. She had not known there was such fluid mystery concealed within the secret passages of her flesh, such tenderness of feeling, such violence of touch. She gripped his shoulders wet with the tears that came from her own eyes.

"Elana!"

He soared and she soared with him. The sky beckoned. She would stretch and touch it, but her hands were for holding him close. She would scream and sing, but she had no voice. She had consigned herself to him.

They rested at last, her body languid and relaxed in his arms, a willing prisoner of his grasp and touch. The woven blue fabric was stained with her blood, and she thought sleepily that now all scales were balanced. He had given his blood for her life, and she had given hers for his love.

"What did you wish?" he asked her sleepily.

"Don't you know?"

She closed her eyes. His shoulder pillowed her head; her hair blanketed his arms.

Chapter 9

THE ROAD TO Sadot Shalom had been roughly cleared by Ezra Maimon and his brothers when he first took possession of the farm. Over the years it had been flattened and widened by the footsteps of visitors and the rolling wheels of carts and wagons, trucks and tractors, the hoofs of horses and the flying feet of Ezra's children. It was only after his return from Switzerland that Ezra had it dredged and smoothed over. More visitors were arriving, and most of them now drove trucks and motor cars. Mazal had cast her artist's eye across the new roadway and arranged for it to be lined with ashlar saplings which created a slender ribbon of shade even on the hottest afternoons. It was through this narrow strand of shadow that Captain Liam Halloran drove his command car late one afternoon.

He waved to Elana Maimon, who was walking down the road carrying a faded purple portmanteau. His grandmother had had such a case, he recalled absently.

"Can I give you a ride?" he called to his friend's daughter. "I don't mind turning around."

"No. It's all right. I'm being met at the bottom of the hill," she said, and he remembered that he had seen Achmed ibn-Saleem waiting there with a traveling bag. "I'm going to Jerusalem to visit my brother," she added.

"Have fun, then," he said and drove on.

Probably she would travel with her brother's friend. It would be good for her to have company on such a long journey. The Arab agronomist and Ezra Maimon's archaeologist son were known to be extraordinarily close. They had been friends since childhood—two bright lads growing up together on this isolated farm, which must have been even more isolated then, when motor cars were a rarity and the road had not yet been developed. Only natural that they should cleave together. Liam Halloran could understand that. His own closest friend in Ireland was Jimmy Foster, a Protestant who lived on a farm adjacent to his own.

That was something those limited idiots in the Colonial Office seemed unable to understand—that bonds of friendship could be forged between people because of proximity and shared adventure. They saw only polarities, adversaries. Catholic versus Jew. Jew versus Arab, and in India the Moslems pitted neatly against the Hindus and Buddhists. It made things all neat and tidy for them, but there was more than that to sorting people out. No doubt that frigging Passfield would find his own friendship with Ezra Maimon peculiar, but he himself was glad of it and well pleased that he had thought to seek Maimon out after all. He had known that night on Gallipoli that the Palestinian farmer could become his friend.

Ezra heard his friend's car approach, and he called out to Liam as he parked.

"Liam, we're out back. It must have been a dusty ride. Come and have something to drink."

"I shouldn't mind a cold drink."

He joined them and held out his hand to Mazal, who sat in the shade of the avocado tree, her sketch pad on her lap and her pencil dancing across the paper. The twins, Tamar and Nachum, chubby, dark-haired children, were rolling a large red ball to each other, and Mazal sketched their activity rapidly, as though fearful that they would tire of the game before she could complete her drawing. It occurred to Liam Halloran that he had never seen Mazal Maimon just sit still as his own Fiona occasionally did, just quietly watching a sunset or looking into the distance. Mazal's hands were always busy, and her eyes darted from place to place.

"I saw Elana as I came. I offered her a ride to the main road, but she wanted to walk."

"Yes. I know. She didn't want me to drive her either. She is going to Jerusalem to stay with the Langerfelds and spend some time getting reacquainted with her brother," Ezra said. "Have you met my son Amos?" A new warmth came into his voice when he spoke of his eldest son, and Mazal smiled. It had taken long enough, but the breach between the two men was healing. Somehow from the moment of Amos's arrival, there had been acceptance and a slow-building affection. Each listened carefully to what the other had to say. Amos had given them a copy of his book, and Ezra had placed it on the top of his bookcase. She had fashioned a pair of enameled bookends for it alone.

"We will add your other works as they are published," she said.

"We expect a full shelf," Ezra had added, and Amos's eyes glittered.

"I met him and heard him lecture just last week on Mount Scopus," Liam went on. "The amphitheater was full, Ezra. You would have been proud. Can't say I understood him, though. It was smart of Elana to leave later in the day and miss the heat. Good that Achmed is traveling with her. Damn boring to make that journey alone. I know. I've done it often enough."

"Achmed?" Ezra asked.

He set his pipe carefully down, and there was a strange edge to his voice that Liam Halloran had not heard before. "Did you know Achmed was going to Jerusalem, Mazal?"

"No. Elana did not mention it," Mazal said, but she frowned. It had been Elana's way, even as a child, to skillfully avoid the truth while managing never to lie.

"Why did you let her go to Hebron that day?" Ezra had asked Daniel Langerfeld.

"She never asked us. She was simply gone when we awoke in the morning."

That had been Elana's way then; it was her way now. *And both times she was meeting Achmed.* The thought flew at her unbidden. When Elana returned, she would have to talk to her.

"I imagine Achmed's going to the general meeting of the Istaqlal party later this week," Liam suggested. "They're expecting a large delegation. Ichsan Bey al-Jabri and Shakib Arslan are coming from Syria. Usual talk of Arab federation."

"More likely rejoicing over the Shaw report," Ezra said. "Your countrymen did everything but pat the Arabs on the head and congratulate them on the nineteen twenty-nine riots."

"Englishmen wrote that report," Liam said stiffly. "There wasn't an Irishman on the panel, don't you forget. I don't disagree with you, Ezra, and all the Irish feel the same. But still, I wear His Majesty's uniform, and a soldier has his job of work to do."

"But it was a terrible miscarriage of justice, wasn't it?" Mazal asked, relieved that the conversation had moved away from Achmed and Elana. "Will you excuse me? I must get some fruit."

Balfouria was in the kitchen peeling cucumbers.

"Balfouria, did you know Achmed was going to Jerusalem with Elana?"

"I suppose so. I saw Elana pack enough food for both of them," Balfouria said. "Do you like my hair the way Elana did it?"

She patted the two bunches of thick, dark curls that Elana had roped with red yarn and tied in place above each ear, and practiced her smile again. She was learning to smile just like Elana, showing only a trace of teeth.

"It's very pretty," her mother said and arranged peaches, plums, and grapes on the large Armenian platter. Probably it was a meaningless oversight. So their departures had fallen on the same day. That was all there was to it. Was she becoming like her old aunt in Saana who was never happy unless she worried over an impending tragedy? "Old Evil Eye" the children had called her, and they had scampered about to avoid her shadow when they saw her coming. Well, no one was going to avoid Mazal Maimon's shadow. She added a sprig of mint to the platter of fruit and rejoined the men.

"The Shaw report was bad enough," Ezra was saying. "But the Passfield White Paper was outrageous."

"But the one led to the other," Liam observed and selected a plum. There were no plums in all of Palestine like those grown on Sadot Shalom. "The Shaw report gave that bleeding heart Passfield the go-ahead he was waiting for. That Passfield worries a lot about mankind—it's men he can't stand."

Liam Halloran himself had been shocked when he read the findings of the Shaw Commission, which had been sent from England to investigate the cause of the 1929 riots. He himself had been among those who had guided Sir Walter Shaw and the three members of Parliament who accompanied him through the riot areas in Jerusalem, Hebron, and Safed. Liam gave testimony, as did other British officers who had been with the skeleton contingents in the other cities. Brave Raymond Cafferata, who had single-handedly held back Arab mobs in Hebron, had testified. All of them had the same perception. The riots had been incited by armed Arab gangs who had laid siege to a vulnerable and almost unarmed Jewish population.

"But surely there was provocation," Sir Walter Shaw had insisted.

The commission chairman was a jurist who prided himself on the efficacy of his court and the supreme fairness of the British system of law. He also congratulated himself that he understood the Middle East. He had served as chief justice of the Turkish Straits settlements, and he often told his wife that he understood thoroughly how the native populations thought and acted. Of course, the Jews weren't really native to Palestine, and that was no small part of the problem. Sir Walter Shaw was no fool—not he.

One couldn't be too careful with the Jews. They had powerful friends in all quarters. They had even sought to influence the public against his own commission. He would not soon forget that letter in the *Times* signed by Balfour, Smuts, and Lloyd George seeking to say what his commission ought to do. It was *his* commission, wasn't it, and chances were those riots never would have happened if those damn weaklings Churchill and Balfour hadn't given in to their Jewish friends. He wasn't a prejudiced man, not a bit. Trouble was, you said anything at all against the Jews and they called you an anti-Semite. He was no anti-Semite. He'd once had a very good clerk who was a Jew. Not a Jew who wanted to come to Palestine, though, thank heavens for that.

"The only provocations were the incidents at the Wall, Your Honor," Liam Halloran had replied. The Irishman was pleased that the commission was sitting as a public court of inquiry and that witnesses were testifying under oath. That hadn't often happened in Ireland. Briefly, he had described the situation at the Wall, the year of tension that had preceded it, and the provocative statements of the mufti.

The commission had listened carefully, but Sir Walter Shaw

had frowned. The mufti had impressed him greatly. There was a native who knew his place, and fine-looking, too, with that trick of sitting absolutely still. Soft-spoken. And he listened carefully when others spoke, not like the Jews, who were forever interrupting and flailing their hands about. The mufti was a serious man who spoke of moderation. He never accused the British of indifference and ineffectiveness as the Jews did. The British government ineffectual! Indeed!

And the mufti had been solicitous of the British and praised their actions. It was true that as an Arab leader he was not pleased by the influx of Jews into Palestine. He hadn't denied that. Well, Shaw for one could hardly blame him. He himself was not too well pleased at the idea of Jews from Eastern Europe filling up the tenements of the East End. And the Americans, he would lay a bet, weren't so happy about their flooding the streets of New York.

True, the mufti might have been shortsighted—perhaps he should have made a greater effort to stop the riots—but to say that he had incited them was stretching it a bit. The implication annoyed Sir Walter. He wondered where he could get a small dagger for his grandson like the handsome one the mufti's bodyguard carried. Well, he might not be certain of everything in this inquiry, but one thing he knew for sure. The heat in Palestine was a good deal more brutal than it had been in the Turkish Straits. *Oh, to be in England . . .*, he thought and fought back a yawn as he listened wearily to the testimony of a one-eyed Jew named David Maimon who had fought the Arabs in the streets of Safed.

"They were armed with scythes and hoes," the Jew said.

"But my dear man, they *are* farmers," Sir Walter interceded, and he was well pleased with the laugh that earned him.

Still, Liam Halloran had been dismayed by the commission's final report. It disregarded almost all the evidence given and concluded that the Arab attacks on the Jewish communities, while unfortunate, were unpremeditated.

"I've been a soldier these twenty years," Halloran's corporal had muttered, "and what I know for certain is that a man who does not think to use a knife and club won't walk the streets flashing the bloody weapons."

The commission had concluded that the riots had been

caused by the "landless and discontented class," and it recommended a check on Jewish immigration until a land survey had been completed. A separate inquiry would settle the issue of the Western Wall, and almost as a footnote the report stipulated that a police force should be maintained at appropriate strength. But what had most incensed Daniel and Nadav Langerfeld was the commission's assertion that the Jewish Agency had no share in the government of Palestine.

"We are back where we began," Daniel Langerfeld had said angrily. "The agency is emasculated. The promise of a national Jewish home is shelved, and instead we get this damn socialist jabbering about a landless people. Who the hell is landless—Saleem? The Arabs in the Galilee for whom we've organized cooperatives?"

"We should never have depended on the British." David Maimon's voice had been harsh. He had not been surprised by the commission's report. "We can depend only upon ourselves. Jews will have to protect Jews, and the League of Nations be damned. We need an army. A defense force. The age of restraint is over. We've got to begin resisting. Damn it, I remember the day we landed in Jaffa. An Arab boy kicked me, and when I tried to pay him back, old Adler, the hotelkeeper, pulled me away. *'Havlagah,'* he said. 'Restraint.' That was over forty years ago. Are we still going to rely on restraint? Shall we wait until our sons are crippled and maimed before we turn to *haganah*—defense?" He had touched his eye patch and flexed his trigger finger. His question had been rhetorical. The answer lay in strength. In arms and the ability to use them.

Liam Halloran settled himself deep within the wicker chair and selected another plum.

"Have you seen your brother recently?" he asked Ezra.

"Saul?" Ezra's answer was cautious. Liam was his friend, but he was a British officer.

"No. David."

"I've seen him."

Ezra knew that Liam could have no liking for David, who had been extremely rude to him, often leaving Sadot Shalom when the Irishman arrived.

"I am not in the habit of consorting with occupying troops," he had said stiffly once, and although Mazal had apologized for him and Liam had laughed it off, Ezra had seen the Irishman's neck grow red and mottled and a new brightness steel his pleasant gray eyes.

"You might tell him, when you next see him, that it's been noticed how often he visits your father's orchards in Rishon."

"David's son Joshua and his family live there now. They manage the orchards and care for my father. It is natural that David would visit them," Ezra replied.

Yehuda Maimon was eighty years old, an aged man who had never resolved the conflicts of his youth. His lips moved in a perpetual self-dialogue, and his children and grandchildren caught only fragments of the arguments he conducted with the dead: "You see my oranges, Father. Then I was right to come, I had to come," he said to his father, the talmudic scholar, whose grave in the Kharkov cemetery had long been untended and overgrown. . . . "Play the piano for me, Rivka. You play so beautifully, Rivka," he said cajolingly to his wife. "See, I promised you a piano in Palestine."

"David Maimon is a most attentive son. He makes the journey to Rishon twice, sometimes three times a week. He, and those who travel with him, carry large cases, wooden boxes that could easily be mistaken for weapon carriers. You might tell him that his activities have been noticed. Just that, Ezra."

"I'll tell him," Ezra said. "You're a good man, Liam Halloran."

"We are not at odds with each other," the Irishman replied. "We both want freedom for our people. One day our causes may merge."

"I think we shall both have to be very patient," Ezra said. "But at least the Irish are already in their country. We cannot even bring our Jews into Palestine. The Passfield White Paper has seen to that."

"They are allowing some immigration. There is a quota," Liam said consolingly.

"A quota!" Ezra laughed bitterly. "Suppose your family were trapped in a burning house and the fire department came and said, 'We can evacuate only your son. Your wife and your other sons and your daughters and your parents will have to burn up because there is a quota on rescue.' That is what

British immigration policy amounts to. Europe is a tinderbox. Any moment now it will burst into flames, and our people will burn because the British have a quota.''

"Come, you're being dramatic, Ezra. No one is going to burn. Germany will be dealt with. The immigration policy will be altered.''

"When? Already over three thousand labor certificates have been canceled and that damned incompetent, Sir John Hope Simpson, has reached the stunning conclusion that there is room in Palestine for only twenty thousand additional immigrant families. Never mind that Jews managed to build a city on the sand and establish farms and settlements in desert and swamps. Hope Simpson does not wish to be confused by fact. A desert will remain a desert, and Passfield happily follows his recommendations—limits on Jewish immigration, an embargo on the purchase of land by Jews. Liam, if your family was in that house, would you accept the verdict of the fire department and let them burn?''

"Do what you must do, Ezra,'' Liam Halloran said quietly, "but do not tell me about it.'' He peeled an orange. "It was all much simpler on Gallipoli, wasn't it, Ezra? We thought that we would pay our debt to Mother England and she would reward us.''

"No, it wasn't much simpler,'' Ezra answered. "But we were much younger, and so we thought it simpler.''

Amnon came up to him then, and he put his arms about his son's shoulders. Amnon was built like Mazal. He was small and slight. He moved swiftly, and his eyes were coal-black in his narrow, finely featured face. The boy drew wondrous pictures and told his brother and sisters intriguing stories in which herons spoke and clever jackals outwitted mountain lions. Sometimes, looking at Amnon, Ezra was seized by an inexplicable fear. The world might prove too much for his slender son, who lived so dangerously in a world of dream and fantasy. He spoke harshly to Amnon at such moments.

"Play ball,'' he told the boy. "Or help Saleem in the fields. Why do you just sit about and dream?''

But now, as he sat on the terrace with Liam Halloran, who had a fondness for song and story, he drew his son close.

"Enough politics, Liam. Amnon, tell our guest the story

you made up about the storks who fly down to Aqaba,'' he
said. ''Our Amnon has written a love story about storks. One
is white and the other is black. Their families, who nest high
on the Hermon, do not approve of their friendship, so they fly
south—all the way to the Red Sea. And they have adventures
on the way, don't they, Amnon?''

''Many adventures,'' the boy said solemnly. ''And I've
given them names now, Abba. I call them Achmed and
Elana.''

The child felt his father's arm stiffen and draw away. He
started as Ezra moved suddenly and the pale blue ceramic bowl
shattered on the stone surface of the patio.

Chapter 10

THE SPACIOUS ROOMS of Haj Salameh's villa on the Alla Uddin road in Jerusalem were so expertly constructed of the most porous stone that even on the hottest day, when the desert wind blew unceasingly, they remained cool. Thick carpets covered the tile floors, and bright cushions were scattered across low couches. Embroidered hangings festooned the whitewashed walls, and a large copper hand hung over the doorway. It was newly polished and refracted the sunlight that danced in through the wide, arched windows. Incongruously, a large, bare conference table stood in the center of the room, but Haj Salameh's guests did not approach it. They reclined on the couches and walked restlessly about. They spoke in muted whispers, as though they were visitors in a house of mourning, and when the barefoot servant boy approached with dishes of nutmeats and dates, they took only one delicacy at a time, as though pledging restraint in all things. Haj Salameh had a gold watch which he drew out proudly and studied carefully. Their guest was not yet late. He had been trained in the ways of the West and would probably be punctual.

"You say that Achmed ibn-Saleem is your cousin?" he asked a young man who sat humbly on a low stool. He averted his eyes from the young man's face. Haj Salameh feared ugliness and illness, and he was repelled by the sticky yellow pus that streaked from Hassan's eyes.

"Yes," Hassan replied. "His mother and my father are brother and sister. But he grew up on the Jewish farm they call Sadot Shalom, and I grew up in the village."

"He is a good Moslem?"

"He is a good Moslem. And a good son to his parents," Hassan said.

"You think he would not betray his people?"

"Who knows another man's heart?" Hassan asked. "But I think he loves his people."

Hassan smiled shyly. His answer pleased him. He had protected himself without betraying his cousin. He enjoyed his new role. It was better to sit in this cool room with the leaders of his people than to spend endless hours in the coffeehouses with his friends analyzing the editorials in *Al-Falastina* and *Al-Karmel*. Their invitation had surprised him at first, but then he had grown accustomed to it. Had not his father often said that he was as smart as his cousin Achmed? It was just that Achmed had had opportunities. Now Hassan's turn had come. These important men listened to him with respect. They recognized his qualities of leadership. They understood that he, Hassan, would have been a powerful effendi if the Jews had not stolen his land. True, they had paid his father and offered him new land, but that farm had belonged to his family for generations. Hassan selected two dates and asked the servant boy to bring him another cup of coffee.

"Achmed ibn-Saleem is here," the servant boy told Haj Salameh.

"Then you will ask him to come in," Haj Salameh ordered. He turned to the others.

"We must listen to him carefully. Musa Alami has spoken highly of him. And the Istaqlal delegation from Syria is not unimpressed with him. He has the ear of the Jewish leaders. He is not unimportant."

"We will hear him out," a soft voice said. "Assuredly we will hear him out."

The quietness of the speaker's tone anticipated absolute obedience. It was not necessary for this man to raise his voice. He expected acquiescence and received it.

He sat, still and silent, in a shadowed area of the room. He had not moved since Hassan's entrance, but the young man had noticed that he occupied the best chair in the room, a throne carved of ebony and padded with red velvet. Its high contours had concealed its occupant, but now he turned his head, and Hassan recognized the perfectly formed narrow features, the slightness of his body. Like many small men, he seemed possessed of a resilience and strength disproportionate to his size. He wore the austere black gown and the white turban of a mullah, and the simplicity of his academic dress made the bright robes and sashes of the other men in the room seem vulgar and ostentatious. Startled, Hassan bowed to the mufti of Jerusalem, who did not acknowledge his gesture but sat as though frozen into immobility, still as a statue.

Achmed entered the room, walking lightly on sandaled feet. He, too, wore Arab dress, a white robe girdled with a black rope belt and a black-and-white keffiyah of fine gauze cotton. Hassan noticed for the first time the coppery light that glinted in his cousin's hair and darted like a fleck of flame on his smooth mustache. His years out of the country had not robbed his skin of its golden sheen.

"We are pleased to welcome you," Haj Salameh said.

Achmed inclined his head to his host and then bowed from the waist to the mufti, who smiled and revealed his small, perfect white teeth. But he did not move. How could a man sit so still? Hassan wondered, and his own coffee cup clattered against its saucer. It occurred to him that the mufti's grace invited the clumsiness of others just as his simplicity emphasized their vulgarity.

"I am grateful to your excellencies for inviting me here," Achmed said and moved toward the conference table. The other men followed him, and for the first time, he noticed Hassan. His cousin's presence surprised him, and he noticed worriedly that Hassan's eyes were badly diseased. He already concealed one eye with a patch, but trachoma would surely ravage both if Hassan did not go to a clinic. Perhaps Achmed could persuade him. He noticed, too, that the mufti did not rise but the table had been positioned so that he had an excellent view from his ornate chair.

"We are interested in learning our brother Achmed's views on Jewish settlement in the land," Haj Salameh said courteously. "We ourselves are only a small group. We call ourselves 'Palestinians Concerned for the Future.' Because you are a learned man, we look to you, Achmed ibn-Saleem. How do you see our future?"

"Our future in this land is a bright one," Achmed said. "Made even brighter by the presence of our Jewish cousins, who are also the children of Abraham, who have returned here from the countries of their dispersion.''

There was an almost audible intake of breath, but Achmed was not perturbed.

''I speak to you as an agronomist, my respected elders,'' he said. ''Have not the Jews helped us develop the land? We have increased our citriculture, and there are more orchards than ever before under cultivation because of advice from the Jews. I myself was educated at a Jewish agricultural school. Our vegetable and grain crops have never been so plentiful. I bring you a gift, El-Haj, from the new Arab cooperative in the southern Galilee.''

He reached into the burlap bag he carried and removed cerise tomatoes, long green cucumbers, baby onions that shimmered like pearls.

''These vegetables came from land we had never cultivated. We had the help of Jewish advisers as to water usage and field cultivation.''

''The vegetables are indeed beautiful,'' Haj Salameh said, but he did not move to lift them or lean forward to examine them further. ''But did not the Prophet teach us that the nourishment of the spirit is more important than nourishment of the body? Shall we abandon the heritage of Islam for a few tomatoes and cucumbers?''

''But the Jews do not ask us to abandon Islam,'' Achmed protested. ''They do not proselytize. They have their religion and they respect ours.''

''Ah, but there is only one true faith.'' The mufti's voice was soft as velvet. ''Do you not believe there is only one true faith, Achmed ibn-Saleem?''

''I believe in the faith of my fathers. But do we not revere Abraham, the first Jew, who was the first to believe in the one God, the Father of us all?''

''We do indeed. You are a good son of your people,'' the mufti responded. His mouth parted in a sliver of a smile, and once again Hassan saw the perfect rows of small white teeth, and he remembered a baby jackal that had bared its fangs at him in the darkness of a long-ago night. Still, the mufti had smiled at his cousin, and he was relieved that Achmed's views had not angered the powerful men who had assembled to hear him.

"You believe that your Jewish friends wish peace?" another leader asked.

"I believe that they wish peace and only peace," Achmed replied. He was not surprised that the Arab leaders knew of his involvement with the Brith Shalom movement. Judah Magnes had told him that the Christian Arab George Antonius reported everything to the mufti.

"It was good of you to visit with us, my son," Haj Salameh said. "We are proud that a son of our people has crossed the great oceans and studied in the United States."

"My studies gave me joy because they will benefit my people, the children of Allah, the blessed faithful," Achmed replied.

"We shall consider well your words. And now you must have some coffee and these sesame cakes baked in the palace kitchen of the mufti himself."

Haj Salameh clapped his hands, and Ethiopian servant boys carrying huge copper trays hurried forward. They offered Achmed coffee and tiny golden cakes and extended great baskets of fruit to him—pearl-white grapes from the vineyards of Silwan and brilliant red pomegranates from the orchards of Abu Ghosh. They bowed and smiled. Achmed drank the coffee and dutifully plucked a cluster of grapes. He answered the questions about America which his elders asked with disarming shyness.

It was true there was a building in the city of New York whose roof disappeared into the clouds. The country was vast and bounded on each side by great oceans, but all the cities were linked by rails of steel across which great trains traveled both day and night. And in the United States people from many countries and of many faiths lived in peace and helped each other.

"Ah, but their land is vast. Our Palestine is but a small state bounded by sea and mountain," a bearded elder said.

"But how vast are the lands of our brethren in Syria and the new kingdom of Transjordan and all across the great stretch of sand of the Arabian desert," Achmed replied and carefully stirred his coffee with the tiny gold enameled spoon the servant boy proffered. "Allah has indeed blessed his people, Islam."

"Blessed be the name of Allah," the mufti said softly. "Come here, Achmed. I have gifts for you."

Achmed set his coffee cup down and approached the velvet and ebony throne. He extended his hand, and the mufti placed within it a tooled leather scabbard and a small copy of the Koran, bound in cloth woven of peacock-blue fabric threaded with gold.

"A man must be armed. Both his body and his spirit must be armed," said the mufti.

Achmed bowed.

"I am your servant, *el-malchun,* O king," he said and passed his fingers across the smooth leather of the scabbard. The Koran he kissed reverently. He removed his dagger and placed it within the new holder.

"Such a beautiful dagger," the mufti said. He did not move, but his almond-shaped eyes saw everything.

"A gift from the Jew, David Maimon. See how well his gift does fit in yours," Achmed said. "I thank you."

Again he bowed and, turning, inclined his head to the Arab leaders who sat about the table.

"*Salaam aleikem,*" he said. "Peace be with you."

"*Aleikem salaam.* Unto you let there be peace," they replied.

There was silence in the room after he left. They listened until they could no longer discern the slap of his sandaled feet against the stone stairway, and then they spoke. Their voices were very soft, and the voice of the mufti was the softest of all.

Achmed hurried through the nightbound streets of the city to the Church of Archangels. Elana was waiting for him in the garden, and he did not like to think of her alone in the fragrant darkness. He did not like to think of her alone at all. She belonged at his side where he could watch over her and protect her. Sweet Elana. Beautiful Elana. His heart pounded and the palms of his hands tingled with pleasure and excitement. He walked more swiftly, almost ran. She would be pleased at his report of the meeting. She had encouraged him to go when the invitation arrived from Haj Salameh.

"If you do not share your views with them, how will they understand you?" she asked with the disarming logic she had inherited from her father, who had never forgotten his talmudic training. "Don't you remember what you told me the morning we left for Hebron—that to acknowledge fear was to embrace it?''

"And you know what happened at Hebron," he replied grimly.

"But we are alive," she said. "We did not die."

Their lives gave proof to his thesis. They were immune to death, her lilting voice asserted. Tragedy overtook the lives of others and magically passed them by. They were young and in love. They had survived danger and distance. Their love made them omniscient. They would fight for peace between their people, and they would win as surely as they had won each other.

It was Elana who had encouraged him to bring the vegetables to the meeting.

"They must see what can happen when we work together. Then they will understand," she had said.

It seemed so simple to her. Sane men did not turn their backs on peace and choose war. They did not see the promise of plenty and select famine. They would not decide on blindness when vision could be theirs. Suddenly Achmed remembered the small boy in the marketplace whom he had urged to go to the Hadassah clinic. "But the Jewish doctors will blind us," the child had said. "The mufti has told us so."

Achmed thought of the delicate man in the black mullah's gown who had sat so still in the velvet chair. Never would such a man want to see a child blind when he might see. Would the soft-spoken mufti allow young Hassan to conceal his diseased eye behind a patch when he could be cured? Surely the child had not understood. The man who had offered him gifts and spoken so gently to him was not a madman. Elana had been right. No one would choose hatred when there could be love.

He saw the small gas lamp on the corner of David Street and increased his pace to a run. A tiny gust of wind whipped the flickering light, and the street was plunged into darkness. He felt a strange surge of fear.

"Elana!" he called as he turned into the church entry.

The boughs of the olive trees trembled, and the leaves were fingers of silver in the light of the newly risen moon. She sat on a wide bench beneath the tree. A shaft of moonlight severed the long, thick plait into which she had woven her hair. Her hands were clasped, and a half-smile trembled on her lips.

"Elana, didn't you hear me? Why didn't you answer?" He was angry now because he had been frightened, because her silence had frightened him. But when she turned her head, his anger melted. She smiled still, that strange half-smile, but he saw the tears that glinted in her eyes, saline jewels of sorrow that slowly spilled over the high curve of her cheeks.

"Elana—what's the matter?" he asked and took her hands into his own. They were icy-cold, and he stroked them gently and lifted them to his lips.

"Achmed, I'm afraid, so afraid," she whispered.

"Afraid?"

He stared at Elana, fearless Elana, who had walked the riot-riven streets of Hebron and hiked the dark night hills of the Galilee. Weeks ago, as they walked back from the shepherd's hut, they had seen the silhouette of a mountain lion poised on a rock-bound cave.

"Are you afraid?" he had asked then.

"I am never afraid when I am with you," she had replied.

Yet now she trembled, and he held her close to him.

"What is it?" he asked quietly.

"I am with child." Her voice was so low that he strained to hear her. "I am pregnant."

"With child?" His tone was bemused, as though he struggled to comprehend her words. Laughter welled within him, but he restrained it. This, then, was the source of her fear, her weeping misery. He was incredulous. His heart soared and his body trembled with joy. Children were the natural gift of love.

He held her tighter, lifted her into his arms, and danced about the olive tree with her. The silver leaves fluttered like the hands of newborn infants. They would have a child. She would be a mother and he would be a father. They had journeyed through their separate worlds and come together to create a life.

"Elana," he said. "My Elana."

He set her down and his mouth traveled across her neck, covering it with kisses, and then moved down to her shoulders, her breasts. He heard her heart beat in sweet staccato, and he rested his head on her abdomen, so covertly flat, concealing the life conceived in the love they had celebrated beneath drifting clouds in a shepherd's hut.

"But why are you crying?" he asked. "We will marry."

"How can we?"

She clutched his wrists and saw that he held a book bound in cloth woven of blue and gold. The Koran that the mufti had given him.

"Our faiths are not so very far apart," he said. "Do we not both believe in one God? Are we not both descended of Abraham? If I worship in a synagogue instead of a mosque, am I denying my belief in the one God who created all the world?"

"Is it so simple, then?" she asked, and he flinched at the irony in her voice.

"It is not simple. But it is not impossible."

"And my father?" she asked. "What of my father?"

Ezra Maimon had wept for his sister, her aunt Sara who had married a Jew but abandoned her faith. Would he accept his daughter if she married a Moslem even if he converted to Judaism? She remembered a girl from Rishon LeZion who had fallen in love with a British officer. He had converted to Judaism. They had married and, yes, Ezra Maimon had danced at their wedding. She felt a brief wave of optimism and then a dizziness that caused her to lean against the olive tree. The church bells sounded just then and she listened to them toll the hours. The hollow metal clang of their tongues were a tintinabulation of her fate. Like a child reading the future in the fallen petals of a flower, she monitored each knell. It will be all right. *Clang*. It will not be all right. *Clang*. All will go badly. All will go well. The metallic concert ceased. The starlit night was still.

"Your father has been like a father to me. Will he turn me away because I love you and I want to care for you?" Achmed asked.

"And your family?" Her voice grew weaker as she spoke.

"They will come to accept you. Our families have a shared history." He knew that it would take them time to accept the marriage, but he did not believe that Saleem and Hulda would reject their son and Ezra Maimon's daughter.

"Amos?" Now her question was a whisper.

"Amos? Amos will dance with joy for us," he said. "I shall

tell Amos myself tonight. Come, Elana. I will walk with you to your uncle's house, and then I will go to see Amos.''

''Are you sure?''

''Quiet. No more talk.''

His lips, his silken, plum-colored lips, came down upon her own, silencing her, muffling word and thought until at last she relaxed in his arms. She surrendered and believed him.

''It will be all right,'' he said again and again. ''Everything will be all right.''

They walked hand in hand through narrow roads where street lights flickered in feathery blaze. A violinist stood on a balcony and played a mournful melody. They paused briefly and listened until the musician lowered his bow and disappeared into the room beyond.

He left her in front of Daniel Langerfeld's house and watched as she ascended the steps. She lifted her fingers to her lips and waved to him. The street was very dark, yet he thought he saw her close her eyes.

''Elana,'' he called, feeling a sudden urgency. But the heavy door slammed behind her, and he could not remember what it was that he had to say.

He hurried then to the Yemin Moshe quarter, where Amos had taken a small flat. As he passed the Montefiore windmill, he saw a young couple embrace, and their joined silhouette moved in a shadowy dance across the windmill's white exterior. Briefly, bitterly, he envied them the ease and openness of their love. They drew apart as he passed, and he saw that the girl's hair was a murky blond and she was short and stocky. His Elana was tall and slender and her hair often floated in a capelet of velvet darkness about her shoulders. How could he envy anyone at all? He was the luckiest of men, Elana's chosen, the father of her child.

The light in Amos's study sent out a friendly glow. Achmed tapped on the door using the code they had developed as boys—a rapid series of beats followed by a long single knock.

''Achmed!'' Amos flung the door open and the two men embraced. ''Come in. Come in. Why the ceremonial robes? Oh yes, you had the meeting at Haj Salameh's villa. How did it go?''

''Well, I think,'' Achmed said. ''The mufti himself was

there. I spoke only briefly—mainly about the benefits to all of us if there was peace between Jew and Arab."

"They were receptive?" Amos asked, motioning Achmed to a seat.

He lit a pipe and offered his friend a short cheroot.

"I thought so. The mufti gave me gifts. This scabbard. A Koran."

"Encouraging," Amos said cautiously. "The mufti's cooperation would make all the difference."

"They asked about the United States, and I told them that there men of many different origins and faiths live and work together. Then is it not possible in our land, I asked? It is the truth, after all, Amos. You and I have lived and worked together."

"We have been like brothers to each other," Amos said, and he reached for his friend's hand. "What is it, Achmed? Do you feel ill? Your hand is so cold."

"I have something I must tell you, Amos," Achmed said. His own nervousness surprised him. This was Amos he was talking to—Amos, the friend and brother of his childhood. Nothing he revealed to Amos could weaken the bonds of love that bound them.

"Yes?"

Did he imagine the sudden guarded edge to Amos's voice, the new erectness as his friend shifted position and carefully tapped dead ashes from the bowl of his pipe.

"You know that Elana and I have been very close."

"Yes. Of course. And I was glad of it."

"You know that I wrote to her during the years I was in America."

"I assumed as much. I knew as much."

"She was a young girl when I left. But even then I was aware of her beauty."

"Elana is very beautiful. As are your own sisters, Achmed. I find Almira beautiful. Fatima is beautiful."

"You do not love Almira. You do not love Fatima. But I, Amos, I love Elana."

"What? What did you say?"

The pipe slipped from the ashtray and clattered onto the tile floor. Amos was on his feet, staring at Achmed as though he had never seen him before.

"I love your sister, Amos. And I want to marry her."

"You must be joking. Tell me that you are joking, Achmed." There was a pleading note in Amos's voice, and his hands trembled.

"I am not joking, Amos." Anger steeled Achmed's tone now. Would he, could he joke about such a thing? "I want to marry Elana. I will become a Jew. We will be married in your faith. Then we will truly be brothers, Amos, as you have always said we were."

"As we have been," Amos replied. "Friends and brothers. But with differences. Great differences."

"What differences?" Achmed's tone was harsh. He tasted a new bitterness, a bilious rage that soured his mouth. "True. You are the son of Ezra Maimon, the Jewish landowner, and I am the son of Saleem, the Arab fellah."

"You dishonor me and you dishonor us both and our friendship when you say that," Amos replied stiffly. Sadness washed over him. Surely this scene was a dream, a transitory nightmare.

"Then what are the differences, Amos? I have said that I would become a Jew."

"Achmed, please try to understand. Such a marriage is impossible, unthinkable."

Achmed stared at him, a new coldness settling in his blue eyes.

"Why is it unthinkable, Amos? How often have you called me brother? I was your brother when we were boys and lived our two lives as one. I was as one of your family when I walked the desert with your uncle David Maimon and brought him to safety. I was your brother when the Turks threatened Sadot Shalom and my family and I guarded it. I was your brother when I saved your sister's life in Hebron. But when I seek to marry her because I love her and because she carries my child, then I am no longer your brother?"

"She carries your child?" Amos's face blanched. Incredulity and anger struggled within him. His knuckles whitened as he balled his hands into fists.

"Our child," Achmed replied defiantly.

"You and Elana? She's a young girl—no more than a child

herself." Now at last, anger triumphed over disbelief. He felt a foreign strength swell within him. "You bastard. You rotten bastard."

Amos's arm shot forward, and Achmed staggered backward. The blow had caught him on the cheek, and he felt a pounding pain near his eye. His own fist clenched, but he did not strike back at Amos, who leaned against the table now, his hands covering his face. Achmed remembered, suddenly, the night Amos had learned of his mother's, Nechama's death. Just so the boy Amos had stood, and shielded his eyes, and wept, and Achmed whom he had called brother had comforted him. But he would not comfort him again, and never again would they call each other brother. He went to the door, closed it softly behind him, and made his way down the steep stone stairway.

"Achmed!"

He heard the door open, heard Amos's strangled voice call his name, but he did not turn around. Elana had been right, and he had been wrong, absurdly wrong, and now he did not know what to do.

Amos visited his sister at the Langerfeld home the next day. They sat in the book-lined study where Daniel Langerfeld composed his elaborate political treatises. Elana stared at the familiar shelves. Two rifles were concealed behind the rows of talmudic volumes. The leatherbound, autographed copies of Bialik's poetry hid cartridge containers. The Langerfelds no longer depended on treaties and agreements.

"Achmed visited me last night," Amos said.

"I know."

"Is what he told me true?"

"It is true."

"What do you propose to do?"

"We want to marry. He will convert to Judaism."

"You cannot marry."

"We will."

He did not argue but rose to leave.

"Where are you going?" Elana asked, fearful suddenly.

"I am having lunch with our uncle David Maimon. He is in Jerusalem on kibbutz business."

"You won't tell him?"

A pleading note crept into her voice. David Maimon frightened her. She had shivered, as a child, when he spoke of the night of the revia, the night that had seen an Arab's bullet smash through his eye.

"They cannot be trusted," she had heard him say again and again of the Arabs. His hatred of them was fierce and implacable. His cheeks burned when he spoke of them. But he felt differently about Achmed, she assured herself. Achmed had saved his life. David Maimon had given him a dagger in gratitude and danced the debka of brotherhood with him at Ezra's wedding. He would never harm Achmed.

"I will do what is best for our family, for our people," Amos replied, and she heard their father's tone in his voice, saw their father's icy determination in Amos's sea-green eyes.

She sat motionless in her uncle's leather chair and watched Amos kiss their aunt and pat Naomi on the head. Dutiful Naomi smiled at her handsome cousin, the famous scholar, and showed him a paper she was writing for her Mizrachi study group on the cultural philosophy of Achad HaAm. Amos took his pen and made a few corrections.

"Still, you have caught the essence of his thought, Naomi," he said approvingly, and Elana felt a pang of envy.

How much simpler her own life would be if she were like Naomi, a schoolgirl still, breathless and giggling, courting the approbation of her elders. Naomi still asked her mother's permission to join her friends for a walk to Mount Scopus and her father's permission to spend two pounds on a sun bonnet. Elana earned a salary from her work with Mazal, and often she had been left in charge of the busy Sadot Shalom household. She walked the fields of the Galilee alone and journeyed to Jerusalem when she chose. But she had paid dearly for that freedom and independence. A wave of sadness swept over her, and she struggled to rise above it, like a swimmer determined to triumph against a compelling current. The price had not been too great. Her fleeting envy of her cousin shamed her and betrayed her love for Achmed.

Naomi, poor Naomi, would never know the beauty of watching the skies through the slatted bough roof of a shepherd's hut as a lover's silken hands and lips wandered across her body. Naomi would not know the heart-turning tenderness of surrender, the surge of tingling joy, the quietness that came after the thundering of unity, and then the drowsy sleep on a fragrant couch of fern and dried grass. Again and again, during those precious weeks, she and Achmed had met at the shepherd's hut. Each encounter had matched the first. Their bodies surged toward each other in a new frenzy of discovery, a new acknowledgment of wonder. His lips kissed her fingers one by one; her tongue found the star-shaped scar on his shoulder. She had been wrong to envy Naomi, to allow Amos to frighten her. There could be no wrong in the sweet tenderness she and Achmed shared. He waited for her now, and she would hurry to him.

"Where are you going, Elana?" Naomi asked. "Do you want to come to the meeting with me?"

"I have an errand to run," Elana said.

Impulsively, she kissed Naomi on the cheek. Poor Naomi, she thought, who would discuss Achad HaAm with a group of girls while she, Elana, walked with Achmed through the silver-leafed olive trees in the Valley of the Cross.

He was waiting for her in the wild glade, wearing Western dress—khaki trousers and a blue cambric work shirt. He resembled the young Jews from Iraq who had arrived recently at Gan Noar. How easily he could mingle with the Jews of Palestine. He was not unlike them physically. Like them, he was a child of Abraham and had been circumcised in accordance with the divine covenant. Amos's outrage would pass. Achmed's conversion would appease her father. Unlike Yehuda Maimon, he did not consider his sister, Sara, dead to him and to their people. He would accept Elana, accept Achmed, rejoice in the birth of his first grandchild. All would be well. The ringing bells had not lied to her.

"Achmed," she called and he hurried to her, pressed her close to him, holding her so tightly that she struggled for breath. She felt the anger in his fingers that clutched her with terrifying tenacity.

"What's wrong, Achmed? What's happened?"

Last night she had been fearful and he had been exuberant. Now she felt his fear, the grip of his sadness. Even her encounter with Amos had not prepared her for the swift and violent change.

He led her to an olive tree, and they sat together in an umbrella of shade. Across the glade an Arab boy passed with a flock of lambs. Black, white, and speckled, they skittered through the fallen leaves and tall sweet grass. Lambs were playful and quick; sheep were plodding and slow. She thought of the frisky toddlers on Sadot Shalom, Tamar and Nachum and Rivka, always running and tumbling, and her slow-moving, cautious grandfather Yehuda Maimon, who thrust a cane before him as he walked. Life slowed you, made you wary and cautious. She did not want to become wary and cautious. The shepherd piped a plaintive tune on his reed pipe. He led his flocks deeper into the valley, and they disappeared over the rise that led to Givat Ram.

"I spoke with Amos," Achmed said. "I told him."

"I know. He came to see me this morning."

"I was wrong. He will not dance at our wedding," Achmed said bitterly.

"Achmed, this is new to him. It came as a shock. When he has time to think—to become accustomed to the idea—"

"No, Elana. He will not change. Nor will your father. Nor will my family. I lay awake all night thinking about it, marveling at my own stupidity. The children of Isaac and Ishmael are not meant to marry."

"Isaac and Ishmael. Thousands of years dead. Gone from the land." Above them two hawks cut a swath of blackness through the cloudless sky. Hawks were a bad omen, Mazal always said. Scavenger birds of death, winged messengers of disaster. Elana averted her eyes from them.

"Nothing changes in the land, Elana," Achmed said. "Lambs are still born black and white and speckled, although Isaac and Ishmael are thousands of years dead."

"Then what can we do?" she asked.

She moved away from him as though fearful that his despair would infect her, rob her of the fragments of hope to which she still clung. Her fingers plucked up long strands of grass. Slowly she braided them and thought of Balfouria. What would poor Balfouria say to yet another infant at Sadot Shalom? But of course, her child would not be a child of Sadot Shalom. Sadot Shalom would no longer be her home.

"We cannot stay in Palestine," he said. "That much I know. If Amos's anger was so great, what will your father say? I deceived myself. I believed what I wanted to believe. Forgive me. I received a letter some weeks ago from the man with whom I shared a room at Cornell. He lives in the United States, in the farm country of Minnesota. He offered me a professorship at the university there, on the faculty of agriculture. We could start a new life there, in a new land. In America, where there are people from so many countries, no one will find our marriage strange. Our child, our children, will be accepted. This morning I cabled my friend Sven, telling him that I accept his offer and that I will come to Minnesota with my bride.''

"To Minnesota?" She stumbled over the strange word. She had never traveled north to the Lebanon or south to Egypt. She had sat on the shores of the Mediterranean, on the beaches of Haifa and Tel Aviv, but she had never thought to cross the sea. Palestine was her home. Its hills had seen her birth. She had learned the secrets of love beneath its skies. She was of the first generation of her family to be born on the land. *Moledet*. Birthplace. How could she leave it and belong again to a nation of wanderers when she was so newly at home?

"I know." His voice was very gentle now, and he took the braided grass from her hand and placed it between his teeth. When he bit down, its sweet juice filled his mouth. "I do not want to leave. But we cannot stay, Elana. Is it even safe to stay?"

"Amos has gone to speak with David Maimon."

"I do not fear David Maimon."

"But you are frightened?"

"There is a saying among my people— 'Only the foolish know no fear.' I am not a fool, my love, nor are you. We must leave. Perhaps one day we will be able to return, but now we must leave. You will return to your uncle's house and pack your things. Tell them that you have decided to return to Sadot Shalom tomorrow. If you see Amos, tell him that you have decided that he was right. That all is well with you and that you have decided to return home and to think of me only as a friend. I will meet you at dawn on the Jaffa Road, and we will take the first jitney that leaves for Haifa. An Italian ship sails tomorrow night. I have arranged passage for us both. Fortunately, I had enough money left from my stipend—enough to get us to America."

"But my travel documents?" Elana asked.

The speed and decisiveness with which he had acted amazed

her. His certainty banished her indecision. His courage extinguished her fear. He was so sure of himself, so sure of their future.

"You have your identity card with you. We will say that you did not have time to arrange for papers. At Cyprus, the British Consulate will issue you a temporary passport. It can be done. It is the only way, Elana. We must start our lives over in a new land. I knew that as soon as I could comprehend what Amos had said to me last night. There will be no forgiveness here, no acceptance, neither by your people nor by mine."

His words rang with truth, and she did not deny them. All her own rationalizations of the morning were crushed beneath the force of his conviction.

"Will you trust me?" he asked.

"I will trust you."

She moved into his arms and he cradled her gently, as though she were a small child who had suffered a terrible and inexplicable loss.

"My Elana," he said and felt the heat of her tears against his shoulder. Gently, he caressed her trembling body. "It will be all right," he said.

The bells of the Greek Orthodox church trilled in metallic chorus through the silent grove. A monk in a brown hooded robe hurried past them. He turned abruptly, and they saw his pale face, his sad gray eyes. He lifted his arms, and his wide sleeves winged the air as he blessed them. He was of an order that prayed for the wayfarer. They bowed their heads and watched him walk toward the red brick church, his bare feet indifferent to rock and twig.

Light lingered in Jerusalem as the day faded stealthily into night. The glow of twilight spread delicately yet inexorably across the rooftops of the city, and the weathered stones were caught in nets of golden light. The long shadows that overtook the hills were filigreed by glowing gossamer strands. A crepuscular halo hovered over the city. Achmed, who loved the evening lights of Jerusalem and knew that he might not see them again for many years, walked very slowly as he descended Mount Scopus. He had spent this last afternoon with Judah Magnes, the American Jew who was president of the Hebrew University and a leader of Brith Shalom. Magnes had been deeply saddened by Achmed's decision to leave Palestine.

"It will be difficult to find someone to replace you," he said. "Musa Alami is a moderate, yet he spends more time thinking of the dangers of Zionism than of the necessity for peace and progress. And I find it difficult to trust George Antonius. He has danced at so many weddings that it is impossible to know when he truly rejoices. But of course you must accept your invitation. It will be a great opportunity for you to teach in Minnesota. I congratulate you."

"There will be other voices of moderation," Achmed assured him. "I was encouraged by my meeting at the villa of Haj Salameh. The mufti himself gave me gifts although surely he must know of my work in Brith Shalom."

"George Antonius tells us that the mufti knows everything—most of it, in all probability, communicated by Antonius himself. Still, your report of that meeting troubles me. Something about it does not rest right."

"Why should it trouble you?" Achmed asked, more harshly than he meant to. "Is it so unusual for Arabs to search for peace? Are we so very different from you, or is it impossible for a Jew ever to truly trust an Arab and deal with him as he would with another Jew?"

Judah Magnes had looked at the young man with new concern.

"What has happened, Achmed ibn-Saleem? You have not spoken such words before. You know that I trust you as I would trust a Jew who had proven himself to me as you have."

But would you let me marry your daughter? Achmed thought bitterly. There were so many mysterious dimensions to trust and acceptance, so many strange limits to the relationship between Jew and Arab, which he and Elana had so dangerously ignored. Yet he was grateful that they had ignored them, for otherwise they would not have found each other.

"Of course. I know that you trust me, Professor Magnes. I am just a little tired. My departure is so sudden, and I have so many arrangements to make."

The lie itself pained him. He had all too few arrangements to make. He would not see his parents, but he would write to them. He would write also to Ezra Maimon. He owed no letter to Amos. All debts of love and friendship between them had been canceled. He stroked his cheek, bruised and tender from Amos's sudden blow.

"I understand. Does your friend Amos Maimon know of your decision?"

"Not yet. And if you should chance to see him before I do, please do not mention it. I would prefer to tell him myself."

"Of course." The American nodded and smiled. He admired the friendship between the two young men, Jew and Arab. It renewed his belief that relations between Jew and Arab could be normalized.

He stood and shook hands with Achmed.

"We will hear great things of you, I am sure," he said. "One day the Hebrew University will have a faculty of agriculture, and I hope we shall welcome Achmed ibn-Saleem as a professor. And now I envy you your walk to the city. This is the best hour of the day in Jerusalem."

It *was* the best hour of the day, Achmed thought as he made his way down the narrow road. He paused at the orderly rows of graves in the British War Cemetery and plucked the weeds from the base of a grave which he chose at random. It was a sin to ignore the dead, and he felt a special sympathy for men who had died so far from their native land, for these sons of Kent and Sussex who were buried in the hills of Judea. He acknowledged, as his fingers dug into the rocky earth, that in all probability he and Elana would live their lives far from the land of their birth.

He shrugged the thought away and brushed the tombstone free of encrusted dust. A globule of hardened sap adhered to the marker, and he took his dagger from the scabbard and scraped it off. He remembered the day David Maimon had given him the dagger, and he knew that he would never forget the day the mufti had given him the scabbard. Only hours had passed since he had first held it in his hand, yet in those brief hours his life had changed forever. He made a brief prayer over the grave and continued on his way.

The light was fading rapidly now, and long shadows engulfed the wadi. A group of Sephardic Jews had just concluded their evening prayers at the tomb of Simon the Just, and he watched as they carefully folded their rainbow-colored prayer shawls and kissed the knotted fringes. He waited until the last of the quorum had disappeared down the hill. He wanted to be alone on the descent, to immerse himself in the silence of the hills. There had been too much talk that day, too many words, too many decisions.

Night came at last, cloaking the hills with sabled darkness. A cool breeze, moist and breathing of salt, drifted up from the Dead Sea. He could see nothing, and he walked cautiously, wishing now that he had thought to bring a torch. The lights of the city glimmered like a distant fairyland. Elana would be packing her case now. He imagined her folding each garment. Was she crying?

He moved slowly, carefully, oddly attentive to the cries of the nightbirds. Once the darkness was pierced by a flash of whiteness as a flock of herons flew to their nesting place on the salt plains of the sea. He stumbled but quickly gained his balance and walked more swiftly, breaking a branch from a tamarisk tree which he used as a walking stick.

And then he heard footsteps moving just above him. A soft but swift rush of movement. He turned but could see nothing. He called out and was angry to discern a tremor in his voice.

"Is someone there?"

His shout echoed in the mountain silence, and he heard an intake of breath, a choking gasp.

"Who are you? What do you want?" he called.

There was no answer. Had he imagined the sounds, then? He continued on his way, gripping the tamarisk branch tightly in one hand and feeling for his dagger with the other. He did not have far to go. The lights teased him, beckoned him. His courage revived, and then a shadow darted out from behind a cactus bush, and he knew that a man stood in front of him. A man who did not move.

He raised his dagger, but even as he did so, footsteps, no longer stealthy, rushed toward him from behind. He swerved, brandishing stick and dagger, and saw that an eye patch as black as the night itself covered the man's right eye.

"David Maimon," he said. "I gave you your life. Will you reward me by taking mine?"

"You would give all the Jews their lives. You would give them our land. You betray your people. You betray the honor of our family."

He saw the white keffiyah now, recognized the deep guttural voice, saw the flash of the steel blade. His cousin Hassan.

"Hassan," he cried. "We are kinsmen."

"You have no kinsmen. You have betrayed your kinsmen."

Three men were with Hassan. Their faces were hidden by their keffiyahs, but he saw the glint of their weapons, heard their muttered curses.

They encircled him. He flailed at the air, striking blindly, sensing the impact of wood against bone. The steel of his dagger sliced into flesh. Blood, not his own, oozed hot and thick upon his hand. He exulted briefly, crazily. He had drawn blood and lived. Then he felt the cold metal against his neck. His arm was ripped back, immobilized. His dagger clattered onto a rock. A hand clamped down upon his mouth and he bit fiercely. A man's flesh was ground between his teeth. He heard the bitter cry of pain. The hand was jerked away. Achmed spat out the bloody bit of flesh and tasted the vomit that gorged up within him. He saw a long sword rip through the night in a streak of silver. It plunged down, and he felt a searing pain in his abdomen. He clutched his stomach, and his hands filled with the pearly ropes of his intestines. He fell into the pool of blood that formed at his feet.

"Listen to me! Let me talk to you," he shouted, but he did not recognize the voice that surely must be his own.

Another stab penetrated his neck, and blood surged in bubbles through his throat. Blood was heavy on his fingers—as heavy as the blood in his dream, the blood that rushed toward him in crimson waves and separated him from Elana.

His fingers clawed the earth of the wadi, struggling toward his pocket.

"Elana," he whispered and drew his hand upward to his lips. The blue satin was so soft, so smooth. "Elana." Her name kissed the fragment of ribbon. His eyes closed.

PART TWO

Ruth and Amos:
A Darkening Sky

1935–1938

Chapter 11

DEATH CAME TO Yehuda Maimon during the season of the citrus harvest when oranges and grapefruits, citrons and lemons, shimmered between the bright green leaves of the slender-branched trees. The mourners, who traveled to the small cemetery at Rishon LeZion from every part of the country, breathed deeply of the bittersweet fragrance that filled the air. His sons and their families came from the Galilee and the Negev, from Jerusalem and Tel Aviv. Members of the Vaad LeUmi, the Jewish governing agency, came to pay tribute to the old farmer who was the last of his generation, a man who had come to Palestine in the days of the Ottoman Empire and settled his family on a barren and deserted farm. That farm was a flourishing orchard now. He had wrested life from the earth, and the sweetest fruit in Palestine grew on the trees he had planted. The very last saplings he had planted had reached full growth at last and bloomed in fragrant tribute to his life's effort, to his life's dream.

"He was a man who thrust himself into history," Daniel Langerfeld said in his brief eulogy. "He suffered greatly, but he prevailed."

There was no need to describe those sufferings because all assembled knew of them. They knew of the death of Yehuda's beloved son-in-law, Avremel, of how the widowed Sara had returned to Poland with her son, Shimon, where she had remarried and abandoned her Judaism. They remembered the days of the Great War, when the Turks had forced Yehuda and his wife, Rivka, to leave the Rishon farm, and how Yehuda had returned to begin again the nurturing of his trees. They recalled that he had quarreled bitterly with each of his three sons—with the twins, Saul and David, whose Zionism was intertwined with a new social philosophy of collective living that had made them founding members of Kibbutz Gan Noar, and with Ezra, who had rejected a scholar's life and chosen to farm alone in the untamed hill country of the Galilee.

But he had made his peace with them at last, and they stood together now beside his open grave, their strong, sunburned faces etched by the mourner's lines of grief and incomprehension. They looked down at the shrouded corpse of the man who had once had the strength to lift the three of them at once (balancing the twins on his shoulders and Ezra, the youngest, on his head) and listened to the words of the mayor of Rishon LeZion.

"Theodor Herzl himself sat in the home of Yehuda Maimon and spoke to him of the dream that would become reality because of men like him," the mayor said and beamed with pleasure at his own words. He was a plump little man whose pompous essays on the reclamation of the soil and the ideals of Zion appeared with alarming regularity in the Friday literary supplement of the Hebrew papers.

Enough already, Ezra thought impatiently. His father had hated speeches and ceremonies and had not been particularly fond of the mayor.

He bent his head as the aged chief rabbi, Avraham Kook, recited the ritual graveside prayer, *El Maale Rachamim,* God Who Is Full of Mercy. That was all right. His father had liked Rabbi Kook, who journeyed throughout the country to discuss the centrality of Jewish nationalism and Zion in Judaism. The old rabbi even visited the kibbutzim of the Shomer HaTzair, where pigs were raised in open (and some said, spiteful) defiance of orthodox law. He carried with him his own hard-boiled eggs and vegetables and patiently discussed religious principles with the kibbutzniks, who listened with grudging respect. Yehuda Maimon had owned a first edition of *Orot,* the rabbi's treatise on aspects of holiness in Jewish nationalism.

"I must ask the rabbi to sign it today," Ezra thought.

He would give the book to Amnon, the only one of his children who was intrigued by mysticism and fantasy. Small, dark Amnon stood very close to Balfouria, his shoulder touch-

ing hers, inviting his sister's protection. His eyes were tightly
closed, and Ezra frowned. His brothers' sons stood tall and
open-eyed, unafraid of their grandfather's lifeless, shrouded
body. But they were older than Amnon, and funerals frightened children, touched them with intimations of their own
mortality. Ezra remembered still how shaken he himself had
been at Avremel's burial, and he had been much older then
than Amnon was now. Still, he had prevailed upon Mazal to
allow Balfouria and Amnon to attend the funeral. Yehuda had
been their grandfather; his life had formed their history. Always the children would remember this burial day, the mournful prayers, the calcite-streaked earth of the newly dug grave,
and the melancholy scent of orange blossoms in the air.

Now Ezra and his brothers moved forward and recited the
mourner's Kaddish.

"Yitgadal v'yitkadash, shmei rabbah," they chanted.
"Magnified and sanctified be His great name."

Their voices were resonant, and the responses of the assembled mourners were startlingly strong. Yehuda Maimon
had lived the length of his days. They had gathered to mourn
his death and to celebrate his life. Elana's voice rose in a sweet
alto that wafted above the others.

"May there be abundant peace from heaven and life for us
and for all Israel," she prayed.

Her voice trembled, and her small son, Shlomo, pressed
against her, burying his earth-colored curls in her skirt. Nadav
Langerfeld separated himself from the circle of men with
whom he had stood during the service. He had seen the quiver
in his wife's lips, the sudden dangerous brilliance in her eyes.
Always, he studied his wife with the absorption of a physician
watching a patient for bewildering and repeated symptoms.

"Are you all right?" he whispered, and it occurred to him
that he had asked Elana that question almost every day during
the three years of their marriage.

She nodded impatiently and bent to pick up Shlomo, stroking his hair, pressing her cheek against the child's. She did not
answer Nadav. He had not, after all, asked a question. He had
reiterated a plea.

Freya Langerfeld watched her son and daughter-in-law
through narrowed eyes. Surely Elana knew that it was bad luck

for a pregnant woman to come to a cemetery, and she knew, too, that it was foolish for her to exert herself unnecessarily. Why did she have to lift Shlomo? And why had she brought such a small child to the funeral? But Freya would say nothing. It was impossible to reason with Elana, and she never left Shlomo alone, even for a few hours. Freya had to admit that she had never seen such a careful mother. Elana carried extra sweaters for the boy, carefully prepared snacks, and covertly watched him at play, plucking him from a rock that might have a sharp edge, guiding him away from thistle and bramble. Yet the child was unusually sturdy, an irony when one remembered how small he had been at birth. The doctors, Freya knew, had despaired of his survival, yet he was a robust, precocious child. He had trotted about when he was only a year old. Six months later he was babbling in sentences, and at three he could read a primer and spout the nursery rhymes Elana's half brothers and sisters taught him. Shlomo's bright blue eyes glinted with mischief, but when he lost his temper, threads of angry scarlet streaked his almond-colored cheeks.

"A farmer's child," old Yehuda Maimon had said when they first brought his great-grandson to the Rishon farm. "He is an earth-colored boy."

The old man's palsied hands had stroked the infant's firm, bright flesh, and his weakened eyes had discerned the colors of the field in Shlomo's skin and hair. But where had the blue eyes come from? Yehuda had wondered, and he tried to remember the color of Nechama's eyes. Yes, perhaps Ezra's first wife, the child's grandmother, had had blue eyes. He could not remember, but it did not matter. In his later years Yehuda Maimon was increasingly amazed at how little most things really mattered. Only his trees were important, his beautiful citrus trees laden with their shining fruit.

"No, he is a farmer's grandchild," Ezra had gently interposed.

He had not bothered explaining yet again to the old man that Nadav Langerfeld, Elana's husband, was a political theorist, not a farmer. During those last years Yehuda's lucidity rose and fell in sporadic waves. The Rishon farm was managed now by David's son, Joshua, a serious, humorless young man who enjoyed clandestine meetings in abandoned khans. Joshua was often visited by intense, solemn young men, whom Ezra knew to be followers of Zev Jabotinsky. Often, on his infrequent visits to the Rishon farm, Ezra would find his nephew strolling through the orchards with such a group. Their heads were bent close together, and they spoke in whispered softness although there was no one to hear them. Conspiratorial tones, mystery, and secrecy were necessary to them. Intrigue nurtured their courage.

"Do Joshua's friends come often?" Ezra had asked Yehuda.

"Sometimes they come, sometimes they don't," the old man had answered vaguely. "But they have taken the guns and hidden them elsewhere." His smile was sly, proud. "They recognized the wisdom of your friend Halloran."

It was on that same day that Yehuda had discussed the news with piercing clarity. His hearing had remained unimpaired, and he listened to a radio commentator discuss the murder of Chaim Arlosoroff on a Tel Aviv beach.

"I don't believe the Arabs murdered him," Yehuda told Ezra as they sipped the tea which Joshua's wife, Luba, brought them. "No. There were too many Jews who did not like him because of his Arab land policy. He thought like your Amos. Compensate the Arabs. Pay them double the worth of the land. Relocate them. Train them. Educate them. It won't work, Ezra. It won't work. The Arabs don't want the land. What did they do with it before we came? My orchards were a dung hill. Rocks grew on Sadot Shalom. It is not what they want that matters. It is what they *don't* want. They don't want us." The old man spat angrily. Petals of blood lodged in the pale green glob of phlegm that floated on Luba's linen napkin. Ezra did not argue. One did not take issue with the dying. Besides, weren't men like Shertok and Langerfeld saying the same thing?

"Not all Arabs want war," he said mildly.

Yehuda Maimon took a lump of sugar and placed it under his tongue.

"All right, there will be some like your Achmed. Poor Achmed. But they will not survive, just as Achmed did not survive. The others will kill them. When an Arab speaks of peace with us, he asks for death."

Yet on other days Yehuda sang softly to himself and chanted

the talmudic passages he had learned as a boy in the Kharkov yeshiva. He called his sons by the names of his brothers, and he clutched Joshua's small daughter, Dahlia, in his bony grasp and called her Sara. Days passed and he did not stir from the Rishon farmhouse, and then, quite suddenly, he would rise and wander through his orchard, plucking an orange from a tree and complaining of its smallness to Joshua, passing his fingers across the rind of a lemon to test it for firmness of texture.

"You see the beauty of our trees, Rivka?" he whispered to the ghost of his wife. His voice quavered with triumph, and small Dahlia, who was charged with following him, looked nervously about, as though her great-grandmother might suddenly appear.

He had died, finally, in the first orchard he had cultivated on the Rishon land. Joshua and Luba had found him at dawn, stretched prone beneath a citron tree. His sea-green eyes stared upward into the delicate network of branches, a single orange grasped in his hand. He held it so tightly that they freed it from his death-stiffened fingers with difficulty, and the men of the burial society complained because they could not completely wash the orange stain from his hand.

The fruit was scarred by the bony ridges of the old man's fingers, and Ezra had wrapped it in flax and placed it carefully in an olivewood box. It bore witness to his father's life, to his achievement. Yehuda Maimon had escaped the hate-rimmed ghetto streets of Kharkov and had redeemed the land and watched sweet fruit grow amid thick-leafed branches. He had raised up a generation in the land, the first Maimons who stood with their own children beside his grave. Now, one by one, they advanced, and each dropped a clump of earth on the frail body in the linen shroud. At last it was the child Shlomo's turn.

"*Shalom, Sabbah,*" he said and turned importantly to the older children. "The great-grandfather has gone away," he said. "He won't come back. Imma told me. Isn't that right, Imma?"

"Yes, Shlomo," Elana said softly and took his hand.

He was only three, but it was important that he understand. Illusions were for fools. The dead did not return and the living walked with danger. She should have known as much—she who had come into the world through a cave of darkness, struggling to life from her mother's death-bound body. But they had sheltered her from the truth, and she had believed herself immune. She had been trusting. She had slept beside her love on a couch of sweet-smelling grass and glimpsed the sky through a thatched roof and thought that she would live forever, Achmed beside her, his hand in hers. His death had changed that, had changed her.

Always she would remember the morning of his death, when she had learned that she was alone and would always be alone. She had followed Achmed's instructions and waited for him at the jitney station, the purple portmanteau beside her, staring expectantly at each approaching passer-by, listening for hurrying footfalls. He would come. Of course he would come. She had not glanced at her watch, nor had she counted the tolling church bells of Jerusalem as one hour had passed and then another. Thirst and hunger weakened her. Waves of nausea came and went. The sun blazed mercilessly and her eyelids grew heavy. Still, she had not moved from the wayfarer's bench, fearful that he would not find her.

. And then, at last, she heard hurrying footsteps, and she rose, her arms open, ready to grasp him, to allow him to envelop her in his lean strength, to tenderly explain away the delay. But it had been her cousin, Nadav Langerfeld, who hurried toward her. He was very pale, and sweat streaked his face and soaked the white student's shirt so carefully ironed that morning by Freya, his mother.

"Elana. Thank God I've found you. You must come home with me." His voice rasped and she saw that he breathed with difficulty because he had been running.

"I can't go home with you," she said calmly. "I'm waiting for someone."

"You are waiting for Achmed?" he asked, and she nodded, strangely calmed by the very mention of her lover's name.

"He will not be coming," Nadav said gently.

"Of course he will. He's just delayed." Her voice was shrill suddenly, strident with fear, like the sound small birds made when they saw scavenger hawks. Briefly, she was ashamed. She saw that her cousin's hazel eyes were soft and moist behind the thick lenses, that his hand trembled. There was a

small tear on his shirt just above the button hole. She looked
up, and a dark cloud drifted lazily by and darkened the sun's
unremitting brightness. A cat howled piercingly. A Jerusalem
cat, descended of those who had guarded the deserted city.
Omens of death. She knew the truth but she denied it.

"It can't be. He's coming," she shouted.

"He's not coming," Nadav repeated. "He's dead, Elana.
He was killed last night by Al-Futuwah—the mufti's people—
as he was coming down from Scopus. I'm sorry, Elana. I'm so
sorry."

His arms were outstretched. He had thought to offer her
comfort, to embrace her. Poor little girl. Poor, beautiful young
cousin. Instead she sank unconscious into his arms, and he
lowered her gently onto the bench where she had waited so
patiently for the lover who would never arrive.

She remembered waking in Amos's whitewashed student's
room and looking dizzily about at the book-lined walls, the
cluttered work table, and finally realizing that Nadav sat beside
her in Amos's leather chair. Somehow, he told her later, he
had found a taxi and taken her there, carrying her up the stone
steps even though he was not a strong man and could only lift
her with difficulty. Still, he had found the strength and had
moved quickly, quietly, before the fainting girl attracted the
attention of passing Jerusalemites. He had recognized early the
need for subterfuge.

"Do you feel better, Elana?" he had asked, looking up from
the manuscript he was reading. Always Nadav could work.
Always he could remove himself from an emotional vortex and
find a peaceful plateau of concentration.

She saw that he had loosened her dress, removed her shoes.
A damp towel lay on the bedside table, and she lay still as he
passed it across her forehead, assigning herself to his care. His
hands were very gentle against her face.

"I will never feel better," she said and her voice, dulled and
heavy, was like that of a stranger.

"You will. Not now. Not soon. But one day. Surely, you
will feel better."

"How did you know where to find me?"

"I didn't. But Amos thought you might have arranged to
leave the city, so we checked all bus stops and jitney stands."

"Amos. Why should Amos care?"

She rejected her brother's concern. He had been against them, against their love. If not for Amos, Achmed might be alive, and she might be walking with him along the beach, with the waters of the Mediterranean licking their bare feet as they planned their life together. But Amos had turned against them and Achmed was dead and she was alone.

"You must not blame Amos," Nadav said calmly. "Achmed's own people killed him. It would have happened no matter what Amos did."

"You think so?" She leaned back. He was so wise, this caring cousin. He peered at their world from behind his thick-lensed glasses and discerned their loves and hatreds, their secret hopes and shadowed discontents. "Whom shall I blame then?" Like an aggrieved child, she sought an assignment of culpability.

"Everyone. No one. History, perhaps. Abraham who sent Ishmael into the desert. The children of Esau who would not trust the sons of Jacob. Chance."

"Chance!"

She laughed harshly and then began to cry. Hot tears coursed down her cheeks, and she held her hands out helplessly. She could not stanch the river of grief that roared within her. She would be drowned in her own sorrow.

He unfolded his white handkerchief and wiped her cheeks with the soft linen.

"It will be all right, Elana. It will be all right," he crooned.

Once, as a small girl, she had visited his family in Jerusalem, and her favorite doll had fallen and broken. He had held her then as she wept and promised her a new one. "It will be all right," he had said then, and her tears had dampened and darkened his jersey. But she was no longer a small girl, and it was not a doll which caused her this rending grief.

"No!" she shouted. "It won't be all right. I'm pregnant, Nadav. I'm pregnant with Achmed's child, and my Achmed is dead. What shall I do, Nadav? What shall I do?"

She was trembling now, swaying like a young tree in a fierce mountain wind. Her dark hair swirled wildly about her damp face. He wiped her cheeks, stroked the tangled curls, and rose to put a kettle on Amos's primus stove. The blue flame comforted them both. Achmed was dead, but fires would be lit, tea would be brewed. Life would inch its way forward.

"You will marry me," Nadav said calmly, dispassionately, as though he were executing a plan long since formulated and held in readiness for this moment, this eventuality.

"How can we marry? We're first cousins," she said. She struggled through her bewilderment to coherence. The tears had ceased at last, and now a deadly mantle of calm settled on her. She felt nothing. There was nothing left to feel.

"No. You forget. I am Daniel Langerfeld's adopted son. You and I share no blood tie. We can marry. And I have always loved you, Elana. You know that I have always loved you. Since you were a small girl."

"I know," she said, and now grief made her cruel. "But I have never loved you. I shall never love you. Can you marry someone who will never love you?"

"I could do anything for you, Elana," he said.

He brought her tea then, laced with jam, just as she liked it, just as he had prepared it for her always.

They were married quietly by a rabbi they had never seen before, and Nadav took her to Cyprus for a honeymoon trip. They sent Marconigrams from Limassol announcing their marriage to the Langerfelds in Jerusalem and the Maimons at Sadot Shalom. Balfouria wept because she had missed Elana's wedding, and Freya Langerfeld bit her lips because she had not escorted her first-born son to the bridal canopy, but Nadav, the shrewd political scientist, knew that a *fait accompli* outweighed the most delicate negotiations.

Eight months later, Shlomo had been born, a sickly infant whose circumcision had to be postponed until he was almost three months old. Elana had seldom left his side, and she awakened often in the night to hover over the child, listening fearfully for the sound of his shallow breath.

"Don't die," she whispered to the sleeping infant. "Don't die," she commanded him fiercely. Her mother had died and her lover had died. She could not lose her blue-eyed child as well.

He did not die but cast off his infant weakness and became a robust, strong-willed toddler. Nadav completed his studies and worked in the political department of the Jewish Agency. Their marriage was strangely calm, and young lovers visited the Langerfeld home and thought that one day they, too, would like to live in such tranquility. Elana was a good wife, a good mother, an efficient businesswoman who busied herself with the Jerusalem office of Chemed Handicrafts.

"She seems happy," Mazal said, after a Jerusalem visit.

"Very happy," Ezra agreed. But where was the laughter, he wondered, and where the gentle touching? Always Mazal's hand found his, his arm encircled her shoulder, her lips were sweet upon his. But his daughter and her husband circled each other like polite strangers. Did they sleep, as he and Mazal did, bodied entwined, limbs knotted, the breath of one warm and sweet against the other's cheek?

He could not know that in the night Elana's calm deserted her. She lay then in dream-tossed madness. Again she was on the floor of the shepherd's hut. Achmed's teeth were sharp against her shoulder, and she felt the full force of his manhood within her, stirring the sources of sweet and mysterious moisture. She writhed, she moaned, and then an echoing vacuum replaced throbbing fullness, despair nudged joy aside, and she awakened, sobbing and trembling, small screams escaping from her throat so that Nadav had to fumble for his glasses and fetch her the tea and jam that always calmed her.

Like many scholarly men, Nadav Langerfeld brooded over dark and secret passions. He struggled to contain forbidden fires. He had promised to protect and to shield Elana, not to subdue her. But there were nights when starlight filled their room with silver radiance and her moans pierced his own sorrow. He seized the moment then and held her tightly. He kissed her tear-streaked face then and whispered softly, cajolingly into her ear. He stroked her gently, his hand tender within the moist secret places of her body, against the rise of her breasts and the delicate seal of her closed eyelids. When she lay narcotized beneath his ministrations, her body lost between dream and reality, he claimed her with a fierceness that exhausted them both. He was violent in his lovemaking, almost threatening, as though through force he would wrest from her all that she denied him when he offered her tenderness and understanding.

"Love me!" he shouted one night, gripping her beneath the

buttocks, kissing her breasts, biting the pearllike lobes of her ears, his tongue frantic across the moist rise of her cheeks.

She did not reply, but her body rose to meet his fierce, insistent thrust, and weeks later she told him that she had conceived.

Nadav had not wanted her to come to Yehuda Maimon's funeral, but she had insisted.

"I must go. He was my grandfather. Amos will be there."

"All right."

She had made her peace with her brother. He had not caused Achmed's death. Achmed had died because life was fraught with danger. Disease and hatred lurked in the long shadows that darkened sun-bright days; grief hovered at the edge of joy. She steeled herself to vigilance. Nadav, her husband, and Amos, her brother, were her allies, sharers of her secret.

Only they saw Achmed as Shlomo scurried about. Their knowledge gave credence to a truth she herself sometimes doubted. Achmed *had* lived, and she *had* loved him. The aqueous blue of their child's eyes was not unlike the color of the Galilee sky on a clear summer's day.

"I am glad you called him Shlomo," Amos had said on the day of his circumcision. Shlomo from the word *shalom*. A child named Peace, whose father had died because he yearned for peace. Achmed would have approved of their child's name.

Amos looked at her now and moved closer to her. He was glad that she no longer condemned him. They had not wasted precious years assigning blame, swallowing bitterness; perhaps she had learned a painful lesson during a childhood of being torn between father and brother. Ezra had blamed Amos for their mother's death. Amos had blamed his father for the loss of Mazal. They had both been wrong, and in their error they had sacrificed years of sharing. Even his grandfather, Yehuda Maimon, about whose grave they gathered, had wasted precious seasons of life quarreling with his sons and he had condemned his daughter without remission.

"Do not tell Sara when I die," he had instructed Ezra. "I am not her father and she is not my daughter."

But Ezra had sent a cable to Oswiecem. Yehuda was dead. His bitterness and hatred had died with him. Sara was free to mourn her father.

Amos walked beside Elana across the path that led from the cemetery to the farmhouse. Shlomo trotted beside them until Amos lifted his nephew in his arms and tossed him playfully above his head.

The child chortled with laughter, and Elana stared at them disapprovingly.

"We are coming from a funeral, Amos," she said.

"Ah, but we are walking toward life," he replied. "You see, Shlomo," he said and pointed to the doorway of the farmhouse where Joshua's wife, Luba, stood holding a pitcher of water which she poured in glinting droplets over the outstretched hands of the returning mourners. "We are washing death from our hands, and we will leave our shoes at the doorway so that the earth of the cemetery does not come into the home of the living."

"I know, I know," Shlomo said impatiently. He sat astride his uncle's head and flattened his fingers on Amos's thick hair. "Your hair is the color of wheat, Uncle Amos."

"That is why your mother used to call your uncle Blond Amos," Ezra said. He fell in step beside his son and daughter. He had lingered briefly at the cemetery and placed a small white stone on Avremel's grave. It occurred to him that Avremel and Achmed had died similarly; daggers of glinting steel had pierced their flesh as they traveled alone through evening darkness. Clearly, their Palestine was a dangerous country for gentle men.

The family gathered about the polished wooden table of the Rishon farmhouse. It was laden with salads and hard-boiled eggs, with deep dishes of herring, round rolls, and pots of fragrant coffee. Shlomo lined up a tomato and egg and rolled the ovoid shapes about.

"Round rolls," he said wonderingly. He had never seen round rolls before.

"We always eat round foods after a funeral," Nadav said softly. "That is because life itself is round and moves in a circle. People are born and people die. There is no beginning and no ending."

He looked at Elana. Nothing was permanent. Grief faded. Love came. New earth was turned, and tilled fields lay fallow. They had today buried Yehuda Maimon, who had coaxed oranges from barren soil. Just so he would coax love from fetid memory. She would care for him. One day she would care for him. She carried his child. She would love him. His throat was dry with the certainty of it, and thirstily he gulped lemonade, freshly squeezed from lemons plucked that morning.

"Eat something, Shlomo," Elana said. She avoided Nadav's gaze as she sliced a piece of coffee cake encrusted with candied orange rind for her son. What did he want of her, the kind cousin she had married? Why had he tricked and cajoled her into this new pregnancy? Did he think it would bring him her love? She could not love him. She brought death to those she loved. Her mother had died at her birth, and Achmed had died even as he rushed toward her. But Shlomo would live. She stood guard over his life.

He shoved the cake aside.

"I'm eating eggs," he said plaintively. "Balfouria peeled them for me."

"Shh." David Maimon's voice was harsh. "It's time for the news."

Even on a day of grief they could not miss the news broadcast. International events ruled their lives, determined their futures. Breathlessly now, they listened to the BBC broadcast from Nicosia. The pleasant Oxford accent of the dispassionate newscaster informed them that a massive rally had been held in Frankfurt, Germany. Ten thousand Germans had cheered the proposals of Helmut Nicolai, president of Magdeburg, who advocated new legislation to govern citizenship in the National Socialist state.

"President Nicolai suggests four categories ranging from full-blooded Aryans to Germans of alien blood," the announcer continued. "The latter group would include Jews, Poles, and gypsies. Such citizens would have the protection of the state but would not be able to hold public office, marry, or have sexual relations with Aryans." The cultivated voice paused briefly as though to ascertain that his script had not betrayed him.

"It's a pattern," Saul Maimon said wearily. "They begin slowly, but the pace will accelerate. This is only the beginning."

"And we will sit by and allow them to do as they please,"

Joshua said bitterly. "Even against the Germans we will practice Havlagah, restraint. The precious Jewish Agency thinks debate is a secret weapon. Weizmann places his faith in writing conciliatory letters to Parliament. And while they are debating and writing letters, the Germans are digging graves."

"What would you have us do, Joshua?" Nadav asked mildly. "Storm the Reichstag? Assassinate Adolf Hitler?"

"I have heard worse ideas," Joshua said sullenly. "We must do something."

"We are doing something," Amos interposed.

His cousin Joshua was a hothead, but there was truth on his side. Now was the time for action. And plans were being made. Children had to be saved. Only days ago he had been summoned to a meeting with Henrietta Szold, Recha Freier, and a grave-eyed emigrant from Germany called Hans Beyth. He had sat beside them, sipping tea from Miss Szold's fine china cup as she outlined the program for a rescue project she called Youth Aliyah. A pretentious name, he had thought, but still, it might work. Children under the age of seventeen could be slipped in without affecting the British quota on Jewish immigrants.

"We need your help with a specific group, Professor Maimon," the old American woman had told him, and he knew that she anticipated no objection, would brook no dissent. A network of blue veins protruded across her hands, and twice during their interview she removed her spectacles and wiped her dark eyes; they were weak and tired easily, she told him apologetically. Her wispy white hair was gathered into a bun, but there was energy and force in her voice. She had, after all, built Hadassah Hospital on a desert hillside. Surely, she could organize the more important task of saving the lives of children.

"Why choose me?" Amos had asked.

Recha Freier laughed.

"But it's obvious. You are the perfect Aryan. How Hitler would like to look like Amos Maimon. You are tall, blond, blue-eyed. Your German is adequate. Your English is impeccable. You will be able to move about Germany easily, without challenge. And you are a scholar of international stature. The Germans will be in no hurry to invoke the ire of the Royal

Academy of Archaeologists or Columbia University by arresting Professor Maimon. Questions would surely be raised in academic circles, even in the League of Nations. They would not risk an international scandal and perhaps jeopardize participation in their precious Olympic games next year. Don't you see?"

Amos had seen. Plans had been made, and today he would tell his family.

"Enough quibbling," Ezra said. "I want to hear the news."

The announcer informed them that President Franklin Delano Roosevelt had assured his countrymen that the United States was on its way to economic recovery.

"Too late for Uncle Morris," Ezra muttered.

His American uncle had died that year, and Ezra had sent a letter of condolence to his aunt and to Sonia and Alex Wade. Alex had written to thank him, enclosing a picture of young Sammy, a teenager now. Sonia had not added even a postscript.

The newscaster cleared his throat importantly.

"The Prince of Wales today reiterated his belief that Adolf Hitler is a man of peace and said that he himself would consider a visit to the German leader's home at Bechtesgaden."

"Why not? From Bechtesgaden there is a wonderful view of Austria. And it's safe for him to go. He's not a Jew." David Maimon tossed an orange peel onto the littered table. "Damn it. Why aren't the German Jews leaving? Don't they see the handwriting on the wall?"

"They see it, but they choose not to believe it. Yet. Still, they are willing to send their children out."

"Yes. Youth Aliyah provides some hope. Hans Beyth told me of your meeting, Amos. Is it decided yet when you will leave?" Nadav asked.

A wary silence settled on the room. Joshua switched off the radio. Balfouria took Shlomo and Amnon outside to play.

"Leave for where?" Mazal asked. Her voice was brittle, and she linked her fingers together because inexplicably they had begun to tremble.

"You didn't know?" Nadav said. "I'm sorry. I thought Amos would have told you."

He blushed. He was not one to reveal another man's secrets,

and he knew there was no danger of betrayal from anyone in that room. Was it necessary to cloak everything in mystery, to talk in riddles? That was Jabotinsky's way. But perhaps he was right, after all. Perhaps they stood now at the frontier of a new era, when all trust was suspended and silence was safer than truth.

"It's all right, Nadav," Amos said calmly. "I was planning to tell everyone today. I am going to Germany soon. There is an international convention of archaeologists in Berlin, and I have been invited to deliver a paper."

"Amos," Ezra said wearily, "if you cannot tell us why you must go to Germany, I will understand. But please do me the courtesy of not asking me to believe that with the world exploding around us, you travel to Germany to deliver a paper on the artifacts of ancient Syria or to chair a seminar on early Mediterranean fertility gods. Such undertakings are peacetime luxuries, and although it has not yet been brought to the attention of the world, the Jewish people are at war. Our battlefronts are scattered. Here in Palestine we fight the Arabs. In Whitehall Weizmann fights the British, and in Europe we must fight this Hitler. So many battlefields for such a small group of people."

"The price we pay for being 'chosen.'" Joshua's lip curled bitterly. "We are 'chosen,' all right. Chosen for death and dispersion, for pogroms and murder. But now the 'chosen' people must show that they have a choice." He pounded the table with his fist. Did Jabotinsky know of this Youth Aliyah operation? he wondered. He would have to send a coded message to Jerusalem.

"You will be careful, Amos?" Mazal said.

Her eyes were dark pools of worry, and she leaned against Ezra, suddenly exhausted. When would they rest? she wondered. When would they stop crossing oceans and continents, forever packing suitcases and checking travel documents? Would their farewells never cease? Would they live always in fear that those who left would not return?

You must come back, Amos, she thought. *Come back to us from Germany, from the darkness of Berlin and the shadowed streets of Frankfurt.* She remembered still the grayness of the sky and the chill of the air as their train had streaked through

Teutonic cities during the long journey from Zurich to London after the Hebron riots. It was Elana over whom they had worried then. Now it would be Amos. Amos who had been her lover and was now her stepson and her friend. Why should they live balanced always on the edge of terror? They were a nation of agile acrobats, striving for precarious balance.

She looked through the window and saw the younger children. They played a game of hide-and-seek, darting through the grove of orange trees. Their laughter filled the air. Amnon teased Balfouria, dashed from the shadow of one tree to the shelter of another. One day they would be consumed with fear for Balfouria and Amnon, for the twins, for Rivka. The cycle of fear was endless, ever deepening and recurring.

"I will be careful," Amos promised. He turned to Elana. "Wish me well, Elana," he said.

"I wish you well, Amos," she replied, and her eyes were strangely brilliant.

"I know you do." He took her hand in his and felt her fingers, ice-tipped despite the heat of the day.

"Come walk with me," he said.

They followed the narrow path that led to the lemon grove.

"I miss Achmed, too," he said. "I loved him." It had taken him these years of grief and regret to articulate the words.

"I know. I should never have blamed you. But I was so frightened, so lost."

"And now?"

"Now I am just lonely."

"Nadav is a good man."

"Nadav is a wonderful man. I appreciate him. But I cannot love him."

"Perhaps one day. One never knows. Time changes all things."

The clichés rolled off his tongue, yet what was a cliché, after all, but an oft-repeated truth? Time did change all things. A decade past, he had not believed that he could look at Mazal without yearning, and yet now he saw her only as his father's wife, his own beloved friend. Just as love faded, so too it might grow.

Gently, he embraced his sister who slept beside a man she did not love. His heart turned for her and for himself as well.

He, after all, slept alone. It occurred to him that their mother, Nechama, had been a woman who cherished solitude, who had been happiest alone in the hills of the Galilee. Perhaps he and Elana were destined to live in the grim shadow of her legacy— lonely and alone—silence and regret the twin companions of their nights. But Elana, at least, would have her children, while he was always alone.

She touched his cheek.

"It will be all right, Amos," she said, but he felt her fingers tremble. She reached into her pocket and took out a small revolver.

"This was Achmed's," she said. "It protected us in Hebron. He would have wanted you to have it."

"Thank you." The weapon was cold to his touch, and he thrust it into his trouser pocket, where it rested, a metallic cancer against his thigh.

Nadav Langerfeld watched his wife and her brother from the window. The fat yellow candle that would burn in its thick glass container through the seven days of mourning stood on the broad sill where once Rivka Maimon had cultivated herbs in tiny ceramic pots. The dusty pots stood there still, the earth within them dry and crumbling.

He placed his hands above the flame and allowed the heat and light to splay across his fingers, all but burning his flesh. As a child he had made wishes over the flames of the Sabbath candles. Even as a young man, he had made such wishes. "Let Elana be mine," he had whispered to the flickering flames on his mother's white-covered Sabbath table.

Now he made a wish over the flame of memory. He wished that the child Elana carried would be a girl, a little girl who would inherit Elana's thick black hair and his own hazel eyes. They would call her Aliza, which means 'joy,' and her sweet laughter and gentle ways would cause his wife to love him at last.

He squeezed his eyes shut, felt the moist heat beneath the lids, and heard a child's lilting laughter. Shlomo stood at the window watching him, his blue eyes blinking against the bright sun which highlighted the traces of gold in his almond-colored skin.

Chapter 12

THE FORESTS OF Europe were ablaze with the fires of autumn. Flame-colored leaves crested huge oaks, and birch and copper beeches shimmered in metallic brightness. But at Tempelhof Airport in Berlin the windbreaks of stately conifers were black-green against the wintry gray sky, and Amos Maimon pulled his plaid scarf tight about the collar of his greatcoat as he descended from the plane. Conversations in German fluttered about him; porters shouted to each other; hasty greetings and farewells were exchanged. Automatically, he adjusted to the demands of the language, muttered his own *bitte*s and *danke*s in the traveler's tentative tone.

It had been seven years since his last visit to Germany, as a participant in the International Symposium on Biblical Archaeology held at the Royal Academy, but the passage of time had not dimmed his memory of the country. He remembered still the pervasive cold and the ambience of grim despair. The symposium had been held in January, but few of the German academics had adequate overcoats, and their jackets were worn thin at the elbows and frayed at the seams. Once in the cloakroom he had encountered a senior lecturer carefully lining his boots with newspaper.

Often, after a session, the archaeologists would convene at a local beer hall. Their wallets bulged with rolls of inflated Reischsmarks but a single round of drinks depleted the packets of flimsy bank notes. The unemployed had congregated on street corners; their gloveless hands were blue with the cold, and their eyes were damp with despair and misery. The war had been over for ten years, but they still could not comprehend their defeat.

"Whose fault was it?" they asked each other, and their sour breath formed clouds of mist in the cold air. Veterans pinned their medals to tattered shirts and jackets and sold their boots and uniforms. Shawled women huddled in the queues of public soup kitchens and kept their faces turned, lest they be seen and accused of the sins of hunger and poverty.

The atmosphere in the country had depressed Amos, although the Konigsfelds, a Jewish family who had acted as his hosts, had assured him that the economic depression was temporary, a phenomenon of transition.

"Soon things will change," Dr. Konigsfeld had said as he poured Amos a cognac from the cut-glass decanter that stood on his gleaming mahogany sideboard. "Germany is resilient. The terms of the Versailles treaty will have to be ameliorated, made more realistic. We will manage, my dear Professor Maimon. We will manage."

He had poured himself another drink and smiled contentedly. His Iron Cross was affixed to his lapel with a wide strip of scarlet satin. He had fought with valor at Nancy and had been duly recognized. He lived in the stone mansion on Donhoffplatz which his grandfather had built, and the walls of the paneled library were lined with portraits of Konigsfelds who had lived in Germany for seven hundred years. In the early portraits, the Konigsfeld men wore decorous high skullcaps, but in the more recent ones they were bareheaded and smiling.

"But aren't you afraid that in the face of this depression, Germans will blame the Jews?" Amos asked guardedly.

"But we Jews *are* Germans," the older man replied patiently. "There have been Konigsfelds in Germany for seven hundred years. Your family has only been in Palestine for forty years. I would say that we are more firmly rooted among the Germans than you are among the Arabs."

"But Papa, Jews have been in Palestine for five thousand years," Liesel, his elder daughter, protested. She was a thin, blond-haired girl who regularly attended meetings of the Maccabi HaTzair. Her father smiled at her benignly but did not bother to reply.

Amos had not pursued the conversation. He was not deaf. It was impossible to lift a stein of beer in any tavern and not know that the Germans blamed the Jews.

"Listen, Maimon, I promise you that when you next visit Germany things will be different, quite different. I have had private conversations with Rathenau. Germany will recover. Come, Liesel, play the piano for us. A little Mendelssohn will reassure our Professor Maimon."

Liesel blushed as she approached the piano. She thought Professor Amos Maimon very handsome; he fulfilled her mental image of how a Jew born in Palestine ought to look: he was so tall and golden-haired, and his green eyes were the color of the coastal waters off the Frisian islands where the Konigsfelds summered.

Dr. Konigsfeld lit a cigar, and wreaths of blue smoke comfortingly filled the room as Liesel played. He sighed contentedly.

"Do you think we must live in fear of the countrymen of Bach and Beethoven, of Schiller and Lessing? Shall we tremble in the land where Felix Mendelssohn was born, where Heine wrote?"

Amos did not reply. It was futile to point out that Mendelssohn had renounced Judaism and that Heine, too, had converted to Christianity with the cynical assertion that baptism was a passport to civilization.

But Konigsfeld had not been entirely wrong, Amos thought now, as he looked about the airport. Germany appeared to have restored itself economically. Well-dressed men and women moved swiftly, importantly, through the immaculate modern terminal. Posters of smiling workers beamed down on them, and brightly lettered placards advised: WORK MEANS FREEDOM and THE COMMON INTEREST ABOVE SELF-INTEREST. He noticed at once the preponderance of uniforms. Soldiers, civil guards, and police patrolled queues and stood beside kiosks and departure gates. Boys in scout uniforms scurried about, saluting each other and grimly helping elderly travelers with their parcels. A huge colored photograph of Adolf Hitler, his khaki-uniformed sleeve sporting the red-and-black armband with the odd swastika insignia, was hung next to the terminal clock. The insignia intrigued Amos. He had seen a similar symbol at the site of an American Indian excavation, and it had been imprinted on the title page of a minor novel by Rudyard Kipling which he had found in a Bloomsbury shop. Why had Hitler chosen it? he wondered. Surely Konigsfeld, who had a whim for the eclectic, would know.

He glanced about the waiting room. He had written his former host, specifying his arrival time, and had expected the courtly German Jew to meet him. In this he had followed the advice of Hans Beyth, the Youth Aliyah coordinator in Jerusalem.

"Write to former friends," Beyth had advised him. "In all probability your letters will be read in official quarters. Try to arrange your schedule in as normal a manner as possible. Maintain always that you are a Palestinian professor of archaeology traveling on an English passport. You are in Germany to attend an archaeological conference and to renew old acquaintances."

"But how will I make contact with your people?" Amos asked.

"Not to worry. They will find you. My people are enterprising." Hans Beyth's tone was brusque. He was a busy man. It was his job to administer all Youth Aliyah activities in Palestine. He had no doubt that clever Professor Maimon would manage admirably in Germany, and he had little time to spare for him. After all, Henrietta Szold had assured him that Amos Maimon was ideal for their mission, and he never questioned Miss Szold's judgment. His wife found it odd that he placed such trust in a virginal old maid who had already celebrated her seventy-fifth birthday, but Hans Beyth, as a banker in Germany, had had long experience managing the affairs of aging maiden ladies. Invariably he found their judgments astute. If Henrietta Szold felt that Amos Maimon could manage, then the archaeology professor could be relied upon.

"But I must have some point of contact." Amos was insistent.

"Here is a phone number. But use it only in an emergency, and call only from a public phone." He passed a card to Amos.

"Here is the name of a hotel. Stay there if your friend Konigsfeld does not meet you."

Amos had placed the card in his wallet, which he touched for reassurance as he sat in the taxi that carried him from Tempelhof to the city. Konigsfeld had not arrived, nor had there been a message from him at the travelers' information desk, and even the brilliant crimson and gold leaves on the trees that lined the newly built Reichsautobahn did not dispel the sudden apprehension he felt. A vague queasiness teased him. The interior of the cab smelled of leather, beer, and the pungent sausage roll which the driver, a ruddy-faced Bavarian, ate with relish as he sped down the superhighway.

"Is this your first visit to Berlin?" the driver asked affably.

"No. I was here some years ago—in nineteen twenty-eight."

"Ah, there have been many changes since then. Wonderful changes, don't you agree?" He gestured out the window. "There was no *Autobahn* in nineteen twenty-eight. I froze my ass off that year. We burned furniture for the kitchen stove. I sold my boots, even my sabre. And me a soldier in the Kaiser's army, three times decorated. But that's all over now. I have my own cab. My boy is in military school. When my wife goes to the greengrocer, there's food in the bins and she doesn't have to carry a basket full of money to pay for it. All because of the Führer. Our Führer." He stretched his arm out alarmingly in salute to a roadside poster that showed the sallow, wild-eyed leader. "Isn't it wonderful what he has done?"

"Remarkable," Amos agreed, keeping his tone even. He had at that moment noticed another poster on which huge block letters proclaimed JUDE VERRECKE.

He made a mental translation—"Jew, Perish"—and remembered that he had seen the exact same slogan scrawled in Arabic across a billboard in Haifa Port. Had it originated with Hitler or the mufti? he wondered, and he realized that his heart was beating rapidly and his palms were sweating. He clutched the edge of his seat as the driver negotiated a sudden swerve. There was just time to read the warning signpost that read "Drive Carefully! Sharp Curve!" Beneath the warning someone had scrawled "Jews 75 Miles an Hour!" The driver read the bit of graffiti aloud and laughed.

"You find that funny?" Amos asked, keeping his voice neutral.

"Of course, it's funny. You know what these Jews are like with their big cars and their weak eyesight. It's about time we made the roads safe from them. In fact, we should make Germany safe from them. If we had put them in their place long ago, we would have won the war. It was their fault that we lost, you know."

"But I have a Jewish acquaintance who has an Iron Cross," Amos interposed.

"He stole it, then. I assure you he stole it. They are cowards, all of them. While our blood flowed on the battlefields, they were at home counting their money."

They reached the center of the city, and Amos was relieved when the driver turned his attention to pointing out the new buildings that had been erected since Hitler took power. Dutifully, he voiced his admiration for the Reich Chancellery, Hitler's residence on the Wilhelmstrasse. His heart stopped when he saw the massive building that extended the length of Leipzigstrasse. The shades of its gaping windows were drawn, and huge Nazi and military flags fluttered from its turreted rooftop; they wafted rhythmically in the wind like the outstretched wings of predatory birds.

"Our Air Ministry," the driver said proudly. "You see the Mercedes in front of it? That belongs to Goering. It flies the banner of the Luftwaffe. That is what I would do if I were a young man. I would join the Luftwaffe."

"An admirable branch of the service," Amos said calmly. "I too, would join the Luftwaffe, I suppose."

The cab had pulled up at last in front of the small hotel just off the Friedrichstrasse which Hans Beyth had recommended, and Amos added a generous tip to the fare.

But in the hotel he was startled to see the Nazi banner unfurled above the registration desk and to notice that the thin-lipped clerk, whose sparse hair barely covered his eggshell-colored pate, wore a small swastika insignia in the lapel of his badly cut cheap suit. He examined Amos's British Palestinian passport carefully and returned it without comment. A thin boy in an oversized uniform carried Amos's bags up two flights to a tiny room. Its single window overlooked a deserted alleyway into which someone had flung an old mattress. Its gray-white stuffing littered the pavement like clumps of soiled snow. The room was cold, despite a small electric heater. He tipped the boy, who clicked his heels together but did not smile as he left. Amos shrugged, lifted the phone, and asked the desk clerk to get him the Konigsfelds' number. He waited a few minutes until the annoyed voice of the clerk told him that their phone had been disconnected. He shivered and delved into his suitcase for a sweater. His fingers curled about Achmed's revolver, which he removed and placed beneath his pillow.

He lay down, feeling now the sudden exhaustion that follows a long journey, an exhaustion compounded by the ambience of danger and hatred he had encountered. Even the heavy eiderdown did not warm him, and he thought wistfully of Palestine, where the fields of Galilee were thick with lush, warm grass and of Shlomo, Elana's son, who loved to run barefoot through the plum groves of Sadot Shalom.

As he drifted off to sleep, he heard the sounds of a radio from a neighboring room. A man's strident voice, arresting in its staccato rhythms, proclaimed the supremacy of the German race, of German concerns. His audience responded to his assertions with a tremulous crescendo.

"Heil Hitler!" they shouted.

"That is Hitler's voice," Amos thought. "I am listening to Adolf Hitler."

He drew the pillow over his head in an effort to obscure the sound and fell asleep as the speech concluded to the strains of "The Badenweiler March."

When he awakened, hours later, evening shadows splayed the pale, flaking walls of the room with gliding strips of darkness. He felt the brief panic of the newly arrived, disoriented traveler and then swiftly remembered that he was in Germany and that he was very hungry. He had not eaten anything since breakfast except for the stale cheese bun and lukewarm coffee which the harassed air hostess had distributed as they flew over the Alps. The hotel had a small restaurant, he knew, but he had little desire to enter the narrow, airless room where gray-leafed plants dominated small tables covered with yellowing cloths.

He had glimpsed it on his way to his room and had also sniffed the gaseous odor of overcooked cabbage and scorched meat.

He remembered now a good, inexpensive student restaurant near the Friedrich Wilhelm University. Liesel Konigsfeld had taken him there during his last visit to Berlin, and he remembered still the taste of the crisp breaded schnitzel and her urgent questions about Palestine. What did his father grow on Sadot Shalom? Did the young people on his brothers' kibbutz, Gan Noar, believe in marriage, or did they simply live together? She had blushed when she asked this, he recalled, and lowered her head so that her golden hair veiled her face. Where was she now? he wondered impatiently and dressed quickly.

He felt better as soon as the door of the hotel slammed behind him and he inhaled the crisp autumn air. He had always thought Berlin a beautiful city, and he remembered vividly the tourist jaunt he had taken up the River Spree in an open flatboat. He had stared, then, at the ancient buildings that lined the riverbanks and marveled that their foundation stones had been wedged into the earth centuries ago. He was an archaeologist who spent months and years sifting the sands of the desert, wresting his people's past from the earth, while Germans could simply stare at the monuments on the Wilhelmplatz and Kreuzberg and know that once their generals had battled Napoleon and that Leibnitz had studied in ancient libraries and strolled beneath the shade of the linden trees.

The Gothic buildings were benevolent guardians of the past. He looked up at the massive structures that lined the Leipzigstrasse and smiled, remembering suddenly his grandfather Langerfeld's pride in the emerging city of Tel Aviv. Always, when he visited, the old man rushed him off to see a new building, a new boulevard. Next to the towering, sturdy edifices of Berlin, the pastel-colored buildings of the seaside city of his boyhood were like children's playhouses, fragile structures that might be knocked down when the summer season was over.

The fear and apprehension that had haunted him since his arrival slowly dissipated as he strolled along Unter den Linden. The smoky, melancholy aroma of autumn, a season lost to

Palestine, filled the air. Young couples walked with their arms intertwined and shared the paper sacks of chestnuts they purchased from the leather-jacketed vendors who warmed their hands over glowing braziers on every corner. Portly businessmen tipped their hats to each other, and women lingered in front of shop windows illuminated by dim fluorescent bulbs.

Groups of uniformed men walked briskly up the broad avenue, and if two such groups met, they thrust their arms forward in military salute.

"Heil!"

"Heil Hitler!"

A group of uniformed boys encircled a tall young man who had dropped a chestnut shell on the street.

"Don't you want a clean Berlin?" asked the tall blond youth who was their leader.

The young man, who was some ten years the boys' senior, bent obediently and picked up the shell. The uniformed leader stroked the swastika emblem pinned to the pocket of his well-pressed brown shirt and pointed with his booted foot to another scrap of paper.

"Pick that up, too," he ordered.

The man knelt lower, and a book dropped from the green burlap student sack on his shoulders. Hastily, he retrieved it, and Amos saw how his hands trembled and his tongue furtively licked his lips.

"What book is that?" the leader spat out. His voice was still the unchanged alto of a boy, but the childish tone was reverberant with authority. His followers drew closer, and their eyes were hard.

"Just a book," the young man replied, and suddenly he broke into a run and dashed across Unter den Linden like a frightened animal. The boys gave brief chase but were summoned back by their leader.

"Let him go. A Jew for sure. Not worth your sweat. We'll get him another time."

The group organized into military formation and marched on, their voices raised in the Horst Wessel song: *"Wenn das Judenblut vom Messer spritzt . . ."* When Jewish blood spurts from the knife . . .

Amos shivered, felt a tingle of fear up his spine as they

passed him. Jewish blood. His blood and that of his family and his friends. He waited until the group of boys had vanished and the sound of their song could not be heard. He understood now the young man's fear, the sensible urgency of his flight. He had fled because he was Jewish and in Berlin, in 1935, a Jewish adult male was vulnerable to the taunts and cruelties of boys barely into their adolescence. He walked more swiftly now, his hand resting on the revolver in his pocket, and he felt an almost giddy relief when he reached the restaurant.

The small eatery was much as he had remembered it. The same clean linoleum cloths covered the wooden tables, and the schnitzel was prepared with the same care. The veal was soft and pink beneath the golden breading, and the potato dumplings were feather-light. The beer was proffered in the same thick glass steins and served with a foaming head. Still, there had been changes. Previously, the walls had been lined with posters and flyers carrying announcements of concerts and lectures, discussion groups and tutorial services. Invitations to seminars and proclamations of international conferences had been tacked up on a makeshift bulletin board. His own lecture on the archaeology of biblical Palestine had been announced on one such mimeographed flyer.

Now, a large photograph of Adolf Hitler dominated the room, and the austerely lettered slogan beneath it read: ONE COUNTRY, ONE PEOPLE, ONE LEADER. The words were vaguely familiar to Amos, and halfway through his meal he remembered that they appeared on the logo of the Palestinian Arab newspaper *Al-Liwa*. Could it be coincidence, he wondered, or was the mufti of Jerusalem in such close collusion with the German Nazi party that even their propaganda was identical? He made a note to write to Liam Halloran about it. It might just possibly be of interest to British intelligence.

When he had visited the restaurant with Liesel, it had been electric with excitement, he remembered. As in all student gathering places, there were intense, dynamic discussions at every table. An art student might sit in one corner, moodily sketching the patrons, while a small group congregated in a booth where a guitarist accompanied them as they sang folk songs. The bustling waiters, many of them students themselves, might pause at one table or another to interject their opinions into the discussions in progress.

"Personally I think Hegel had everything upside-down. There is no dialectic to the historic process."

"You actually prefer Feuchtwanger to Mann? You must be crazy. How can you even compare them?"

"What does he know of music? He didn't understand the way Bruno Walter conducted the Beethoven last week."

Good-natured derision, febrile intensity, danced through the discussions, and the students joked that the waiter was likely to slop soup or drip beer on those with whom he took issue.

Now Amos noticed the hushed quiet of the restaurant, although every table was occupied. People ate in silence, or if they spoke, they whispered to each other. The waiters solemnly and swiftly set down full platters and removed empty ones. But of course, the conversations would have been different in any case. Thomas Mann had left Germany, Bruno Walter had been prevented from conducting a concert in Leipzig, and Feuchtwanger's manuscripts had been seized. Hegel, Amos had no doubt, would be considered a deviant intellectual. After all, the Thousand-Year Reich of Hitler's dream would be undermined by the Hegelian philosophy of a dynamic history always in the process of synthesizing. What would happen to Hitler's government in historic synthesis?

The waiter who brought Amos his stewed apples smiled thinly as he set it down.

"You look familiar, *mein Herr.*"

"I used to come here when I was in Berlin for a conference, some years ago. Nineteen twenty-eight. With a friend, Liesel Konigsfeld."

"I knew her. I worked here then too," the waiter said. He glanced nervously about, brushed the table free of crumbs, and refilled Amos's water glass.

"But things have changed. There is prosperity."

"There are jobs. But I have no great desire to work in a munitions plant or join the army. I prefer to serve schnitzel and soup and keep my ears open."

"I see," Amos said noncommittally. "I tried to call Liesel, but her phone has been disconnected."

"Many phones have been disconnected."

The door was suddenly thrust open, and a gust of wind ripped through the room. Several patrons looked up in annoyance, words of protest on their lips, but they turned back to their meals as a group of officers strode in, selected the largest table, and called loudly for a round of beers. When their drinks arrived, they stood as one, clicked their heels, and raised their glasses to the portrait of Hitler. In resonant tones they sang "Deutschland über Alles." Hastily, the other diners rose and joined in the song. Amos, too, stood and moved his lips, although he did not know the words. A glass of beer on their table overturned, and an officer grabbed a napkin from a neighboring table and spread it over the mess. The man from whom he had taken it voiced no protest.

Amos noticed their highly polished boots, the elegant cut of their gray uniforms, the death's-head insignia on their caps and epaulets. He had not seen such uniforms before.

"Who are they?" he asked the waiter.

"You don't know? They are Schutzstaffel, political police, the SS," the waiter replied, and he hurried away because one of the officers had called for an order of pickled eggs and sausages.

Amos left a large tip and walked out of the restaurant. Almost instinctively he put his hand in his pocket, and his fingers fondled the cold steel of the revolver. He was ashamed to find its weight welcome, reassuring.

He wandered the streets aimlessly and found himself once again on Unter den Linden. The atmosphere in the restaurant had depressed him, and he had no desire to return to his narrow, empty room, to slink past the curious gaze of the sallow hotel clerk. It was interesting, he thought bitterly, that the clerk had not offered to procure a woman for him, but then he knew that Amos was Jewish. How could an Aryan prostitute share the bed of a Jewish archaeologist?

Amos thrust his shoulders back. The loneliness that had adhered to him like a tenacious shadow since his separation from Mazal was heavily oppressive tonight. He wearied beneath its weight and looked expectantly into the faces of those who passed him as though searching out a lost companion, an absent friend.

As he neared the University of Berlin, he realized that despite the lateness of the hour, there was an unusual amount of activity in the city. He encountered groups of students walking two and three abreast, some wearing the blazers of their academic societies. Youngsters in the brown-shirted uniforms of the Hitler Jugend movement stomped down the avenue. Their cheeks were ruddy and their eyes bright. They carried blazing torches, cornucopias of flame which they thrust skyward, as though to challenge the few pale stars adrift in the dark skies. Were the heavens themselves fearful of the Nazis? Amos wondered. They sang as they walked, and the words of one song blended harshly with those of another. Like raucous children, indifferent to meaning, their voices rose in nationalistic anthems, resounding hymns, foolish ditties.

> *Knalt ab den Walter Rathenau*
> *Die Gottverdammte Judensau.*

> (Mow Down Walter Rathenau
> The goddamned Jewish sow.)

That Walter Rathenau had indeed been mowed down and that the Weimar Republic had vanished into the footnotes of history was irrelevant to the chanting marchers. Amos wondered if they even knew who Rathenau was. He found himself walking behind a group of youngsters who carried a large red banner emblazoned with a swastika and the words "Students for a Clean Germany."

A beautiful girl, her hair swept upward into a gleaming golden topknot, her full breasts straining against the harsh cloth of her brown shirt and jacket, smiled at him. Her teeth were extraordinarily white against her flame-tinged skin.

"Join us, comrade," she said and walked beside him. He glanced at the circular she pressed into his hand. The crude mimeographed sheet proclaimed a campaign against any concept ". . . which acts subversively on our future or strikes at the root of German thought, the German home, and the driving force of our people."

"Surely you agree with us?" his companion asked.

"An ambitious program," he said cautiously.

"Perhaps. But then, we are ambitious people. I especially. I am very ambitious."

She glanced at him teasingly, moistened her lips, tucked a stray tendril into place. He smiled back, on familiar ground now. He recognized her type. The buxom student who always sat in the front row and smiled engagingly while toying with the top button of her blouse and ingenuously lowering her eyes. Once, during the first year of his sojourn at Columbia, he had taken such a student to bed and discovered that she lay rigid beneath his caresses, that the breasts which had jutted teasingly out at him in the lecture hall were flaccid and dead to his touch. He had given that girl a decent grade, he recalled, and had been relieved when she did not appear in his lecture hall the following semester.

"Do you teach?" she asked.

"Yes."

"I am a student," she said proudly. "I study astrology. Like the Führer. Do you believe in astrology, Herr Professor?"

"Perhaps. I believe in the secrets of the heavens and of the earth, Fräulein."

His answer pleased her and she smiled; she lowered her torch and he saw gold flecks in her brown eyes.

"You must call me Lotte," she said. "Perhaps when this is over, you would like to come home with Lotte?"

"Perhaps," he said and wondered that he felt no desire. Fear had stilled his yearning. When *what* is over? he wondered, and his heart beat faster as he raced to keep up with her.

The street was bright with firelight now, and the shouts and songs were more vehement. They had reached a lovely square opposite the University of Berlin. Once he had sat with a colleague on a bench in that very square and argued an obscure point in biblical archaeology, producing books from his briefcase to bolster his arguments. Now, too, that bench was piled with books, and in front of it huge piles of volumes formed uneasy pyramids. The marching students approached the books and tossed their flaming torches onto pile after pile. Within minutes a massive bonfire was burning. The crimson flames danced in fiery balletic spirals, grew tinged with rims of blue, and emitted acrid gaseous odors. The leather bindings, reluctant to burn, hissed and writhed within the flames like small struggling creatures. Now and again a cloud of ash soared upward as though the volcanic fire could not contain it. The students shouted wildly and threw more and more books onto the flames, gathering them up in a frenzy of excitement. They called out the names of the authors in strident voices that gradually grew hoarse as they competed with each other in orgasmic zeal. Beside him, Lotte shouted wildly. A rivulet of snowy saliva trickled down her full red lips, and her brown shirt was soaked with sweat and clung to her body.

"Thomas Mann!" she shrieked. "Stefan Zweig! Arnold Zweig!"

She swayed above the pile of books and tossed them volume by volume into the blaze.

"Here." She put a slender volume into Amos's hand. "You throw it."

He looked at the title. *The Journey to Zion* by Yehuda HaLevi. Stealthily, he moved away from her and concealed the book beneath his jacket. His mother, Nechama, had read him those verses, in the garden of Sadot Shalom.

The passionate chorus grew louder, but one voice dominated. He called a name and they echoed it.

"A clean Germany. Down with Lion Feuchtwanger." The leader's voice was bell-clear. One by one he lifted the books, called out the names of the authors, and consigned them to the flames. "Jack London. Sigmund Freud. Marcel Proust. Arthur Schnitzler. Heinrich Heine. Walt Whitman. William Shakespeare."

The crowd moaned in ecstasy, and the flames billowed, soared upward in glowing waves, cavorted in fiery frenzy. Then a sudden silence fell, and a short, bespectacled man mounted a makeshift podium. He wore a bemedaled uniform, and flashes of flames were reflected in the leather brim of his officer's cap. He spoke the guttural German of the Ruhr district, and his words were dry and passionless, yet the crowd of students listened with rapt attention.

"I congratulate you on your brave act. Now once again the soul of the German people can express itself. These flames not only illuminate the final end of an old era—they also light up the new. *Heil Hitler!*"

He clicked his heels together and stood at attention, his arm outstretched in centurion salute.

"Heil Hitler!" the young people shouted back. They, too, stood at attention and returned his salute.

"Heil Goebbels!" A group of young girls shrilled their adulation, and Amos recalled reading somewhere that the propaganda minister had a loyal following among very young women.

Now the book burning resumed with new enthusiasm. The words of Helen Keller, Margaret Sanger, and Bret Harte were catapulted onto the flames and reduced to ashes amid triumphant screams.

"More!" the students cried. "More!"

The girl Lotte swayed dangerously and danced before the flames as though praying to a fiery god. The students had stormed the gates of the university library and were bringing out more and more volumes. Philosophy and poetry. Psychology and sociology. Music folios. Sickened, Amos imagined the flames releasing each note so that the flying symbols filled the air with a dissonant cacophony.

"The original sonatas of the Jew Mendelssohn," shouted the leader, and the crowd applauded wildly as the pages of musical notations curled and shriveled into ashes. Wisps of blue smoke trailed skyward, above the city whose streets had been familiar to the composer's grandfather, who had translated the Bible into German and advised his sons to be Jews at home and Germans in the street. Moses Mendelssohn could never have envisioned that one day, in the streets of his city, Germans would be burning his books.

Now art books were being brought out.

"Original Matisse lithographs!"

A cheer went up, but as the heavy prints fluttered toward the flames, a young woman thrust herself forward and seized the folio sheets.

"You can't," she said. "You mustn't."

Tears glittered in her eyes, and her slender white hands became a protective shield about the pictures, which she clutched to her breast, drawing her blue velvet cape about them.

At once she was surrounded. Furious hands clawed at the cape and pried the pictures loose from her clutching fingers.

An open palm slammed against her face, and the frenzied Lotte pulled at her silken hair, the color of moonlight. Amos dashed forward and encircled the trembling girl in his arms. Impatiently, he pushed Lotte away.

"Leave her alone!" he shouted, and the fierce authority of his own voice amazed him.

The mob stepped back, startled briefly into confusion. Still shielding her with one arm, Amos reached into his pocket and removed his revolver.

"Stay back," he commanded tersely.

His voice was steady now. Lessons of his childhood, unbidden, resonated. He was on Gan Noar, and his uncle David was teaching him how to shoot. *Hold your hand steady. Don't relax your trigger finger.* He walked the plum orchards of Sadot Shalom with Ezra, his father, who advised him on how to deal with the older boys who occasionally teased him at the Gymnasia Herzliah. *Always stare a bully down. Nothing confuses them more than courage.* He kept his hand steady now and stared them down as he edged the girl out of the crowd, moving slowly, carefully.

His heart pounded with harsh staccato beats and his fingers were clammy about the revolver. His shirt was damp with sweat, but he forced himself to keep his gaze steady, his pace even. They had almost reached the edge of the crowd. Within minutes they would be out of the square and back on the broad expanse of Unter den Linden. She trembled within his grasp and her hot tears seared his knuckles.

"Soon. A few more minutes," he whispered encouragingly, but behind him the crowd muttered and moved menacingly forward. The smallest mistake could release their fury.

"*Schwein!*" A tall SS officer moved in front of him, his fist clenched and raised. He smashed his knuckles against Amos's chin and wrenched the revolver from his hand.

"Run!" Amos shouted to the girl and thrust her forward. She streaked off, her cape flying, her silvery hair streaming behind her.

He himself stumbled, tasted blood in his mouth, thick and salty. Disoriented, he anticipated another blow and braced himself, but none came. The SS officer had melted into the crowd, which had lost its interest in pursuit and punishment and worshiped again at the altar of leaping flames. Amos broke into a run, following the girl. Footsteps moved behind him, pacing and outpacing him, and he ran faster, but his pursuer came abreast and whispered into his ear.

"Potsdamplatz," he hissed. "Wait at the corner."

He sprinted past him and Amos recognized the voice of the waiter who had served him his beer and schnitzel earlier that evening.

They were waiting for him when he reached the corner. The girl's cheek blazed red where she had been struck, and her palms were black, cinder-streaked by the lithographs she had plucked from the fire.

"I want to thank you," she said. Her voice was very soft, and Amos wondered if it was the shadow of fear that tinged her wide blue eyes with markings of violet. "I am Ruth Niemoeller. This is Ernst Kramer."

"And I am Amos Maimon."

"It would be safest if you went directly to your hotel, Professor Maimon," Ernst Kramer said. "Use the side streets. I will see Fräulein Niemoeller home."

"But promise you will come to see me tomorrow," she said. "Please. My parents will want to thank you." She handed him an engraved calling card.

"I promise," he said gravely. "But hurry now. That mob will soon be dispersing."

"Come, Ruth." Ernst Kramer pulled her gently away. She followed him but turned back as they reached the corner and waved her hand shyly, tentatively. He stared after them until they vanished into the swirling night mist, then he, too, hurried away. He tucked Ruth Niemoeller's card into his pocket, and his hand once again met the cold metal of his revolver. He had been certain that the officer had wrenched it from his hand. How had it made its way into his pocket again? He shrugged in puzzlement and wearily made his way back to the hotel. To his relief, the sallow desk clerk was asleep, and he stole unnoticed up to his room.

Only when he had closed and locked the door behind him did he begin to tremble. The room key dropped from palsied fingers and clattered to the floor. His teeth chattered and he hugged himself in a struggle for control. He slept fully clothed that night, the revolver within easy reach.

Chapter 13

THE ADDRESS ON the engraved card was in Charlottenberg, and the taxi he engaged the next afternoon traveled the length of the Kurfürstendamm to carry him there. The driver was a wizened old man who proudly pointed out the avenue's more famous emporiums.

"There, on the right, you see Israel's Department Store," he said.

The enormous plate-glass display windows shimmered in the autumn sunlight, and the revolving doors spun constantly as customers entered and left. Chauffeured cars waited at the corner. In the central window, a window dresser, oblivious to the stares of the small crowd, draped a length of bright green fabric over a naked plaster of Paris mannequin.

"A very elegant store," Amos said as the cab moved on.

"Yes. The Jews do know how to do things, but then they all work together, so why shouldn't they? Their cousins in other countries send them money and business. That's how they succeed, you know. I read a book that explains it all."

"Really?" Amos's tone was neutral.

"The *Protocols of the Elders of Zion,* it's called. It makes everything clear. Why shouldn't they succeed? They conspire together. They control banks, newspapers. They want to control the world. It was they who caused the depression after the war. The Führer does not hate them for nothing. He has reason, proof. It's all in this book. Where are you from, *mein Herr?*"

"From Sweden," Amos said. It was simpler and safer to lie.

"But you read German?"

"Of course."

"Please. You may have this as a gift."

The driver passed Amos a mangled pamphlet. The Nazi edition of the *Protocols*.

"I can get another one at party headquarters. They are free," he added, as though to apologize for his munificence. He did not want to be thought a fool, a man who gave something for nothing. "Ah, we are at your address. One of the new villas. Your friends must be important people."

Amos looked at the imposing brick residence set well back on an expansive lawn.

"I imagine so," he said and pressed an extra ten marks into the driver's hand.

"I thank you. When you return to Sweden, tell your people what you have seen in Berlin. Tell them that a new world is being born and that Adolf Hitler is its father. *Heil Hitler*."

"Heil Hitler," Amos replied, startled at how easily the words came to his lips, a verbal reflex, a conditioned response.

Ruth Niemoeller herself answered his ring.

"Professor Maimon. I am so pleased to see you," she said.

Her long silver hair hung down her back in a single braid, and she wore a lilac-colored wool dress that matched her large, widely spaced eyes. Her eyebrows were dark, bold slashes against the ivory sheen of her skin, and her features were delicately molded, reminding him of the Dresden doll which Ezra and Mazal had bought for Balfouria in Switzerland. She held her hand out to him and he took it gently, conscious of the fragile bones of her slender fingers, the velvet softness of her skin.

"I wanted to make sure you were all right," he said.

"I am fine. Please come in." Her voice was very soft and very clear. It had the sweet authority of the only child whose parents and nursemaid had always given her full attention, who had never had to compete with the raucous tones of siblings.

He followed her through a hallway that smelled of beeswax and burnished leather, treading on a thick Oriental carpet that covered the highly polished floor. Softly lit paintings hung on the paneled walls. A somber van Eyck portrait. A star-studded skyscape by Matisse. Once, a visitor to Sadot Shalom had brought Amos's mother a folio of impressionist paintings. Amos had sat beside her and studied the prints. Always, Nechama had paused at the Matisse skyscape, and finally she had it framed in Tel Aviv and hung it in the dining room. Mazal had not removed it.

"My mother loved that painting," he told Ruth Niemoeller.

"I am glad," she replied. "It is one of my favorites."

Like his mother, she spoke in a mild, gentle tone, stood tall, and moved with startling courage. How had she dared to dart forth in that maniacal crowd of haters and try to rescue the lithographs? Nachama, too, he imagined, would have done as much, and he was ashamed because he himself had watched the burning of the books and had only stealthily rescued the single volume of HaLevi.

She led him into a small sitting room furnished in graduated tones of green. Velvet draperies, the color of a spring forest, hung at the wide windows and were closely drawn despite the brilliance of the day. Moss-green polished cotton covered the small sofa, the straight-backed armchairs; a crystal bowl sparkled on the small cherrywood table. Rows of bookcases lined the walls, and he studied the titles with a scholar's automatic interest.

Men revealed themselves through their libraries, through the way they cared for their books. The most important item of furniture in the Sadot Shalom farmhouse had always been the glass-enclosed bookcases. The shelves in his own Jerusalem room were carefully crafted, planed to perfect smoothness. He remembered then, with a shiver, the previous evening and the tongues of flames that had licked ferociously at the darkness as the maddening crowds had tossed volume after volume into the consuming flames. What could one say of a nation that burned its books, pillaged its own history?

The Niemoellers were careful with their books. The leather bindings were rubbed to a soft smoothness, and the books which concentrated on philosophy and art were loosely ranged so that they might be removed and replaced easily. These were books that were often referred to, a collection that had been carefully built up, perhaps over generations. Only a single framed drawing hung in that room—a working sketch by Rembrandt of an aged Jew. Amos stared at it, and it occurred to him that his grandfather in Kharkov might have resembled the white-haired elder with the flowing beard.

"That is a wonderful drawing," he said.

"Yes. My mother bought it many years ago in Amsterdam.

We thought it would go well in this room. We hung it here only last week.''

"Then you are new to this house?"

"Yes." She averted her eyes. "My father was on diplomatic assignment abroad for many years. When we returned to Berlin, we were told that our home in Leipzigstrasse was needed for a high-ranking government official and had been appropriated. We were lucky to find this villa."

"Can a government arbitrarily take away a family's home?" he asked.

"You were at the university last night," she said bitterly. "This government can do anything."

She fell silent as the door opened and a uniformed maid brought in a coffee tray and arranged the sterling silver carafe, the delicate Meissen cups and saucers, the blue-and-white Delft sugar bowl and creamer. Amos fingered the gold sugar tongs. The furnishings and appointments of the Niemoeller home exuded an ambience of wealth and history, of one generation neatly continuing the elegant tradition of another.

"I will pour myself, Mathilda," Ruth Niemoeller said. "Please close the door as you leave."

"Yes, Fräulein," the maid replied, but she left the door slightly ajar.

Ruth rose to close it. She listened for a moment before she returned to her seat. Amos understood. This was a room where the drapes were always drawn, a room whose heavy doors were kept tightly closed and whose carpeted floor cushioned the sound of footsteps.

"You are recently returned to Berlin?" he asked, and the directness of his own question startled him. He was a man who prized his own privacy and was respectful of that of others. But he was consumed with curiosity about this delicately boned young woman whose silver-blond braid fell gracefully to her shoulder. He wanted to know everything about her. What countries had she visited? What had she studied? What languages did she speak? Did she like chamber music? he wondered. What was her favorite time of year? He watched with intense interest as she poured cream into her coffee and laced it lavishly with sugar. He smiled, certain that her breakfast croissant was thick with marmalade and that she had a passion for sweets and thickly whipped cream. On his next visit he would bring her a box of chocolate-covered Kron cherries.

"If I had not been so recently returned, I would not have acted so foolishly last night," she said.

"You acted bravely," he replied.

"No. Bravery is when you know the danger which you confront, yet you continue to confront it. I simply did not know. You see, my father was with the German embassy in Ecuador for some years as cultural attaché. It was not considered an important posting, and even when the Rathenau government fell, he was not recalled. I suppose the Nazis did not think it was worth the bother, and besides our family name is not unknown."

"Niemoeller," Amos repeated with sudden recognition. The Reverend Martin Niemoeller had praised Hitler's triumph from the pulpit. The sermon had been reprinted in the *Palestine Post*. Hitler's election, the clergyman had said, meant the end of "years of darkness" and would herald "a national revival."

"We are distant cousins of the reverend. We thought that connection would protect us during this interim period."

"Interim period?" Amos took his coffee black. His tongue curled against its bitterness.

"This is only transitory—this flirtation the German people are having with Nazism, with totalitarianism. It cannot last."

"Surely you don't believe that?" Amos said gently. "Hitler has been in power for two years and grows stronger every day."

"Amos Maimon, am I correct in thinking that you are a man of letters?"

"I am a professor of archaeology," he acknowledged. "At the Hebrew University of Jerusalem."

"Then you know of the German contributions to world culture. Do you think that the nation of Goethe and Schiller, of Mozart and Beethoven, will continue to tolerate the philosophy and actions of the Nazis?"

Her words rang with familiarity. He remembered Konigsfeld summoning his daughter to play the piano and to banish fear of the present with memory of the past.

"As you said, Fräulein, we were both at the university last night. The book burners are citizens of the nation of Goethe and Mozart. You know that they would have killed you. It is a miracle that you are alive."

"No. It is not a miracle. It is because of you. I owe my life to you." She bowed her head, and he saw the swanlike curve of her neck and the web of shimmering tendrils of silver-blond hair that had escaped her braid.

"I had an Arab friend," he said, "who believed that to save someone's life was to become responsible for that person forever." How would Achmed have reacted to the bonfires of books and the screaming frenzied crowd? he wondered, and felt with renewed sorrow the loss of his childhood friend who had known the name of every flower that blossomed in the Galilee.

"You are not responsible for me, Amos Maimon," Ruth Niemoeller said. "I am responsible for myself. For myself and for my country—the Germany that is the true Germany. That mob last night was made up of wild youngsters, crazed fanatics—not of thinking men and women."

"I am afraid I cannot be as charitable and optimistic as you are," Amos said. "I do not think that it is only the fanatic young who are infected with Nazism. I am a Jew, and my perspectives are different from yours. I cannot afford to hope for the best."

"But I, too, have Jewish blood," Ruth Niemoeller said very softly.

She pulled her chair closer to him and told him, in an almost breathless whisper, that her mother, Inge, had been born into a Jewish home. Inge's father had been a Jewish judge who had served briefly as the personal legal adviser to Kaiser Wilhelm. There had been little emphasis on Jewishness in her home.

"The religion of this household is knowledge and culture," Inge's father, the judge, had often said, but this did not prevent him from donning his cutaway and top hat each year on the Day of Atonement. He tucked his blue velvet case under his arm and went to the synagogue that nestled in the shadow of the Kurfürsten bridge.

Inge attended a small private academy for young women of good families, and her closest friend was the daughter of a baron who often invited her to spend holidays on the family estate in the Ruhr Valley. No one thought it at all strange that a

Jewish girl was the baron's guest, but then Inge never thought of herself as Jewish. She felt herself to be somewhat superior to the baron's daughter because she could recite endless passages of Schiller by heart and play Mozart without even glancing at the music.

It was on the baron's estate that she met Hugo Niemoeller, a young diplomat who shared her love for literature and painting but whose consuming passion was for art history. They were married quietly by the Reverend Martin Niemoeller, and the judge and his wife were not discomforted when their daughter knelt in the small family chapel and the purple light of the stained-glass window streaked her pale hair with violet rays. It was a German ceremony they were witnessing, not a religious one. The judge wore the medal he had been awarded by Kaiser Wilhelm for personal service to the royal family (he had arranged for the kaiser to be excused from an embarrassing gambling debt) and gave the young couple a Meissen coffee service and a thousand pounds sterling which he deposited in their name in a Zurich bank. The judge's family had always maintained a Swiss bank account. The judge had been vaguely surprised when Inge named her only child Ruth, after his own mother.

"It is, after all, a very Jewish name," he said mildly.

He would have preferred a more classically German name or even an English one. He was partial to the name Victoria because he had a particular fondness for the English princess whom the kaiser had married. But he adored the child, Ruth, and somehow often found himself telling her stories of her grandmother Ruth, his own mother, who had always lit Sabbath candles and covered two braided loaves of fragrant white bread with an embroidered cloth each Friday evening. Once, to his surprise, he had wept when he remembered how soft and sweet that Sabbath loaf of his childhood had been, and Ruth had taken his large hands into her own small palms and kissed his finger, heavy with the signet ring that bore the seal of the University at Heidelberg.

"I will bake you a Sabbath loaf, Opa," she promised, but she had never done so. He died just after her tenth birthday, and six months later her Jewish grandmother was also dead. At their funerals Ruth heard Hebrew for the first time. A man who wore a black academic gown and a large black hat sang a song of mournful beauty, and she wept, although she could not understand the words. Still, she repeated them to herself night after night: *"El maale rachamim,"* and a Jewish classmate finally told her that the words meant "God who is full of mercy." She felt better then about not having baked her grandfather a Sabbath loaf. God in His mercy would surely give him one in heaven.

Her father was posted to minor embassies abroad, and gradually, memories of her Jewish grandparents faded. Her travels abroad intensified her love for Germany and all things German. Her mother taught her music and literature, and she trailed behind her father as he visited galleries and museums. He was building a small collection of Impressionist art and occasionally acquired a minor classic drawing like the Rembrandt sketch of the Jew. His diplomatic work required minimal effort. Art was his calling, his passion. He seldom read the briefings that arrived from Berlin. Art became Ruth's own passion. She had only a modest talent for drawing and painting; it was art history that engaged her. She read Gombrich with absorption, and during their last posting in Ecuador she wrote a monograph which traced the influence of the Inquisition on El Greco's painting. It was published by a prestigious journal, and her father ordered twenty-five reprints and had them bound in Morocco leather and sent to friends and relatives in Berlin. One was sent to the foreign minister. Within weeks they were recalled to Germany.

"Ernst Kramer thinks it was because I wrote with sympathy of the Jews and other heretics during the Inquisition," Ruth said.

"How did you come to know Ernst Kramer?" Amos asked, remembering the waiter who had spoken to him so sadly in the restaurant and then materialized so suddenly in that frantic crowd.

"I met him in the Schloss Museum. We sketched together, and he introduced me to some of his friends—young people who feel as I do, as he does. They know that the Nazis cannot last. The good people in Germany will not tolerate it. They foresee a new day in Germany, and we work together toward that day."

Amos was pierced by a shaft of jealousy. He recalled the

deep warmth in Ernst Kramer's dark eyes, the thickness of his hair.

"Do you meet with him—with them often?" he asked.

"We are working together. We both believe in Germany. But now I should like you to meet my parents."

She pulled the green satin bell cord, and the servant girl, Mathilda, came in. Too quickly, Amos thought. Surely, she had been lurking just outside the door. Her face was flushed and her cap was askew. A dust curl clung to her white stocking.

"Please tell my parents that I should like them to meet my guest," Ruth said.

"Yes, Fräulein." The girl glanced sourly at Amos as she left.

"She was listening at the door," Amos said.

"Of course she was," Ruth agreed. "She is a dutiful Nazi. If children are encouraged to eavesdrop on their parents and report them, surely servants must inform on their employers. But it makes no difference. She did not learn anything they do not already know."

The sitting room door opened and Ruth's face lit up with a smile as her parents came in. It was remarkable, Amos thought, how pervasive the family resemblance was. All three of them shared the same delicate features, the fair hair and slender fingers. Inge and Hugo Niemoeller were tall and thin, and they moved with the easy grace of those who have never had to hurry, because always doors would be held for them and vehicles would be delayed to suit their convenience. Inge wore a blue silk dress that matched her husband's cashmere pullover. As they stood together, they resembled a brother and sister, and Ruth, who moved toward them, might have been a younger sibling. Their faces were calm, relaxed, perhaps because they had lived so easily, floating through a privileged existence on a serene surface, ignoring the waves and ripples that unpleasant political reports might have created.

"We want to thank you for rescuing our Ruth last night," Hugo Niemoeller said. "It was a foolish thing for her to have done." He spoke as though Ruth had been guilty of an adolescent escapade and Amos had extricated her from a negligible embarrassment.

"She was in great danger," Amos said gravely.

"We are newly returned to Germany. Ruth was not aware of the passions of these people," her father said. "It will not happen again."

"Of course not. All this will soon be over," Inge Niemoeller added. She busied herself with arranging the lilies that floated in the sparkling crystal bowl, plucking a dead leaf from one flower, pinching the wilted petal of another. "How much longer can it last? People will see the truth and the Nazis will be finished."

"With all due respect," Amos said, "I think not."

"But you are wrong, Professor Maimon," Hugo Niemoeller insisted. "I have friends who are abreast of the situation. They are men of insight and importance. We feel that the tide is turning. Hitler himself recognizes it and is growing more moderate. Hasn't he promised Anthony Eden that he will reduce the military and that there will be a system of inspection? Now that he has stabilized the economy, there will be changes. This is, after all, only a transition period. Germany is a great nation, and great nations do not suffer barbarians for long."

"But measures against Jews are intensifying," Amos said. "You must realize that. Your own family is in danger."

"My family?" Hugo Niemoeller's voice grew icy-cold.

"Your wife is Jewish. Ruth is half-Jewish, a *Mischling*."

"My wife enjoys my protection. She was baptized and we were married in a church. There are documents—our marriage license, her baptism certificate. Ruth is therefore a non-Jew, an Aryan, if you will."

"Only by your definition," Amos said harshly. "Not by theirs."

"Amos, please," Ruth said softly. His name was a caress on her tongue, and her use of it startled and silenced him.

"I am sorry," he said. "I have no wish to upset you or frighten you."

"My family has lived in Germany for seven hundred years," Inge Niemoeller said. "My father was decorated by Kaiser Wilhelm and awarded an Iron Cross. How many Nazis can say as much? They are vermin, Professor Maimon. We are repelled by lice and roaches, but we do not fear them. Why should we fear this Nazi rabble?"

"It is always prudent to be vigilant," Amos said carefully.

"I hope, Herr Niemoeller, that when you and your friends meet, you are careful."

"We are exceedingly discreet," Ruth's father replied. "May I ask the nature of your business in Berlin, Professor Maimon?"

"I am here for an international convention of archaeologists at the university and to conduct some seminars. I teach at the Hebrew University in Jerusalem."

"It is an odd time for a Jew to visit Berlin."

"I travel under a British passport, and of course I enjoy the protection of my professional organization. I thought it safe to come because the Nazis do not want to anger the British by interfering with a British citizen. They want Prime Minister Chamberlain's cooperation. And they would not want to risk incidents before the Olympics."

"Of course." Hugo Niemoeller smiled. "Our home is open to you."

"Thank you," Amos said. He shook hands with Ruth's father and pressed her mother's fingers to his lips. They were like fragments of ice to his touch.

Ruth walked him to the front door, and once again he glimpsed the maid darting out of the shadowed hallway.

"The truth frightens them," she said. "But they are not entirely wrong. The German people will soon see the truth."

"I hope you are right," Amos said. "Try to convince me at lunch tomorrow. Twelve o'clock at the restaurant where Ernst Kramer works."

"All right."

"Goodbye, then." He stretched his hand out and touched her hair. His own temerity startled him, but she smiled and inclined her head, at once submissive and inviting. He tilted her chin and his lips brushed hers—petal-soft and moist.

At his hotel there was a message from a Dr. von Sud, inviting him to a meeting at a nearby *Konditorei* in an hour's time. *Sud* was the Hebrew word for secret. A quiver of excitement ran through him. He glanced around the empty room and realized, with startling clarity, that for the first time in years he did not feel alone. The narrow bed did not sadden him, and the ticking of the clock on his bureau reminded him that time was moving swiftly forward. He would go to his meeting. The day would pass, the night would come, and on the morrow he would see Ruth Niemoeller again.

Chapter 14

THE ONLY CUSTOMERS in the Konditorei were two middle-aged businessmen who sat at a corner table, leisurely drinking large cups of coffee on which islands of whipped cream floated. Their worn and laden briefcases rested beside them. They were clearly busy men of affairs snatching a brief interlude of leisure from the demands of a busy workday. The older of the two smiled broadly and waved as Amos entered. Taking the cue, Amos walked purposefully to their table and extended his hand.

"Dr. von Sud, I hope I have not kept you waiting."

"Not at all. Won't you take a seat, Professor Maimon?"

The waitress, a pouting blonde in an ill-fitting milkmaid costume, appeared and recorded Amos's order for coffee and cheesecake.

"An excellent choice," the second man said. "I am Joachim Deutsch. Hans Beyth is a relation. Please give him my regards when you see him in Jerusalem."

"Of course," Amos said. He wondered what von Sud's real name was. The tall, silver-haired man wore an elegantly cut gray suit, but his palm was cracked and callused. A farmer's hand. His eyes were narrowed as though he had spent too many years squinting against the sun's brightness. He was a Palestinian, Amos was sure, most likely a secret agent whom the Haganah had planted in Germany.

"Your brief stay in Berlin has not been uneventful," Joachim Deutsch said. "We heard about your experience at the book burning."

How had they heard? Amos wondered, but then, they were in the business of gathering information.

"I commend you on your gallantry," the man who called himself von Sud said, "but in the future please forego such acts. You attracted attention. You might have been arrested, and then our entire operation would have been jeopardized."

"But a girl's life was in danger," Amos protested.

"That young woman is related to influential Nazis. She may have been planted there."

"No," Amos said firmly. "She wasn't." The certainty of his tone brooked no further discussion. "But perhaps we might discuss this 'operation.' I was told very little in Jerusalem."

"Yes. In a moment. Someone will be joining us," Joachim Deutsch said, and he glanced at his watch and then at the doorway.

Amos followed his gaze. Briefly, his view was obscured, and then he saw the uniform, the highly polished boots, the death's-head emblem on the newcomer's epaulets. His heart sank as the SS officer entered the Konditorei. He recognized his assailant of the previous evening, and instinctively he stroked his chin, still tender where the officer had struck him. He heard the waitress's fluttery welcome, her subservient giggle.

"A table near the window, Captain. We have apple torte, and there is fresh whipped cream today." She beamed expansively and played with the ribbons at her bodice.

"I am joining friends. Ah, there they are."

The officer approached the table, and Amos's heart pounded. They had been betrayed. He had no way of knowing who his two companions were. They might be agents working with the SS officer. Perhaps that was how they had known about the fire and about Ruth Niemoeller. His fingers curled about the revolver. If necessary he would shoot his way out of the café. Already he was measuring the distance between the table and the door.

"It is good to meet you, Professor Maimon," the SS officer said and extended his hand.

Confused, Amos took it.

"Professor Maimon, Captain Schmidt. Our brave and valued comrade," von Sud said.

"We did meet briefly last night," Captain Schmidt said softly, lighting a small cheroot. "I hope I did not strike you too hard, but I had to deflect the interest of that mob. They would have been after you if I had not intervened. Fortunately, I recognized you from the photograph which the Haganah sent."

"I see," Amos said.

He was weak with relief. He took his hand out of his pocket, and his fingers, which had remained steady when he had thought himself in danger, trembled now; a ridge of sweat formed at his neck and trickled down his back. An urge to laugh wildly grew within him. SS Captain Schmidt, by some miracle, was working with the Jews.

The handsome officer smiled graciously at the waitress as she served his cake and coffee. He discussed the weather as she refilled their water glasses. Fall in Berlin was beautiful. He hoped that it would not rain during the professor's visit. But when she left, his voice dropped so low that they bent forward to hear him.

"You must move very quickly," he said. "Even now they are drafting laws which will totally disenfranchise the Jewish community. Jewish assets will be confiscated, and every Jew will be forced to register. To what purpose, I have been unable to discover. But there are plans to expel the *Ost-Juden*—the Jews from Poland. Every day you wait is a day lost. There is no time."

"We are still hopeful of compromise," Joachim Deutsch said. "We have scheduled a meeting with Adolf Eichmann and Karl Hasselbacher. Eichmann hinted that they want to discuss arrangements for transporting Jews out of Germany."

"Only Jews with money," Captain Schmidt said impatiently, even as he smiled charmingly at the waitress, who now escorted a handsome young couple to a table at the other side of the room.

Amos watched as the young man took his companion's hand, touched her cheek, smiled at her across the table. Would he one day sit across a table from Ruth Niemoeller, stroke her slender fingers, and watch the autumn sunlight drift across her silver-blond hair? He yearned for normality, for an end to intrigue, to conspiracy. But normality was a luxury, and he and Ruth had met in austere and hazardous times.

"It's quite simple," Captain Schmidt continued. "For some time now the government has been allowing German Jews who emigrate to Palestine to withdraw their savings and use them to purchase German goods—refrigerators, sewing machines, household appliances. German manufacturers got the money, and in Palestine such items were sold for British currency. Sixty-three million pounds sterling left Germany in this manner. But now the government has had second thoughts. Why should the Jews take any money at all? It is a simple matter to simply impound their bank accounts. Hitler is pleased with this idea. He gets the money and gets rid of the Jews. He cannot see why the Jews are not also pleased. In exchange for mere money they are allowed to keep their lives. But what happens to Jews who have no money to trade? What about the young people whose parents cannot afford to buy their way out?''

"There is Youth Aliyah," von Sud said.

"Youth Aliyah is designed for youngsters who are seventeen years old or younger. By the time the British have approved their visas, many of our youngsters have passed their seventeenth birthdays. We have such a group waiting now—forty young people—strong, talented, and over seventeen. The Germans will not let them leave, and if they manage to get out, the British will not let them enter Palestine. A peculiar dilemma," Joachim Deutsch said. "We hope that you will help us out of it, Professor Maimon."

He lit a cigar and contemplatively blew a smoke ring. His hands were spread out in the helpless gesture of a businessman who has encountered a troublesome obstacle during complicated negotiations.

"Professor Maimon will help us with that particular group," von Sud said, "but Captain Schmidt is right. With the passage of these new laws, everything will be tightened. More rigorous security measures will be taken. You will not be able to work with us much longer, Captain."

"I will be across the border before the 'Law for the Protection of German Blood and German Honor' is passed," the officer replied. "I prefer to protect my own blood and my own honor. We expect the law to be ratified by the Reichstag Assembly at Nuremberg in November. You have almost six weeks. Work quickly." He scooped the last of the whipped cream from the rim of his cup and stood, clicking his heels with automatic precision. "Delicious coffee. Wonderful torte," he said in a loud voice. "So good to meet with all of you. *Heil Hitler.*" He saluted sharply and they raised their arms almost in reflex response. "Good afternoon, Fräulein.

You are the most beautiful waitress in Berlin.'' He tapped her rounded buttocks with his leather crop and left the Konditorei.

"Who is he?" Amos asked wonderingly.

"His name is Klaus Schmidt. He was a doctoral candidate at the University of Berlin who became interested in the Nazi movement on a purely theoretical level. He had chosen to write a thesis on youth movements and nationalism, and he realized that he had a living laboratory in this country. He attended a few party meetings, read *Mein Kampf* carefully, and realized very early what was happening. He infiltrated the party on a high level, got himself onto the Schutzstaffel, and established contact with us. He manages to stay one step ahead of them, but of course his days of effectiveness are numbered. He always knows when we are planning an operation but never the details," Joachim Deutsch said. "We cannot risk that."

"And what is my operation?" Amos asked.

"It involves that group of forty youngsters we spoke of. It will be your job to get them out of Germany and then into Palestine."

"But they have no visas for Palestine."

"Never mind that," von Sud said curtly. "The British are the least of our worries. Somehow we will get them into Palestine. We have done it before and we will continue to do it. There is no choice."

"How will I get them across the border?" Amos asked.

"You are an archaeologist. Archaeologists make many field trips. Professors must demonstrate digging techniques. Am I correct?" Joachim Deutsch now wore the happy look of a businessman who has perceived a solution to his problem and can reopen negotiations. He smiled pleasantly and twirled his gold watch.

"You are," Amos said. "I have often taken my students on such trips."

"Good. You will take these forty youngsters, all of them archaeology students, off for a weekend dig in the Saar. There is much speculation about the Roman fortifications there. They will all have valid student identification cards, and a group visa will be issued by the Ministry of Education. Among our people is a master printer who is not an unskilled copyist and calligrapher. Of course, it will take a bit of time to get everything in order, to produce the required documents. A few weeks, perhaps. In the meantime you will give your scheduled lectures, meet with your colleagues, attend some seminars. You will purchase proper equipment for the excursion. In short, you will be the visiting academic. The youngsters, too, will be coached in their roles. By the way, one of them, a young girl, is acquainted with you. Liesel Konigsfeld, I believe,'' Deutsch said, consulting his notebook. ''Yes. That's right. Konigsfeld.''

''Yes. I was a guest in her parents' home.''

''Her parents were arrested and sent to Dachau. Some trumped-up tax charge. The father was publicly humiliated. But we managed to hide Liesel successfully.'' Joachim Deutsch sighed deeply. He stood and took his leave. ''We will be in touch, Professor.''

''Yes. Of course,'' Amos said but he was still stunned by the news of the banker's arrest. It occurred to him that the Konigsfelds had expressed exactly the same sentiments as the Niemoellers. They, too, had refused to believe that the nation of Goethe and Mozart could also be the nation of Dachau and the SS.

Von Sud also stood. ''I will leave messages at your hotel from time to time, Professor. Meanwhile, enjoy Berlin. These fall days are very beautiful, but November will bring the winter. A terrible winter.''

''I will try,'' Amos said. They did not shake hands. Their work had only just commenced.

Minutes later, he, too, left the Konditorei. Furtively, he glanced over his shoulder. He took an indirect route back to his hotel, turning in at obscure corners and exiting through the rear exits of large shops. The ambience of conspiracy had claimed him, and he no longer questioned its validity or its necessity. He did not chide himself that night for sleeping with his revolver close at hand. Indeed, he checked the bullet chamber twice to make sure that it was properly loaded.

Ruth was waiting for him at the restaurant the next day. He watched her for a moment from the doorway as she sipped a glass of sherry and turned the pages of *Der Sturme*, frowning at the crude caricatures which the tabloid featured. She wore a navy blue wool suit, and the darkness of the color and the nubby roughness of the fabric contrasted sharply with the delicacy of her skin and the porcelain pallor of her complexion. A navy blue satin headband held her silver-blond hair in place, and he was reminded of the illustrations in the copy of *Alice in Wonderland* which he had bought for Balfouria in a Fourth Avenue bookstore in New York. He approached the table, smiling at the thought. She looked up at him quizically.

"What amuses you?" she asked as he slipped into the seat opposite her.

"I am just pleased to be here," he replied. "Pleased to be seeing you again." *My Alice*, he thought, *whom I will never allow to vanish through a looking glass or to scamper down a rabbit hole.*

"I am glad. And I am pleased to see you," she said. "Amos." Again she used his first name, softly forming the syllables with tremulous inflection, with touching shyness, as though testing their sound.

"Ruth." Her name came easily to his lips. He had always loved the single-syllabled name and the story of the young Moabite widow who had gathered up the gleanings in handsome Boaz's fields. Amos did not often go to synagogue, but during the Feast of Weeks, when the Book of Ruth was read, he managed to attend a service so that he might listen again to the tale of loyalty and devotion, of planting and harvest.

"Did you know," he asked her teasingly, "that Ruth was the great-grandmother of King David?"

"No," she said, "I didn't know that. But I do know that I'm hungry."

"Then we shall order at once."

Urgently he summoned the waiter and ordered mushroom omelets for both of them and a salad of sweet-and-sour red cabbages, apple tarts, and a pot of coffee. He did not consult her but ordered with the protective benevolence of a concerned guardian. As they ate, he was pleased that they were sharing the same taste sensation. He wanted to share everything with her—food and music, sunsets and the breath of the autumn wind. He felt mildly aggrieved when she ordered tea instead of pouring a cup of coffee.

"Tell me about your country," she said.

He told her then about his father's farm, where plums grew in purple clusters on thick-leafed trees and apricots dangled in golden obloids on slender branches. He described the fields of golden grain and the lazy, meandering cattle that grazed in the meadowland. He told her of Jerusalem as it looked brushed with the rose-gold light of sunset and of his grandfather's citrus orchards and how the air of Rishon LeZion was filled with the fragrance of orange blossoms. Her eyes widened as he described the barefoot children running through the orchard in the season of harvest, plucking ripened lemons from the trees. They tossed the golden fruit from hand to hand until at last a kindly mother offered them a dish of granulated sugar. Then they cut the lemons into small pieces, dipped them into the sugar, and ate them like candy.

They left the restaurant and made the way back to Unter den Linden. As they strolled the wide thoroughfare, he told her of Jerusalem's narrow streets and of its ancient cobbled squares where stone houses squatted in the shadows and majestic cypress trees jutted skyward.

"You love your country," she said.

"Yes." Sunlight spangled the street and danced in radiant beams about the arched windows of the majestic buildings, but his heart yearned for the hills of Judea and the Wilderness of Seir.

"Would you die for it?"

"Yes."

"And I, too, love my country and would die for it," she said with a nervous air of triumph.

Together they looked at a group of youngsters, dressed in the scout uniforms of the Hitler Youth movement. The boys goosestepped up the avenue, following a color guard—two older youths who carried the red-and-black swastika banner. They sang as they marched, and their voices had a shrill sweetness. Their skin was soft and smooth, unmarred by the hint of facial hair. One of them toyed with his red neckerchief. Another impatiently hitched up knickers that hung too low. They stood on the frontier of childhood, sweet-voiced and bright-eyed, yet already they had achieved hatred and dreamed of death and destruction, war and power.

"Deutschland, Deutschland über alles," they sang in uneasy crescendo. "Germany, Germany above all else."

"They sing of a different Germany from mine," Ruth said fiercely.

"All right." He put his arm around her shoulders. He did

not want a political discussion. He wanted only to continue walking with her up the tree-lined avenue, her hand tucked in his. A strand of her silver-blond hair gleamed against the dark wool of his jacket sleeve like the metallic thread which Arthurian maidens offered their knights as talismans of luck. He thought to pluck it off and conceal it in his wallet, but an antic wind blew it loose.

They went to a concert that night and heard a stirring performance of the *Messiah*. The audience trembled in ecstasy as the chorus sang out in rich unison—*"Alle menschen sind Brüder"*—all men are brothers.

Women in velvet evening dresses, men in striped trousers and tails, students in tweed and wool, uniformed men and working people dressed in their best, applauded together, until their palms were sore and tears coursed down their faces. Their faces were luminous in the blaze of light from the opera house's crystal chandeliers. Ernst Kramer applauded from a balcony, and the girl called Lotte leaned heavily against an officer, whose hand rested on the ice-blue satin bodice of her dress. In this world, where coincidence had become the norm, Amos half expected the officer to be Klaus Schmidt, but it was a man he had never seen before.

Ruth, flushed with excitement, clung to him as they left the opera house.

"This is my Germany," she said.

"And is this also your Germany?" he asked and pointed to a poster which carried an announcement of an all-Mahler concert. A sticker reading CANCELED! obliterated the date, and beneath it someone had drawn a crude caricature of the composer with tiny Jewish stars for eyes and the symbol of a dollar for a nose. A black crayon scrawl had been added: *"Die Juden sind unser Unglück"*—The Jews are our misfortune.

"That is an aberration," she said. "If you will come with me to a meeting tomorrow night, you will understand that there are Germans who still struggle against this mindless hatred."

"It is hardly mindless," he said. "It is, in fact, most expertly programmed. But yes, I will come to your meeting."

They had reached her Charlottenberg home, and they stood beneath the portico. A shaft of moonlight rested on her face, and he touched the slatted silver ray with his fingers and then moved his hands slowly across her face, touching cheek and mouth, tracing the line of her brow, the curve of her lips, like a blind man who seeks to capture impression and memory within his fingertips. Her long eyelashes fluttered, but she stood motionless, almost breathless. His hands came up to her ears, tiny fragile shells. He cupped her head in his large palms, slipped the satin headband loose, and lifted her hair. The pale sheaths, the color of winter wheat whose new, sweet kernels shimmer in the darkness, swirled about his fingers.

"Ruth."

His lips found hers and his arms encircled her body. Why did she tremble? Her face was moist. Why did she weep? He held her closer to shield her from fear, to protect her from grief. His lips moved urgently across her face, capturing her tears as they fell, until his tongue was salty. She rested briefly, relaxed against the bracelet of his arms.

"I must go in." But she did not move.

They saw an inch of drapery stir, revealing amber lamplight.

"You must go in," he said. Again his hand moved across her face. She had shivered, yet her skin was burning hot. She had wept, yet a smile danced across her lips.

"Till tomorrow, then," she said.

She slipped into the house, and he heard her father's muted voice and her own reply. The door closed, and he walked slowly to the corner. When he turned back the house was dark, and he walked back to his hotel repeating her name in breathless whisper.

"Ruth. Ruth. Ruth."

Boaz had marveled at the courage of the biblical Ruth, who had left her parents' land and "come unto a people she had not known before." He marveled at his own Ruth, who had the courage to live in her parents' land. He would see her again tomorrow, and he longed for the hours to pass.

He joined the Niemoellers for dinner the next evening. They gathered in a dining room too small for the heavy mahogany furniture. The huge table was covered with damask cloth woven through with golden thread that was reflected in the heavy carved silver.

Hugo Niemoeller raised his crystal wineglass in a toast.

"To Germany," he said. "To the Germany of Goethe and Beethoven."

"To Germany," Inge and Ruth replied, but Amos remained silent and did not lift his glass.

Mathilda, the serving girl, watched them contemptuously and slammed the kitchen door.

"She has given notice," Inge Niemoeller told him. "She says she has found better-paying work in a munitions factory. Krupp is offering very high wages."

"I think it is more likely that she has been informed that the new laws will forbid Aryans to work for Jews," Amos said.

"I have told you before, Professor Maimon, my wife is not Jewish. Nor is my daughter." Ruth's father's voice was steely-edged. He would not be rude to a guest in his home, to his daughter's friend who had extricated her from danger. Still, the man presumed too much. These Palestinian Jews were too blunt, too outspoken. Inge's family had not been like that.

"How are you keeping busy in Berlin?" Inge asked, ever the diplomat's wife. The dinner table was no place to discuss politics or religion.

"I have arranged some lectures at the university, and I am conferring with my colleagues on the faculty. They have told me of some interesting excavations in the Saar valley, some ancient Roman and perhaps even Celtic fortifications. I am most anxious to organize a field trip and demonstrate new techniques we have developed in Palestine for working at the site of such an ancient dig," he replied, offering the same speech he had given others who expressed curiosity. His interest in the Saar region was becoming known. There would be no surprise when his expedition traveled there.

"How interesting."

Inge Niemoeller served a spinach and mushroom salad, carefully spooning the crisp leaves and delicately shaped crescents onto hand-painted china plates.

"How beautiful your dishes are," Amos said.

"Thank you. They belonged to my great-grandmother." Inge stroked the edge of her plate. "You think us foolish, perhaps. We are much attached to our things."

"Why is it foolish?" Her husband's voice was irritable. "In our possessions are the secrets of our history. Of course, you may not understand this, Professor Maimon. You are a pioneer. Your community in Palestine has no history.''

''I think you will concede that both Jesus and Moses belong to history and, in fact, to the history of the Jewish community in Palestine,'' Amos replied. He had often made similar answers, in seminar rooms in New York and in Oxford, at dinner tables in Brussels or in Copenhagen. ''But it is true that in Palestine my people are looking to the future. That, I think, is the great difference between us. Here in Germany you look to the monuments of fallen heroes. You drink toasts to Goethe and Beethoven. You hang heavy draperies at your windows so that you will not see the present, and you turn in fear from the future. In Palestine we do not fear the future. We embrace it.'' He spoke very softly, aware that the door to the kitchen was ajar. Mathilda's shadow fell across it.

Ruth rose and gently shut it.

''We do what we can,'' Hugo said. ''I have friends who feel as I do. We meet. We discuss. We will be ready when the Germans have exhausted their infatuation with Hitler, when the Nazis fall from power.''

''But they will not fall from power,'' Amos said. ''Herr Niemoeller, you and your friends mean well, but you are like frightened forest dwellers who see a great fire, a holocaust if you will, moving toward them. What do they do? They pray for the wind to shift while they fill very small buckets with water.''

''What would you have us do?'' Inge asked, and for the first time Amos saw fear in her eyes.

''It would be wiser to leave the forest. Seek refuge before the flames consume you.''

''Unthinkable,'' Hugo said angrily. ''Germany is our home. We cannot leave.''

His eyes traveled the room, pausing at the silver tea service, the thick Persian carpet, the tapestry of Saxon warriors that hung above the sideboard. Amos remembered how his grandmother Rivka, until the day of her death, had mourned the loss of the elegant furnishings of her Kharkov home. She had sighed deeply as she sat in the small sitting room of the Rishon farmhouse and told her grandchildren of the crystal chandelier and the abandoned hand-carved furniture of her Russian parlor. She would have understood Hugo and Inge Niemoeller.

"You mean that you will not leave," he persisted. "Others have started over."

Mathilda came in then to clear the table, and the tenor of the conversation changed. They spoke of music, of the approach of winter, of Mussolini's surprising campaign in Abyssinia. Inge Niemoeller confided that she did not like Mussolini, whom she had met at a diplomatic reception. He wore cologne. She grimaced charmingly.

"How does Germany feel about the Italian invasion?" Amos asked.

Hugo Niemoeller smiled slyly.

"I should imagine that there is little distress on Wilhelmstrasse. If the Duce is concentrating his energies in Africa, he cannot bother with Austria, and that will leave Hitler a clear field. And of course, he jeopardizes his relationship with both France and Britain, so he will have no choice but to ally himself with Germany. The chessboard is intricate but not mysterious. Germany, I believe, has the next move and is in no danger of moving into check."

He leaned back, pleased with himself, the superior player who contemplates other people's games but does not care to play himself. Amos imagined that Ruth's father had often delivered such piercing evaluations of the political scene as he presided over embassy tables in the tiny duchies of Europe and in the torpid South American countries of his minor postings. But still the man saw everything clearly. Damn it, why didn't he act on his insight?

He and Ruth left early after dinner for the meeting in Ernst Kramer's flat. They climbed the narrow stairwell of his apartment building, and Ruth tapped three times sharply and then kicked the door lightly—the same signal his cousin Joshua used for his Irgun meetings, Amos remembered with amusement.

The shabby, ill-lit apartment was crowded with young men and women who sat morosely about, clutching the crudely mimeographed pamphlets that littered the room. Their faces were chalked with the parchment pallor of the serious graduate student, and their voices were either too loud or too soft, as though the long hours in libraries and lecture halls had damaged their perceptions of proper speech. They spoke vaguely to each other of taking a stand. Perhaps they would hold a protest meeting on behalf of their Jewish colleagues who had been dismissed from university posts.

"Just a token protest," a bespectacled young man said.

Others demurred, objected to suggested times and places. Someone observed that a protest might lead to arrests, and many arrested dissidents were being sent to detention camps at Dachau and Sachsenhausen. The mention of these places made them uneasy, and they shifted position and avoided each other's eyes.

The room was very small, and too many people were smoking. The air grew gray and sour. Someone spilled beer on the tattered arm of Ernst Kramer's sofa, and the bare scarred floor was littered with crumbs and peanut shells. A girl whose fingernails were bitten down to bloody rims tore the pamphlets into long strips that curled like paper winding sheets.

"Where is Walter?" Ruth asked.

"He left the country last week. They say he crossed into Switzerland."

"And Clara?"

"She was arrested."

"No. She was detained for questioning."

"Same thing."

"Yes. The same thing."

Ernst Kramer tried valiantly to pursue an agenda. He introduced a political theoretician, who advised them that there was reason to believe that once the economy had stabilized the Nazis would grow more moderate. He, too, quoted Hitler's exchange with Anthony Eden. As the group listened, their faces were intense with the desire to believe, but their eyes glinted with the certainty that he was wrong.

Ernst asked for a decision as to whether they should print more leaflets. Amos glanced at the one he held. It called for a return to the democratic ideals of the Fatherland and for a positive affirmation of the great German cultural tradition that had given the world Goethe and Beethoven.

Again, Goethe and Beethoven, he thought impatiently. Again this craning backward into the past. They would all be trapped behind a barrier of flames, hypnotically repeating the names of their cultural heroes—Ruth's parents in their elegant Charlottenberg villa amid the relics of their elegant past, prisoners of their silver and their paintings, and Ernst Kramer and his friends in their dreary student lodgings with posters of Rosa Luxemburg peeling on the walls and tattered treatises by Karl Kautsky moldering on makeshift bookshelves. But he would not allow Ruth to be trapped with them. He touched her arm and they slipped quietly out of the room.

"Now do you see what I mean?" he asked as they walked the silent streets. "Your friends are terrified. They are exhausted, but they will not move to another part of the forest."

She did not reply but clung tightly to his arm as they stood beneath the portico. This time it was her long fingers that traveled across his face, that drew his neck down. His mouth bruised hers in fierce, desperate assault; her nails dug into his flesh, and her teeth nipped wildly at cheek and ear lobe.

The weeks that followed were fraught with activity. Amos prepared and delivered several lectures at the University of Berlin, although the small auditorium was only half filled and very few of his colleagues attended. He remembered the huge crowds that had flocked to hear him at the same auditorium a few years before, when scholarship and religion were discrete issues. Still, there was no open rudeness, and he was given full library courtesies. He posted a notice on the bulletin board of the Archaeology Department announcing the organization of a field trip to the Saar. He also placed a small announcement in the student newspaper, but although he checked his box each day, to his relief there were no applicants. He and von Sud had not discussed what they would do if legitimate students applied.

He purchased equipment, spades and pick axes, canvas specimen bags and hand lenses.

"A strange time of year to dig," his supplier commented. "It is winter. The ground will be hard."

"I will not be here in the spring, and I have a theory about the location of the Aqua—the Roman baths," Amos replied.

The supplier shrugged. Jews had a streak of madness. The Führer was not wrong. They belonged in Palestine or Madagascar—on an island or in a desert where they could do no harm.

Amos was invited to confer with Karl Hasselbacher, the bureaucrat at Gestapo headquarters who headed the desk for dealing with émigrés and Jews. The invitation unnerved him, but von Sud urged him to accept it.

"In effect you have no choice. He asked to see you because you are a distinguished Palestinian visitor. Perhaps he wants to show you how reasonable he is being so that you will report favorably to the British. The Olympics are much on Hitler's mind these days."

Von Sud was not wrong. The pudgy official was affable and offered Amos coffee served in chipped commissary cups.

"My superiors, Rudolf Heydrich and Adolf Eichmann, will be most disappointed at missing you, but they were called to Bavaria. They are both most interested in Palestine. Adolf Eichmann, you know, is our expert on Zionism. He has visited Palestine."

"I am aware of that," Amos replied. He did not add that Eichmann had not "visited" Palestine but had served with the defeated German army in Syria.

"They wished you to have this directive which we are issuing to all police offices," Hasselbacher said proudly. He read it aloud in a stentorian tone: "The activity of Zionist-oriented youth organizations that are engaged in occupational restructuring of the Jews for agriculture and manual trades prior to their emigration to Palestine lies in the interest of the Nationalist Socialist state's leadership. These organizations therefore are not to be treated with that strictness that it is necessary to apply to the members of the so-called German-Jewish organizations."

"How very generous of you," Amos said, and the German beamed.

Amos inured himself to the sights that daily grew more commonplace on Berlin's streets. The prestigious Wertheimer Department Store was plastered with notices warning shoppers not to buy from Jewish merchants. JUDE was crudely scrawled on shop windows with a spattering of yellow stars and large-nosed caricatures. Small boys dashed into such Jewish-owned shops and snatched merchandise from the counters. He saw a well-dressed businessman push a broom the length of Potsdamplatz, bent beneath a placard emblazoned with yellow stars. He watched a crowd of boys in Hitler Jugend uniforms chase a small girl up the street. He saw an old man assigned to scrub a storefront with his beard while a crowd of teenagers taunted him. Amos's heart pounded, his stomach turned, but he did nothing. Von Sud had warned him that it would be dangerous to their mission for him to call attention to himself.

He spent all his spare time with Ruth and told her always what he had seen. He would spare her nothing. One evening he told her that he had seen a mob of children pursuing a small boy and shouting, *"Jude verrecke!* Jew, perish!"

The child had stumbled and lost a shoe. Weeping and limping, his face distorted with fear, he had hurtled past Amos, his eyes glassy with terror, a small, frightened animal pursued by a scavenger pack.

Ruth's hands contorted into fists, and her large violet eyes were moist. Weakened, she rested her head against his breast while he stroked her silver-blond hair.

"It will pass," she insisted, but there was no conviction in her tone.

"No. It will get worse," he replied. "You must leave the country when I do."

In the next room her parents listened to baroque music on the phonograph and turned the pages of their books. Her father had abandoned his visits to the Foreign Ministry and had begun research for an article on an obscure Renaissance artist. The maid, Mathilda, had left, taking with her the sterling silver sugar bowl and creamer, but they had not reported the theft to the police. A film of dust covered the heavy, dark furniture. The only daughter of the Jewish judge had never learned how to clean a house. Ruth did the shopping, cooked the meals, and struggled to maintain a semblance of order. Her pale hands were reddened and coarsened by carbolic laundry soap, and ashen circles of fatigue lined her eyes.

"How can I leave them?" she asked pleadingly.

"How can you stay?" he asked in return.

The questions became an exercise in echolalia, repeated again and again. His arguments balanced her protests, and all the while their arms were tight about each other's bodies, as though to relinquish their grasp were to relinquish hope.

They strolled along Unter den Linden one afternoon. It was early November now, and the branches of the graceful trees were denuded. Yet here and there a few leaves clung to slender wands of wood, and although they were withered and dried, some few still retained pale veins of green, as though they struggled to endure past their brief season of life. As they walked, a lambent wind lifted the fallen leaves, and the brittle debris swirled about them in mischievous dun-colored clouds. The cloying fragrance of decay filled the air and mingled with the smoke of a small fire burning on a side street. The flames danced in curling spirals, and the children who had set the fire, in imitation of their elders, laughed and tossed copybooks and primers into the small blaze. They sang and clapped their mittened hands as the books burned. Some tossed leaves onto the fire, and an acrid stink filled the air.

"The smell of death," Amos said bitterly. "Of dying Germany."

"Of dead Germany," she added in a small voice. Her shoulders slumped in defeat. She had hoped for the hopeless.

"Then you'll leave with me?" he asked.

"They will be alone. How can I leave them?" But for the first time he was comforted. She had not said no.

"I love you." The wind bruised their faces. Her head was turned, but he saw how her lips trembled and the dangerous glitter in her violet eyes.

"I love you, too." But there was no joy in her voice. Their love had come in the season of death and had been proclaimed on an avenue carpeted with putrescent leaves.

He met with von Sud. Again they sipped their mugs of coffee in an overheated café and smiled too cordially at the waitress who brought them a bowl of whipped cream to spoon onto their pastries.

"Only in Germany is there such wonderful pastry," von Sud observed.

"Yes. Only in Germany," she agreed and smiled prettily.

She turned to an old man who had sat down at a neighboring table.

"I am sorry, Herr Maier," she said, "but we no longer serve Jews here." Her smile did not alter as the elderly man shuffled to his feet, his cheeks blotched and his eyes atwitch, and left the café.

"You leave in two days' time," von Sud said. "It is all arranged. All the papers are in order—student identity cards and passports. You travel in distinguished company. We have endowed some of our youngsters with noble names. A von Stumpf travels with you, and a Giesseking. If asked, he will say that he is a distant cousin to the pianist. They are, of course, both *Ost-Juden* and tone deaf. You will place a notice on the archaeology bulletin board announcing that the expedition to the Saarland will meet at the railroad terminal at nine P.M. Your group will travel third class on the night train to Ratstaat. I do not think that a group of students and their professor, carrying only knapsacks, archaeological equipment, and texts, will attract much attention. Ratstaat borders the Alsatian town of Hagenau, and of course in Hagenau there are fascinating remnants of Roman fortifications. You will take your students to the student hostel at Ratstaat, where they will leave their possessions, and you will announce your intention of spending a few hours working in Hagenau. The groundwork has been laid—I am sure no question will be raised. Why should a group of students pursuing a well-publicized field trip be denied the border? Once across, you make your way through the Forest of Hagenau. There is a train station at the other side of the forest, and you will travel to Marseilles where the *Hanna Maru*, a Japanese freighter, will be in dock. Passage has been booked for all of you to Port Said, and from there other Haganah agents will guide you northward to Palestine."

"A neat plan," Amos said. "Too neat, perhaps?"

"It will work," von Sud replied and licked a rim of whipped cream from his upper lip. "It must work."

"I have a request," Amos said. "I want a set of papers prepared for Ruth Niemoeller."

"She is going with you?" Von Sud frowned.

"I think so. I hope so."

His heart beat faster. Only two days. She would have to go with him. He could not, he would not, leave her behind.

They met for lunch as usual the next day and afterward took the tram south to Schoneberg. They sat side by side on the wicker seats, and her gloved hand rested lightly on his open palm. They might have been a young married couple, taking a half-day holiday to visit aging parents in a peaceful suburb. How wonderful that would be, he thought, to be ordinary, living a simple, conventional life. He looked with jealousy at the other passengers, and his gaze lingered on a cheerful family group returning from a shopping expedition—the plump, harried mother surrounded by packages, and the children playing tag and jumping boisterously from seat to seat. They were red-cheeked and gay-eyed, and each wore a homemade swastika armband about the sleeve of a bulky winter jacket. The mother smiled apologetically at Ruth and Amos.

"I hope they are not bothering you. Children have so much energy," she said. "Do you have any children?"

"No," Ruth said softly. "Not yet. We have no children yet." Wistfulness weakened her voice, and he pressed her hand.

The woman chided the eldest boy and reached out to straighten his armband. Amos watched her stonily. What would she say, he wondered, if he told her that if he and Ruth did have children, her own youngsters would torment and chase them? He thought of the small, tearful boy who had scurried past him down the Donhoffplatz. Still, they nodded pleasantly to the woman as they descended from the tram.

They climbed the Kreuzberg and at its summit rested on a bench and looked down at the city. The air was cold and had the rare clarity peculiar to the bright first days of winter. The few drifting clouds were silver-edged. Birds flew southward in formation, streaking their way darkly through the white sunlight. Now and again one or two broke flight and settled briefly on the stripped skeletal branches of the birch trees, where they sang mournfully before flying on.

Ruth rested her head on his shoulder. She wore her blue velvet cape, and he slipped his hands within its folds and felt the fragile contours of her body, the winged tips of her shoulders, the slender, silken length of her arms, bare except for a narrow gold bracelet, his only gift to her.

"They are starlings, those birds," she said. "Are there starlings in your Palestine?"

"There are wonderful birds in my Palestine," he replied. "Doves and swallows, egrets and storks." He told her how once he and Achmed had found the bleached skeleton of a young stork.

"Achmed. Who loved your sister, Elana," she said dreamily.

"Yes." He pulled her even closer so that she might shield him from the pain that pierced him anew with each memory of his boyhood friend.

"Poor Achmed. Poor Elana," she said sadly. "Star-crossed lovers. Like us, Amos."

"Not like us. We are together. We will be together."

"No. It's not possible. You have your work to do. You must return to Palestine. And I cannot leave my parents. It would be death for them. They cannot manage without me. My father had to replace a pair of shoelaces. He did not even know where to buy them. Always a servant took care of him, and now there are no servants. His own business affairs confuse him. Today he gave me the account book for his savings in Zurich. He is short of funds and wants to transfer some money to Berlin, but he is not sure how to do this. His business manager always took care of such things, but he wrote to my father and told him he could no longer handle his affairs—at least as long as he is married to my mother. Others in his family have suggested that my father divorce her—many Aryans are divorcing their Jewish wives—but my father, of course, will not think of it. I will have to arrange for the transfer of funds. How would they exist if I left? They are helpless."

"Ruth, you yourself are in danger. Ernst Kramer was arrested this morning. The Gestapo is clamping down on dissident groups."

They would clamp down on Hugo Niemoeller and his friends as well, those gentle intellectuals who believed in the brotherhood of men and the civilization of Germany. Soon, like Ernst Kramer, they would answer a knock at the door and find themselves en route to Dachau or to Sachsenhausen.

"Then my parents are in danger as well. Tell me, Amos, could you have abandoned your parents to danger?"

He did not reply. For years his father, Ezra, had in fact accused Amos of abandoning his mother to danger. He had blamed Amos for Nechama's death because Amos had not been at Sadot Shalom, and Ezra had been unable to leave her and ride for a doctor. Amos remembered still the terrible burden of that guilt and the bitter remorse and regret that had cloaked his youth and young manhood in a miasma of misery. His father would not forgive him, and he would not forgive himself. Sensitive, delicate Ruth would sink beneath such a burden. She was like the biblical Ruth, a fiercely loyal daughter, a Ruth who would not desert those who had sustained her.

"I cannot persuade you?" he said, and the question acknowledged defeat. She would be lost to him—as Mazal, his first love, had been lost, as Achmed, his friend, the companion of his boyhood, had been lost. Always he would be alone, accompanied only by shadowed memory.

"I'm sorry."

Misery thickened her voice. She trembled. He drew her still closer, and they sat in mute companionship on the hillside and gazed down on the twilit silhouette of the city of Berlin rising in dark majesty on either side of the silver ribbon of the River Spree.

They spoke little during the short journey back to the city. It had rained briefly, and moisture streaked the windows of the tram. A dancing arc of fading sunlight careened into a tiny rainbow that shimmered across the loosened knot of Ruth's silver-blond hair. A rainbow was an omen, a promise. He reached to touch it, but as suddenly as it had appeared, it vanished.

"When do you leave?" she asked.

"Tomorrow."

"Tomorrow?"

The word weakened her, filled her with despair. Tomorrow. He would leave, and she would never see him again. She would be left with only the memory of his hands upon her hair, his lips traveling across her face, his voice, so soft and yet so resonant, telling her of his country, of Palestine, where golden oranges grew in thick profusion and white-winged storks soared above date-laden palms. They had never even slept beside each other. They had shared no love-darkened nights, had never awakened to the filigreed light of earliest dawn. At least Elana had shared sweetness with her lover, Achmed. But she and Amos had been doubly cheated.

Bitterness welled within her as they walked the length of Kurfürstendamm to Charlottenberg. Her eyes were downcast, and only the pressure of his hand upon her arm directed her. She walked as though she were blind. She was training herself. From tomorrow all would be darkness for her.

They had reached her corner. She recognized the oak, with a swastika patriotically carved into its trunk, the glow of the street lamp always lit too early so that its harsh light rivaled the soft luminosity of the afternoon's end. It was only steps now to her door, to their parting. They would say goodbye. They would not kiss. She could not bear a farewell kiss. She would melt beneath its tenderness.

"Ruth! Stop!" His voice was an urgent whisper. He thrust her back against the wall of a building. "Don't move!"

His hand was in his pocket. She saw the outline of his revolver and moved to touch him, but his body pinioned her against the wall. A black Mercedes was parked in front of the Niemoeller villa. A uniformed driver sat at the wheel and an officer leaned against it, tapping his booted foot impatiently. The death's head glinted at his epaulets, and his fingers beat out an odd staccato rhythm.

The door opened and Ruth's parents slowly exited, each accompanied by a soldier. Hugo Niemoeller wore his white silk scarf and a dark gray cashmere coat. Inge Niemoeller was wrapped in a tweed cape. A tiny hat fashioned of feathers the colors of an autumn forest was perched on her upswept pale hair. They each carried a small valise.

"Do you have everything, my dear?" Ruth's father's tone was solicitous. He ignored the soldier who held his arm, as he would ignore any underling, any social inferior.

"Yes. I think so."

The SS officer moved forward and attempted to help her into the Mercedes, but she withdrew from his touch. The judge's daughter did not like strangers to hover too close. The car door slammed, a lock clicked into place. The car's windows were of smoked glass, but as it pulled away, they saw Frau Niemoeller's face at the window, and she lifted her white gloved hand in gentle gesture. Amos kept a restraining grip on Ruth and knew that always she would remember the ghostly outline of her mother's hand against opalesque glass.

They stayed huddled in the shadow of the building for long, aching minutes, Ruth's eyes squeezed shut yet tearless. Then they retraced their steps, treading lightly, like fugitives in a dangerous wilderness, wary of predators. The street lights of Berlin were aglow now, and their long shadows danced through the circlets of lights as they walked back into the city. Ruth had not once looked back at the house, where moss-green drapes hung at gabled windows and Rembrandt's drawing of an aged Jew hung on a cream-colored wall.

Chapter 15

THE YOUNG PEOPLE glanced nervously about them as they stood before the information booth at the Potsdam Terminal. The thin yellow light cast by low-wattage bulbs jaundiced their faces, and their hands trembled with nervousness as they waited for Professor Amos Maimon. One of their number, a tall, dark-haired youth, had already left.

"This will never work. A crazy scheme," he had muttered.

His defection had unnerved them, and they looked at their watches and moved uneasily about the cavernous waiting room, sweating profusely beneath the many layers of clothing they wore. They knew that all their luggage, even their book bags and knapsacks, would have to be left behind at the student hostel in Ratstaat and that they could effect their escape with only the clothes on their backs. Birth certificates, snapshots of parents and brothers and sisters, photographs of houses and gardens were sewn into the hems of their long coats, and small pieces of jewelry were concealed in footgear and undergarments.

Liesel Konigsfeld's feet were icy-cold within her fur-lined boots despite the three pair of socks that covered them. But warmth surged through her when she saw Amos Maimon hurrying toward them, accompanied by a sad-faced young woman whose silver-blond hair hung like swathes of moonlight across the dark blue velvet of her cape. Liesel had not seen Amos for years, yet she restrained herself from rushing to him. They had been warned that they must be very casual and act as though their journey were a routine student excursion.

Amos, in turn, greeted them with professorial reserve and

distributed the equipment he had brought with him. Small rock hammers and hand shovels. Sifters and specimen pouches fashioned of soft chamois. They compared items and chatted among themselves. Liesel smiled shyly at Amos and was grateful for the recognition and compassion that glinted in his sea-green eyes.

"This is Ruth," he said, and the two young women had pressed each other's hands. By a sheer effort of will they did not stare when a group of prisoners flanked by SS officers walked by in pseudomilitary formation.

The men and women prisoners had been divided into two separate flanks, and each carried a small satchel. Their faces were pale and expressionless, and they marched in step, lifeless automatons, glancing neither to the right nor to the left. The young people averted their eyes and talked to each other with nervous animation, their voices too shrill against the silence of the almost empty terminal. Liesel's fingernails bit down on Ruth's soft palm. Her favorite aunt marched in that funereal procession of the defeated and the damned.

Later, Amos had told Ruth that one of the boys in their group had seen his mother and almost choked on the bilious vomit that welled within his throat. Ruth had wondered, then, what she herself might have done if her parents had been among the prisoners. Nothing, she bitterly supposed. Her courage had died the night of the book burning, and all that remained of it was the pale crescent of a scar that a welt had left on her palm.

At last their train was announced, and they boarded and found their seats in the third-class compartment. The lights of Berlin vanished, and the train streaked southward. The students presented their tickets and were not asked for identity cards. Ruth leaned against Amos's shoulder and fell into a weary sleep.

At Magdeburg the train took on additional cars, and the Jewish prisoners and their guards left the train. Amos was glad that most of his group was asleep and did not see the small, forlorn column of men and women, their faces bleached masks of despair, march across the platform, clutching their pathetic satchels.

At Göttingen the station lights were dimmed, but the silver

spire of the university cathedral glinted in the darkness. Were prayers still being said there? he wondered. Were the intellectual theologians still praying for their country, which was spiraling toward hell?

At Frankfurt they screeched to a halt. The train lights were turned up, a siren sounded, and there was great commotion on the platform. Uniformed police flanked the halted cars, and searchlights illuminated the interstices. Amos slid open his compartment door, lit his pipe, and stood smoking in the corridor.

"What's happening?" he asked a conductor who strode by importantly.

"They wired from Magdeburg that two of the Jewish prisoners are missing. Those damn conniving cockroaches. They know how to crawl through the narrowest of openings. A damn nuisance. We lose time while we're stopped here, and now they are talking about checking papers. I don't need to see papers. I can spot a Jew anywhere." The conductor snorted his irritation and searched in his pockets for a tin of snuff, which he packed into his nostrils. "I just hope your students won't be inconvenienced, Professor. Such fine-looking young people. It is for our Aryan youth that we must fight for a pure Germany."

"Indeed," Amos said politely. "We are grateful for your efforts."

He returned to the compartment, apprised the youngsters of the situation, and was pleased that they did not panic.

"Just remember the names and dates on your papers," he advised them. "I am sure there will be no trouble." He was surprised that he himself felt no nervousness. Was it calm or numbness? he wondered.

"Papers!" They heard the harsh command and the thundering of boots in the next carriage. The sliding door was wrenched open and slammed shut.

"Papers!"

An SS officer pushed his way into their compartment and leaned against the door, his thin lips twisted into a knot of official boredom. Two soldiers edged past him, each holding in check a slavering dog that strained at the leash. Amos's heart stopped. Behind the SS officer stood Lotte, the avid Nazi he had met at the book burning and glimpsed again at the concert. Surely, she would remember Ruth.

The young people produced their papers, and Amos admired von Sud's thoroughness. The documents had been placed in tattered and worn cases. Ink was smudged in appropriate places, and the photo attached to each identity card was officially bleak. As though by agreement, the officer glanced cursorily at the cards belonging to the young men, and Lotte, in paramilitary dress, seized the papers offered by the women. When she reached Ruth, she paused and stared hard at her.

"I know you," she said slowly, ominously. "And you are not a student." She spoke softly, and Amos was grateful that the SS officer was at the other end of the car and did not hear her.

"You are right. She's not. She's my present to myself, Lotte. It is Lotte, isn't it? I never forget a beautiful girl's name." He smiled confidingly at her. "You know how it is. She's my bit of fun for this field trip." He tweaked Ruth's chin, allowed his hand to linger on her breast, and invited Lotte to share his lascivious glance. "But it's you I've been thinking of, Lotte. I will see you in Berlin. You must write down your telephone number. Perhaps you will chart my horoscope."

"I'll look forward to it," Lotte replied and scribbled her phone number on a card. She did not look at Ruth's documents but tossed them contemptuously back at her. "You must have an interesting fate, Herr Professor." She licked her lips and straightened her cap, pleased that Amos had remembered her interest in astrology. There was no need to bother with his silver-blond tramp. She was the professor's weekend whore, but it was Lotte he would take to dinner. He was an important man, she knew. A visiting professor from some Eastern land. She had caught a glimpse of him once, through a café window, having coffee with an SS officer. Klaus Schmidt, she remembered now. He was no longer in Berlin. It was said that he had been sent abroad on a direct special assignment from the Führer. This professor could be trusted, then. She winked conspiratorially at him as she left the compartment with the officer and the other soldiers. The dogs yelped in fierce staccato sequence. Then, slowly, the motor roared and the train left Frankfurt at last. They sat in silence as it continued on past Mannheim and Karlsruhe to the tiny rural depot in Ratstaat.

There they breakfasted on hard rolls and bitter coffee at the student hostel as they loudly and gaily discussed their venture. The hostelkeeper, a large-bellied Rhinelander, offered his own archaeological theories. The Romans had withdrawn from Germany, he asserted, because they had recognized themselves to be inferior to the resident population. He was certain that if inscriptions were found at the Aqua, the Roman baths, they would prove his theory. Although it was early morning, he drank a lager of beer and offered them sausage from his private store.

"Take. Don't worry. There's plenty more. There are plenty of Jewish cattle farms near Ratstaat. We'll always have meat."

He laughed, and they laughed with him. They accepted the sausage because they dared not refuse it, but in the Forest of Hagenau, Liesel vomited the pig meat onto a pile of pine needles. There was no problem at the French border. Only Amos was asked to identify himself, and the border guard accorded him the respect reserved for academicians in a country where bookkeepers addressed each other as "Herr Doktor."

"Have a good excursion, Herr Professor. It's wonderful to travel with the young."

He smiled approvingly at the students, who grinned in return and sang the Horst Wessel song. At the conclusion of the last stanza they passed a windbreak of conifers, and the soil beneath their feet became French.

Ruth breathed deeply of the mingled fragrance of the giant evergreens and the dried juniper that filled the forest. The autumnal odors carried the fresh, wild scent of freedom, and they drew it in like refugees from a gas-filled room inhaling fresh uncontaminated air. The pine needles were soft beneath their feet, and in the sky above, soft clouds drifted. In Germany they had lost the habit of looking up at the sky. They walked rapidly through the forest, singing Hebrew songs, calling to each other by name, for the sheer joy of raising their voices without fear.

"Who will build the Galilee?" one group shouted.

"We will!" The Hebrew refrain was joyous.

"Who are we?"

"Israel!"

Beneath a giant oak, its naked branches stretching skyward, Amos Maimon took Ruth Niemoeller into his arms. He kissed her violet eyes, caressed her hair.

"Let us be married in Marseilles," he said.

"In Marseilles," she echoed and relaxed in the circle of his arms, her life committed to his.

An aged rabbi married them in a small Marseilles synagogue. The scent of the sea clung to the red velvet curtains that covered the holy ark. The rabbi's wife wept when she heard their story. A son of the Land of Israel had led this group of children through the dark Forêt de Hagenau to freedom even as Moses had led the children of Israel through the Sinai. And now the brave Israelite was marrying the most beautiful of the young women and taking her with him to Zion. The rabbi's wife served them wine and newly baked challah. Her cambric handkerchief grew damp with tears, and because she could find no other gift, she gave them a Sabbath cloth of her own embroidery. Ruth was deeply moved by her tenderness and warmth.

This, then, was what it was like to be Jewish. Mysteriously, she belonged now to a family of caring strangers who wept at her sorrow and rejoiced in her marriage, who offered her sweet wine and Sabbath loaves like those for which her Jewish grandfather had yearned.

The next day, in an austere maritime banking house, she arranged to withdraw all the funds in the Swiss account which her Jewish grandfather had opened on her parents' wedding day. She and Amos took the pile of fresh new franc notes to a small quayside shop where a somber-faced Alsatian sold them fifty carbines and neatly stacked wooden boxes of bullets. She watched Amos examine each weapon, his finger deft on triggers, safety locks, his attention concentrated. A dark line of oil streaked his palm.

"So many guns," she said.

"Not enough." He sighed. "But we could not get more into the country. Our Jewish army is illegal, of course."

"Is it so dangerous, then, in your Palestine?" she asked.

Her voice was very soft, made fragile by fear. She had seen enough danger. She did not want the oil of weapons to stain her husband's palm.

Still, she helped Amos to pack the carbines and ammunition into cases where they were concealed by linens and comforters.

"My trousseau," Ruth told the captain of the *Hanna Maru* when they at last boarded the Japanese freighter that carried them to Port Said.

"Gifts for my family," she explained to the Egyptian customs official.

"You don't expect me to begin married life without proper linen," she teased the British immigration officer who examined her belongings when she descended from the train in Jerusalem. As Amos's wife, she was able to enter Palestine openly, exempt from the harsh British quota. The others in their group were smuggled into the country in private taxis driven by Egyptians who knew secret roads across the desert. Some traveled by camel caravan, disguised as Arabs, and others were concealed beneath the tarpaulins of produce wagons. But all of them had gained entry, and within weeks the entire group assembled in the Maimons' Jerusalem flat. The long journey that had begun at the Berlin railroad station was over at last, and at that reunion they lifted tumblers filled with wine from the vats of Rishon and toasted Amos and each other joyously.

"*L'chaim.* To life. To a new life in our own land!"

Some wept as they tasted the sweet wine, and others laughed. But both Liesel and Ruth remained silent, thinking of those left behind. Ruth, remembering still her mother's raised hand (the glove so white, her mother's face so pale), struggled against the knowledge that the opposite of life was death. She shivered, although the day was warm and Amos's protective arm covered her quivering shoulders.

Chapter 16

"FLOWERS, ADONI?" The toothless Yemenite woman smiled coaxingly at Amos Maimon and beckoned to him with a bouquet of yellow roses. She shook her head from side to side as though to mesmerize him with the rhythmic swing of her dangling golden earrings. "Flowers for *Shabbat*. How can you go home without flowers for the Sabbath table?"

Amos paused and studied the rainbowed array of blossoms that blanketed the hand cart she had parked on the busiest corner of Dizengoff Street.

"Yes, *Imma,* you are right. Of course I need flowers for Shabbat," he said.

She flashed a grateful smile at him, revealing a single gold tooth mysteriously ruling the corner of her mouth. He wondered briefly how many flowers she had sold to pay for it and then turned his attention to her wares. Carefully, he selected three separate bouquets. The pale violet irises that grew among the foothills of the Galilee were the color of his wife's eyes. The flowers would not survive until their return to Jerusalem in two days' time, but that did not matter. Ruth would fashion them into a small corsage to be pinned to the shoulder of the pale gray silk dress which Mazal had designed for her to wear to the Toscanini concert.

The tall white primroses, their petals rimmed with red, would look well in the blue vase which Elana always placed on the center of her dining room table. His sister was strangely partial to the color blue and had even hung a blue donkey bead above the crib in which her small daughter, Aliza, slept. Amos had teased her about it, accusing her of believing that the hue

of heaven warded off the evil eye, but Nadav had raised a
warning finger. The bead had been a gift from Achmed's
mother. Besides, the dangling bauble made Aliza laugh, and
the energetic childish chortle lightened the faces of her parents.
Shlomo, a serious child, seldom laughed.

Amos selected a nosegay of sand lilies for Mazal. He was
surprised to find the pure white bell-shaped blossoms. It was
December now and long past the season when they blanketed
the sand-encrusted coast of the Sharon plain. He studied them
questioningly, but the vendor, as though fearful he might
change his mind, snatched them from his hand and wrapped
them in yellowing copies of *Davar*.

"You are lucky to have these. I have not seen lilies since the
summer but today an Arab came to the Carmel flower market
with them. I bought a bushel and sold them within the hour.
You are lucky to have the last of them."

"He must have brought them down from the Lebanese
coast," Amos said thoughtfully, and his brief pleasure in the
beauty of the fragrant lilies was diluted. It was more than likely
that the flowers had served as camouflage for the weapons the
Arabs were bringing southward into Palestine from Syria and
the Lebanon. Grenades and dynamite, Brownings and hand
guns were neatly blanketed beneath bright coverlets of lilies
and primroses, gladioli and wild orchids. Nadav, who served
as an intelligence officer in the Special Jewish Constabulary,
had told Amos of intercepting two such wagonloads during
recent weeks.

"Be careful when you buy from the Arabs, mother," he
advised the vendor as he paid her for the flowers.

"Of course I am careful," she retorted indignantly. "Who
knows the children of Ishmael better than I who was born
among them? You Ashkenazim were surprised by the general
strike, but we were not surprised. We know the Arabs—*ya la*.
We know what they can do—what they *will* do. Still, I am in
business. I buy flowers from those who sell them. May your
women enjoy my flowers. *Shabbat shalom, adoni*."

"*Shabbat shalom, Imma*," he replied and then impulsively
plucked up two single scarlet roses and pressed additional
coins into her outstretched hand. Balfouria and Liesel Konigsfeld would be glad of the full-petaled flowers.

"Ah, the *adon* has many women," the vendor cackled after him. Her almond-colored, wrinkled face creased with laughter, and the single gold tooth glinted. Amos laughed, too, and hurried on, anxious suddenly to be with Ruth, to offer her the flowers and see her press their softness against her cheek. As he crossed Dizengoff Street, a small girl dashed up to him and sniffed at the sand lilies, which exuded their rare, heavy fragrance.

"Leah! How many times have I told you to hold my hand and not to go near strangers," the child's irritated mother snapped. "No offense, sir," she murmured to Amos, "but you cannot be too careful these days."

"Of course not," Amos agreed and gave the child a lily.

The woman's vigilance did not surprise him. Danger and fear haunted the country. A bus journey from one hamlet to another was perilous. An outing to the cinema might end in violence and death. Householders double-bolted their doors at night and slept with weapons at their side. Arab unrest had peaked that spring, and the flower vendor had been right. The Jewish community had been startled, unprepared. Amos had once been caught up in the terror so narrowly escaped in Germany, but now, in nightmare races, he darted between menacing Nazis and attacking Arabs, awakening with his throat dry and Ruth shivering and weeping in his arms. Still, Nadav Langerfeld, the student of history and political theory, had not been surprised.

"It was bound to happen," Nadav had told him calmly one afternoon, not long after the escape from Berlin, as they sat in Jerusalem's Café Atara, sipping hot chocolate and eating the cheesecake for which the café was famous. "The Italian invasion of Ethiopia has paralyzed trade in the eastern Mediterranean. The Arab fellahin don't blame the Italians because there is no market for their crops. They don't even know where Italy is, the poor buggers. And the Arab stevedores don't blame them because there's no regular routine for shipping. They only know they have no work and no money, and then the mufti and the Arab fascists in Italy broadcast over the radio and explain it all. It's the fault of the Jews. That's easy enough for a Palestinian Arab to believe."

"Interesting about those broadcasts," Amos said. "The exact language being used in Germany. I've spoken to Halloran about it."

"It's not surprising. The language of anti-Semitism is universal," Nadav said in the weary tone of an instructor trying to impress a slow student with a salient point. "The mufti gets his scripts straight from Dr. Franz Reichert, the director of the German News Agency. We know that, and the British know that, only the British tend to be selective about what they choose to know. The Arabs only see that their unemployment rate is rising, and at the same time more and more Jews are coming into the country. The Templar knights are only too happy to keep them aware of that. Fascism is the most important thing to happen to the Templars since Ivanhoe. It can all be traced back to our friend Hitler, and it's in his best interest to keep the Arabs of Palestine restless."

"Restless? Is that what you call it?" Amos laughed harshly and held up that morning's edition of *Davar,* but Nadav did not even glance at it. He had already analyzed the headlines and the news stories and written a précis of them which he had dutifully submitted to Sir Arthur Wauchope's office at noon. It was rumored that Wauchope went through his dispatch case at lunch. Not that Wauchope would take any action.

The British, after all, had made only the most cursory investigation of the murder of two Jews on a bus waylaid by Arab highwaymen. There had also been no official reaction when a dozen orange groves owned by Jews had been inexplicably uprooted during a spring night. "Surely, you don't expect His Majesty's government to intervene whenever neighbors quarrel?" a British colonial officer had impatiently asked Nadav. He had served in Burma, where it was common practice for quarreling families to ravish each other's fields.

It was true that Wauchope had been visibly upset when a riot had erupted in Tel Aviv at the funeral of the two murdered Jews, but then that riot had been responsible for the deaths of twenty Jews and might lead to parliamentary questions about the efficacy of Wauchope's administration. There had been a scattering of arrests then and the pronouncement of veiled warnings, but neither the arrests nor the warnings had deterred the Arab arsonists who set fire to a Jewish cinema or those who forced their way into a Jewish clinic and opened fire on nurses and patients. A roller coaster of terror had been set in motion, and no one knew when it would gather additional momentum and increase its speed. But one thing was certain. It would not be slowed by the six-month general strike that the mufti had ordered if Jewish immigration was not suspended.

"All right. 'Restless' is a bad choice of word," Nadav had admitted. "But then I am a diplomat, Amos, and I must speak moderately and keep as many options open as possible."

He put aside the newspaper with its screaming headline about the rape of a Jewish girl standing guard at a northern kibbutz. The girl had been sixteen, not much older than Balfouria, who yearned to join just such a settlement. Would Nadav be as calm if it had been his wife's sister who had been violated? Amos wondered. Still, his brother-in-law's stoic forbearance filled him with a grudging admiration. And it had, after all, stood Nadav in good stead. It had enabled him to marry Elana and to raise blue-eyed Shlomo as his own child and to sit dispassionately in conference with the English, the various factions of the Jewish community, and even with the few moderate Arabs who still secretly conferred with Jewish representatives. Nadav's calm was imperturbable, vulnerable only to the child Aliza, who filled him with wild gaiety and pride.

"How is Elana?" Amos had asked.

There was nothing more to be said about Arab terror, just as he and Ruth had reached a despairing silence about German terror. Words only emphasized their own impotence.

"Elana is pleased to be in Tel Aviv, I think," Nadav had replied carefully. "She enjoyed fixing up Grandfather Langerfeld's house, and Shlomo and Aliza love the beach. It is, of course, more convenient for my work, and there are fewer memories for Elana in Tel Aviv."

A silence had fallen between the men. They would not speak of Elana's memories, of the ghost of Achmed that hovered over them. Too often their eyes met as they turned away from Shlomo's gaze, oddly unnerved by the clear blue of the small boy's eyes.

"And Ruth?" Nadav had asked in turn. He liked Amos's beautiful German-born wife although her sadness and pallor oppressed him.

"She is adjusting," Amos had said curtly then.

Now, months after that conversation at Café Atara, as he hurried through the streets of Tel Aviv on the eve of the Sabbath, he tried again to convince himself that it was true. Ruth *was* adjusting to life in Jerusalem. Still, it would take time. She had been through so much, his lovely Ruth, his silver-blond princess, but she would weather it all. His land would become her own. She could now speak and read Hebrew with some ease, and she had seemed to enjoy furnishing their small Jerusalem flat. Now that Elana was in Tel Aviv, Mazal relied on Ruth more and more to manage the Jerusalem affairs of her handicraft business, and Ruth enjoyed the work. And this weekend there was the concert. Arturo Toscanini himself would conduct the newly formed Palestine Symphony. Ruth would see her parents' old friend, the violinist Bronislaw Hubermann, and she would hear again her beloved Brahms and Mendelssohn, her Schubert and the Rossini which her mother had played flawlessly on the Bechstein that dominated the Charlottenberg drawing room. Surely that would make her happy. Perhaps, at last, she would shrug off her persistent melancholy and turn to him with laughter in her eyes. Perhaps, at last, there would be an end to tears in the night, and to the small sighs that wrenched him awake from deepest sleep.

An ancient dwarfed beach palm dominated the small garden behind the Langerfeld home. The tree had stood there in ponderous gracelessness when Elana's grandfather selected the site for his home in the new city of Tel Aviv. The old man had resisted the urging of the architect that he cut it down.

"It has no beauty. It will take up space in the garden. It will not give sufficient shade," the weary architect had argued.

"Let it stand." The old man had been insistent. "It will bear witness that we built a city on the sands."

And so the tree had remained, casting its diminutive pyramids of shade and producing clusters of amber-colored dates which the Langerfeld women made into a sweet jam to be spread on apples at the feast of the New Year. Its fronds had neither withered nor multiplied. Only weeks before his death, the old man had carried a huge piece of bleached driftwood up from the beach and placed it gently against the coarse-grained trunk. The impact of endless waves had smoothed the wood to a satin finish; two pale branches jutted forth from it, like hands outstretched in anguished prayer. The old man, who had throughout his life turned his eyes away from graven images, was comforted and intrigued by the wood, and when he died his children had not moved it. The child Shlomo, his great-grandson, who now lived in the house, often sprawled across it and stroked the smooth grain while he stared up at the strips of sky visible through the closely grown fronds.

On the other side of the tree Nadav Langerfeld had placed a slab of pink Jerusalem marble. The textured stone brought him closer to the city of his birth, which he missed with an almost palpable ache. Often he sat upon the marble in the evening, and in his mind's eye he saw the mountains of Jerusalem, although the sound he heard was that of the waves of the Mediterranean licking the shore.

Always, at the evening hour, the family gathered beneath the tree, and now Amos paused in the house only long enough to set down his briefcase and sniff the aroma of the Sabbath meal before hurrying out to join them. Always, he rushed to meet Ruth as though fearful that his slender wife would some-how have been spirited away and lost to him. That had almost happened once, and he lived in irrational terror that it might happen again. He recognized his anxiety and did not disparage it. They lived, after all, in the season of fear. He had taken Ruth from one frontier of jeopardy to another, and when she lay quivering in his arms, wakened by fearful dreams, he cursed himself because he had no sanctuary to offer the fragile woman he had married.

Hearing his step, Ruth turned and smiled. She held Aliza on her lap. Her fingers stroked the child's hair, and she sniffed the sweet scent of newly washed garments and fragrant powder. This, then, was what it was like to hold a baby close, to hear the rhythm of tiny heartbeats and feel the soft, curling clutch of little fingers.

She rose to greet Amos, surprised at how heavy the child felt when she stood.

"Here. Let me take her," Elana said.

Always Elana stood close by her children, hovering expectantly. Her vigilance irritated Mazal. The Maimon children had always scampered freely through the fields of the Galilee without coming to harm. Even now, as the adults gathered in the garden, Amnon dashed across the beach with the twins and Rivka. Shlomo had wanted to join them, but as always, Elana had objected.

"Stay and visit with your aunt Ruth and your grandmother," she had said coaxingly, and dutifully, the child had remained in the garden, sprawled across the driftwood, his eyes screwed up against the fading gleam of the wintry sunlight. Elana avoided her stepmother's glance. Mazal thought her too cautious, she knew, but then Mazal walked fearlessly through the shadows that hovered over this promised land of theirs. Ruth, however, might understand her fear. Elana had heard familiar tremors in Ruth's voice and observed her as she stood at a window waiting when Amos was delayed. Ruth had known loss. She, too, anticipated the dangerous, the untoward. She touched Ruth's arm lightly as she reclaimed Aliza, and saw the flash of relief in her sister-in-law's eyes as she turned to Amos.

"You're late," Ruth said, but there was no accusation in her voice, only a breathless relief.

"I stopped to get these flowers," he replied and offered her the irises. She pressed them against her cheek, and he saw that he had been right. The flowers matched her eyes.

Mazal and Elana exclaimed over their own bouquets, and Balfouria stuck her long-stemmed rose in her mouth and danced a mock tango. But Liesel Konigsfeld sat quietly on the pink marble slab, holding her flower in her hand as though it were a magic wand that might give her some power over her destiny.

"It's beautiful, Amos," she said. "Do you remember the hedge of rose bushes in our Berlin garden? I wonder if anyone prunes them. They had to be done so carefully—once in the spring and then again in the fall."

Liesel's voice grew vague as she worried over the distant, lost rose bushes, and Ruth was surprised. Not once in the three years since they had fled Berlin had Liesel referred to her family. But then, of course, it was easier to worry over the fate of a flower bed than to think of one's parents in a concentration camp or a detention center. Ruth, too, had schooled herself against speculating about her mother and father, although she often worried about the Rembrandt sketch that had hung in the sitting room, and she wondered occasionally if the moss-green drapes had faded as her mother had feared they would. It was only in the night that the faces of her parents haunted her.

They wafted then, in cloudlike death masks, above the blazing fires that seared her uneasy sleep. In her dreams, she rushed through flame and sprinted, as though to reach them, but they floated on. They were helpless clouds driven by cruel and deceptive winds. In one such dream, her mother had wept; the tears became raindrops that cooled Ruth as she ran. Yet she knew that even as she pursued the fleeting clouds, they would elude her and vanish, just as her parents had done. Liesel, too, writhed in the grip of nightmares, Ruth knew. She had slept beside Liesel during their flight from Berlin and had felt her tremble in the night and moan softly with secret fear.

Three years had passed since Ruth's arrival in Palestine, but still she awakened each morning newly startled by the brightness of the sunlight, the warmth of the air, the lilting cadences of the Arab vegetable vendors who passed beneath her window. She had learned some Hebrew and spent a few weeks on Sadot Shalom. Mazal Maimon had embraced her and wept openly at their first meeting.

"Now Amos will be happy," she had said, and Ruth was deeply moved that her husband's stepmother should care so deeply for him. When Elana and Nadav moved to Tel Aviv, she had taken on the Jerusalem operation of Chemed Handicrafts, and it had been her idea to organize a cooperative gallery for painters and sculptors.

Yet despite everything, melancholy clung to her, draping her in a clinging, tenacious veil of sadness. Even at the peak of joy, as she lay beside Amos, sated and quivering, his golden arm stretched across her pale breasts, even then she felt that drifting sorrow, that compounding of loss. She had felt it that afternoon when the pleasant Tel Aviv obstetrician had smiled benignly at her and confirmed her suspicion. She was indeed pregnant.

Her heart had leaped with gladness, but within minutes, the familiar grief tugged at her. She would be a mother, but she herself had lost both mother and father. She had abandoned her parents to danger, and the child that she birthed would be born into danger. Germany had betrayed her—Palestine filled her with uneasiness.

When she shopped for vegetables in Jerusalem's Machane Yehuda, the busy open air food market, she heard the harsh shouts of frantic Jewish and Arab housewives, each thrusting her own produce forward. She remembered then the orderly queues in the spotlessly clean greengroceries and butcher shops of Berlin. Occasionally, when she had been rudely shoved or her place on a line preempted, she caught herself thinking angrily, involuntarily, "These Jews—why do they behave this way?" Immediately she had been ashamed.

She herself was Jewish, according to law, according to choice. The rabbi in Marseilles had assured her of that: "If your mother was Jewish you are Jewish." Yet so many of the Palestinian Jews, with their startling frankness, their rough assertiveness, were alien to her, and their raucous boisterousness intimidated her. Perhaps her own child would be a stranger to her, chattering rapidly in mysterious, guttural Hebrew, dashing barefoot through fields of wild meadow grass like the younger Maimon children, Amos's half brothers and sisters on Sadot Shalom.

And the violence in Palestine frightened her. She trembled when she read of the exploits of Fawzi Kawakji, the Syrian terrorist and his night raiders who swept down on unarmed settlements and killed women and children. Mazal Maimon had been a passenger on the Haifa train that had been bombed as it left Kalkilleh Station. She herself had been unhurt, but she had told Amos and Ruth of the injured children, the frightened, weeping women.

On their first wedding anniversary Ruth and Amos had gone to see *Gunga Din* at the Edison Cinema. It was pleasant to sit in the Jerusalem darkness, imagine themselves in India, and reflect, hand touching hand, that a year had passed since their marriage in the seaport synagogue. Suddenly shots had rung out and the house lights flashed on. Four cinemagoers sat slumped in death. A small boy, seated two rows behind them, moaned in pain. Blood spurted from his forehead and drenched the floor in crimson flow. Ruth's sandals were stained with death, and she left the strapped shoes in the street and ran home barefoot.

She had wept in Amos's arms that night.

"It's just like Germany. They hate us. They would kill us without cause, without reason."

"No, it's different," he replied soothingly. His large hands stroked her long silver-blond hair. "Here we are not afraid to fight back."

Beneath their bed lay the huge crate so carefully packed in Marseilles. The carbines were still concealed beneath silken comforters. Only a few leaders of the Haganah knew of their existence. But the weapons brought Ruth no comfort, no reassurance. She seethed with secret rage; she struggled to balance alternatives. Were their only choices those of flight or combat? Was it not possible for them to live out their lives in peace? There were other countries which held out hope of refuge and safety, where a child, even a Jewish child, might grow up free of fear. Amos had family in America. She had distant relations in South Africa. There were choices to be made, and the knowledge of her pregnancy gave sudden urgency to such choices. Still, she would not think about that this weekend.

She would, instead, relish her secret, enjoy the family reunion, and sit beside Amos at the Toscanini concert.

Arturo Toscanini was very tired. He was the quintessential European, and the frenetic Middle East bewildered and exhausted him. Besides, he had spent much of the year traveling. He had understood his wife Carla's resistance to Bronislaw Hubermann's invitation to conduct the newly formed Palestine Symphony. Still, he had accepted immediately.

"I can't refuse it," he had said. "This is not an ordinary invitation. This is an invitation to Jewish Palestine, to Tel Aviv and to Jerusalem, the city of God. It is also a splendid opportunity," he added with a wry smile, "to spit in Hitler's face."

Carla Toscanini had abandoned her argument. Her husband's war against Fascism had begun back in 1931 in Bologna when he refused to play the Fascist hymn "Giovinézza." And when German authorities refused to have performances led by Bruno Walter broadcast from Salzburg to Berlin, Toscanini had responded in kind. If any Salzburg performances at all were broadcast to Berlin, he would leave the festival. Anti-Semitism enraged him and touched a rare nerve of vulnerability. After all, his own daughter, Wanda, was married to Vladimir Horowitz. Were the grandchildren of Arturo Toscanini to be refused the podium because they had Jewish blood? He would be proud, he wrote to Hubermann, to conduct an orchestra of Jewish musicians, many of whom had been forced to leave Germany.

On the Saturday night of his concert, as he studied the audience that filled the concert hall on the Levant fairgrounds in Tel Aviv, he acknowledged that despite his weariness, he was glad he had come. The musicians were excellent and they responded to his baton with sensitivity and obedience. He remembered how on the first rehearsal morning, the exposition hall had been filled with nightingales, fluttering about the rafters and singing with a sweetness that caused him to lower his baton.

"Please," he said softly to his musicians, "let your instruments sing like those birds."

When he raised his baton again, the birds were silent and the string section joyously and flawlessly bowed the prelude to the nocturne and scherzo of Mendelssohn's *Midsummer Night's Dream.*

"Ah, Jewish birds respect the music of a Jew. How much wiser they are than Herr Hitler," the conductor had quipped, and the musicians had smiled bitterly. The Nuremberg Laws made it a crime for anyone to play or listen to the works of Mendelssohn.

He had been deeply moved by the rehearsal audiences. Each day the hall was packed to capacity well before the appointed hour. Young parents carried their children in their arms. Shopkeepers and farmers, olive-skinned Jews from the lands of the East, Yemenites and Moroccans and pale men and women from the ghettos of Europe, elegant German Jewish matrons and kibbutz women wearing overalls, their hands hardened and reddened, sat side by side or stood shoulder to shoulder and listened to the music in absolute silence. No paper rustled, no whisper was heard, no child whimpered or cried. The air belonged to the musicians and their music, to the concentrated, agonized efforts of the little Italian conductor whose baton had become a weapon in defense of truth and beauty.

Surely, the audience tonight would be as good, Toscanini thought, as the hall filled. He peered at the arriving crowds through a slit in the curtain, and his old friend William Steinberg pointed out the dignitaries.

"There in the first row center, Commissioner Wauchope and his family. Ah, the entire Vaad LeUmi is here, maestro. Even David Ben Gurion, and they say he is tone deaf. Do you see the dapper-looking little fellow with the Vandyke beard and the dress suit?"

"A Savile Row tailor," Toscanini replied. "I can tell it anywhere." He himself was dressed, as always, in black. His small body would be absorbed into the darkness of the concert hall, and only the graceful white butterflies of his hands would be seen, flitting now to the brasses, now to the string section, beckoning piano and woodwinds.

"Yes. That's Dr. Chaim Weizmann."

"And who are the English officers with him?"

"One of them is Orde Wingate and the other is an Irishman—Liam Halloran. I've heard rumors that he and Wingate are setting up some sort of self-defense unit for the Jews."

"Certainly something of the sort is needed," Toscanini said. "Do you know who these beautiful women are?" he asked, pointing to three women who had entered together and were threading their way through the rear mezzanine.

"Oh yes. Those are the Maimon women. The wife, sister, and stepmother of Amos Maimon, the archaeologist."

"Maimon," the conductor said musingly. "I know the name. Years ago I met a man named Ezra Maimon at Justice Brandeis's home. He was raising funds for the Jewish Brigade, I believe." He remembered the tall Palestinian who had spoken so passionately of his homeland. Toscanini had been asked then to conduct a benefit concert on behalf of the Jewish force, but his schedule had been too busy. Well, he was making up for it now, and the presence of the Maimon women in the audience was a pleasant bonus. It was the conductor's habit that when he faced his audience, he would seek out a beautiful woman and fix his dark-eyed magnetic stare on her, his baton stretched commandingly forward. Inevitably, even in the dark-

ness, he could discern her awareness of his attention, and he
would feel a twinge of pleasure.

Now he saw Ezra Maimon and recognized him at once. The
small woman in the stark black dress beaded with gold thread
at waist and bodice greeted Ezra with a brilliant smile and
rested her head on his shoulder as they were seated. She held a
program out to a tall younger woman whose silver-blond hair
was braided into a regal coronet. A corsage of pale irises was
pinned just above the soft rise of her breast, and a single white
primrose caught at its center matched her pale skin.

*I would cast her as a war maiden in the "Ride of the Val-
kyrie,"* Toscanini thought, *if only she did not look so sad.*

The third woman in their party was also tall, but her glossy
hair was dark and hung loosely about her shoulders. She was
full-figured, and her skin was honey-colored. She sat erect, yet
there was a strange furtiveness about her. Even as Toscanini
watched her from behind the curtain, he saw her eyes dart
about the huge hall as though searching out signs of danger.
But then, of course, it would be difficult to live in Palestine
without being constantly vigilant, constantly fearful, he
thought and sighed deeply.

He listened to the sounds of the musicians tuning and prim-
ing their instruments. The first violinist's A string was spread
too tautly. He hurried over to him, saw that it was properly
adjusted, and then stepped onto the podium. He signaled the
stagehand and bowed slowly from the waist as the curtain
opened. The applause was overwhelming. Tears trickled down
his cheeks as he lifted his baton, and the orchestra played the
bell-like introduction to Rossini's *Scala di Seta*.

Ruth sat motionless throughout the concert, only vaguely
conscious of the pressure of Amos's touch on her open palm,
and of the slight breeze that whistled through the open rafters
of the improvised concert hall. She had heard Toscanini conduct before, both at Bayreuth and at Salzburg, but never had he
controlled the music with such passion, such fervor. When he
completed the nocturne and scherzo to Mendelssohn's *Midsummer Night's Dream*, tears glistened on many faces in the
audience, and when he turned to face the deafening applause,
his own eyes were brilliant; slowly, he extended the baton to
his listeners and lowered his lionesque head. The black tur-

tleneck jersey, damp with sweat, clung to his torso, and she saw that his lip was cracked and a twitch quickened his cheek.

"Bravo!" A man's thunderous voice rang, unrestrained, exuberant.

Ruth turned her head and saw that it was the English officer in full dress uniform sitting next to Chaim Weizmann who shouted with such enthusiasm.

"Orde Wingate," Amos whispered, his eyes following her own. "A very uninhibited man, Liam tells me."

Ruth did not answer. She did not like the tall Irishman whose uniform was always so neatly pressed. Tonight, in honor of the concert, he wore all his decorations, including the narrow blue-and-white ribbon that marked his valor at Gallipoli. She did not like him, she acknowledged, because uniforms repelled her and because Liam's involvement with the Maimon family gave her a ghostly presentiment of danger. And he was too often alone with Liesel Konigsfeld. Liesel was a lonely girl, seeking comfort, but Liam, older and married, should exercise restraint.

Toscanini had turned his back on the audience and bowed now to his musicians, motioning the leader of each section to rise in turn. The musicians rose and the applause reached a crescendo, then subsided into expectant quietude. Perhaps there would be an encore. Silence filled the exposition hall, and then suddenly they heard the flutter of wings. A flock of nightingales flew in, settled on the rafters and filled the hall with passionate bursts of sweetness. Smiling, Toscanini raised an appreciative hand to the tiny winged songsters and swiftly left the podium. Those in the front rows saw the tears that streaked his cheeks.

The champagne reception was held in a tent on the fairgrounds, and Ruth moved through the crowd on Amos's arm, walking cautiously so that the narrow heels of her evening shoes would not be caught on the rough-hewn boards of the platform. Mazal's workshops had fashioned gold cloths to cover the improvised plank tables, and the long poles had been threaded with fairy lights whose incandescent colors lit the excited faces of the celebrants.

"Not quite the Hotel Franz Josef, but then at the Hotel Franz

Josef we could not smell the salt odor of the Mediterranean. How are you, Ruth?''

The violinist, Bronislaw Hubermann, her father's oldest friend, bowed deeply before Ruth and then kissed her on each cheek.

''Herr Hubermann. I am honored. I was so happy to receive your letter.''

''The happiness was all mine, to learn that you were safe in Palestine. And this must be your husband, the notorious Professor Amos Maimon.''

Amos smiled and held his hand out to the violinist.

''An honor, sir,'' he said. ''But why am I notorious?''

''I use the word as a compliment, Herr Professor, although other Germans may not. Do not return to Germany. The archaeology professor who spirited forty Jews across the border is no longer welcome there.''

''No matter. We would not go back to Germany, of course,'' Ruth said, ''unless we could help my parents.'' She sipped her champagne, surprised by the lightness of its taste. A German vintner newly arrived at Rishon LeZion had introduced the effervescent drink. Hitler had sent champagne and music to Jewish Palestine. An irony of history, she thought and drained her glass.

''But surely you have heard about your parents,'' Bronislaw Hubermann said softly. He looked at Amos in mute appeal, but Amos shook his head from side to side. Whatever had to be said must be said. He stretched his arm across Ruth's shoulder and held her close as though to brace her against an untoward blow. His fingers touched the soft petal of the purple-throated iris. He felt himself powerless. He could protect her from danger but not from sorrow.

''No.'' Ruth's voice was barely audible, a whisper lost amid the noisy excitement, the laughter and chatter in the festive tent. An accordionist struck up a folk tune. The floorboards rocked as a small group danced a hora.

''I am sorry to be the one to tell you. I myself heard it from a composer who was interned at Sachsenhausen but was released. Your father's family visited Hugo at the camp. They pressured him to divorce your mother. Such divorces between Jews and Aryans are not uncommon now. But your father refused. The next day he and your mother went off together. They were found hours later in a small wooded area. Their fingers were on each other's lips. They had fed each other poison. Cyanide. They say that cyanide kills swiftly.''

Hubermann told the story in a monotone. He remembered once telling small Ruth Niemoeller a fairy story. "I don't believe you," the child Ruth had said. But the adult Ruth, pale and beautiful in her shimmering gray silk dress, she believed him. He saw credence in the sorrow that shadowed her violet eyes, in the sudden sway of her body.

"I thank you for telling me," she said, and her soft voice was steady.

Now, at last, the floating cloud-faces of her dreams would come to rest. They had drifted past all danger—cruel winds would no longer buffet them. The grief she felt was for herself, for her own loss. She did not grieve for her gentle parents, who had been spared an existence they could not endure.

Amos led her to a chair, and he and Hubermann talked softly. Their voices drifted about her like the buzzing of distant bees. Hubermann asked if it was possible for them to take Toscanini and his party to the settlement of Ramot HaShavim the next day. She saw Amos hesitate and leaned forward.

"Of course, we will go," she said and listened to her voice as though it belonged to a stranger.

"Will you be up to it?" the violinist asked kindly.

She nodded and took his hand in hers. He had been her father's friend. He was a last link to her childhood, to the golden magic years in a vanished time, a vanished country.

"We shall see you in the morning, then." He struggled for words of condolence, but in the end he simply kissed her on the cheek.

She sat for a few moments longer, her hand resting lightly on her abdomen. Strange, how in a single weekend she had been apprised of impending life and distant death.

Chapter 17

THEY LEFT FOR Ramot HaShavim at sunrise because Toscanini had to be in Jerusalem that night. They traveled the coastal road, crossed the iron bridge that straddled the Yarkon River, and emerged onto the verdant plain of the Sharon. Carla Toscanini's knitting needles flashed as they drove. She was knitting a bright yellow cardigan for her husband. She had heard that it was cold in Jerusalem.

The conductor perched on the edge of his seat, his dark eyes darting from place to place, marking the flight of a flock of egrets, the drainage sewer under construction north of Petach Tikveh, the plodding progress of a procession of sheep from Ramathaim to Kefar Malal.

"*Avventura*," he pronounced at last. "This whole country is an adventure. How fortunate you are to be part of it, Professor Maimon."

"Fortunate?" Amos asked hesitantly. "Yes, I suppose you are right."

The small conductor's enthusiasm was contagious. Amos had not often thought of himself as being fortunate. Often, traveling abroad, he had envied others. Wars did not threaten the family life of his American cousins. He had coveted such safety, such seeming normality yet, he admitted now, he would not have forgone the excitement of his life, his work, his love for Ruth and the land in which they lived.

He touched his wife's arm. Somehow the knowledge of her parents' deaths seemed to have strengthened her, absolved her. She knew now that she could not have helped them by remaining in Germany. Their deaths, however tragic and painful, had been less terrible than her imaginings. Truth was a great liberator, Amos thought and remembered his own relief when Dr. Menzies had released him from the guilt which had enmeshed him with his mother's death. His sorrow had not been mitigated but the bitterness of self-indictment had vanished. So, too, it would be with Ruth. He held her close, and she turned her serious violet-eyed gaze on him. There was a new glow about her today, a new softness.

At Ramot HaShavim the children of the settlement waited impatiently and flourished the blue-and-white single-starred Jewish flag and the red, green, and white tricolor of Tuscany.

"*Shalom! Shalom!*" they called happily.

Carla Toscanini waved her knitting, and the conductor rummaged in his briefcase and triumphantly brandished his baton.

The sixty families of the settlement had assembled to greet the conductor. The mayor, an autocratic man who wore a gold watch draped across his too-abundant midsection, welcomed Toscanini and presented him with the title and deed to an orange grove. The children sang a song of welcome composed especially for the occasion. A boy tenor sang one stanza in solo, and Amos recalled the stories he had been told about Theodor Herzl's visit to Rishon LeZion and how his cousin Shimon's voice had caused the great man to weep. Shimon was a middle-aged man now, a physician, living in Oswiecim. Would his cousin ever sing again beneath the skies of Palestine? Amos wondered.

Since Hitler's rise, Ezra had sent urgent letters to his sister in Poland, pleading with her to leave. Sara's replies were always perfunctory, almost impatient. Hitler was a crazed despot, ranting and raving across a foreign border. What effect could he have on their life in Poland? Casimir, after all, was a member of the Diet, Shimon a respected surgeon, and her other children were all well married and established. She herself was an old woman. She had no desire to return to a land where she had known only death and grief.

His aunt and cousins in Poland were mythical creatures to Amos, their existences verified only by the sepia-tinged photographs that arrived in strangely shaped envelopes encrusted with colorful stamps. He had studied the pictures which Sara sent dutifully each year and had been struck at how closely he and Shimon resembled each other, at how like Sara Elana looked. Yet he felt no real tie to these relatives whose lives were so different from his own. His aunt had submitted to fear, and Shimon had been forced to surrender his legacy. Toscanini had been right. He himself had been fortunate. He could never leave this land of his birth. No danger could divert him from the adventure of his life. Ruth was not happy here, he knew, but she would adjust in time. He was an archaeologist and had faith in the passing of years, the gradual layering of days.

The mayor led them to the southeastern edge of the settlement, where a group of children were gently setting saplings into the moistened, newly turned earth. Toscanini sank to his knees, took up a young tree, and placed it into a furrow. He patted the earth into place about it with his baton. As he arose, a small boy and girl approached, each carrying a basket filled with oranges and grapefruits, honey and eggs.

"All produced on our settlement," the mayor said proudly. In Frankfurt he had been the proprietor of a large leather goods factory, but his smooth, expensive pigskin wallets and suitcases had never given him the pleasure which the produce of Ramot HaShavim brought him.

Before they left, Toscanini signed his name in the leather guest book and added a bar of music—the opening notes of "HaTikvah." An appropriate inscription for Ramot Ha-Shavim, Amos thought. There were more pianos than tractors on the little settlement.

"Will all the settlers stay?" Carla Toscanini asked as they drove southward to Jerusalem. "The life here is so different from what they knew in Germany."

"Not only different but dangerous," Ruth said guardedly.

"Your life is also different and not without danger. Yet you are staying," Toscanini said. His dark eyes were riveted to Ruth's face, and she blushed, certain that he had penetrated her most secret fear, her doubts, her amorphous plans.

"For now," she replied, and Amos looked at her with narrowed glance.

They were silent then. Amos drove slowly, carefully, and the Toscaninis slept, Carla's knitting needles crossing her husband's baton, lightly caked with the earth of Ramot HaShavim. Ruth, too, dozed, and Bronislaw Hubermann studied a score.

It was only Amos who noticed the flutter of white linen among the date palms that bordered the Arab village of Deir Ghassana. Village elders smoking a narghile in a patch of shade, he supposed. But then he saw the leaves of a thorn bush move although the air was still, unsettled by even the slightest breeze. He slowed the car then, his eyes raking the road. He discerned nothing, but still, instinctively, as he drove past the date palms, he swerved suddenly to the right. The car rolled to a halt in a ditch. Inches from them the road erupted. Flame and cloud filled the air. A mixed debris of metal pellets exploded and showered the tarmac with glowing embers that ricocheted in wild ferrous dance. An Arab child dashed across the road.

"Back!" a voice from behind the palm trees shouted, but the warning came too late. A whirling fiery bolt slammed against the small boy. With frenzied shriek he fell amid the molten detritus.

Amos ran to him, but the child had no pulse and his foot had been blown away, severed from his leg by the force of the explosion. Trembling, Amos moved the blackened piece of flesh back to the bloodied stump of leg and tucked it beneath the child's grimy robe, now become his shroud. Perhaps the child's mother need never know.

He glanced about and saw at once the source of the massive explosion. It was the usual sort utilized by the mufti's followers. Tin canisters had been packed tight with nails and explosives and tossed onto the road as their car approached. A simple enough endeavor designed to kill the famous conductor and thus deter any foreign visitors who might be sympathetic to the Jewish cause.

The villagers of Deir Ghassana thronged the road, and a woman's throaty voice emitted the wild keening screams of grief. She tore at her cheeks and spread her body across that of the child. Slowly, Amos walked back to their car.

"Are you all right?" he asked.

"We are fine," Toscanini said in a strong voice.

"But maestro, we must revise our plans for your tour of the country," Bronislaw Hubermann said. The violinist's face was ashen, his dark serge jacket stained with sweat.

"Nonsense," Toscanini said brusquely. "We will not let them frighten us out of this land."

Ruth Maimon leaned against the car and pressed her face against the coolness of the window. Her arms were wrapped about her abdomen as though to shield the fragile life she carried. Now she turned hesitantly and saw that the dead child had been carried away and a fire blazed on the road. Once before, on the night that Amos had come into her life, she had run away from flames. She could not run forever. A stand had to be taken against fear, against terror. Toscanini was right.

"Ruth, you're all right?" Amos held her close, his hand cupped her chin, stroked her cheeks.

"I'm fine," she said. "Don't worry. We will not let them frighten us out of this land."

She looked at Toscanini, whose words had become her own. He smiled at her.

"In a year's time," he said, "I shall visit Palestine again. I want to celebrate the first anniversary of the Palestine Symphony. And I want to harvest the oranges from the trees in my grove."

"We will look forward to welcoming you," Ruth said. "In a year's time."

In a year's time she would hold their child in her arms—a second generation of Maimons born on this land, this promised land, from which one day they would surely wrest peace and permanence.

PART THREE

Balfouria:
The Onset of War

1939–1941

Chapter 18

A LIGHT RAIN spattered the canvas shelter, and Balfouria, always a light sleeper, stirred within her nest of blankets and peered through the narrow tent flap at the deceptive darkness. The rain would be brief, she knew, and even as she listened, the rhythmic downfall diminished. Still, she did not go back to sleep but lay awake in the moist, sweet darkness and waited for the narrow wedge of first light to inch its way eastward.

"We must be ready at dawn," Moshe Dayan, the Haganah leader assigned to her group, had told them at the reconaissance meeting the previous evening.

The others in the group—many of them new to the demands of rural life—had groaned, but Balfouria felt a thrill of anticipatory pleasure. She had always loved the silver nascence of dawn on the highlands of the Galilee. Even as a small girl, she often awakened early in the room she shared with Elana and watched the first rays of timorous sunlight pierce the darkness and tremble in gossamer star-colored thread over the sloping hills and terraced orchards of her father's farm. She would fall asleep again as the sky drifted from an aqueous green to the pale rose color of the hollyhocks that grew wild in the northern meadowland.

Occasionally, she had tiptoed past her sleeping sister and stolen outside to breathe deeply of the new dawn. At that hour bright beadlets of dew moistened her bare feet, and the day's beginning warmth teased her outstretched arms. Always then, she turned her gaze northward, where the mysterious purple hills of the Lebanon shadowed Palestine's northernmost border. Jewish settlements would flourish there one day, she knew, and she imagined herself walking there, a young man beside her, tall and lean, his step matching her own. They would progress through a virgin field, and the earth beneath their feet would be firm and fragrant with the promise of new plantings and new gleanings.

That would be the great thing, Balfouria had thought, to create a settlement where none had existed, to harvest crops from resistant earth, to reclaim abandoned land and to do all that in joyous comradeship. The adventure was gone from her father's farm. Sadot Shalom was a prosperous and established homestead. Besides, Balfouria disliked the loneliness of life on a homestead. She loved being in a group. The exchange of talk and laughter, of music and ideas exhilarated her. Even her flute sounded sweeter when she played for others. Ezra, her father, could spend hours alone reading and writing. Her mother, Mazal, was happiest alone with her sketch pads and watercolors, but Balfouria craved company. People were as necessary to her as the wild green landscape of the Galilee.

"How can you live in a city, Elana?" she asked her sister during a visit to Tel Aviv.

The young city expanded day by day. Streets replaced sand dunes and open kiosks became enclosed shops. Buildings pressed close upon each other, and the sounds of many lives converged in a strident cacophony of urban sound. Balfouria, bored and restless, pulled a hose through Elana's garden and watered the roots of the ancient beach palm. Glinting bits of shell peppered the dry, crumbling soil where Elana's tomato plants withered and her straggling cucumber vine yellowed and died.

"It is safest in the city," Elana replied mildly. "Careful, Aliza," she called to her daughter, who happily dashed after Shlomo as he rode his wooden-wheeled tricycle up and down the narrow road.

Balfouria sighed impatiently. Elana judged every situation by the security and safety it offered. She checked restaurants and cinemas for fire exits and clutched her children's hands tightly at every crossing. Often, during her visit, Balfouria had heard her sister prowl the house at night, opening and closing windows, now fearful of a draft, now surveying the street against strangers because an Arab carrying explosives had been apprehended on a neighboring street. Everyone in Palestine was cautious, but with Elana caution had become an obsession, one which laughing, daring Balfouria could not comprehend.

How foolish to live always in the shadow of fear when the country was filled with excitement and adventure. There was new land waiting to be claimed and redeemed, new settlements to be built, new songs to be sung beneath starlit skies.

Balfouria was equally impatient with the life which Amos and Ruth had built for themselves and for their small daughter, Miriam, in Jerusalem.

Amos taught at the university and hurried from seminar room to the newly built library on Mount Scopus, occasionally breaking his academic routine for mysterious journeys to the north. Balfouria knew that her brother was involved with the Haganah. Occasional meetings with Yitzchak Sadeh, Chaim Shturman, Yigal Allon, and Moshe Dayan had been held at the Sadot Shalom farmhouse. Now and again they were joined by Orde Wingate, the British officer who insisted on speaking a peculiarly accented and archaic biblical Hebrew.

Balfouria and her brother Amnon hid behind the door and watched the short, sandy-haired Englishman, whose field khakis were always unironed, chew huge clusters of grapes and spit the seeds into Mazal's copper bowl. Many landed on the polished floor, but Ezra Maimon, who had the farmer's fastidiousness in domestic matters, said nothing. Orde Wingate had special privileges.

The men spoke softly of forming new patrols, special night squads that would retaliate against the Arab marauders.

"You must forget retaliation and strike first," Wingate had said.

"Not so quickly," Chaim Shturman, the veteran leader of Kibbutz Ein Harod had remonstrated. "You know the Bible, Wingate. Doesn't the Bible tell us that we must treat the stranger who dwells among us as we would treat ourselves? The Arab is that stranger."

Balfouria remembered, too, how Wingate had sat at their table and wept openly when Chaim Shturman, who had counseled love and moderation, stepped on an Arab land mine and was killed instantly.

"I'll want your carbines," he had said then, and Amos had

driven to Jerusalem and returned with the crates so carefully packed in Marseilles.

It was true that Amos's life had its secret excitements, but the pattern of Ruth's days was unchanging, uneventful.

"How can you spend your days like that?" Balfouria challenged Ruth, who seemed always to be indoors. Amos's silver-haired wife totaled up the daily receipts of the Jerusalem Chemed shop and then turned her attention to the portfolio of a young Bezalel artist. She smiled pleasantly at her young sister-in-law.

"I like my work," she replied patiently.

Balfouria shook her head in disbelief and went out to the balcony of their flat, where little Miriam played with a speckled kitten.

"When you visit us at Sadot Shalom, Miriam," Balfouria told her niece, "I will give you a kid goat of your very own."

Small animals and newly sown fields had always interested Balfouria more than her studies at the district school or her mother's flourishing craft enterprise. She grew bored when Mazal, Elana, and Ruth discussed new markets and materials, new artisans and workshops. She longed to be outside, working with her animals or in her garden.

"All right. She's a farmer's daughter and wants to be a farmer," Ezra said mildly when her teachers spoke despairingly of Balfouria's inattention. She excelled only at music, and although she practiced diligently on the silver flute Ezra had brought her from Switzerland, she was happiest astride her horse, galloping bareback through the northern hills.

At fourteen she had suddenly shed her baby fat, and her figure beneath her dirndl skirt and peasant blouse was supple and full. Her thick black hair clustered about her head in thick, irrepressible curls, and the sea-green Maimon eyes sparkled sharply in the desert darkness of her skin. She laughed swiftly and easily, yet she fought with fierce determination for what she wanted.

Ezra and Mazal had raised minimal objections when Balfouria decided to attend the agricultural school at Nahalal. They had each fought resistant families to establish their own lives, and they had decided early that their children's lives would be their own. Their objections had been more vigorous when, after two years at Nahalal, Balfouria announced that she wanted to leave the school and join a group that was to found a kibbutz on the Lebanese border.

"You're too young," Mazal had objected.

"Liesel Konigsfeld is part of our group."

"Liesel Konigsfeld is years older than you. And she has been through a great deal. You're a child."

Laughter spurted from Balfouria's wine-red lips and filled the room with golden sound.

"I'm not a child at all. I'm a woman and I'm in love."

Buoyantly she had sailed across the room, her dark brown legs flashing against her bright red skirt, her full breasts taut against her white cotton blouse. She seized Amnon's hands, beckoned to the twins and spindly-legged Rivka.

"Come, let's dance," she cried. "I'll teach you a new dance."

They followed her as she moved in intricate step, circling the room, slapping the wood floor with her bare feet after executing spritely turns and jumps.

"Hear the voice of my beloved," she sang and the younger children joined her in the chorus: "Behold he cometh, leaping upon the mountains, skipping upon the hills. . . ."

She leaped and skipped the length of the room, her body rising and falling in joyous motion, her hands raised to a sharp clap, her fingers snapping.

"What's your beloved's name?" Rivka giggled, when they fell exhausted onto the woven pillows which Mazal kept scattered in corners of the sitting room.

"Daniel," Balfouria said, carefully emphasizing each syllable, and Mazal smiled. *Ezra, Ezra*, she still repeated softly to herself. A lover's name assumed a special mystery, a wondrous sweetness of cadence. Often she sought excuses just to use her husband's name—"Ezra says . . . Ezra thinks . . . Ezra. Ezra." She listened carefully to her eldest daughter.

"Daniel Alkilai," Balfouria said, and the separate syllables became a poem, a verbal caress.

Ezra looked across the room at his daughter. She was only sixteen, but they lived, after all, in an age of haste. Danger accelerated their lives, sensitized them to the swiftness of passing days, the brevity of changing seasons. If they ran quickly enough, they evaded fear and snatched at brief and precarious happiness. Battle drums rumbled from a distance and spurred them on. Adolescents stood beneath the marriage canopy on starlit nights, smashed the wedding glass with booted feet, danced whirling nuptial horas, and hurried off at dawn to stand guard at a border settlement, to row a long boat to a secret cove and wait patiently for signals from a ship laden with illegal immigrants. Someone had written a plaintive song about young women widowed before they became wives.

Ezra would not prevent Balfouria from hurrying toward her adventure. He was fond of Daniel Alkilai, the thin-faced young man whose thick, dark hair inevitably tumbled down his broad forehead into his clear gray eyes.

"What is the name of your settlement?" Ezra had asked.

"Hanita."

"Go, then, to your Hanita."

"But be careful, Balfouria. Be careful." Mazal's admonition was a plea, a fearful, tearful prayer.

Always they pleaded with their children to exercise caution although they recognized the impotence, the invalidity of their words. They lived in a land where caution could not prevail and in a time when the sour winds of war breathed with fearsome strength across oceans and frontiers. Danger claimed their children, and they themselves were caught between fear and pride. They were proud of the young adults whom they had nurtured and raised to courage and responsibility, yet fearful that their courage might lead them to death.

"Let her be alive," Mazal had prayed during the Hebron riots when Elana had been caught in the crossfire.

"Let him return safely," they had whispered to each other in the darkness during Amos's rescue mission to Germany.

Keep Balfouria free from danger, from illness, they said silently, because to utter the words aloud would be to give them reality, credibility, to make visible the specters of malaria, of Arab terrorism.

"I'll be careful," she had promised.

She went off to join her group, and they remained alone on Sadot Shalom. Each evening they read the paper and passed sections to each other without comment. Each news story was a personal threat, a dark foreboding. They awakened in the

early morning and moved through the darkened bedrooms of
their house where their younger children slept, briefly encased
in the safety of childhood.

But Balfouria, who watched the dawn now break in silver
shards across the darkness, felt no threat, no danger. She
dressed quickly, flushed with excitement, anticipation. The
day of their beginning had arrived at last. Today they would
claim Hanita.

Daniel Alkilai shivered in the chill of the March dawn and
moved closer to the cooking fire which glowed with a muted
blue flame. He had often built such fires in the hill country of
Bohemia where he had gone to summer camp, and he carefully
added a slow-burning log as his counselors had taught him. His
Czech classmates would be planning their spring excursions
now, and the delicate white chestnut blossoms would tremble
in new bloom along the boulevards of Prague. He wondered
vaguely if he would ever see them again, if he would ever
again stroll through the springtime streets of the city where he
had been born and spent his boyhood. But then it was Daniel
Appelfeld who had lived in Prague. He was Daniel Alkilai
now; he had a new name and a new life in Palestine.

Daniel's father had been a professor of physics at Prague
University. His work was widely respected, and his major
paper on molecular formation had received international recognition. An invitation had arrived from the Institute of Mathe-
matics in Basel, where Professor Appelfeld's friend Albert
Einstein was doing interesting work, but it had been refused
without hesitation. The chairmanship of the physics department in Prague was due to fall vacant, and it was a position
which Daniel's father had coveted since his student days. He
worked feverishly toward its achievement and published two
monographs in a single year. One of them earned him a letter
of commendation from Edward Benes.

Encouraged, confident, he removed his long black academic
gown from the cedar closet, noticed that its velvet cowl was
frayed, and took it to the tailor for repair. His old father cautioned him against optimism.

"Remember, you are a Jew," Daniel's grandfather said.

He himself had come to Prague from the mountains of Carpatho-Russia. Jews fleeing the pogroms of Kishinev had found refuge in his parents' new home. He had married young, a refugee girl whose pale back was scarred with welts made by the Cossack who had raped her and then pressed the glowing embers of his cigar into her flesh, searing her skin with Cyrillic letters that spelled ZHID—Jew. When he lay beside his wife, his fingers traced those scars and he reminded himself harshly that he was Jewish, that he was vulnerable.

He reminded his son of the same thing at every opportunity, but the proud professor of physics, whose picture often appeared in the scientific columns of the weekend *Tribuna*, brushed his father's remonstrations aside. The Kishinev pogroms were long past. The Jews of Czechoslovakia had complete economic and political freedom. In Carpatho-Russia they even operated their own religious schools and had the right to claim separate nationality. They were the most secure Jewish community in the entire world.

"There is no secure Jewish community," the old man muttered. "Secure" and "Jewish" were contradictory terms.

Still, Professor Appelfeld would not be deterred. He prepared a speech of acceptance and decided to give a small reception to celebrate his appointment. A wine and cheese party, perhaps. His son, Daniel, an accomplished violinist, would play for their guests.

In the corridors of the university, colleagues offered him their congratulations—prematurely, of course, but then no one else qualified for the post, they assured him.

On a Monday morning in June the new appointment was posted on the department bulletin board. A young man of impeccable Czech and German antecedents and very modest talent, who had never published a paper, was named chairman. Professor Appelfeld rushed into the office of the provost, an old friend, who was perturbed and embarrassed.

"I agree with everything you say, my friend, but it would have been impossible to appoint you. The university is vulnerable just now. Konrad Henlein would never accept a Jew as a department chairman. It is better just now for Jewish academics not to call attention to themselves." He reddened as he spoke and studied the papers on his desk.

"I am a Czech," Professor Appelfeld replied and realized

with chagrin that he was standing at attention. Konrad Henlein, the leader of the Sudeten Nazi party and an overseer of the University of Prague, was always photographed in such a manner. He relaxed then and lit a cigarette, and offered one to the provost, who shook his head and looked at him sadly.

"To Henlein you are a Jew."

"And to you, Herr Provost—am I a Czech or a Jew to you?"

"To me you are a fine physicist, a good friend."

"You have not answered my question," the professor replied, and he turned on his heel and left.

He and the provost had been undergraduates together. They had attended each other's weddings. But after that June afternoon they never spoke again.

On his way home that afternoon he stopped at a university bookstore and bought a Hebrew dictionary and a grammar. That same evening he wrote a letter to his former Prague colleague, Professor Hugo Bergmann at the Hebrew University, and within weeks he received an invitation to join the physics department in Jerusalem. That fall the family settled into a flat on King George Avenue, and Daniel was enrolled at the music conservatory.

"You will never be denied a position here because you are a Jew," the professor told his son.

He hung a lithograph of the Vysehrad Castle on the wall of his study and retained his subscription to the *Tribuna*. He had not come to Palestine out of love for Zion or because he feared for his life. He had come because he was a trained scientist, attuned to the study of theorems, the validity of proofs. Scientific deduction ruled his thinking, and he had deduced that Jews had no choice but to create and live in a Jewish state.

It was Daniel who insisted that they change their name to Alkilai, selecting the name of an early rabbinic Zionist philosopher. The physics professor was indifferent to Zionist theory, but the new name pleased him. His son's progress also pleased him. A year after their arrival in Palestine, Daniel substituted for an ailing violinist during an important concert of the Palestine Symphony Orchestra. He played the solo with such melodic ease that the conductor lowered his baton and gave the boy musician full sway. He was given a permanent position and became the youngest member of the orchestra. He played during Toscanini's second visit to the country, and the great Italian conductor summoned Daniel and his parents to his hotel room.

"I will make arrangements for you to study at the Juilliard School in New York," he said.

Daniel Alkilai did not hesitate.

"I would never leave Palestine."

His parents did not intervene. They had left parents and friends behind in Prague. They did not want their son to leave them behind in Jerusalem. Besides, the professor believed deeply in his theorem. Jews had no choice. Survival and Zionism formed a comprehensive, unalterable equation.

The Palestine Symphony traveled northward to Haifa and the Galilee. They performed in the port city and in makeshift tents and on wooden platforms erected on newly cleared fields. Their music vaulted up to star-encrusted skies.

Daniel Alkilai loved the wild countryside of the north. In fitful sleep he dreamed of profusions of wild orchids, of crimson poppies and buttercups the color of sunlight. Back in Jerusalem he longed for the Galilee. He practiced scherzos and crescendos and thought of the newly planted fields of the young settlements.

He composed a dance which caused his listeners to think of sheaves of wheat tensed against a mountain wind. The symphony was invited to play at the harvest festival in Nahalal. Daniel wrote an étude which he called "Gleanings," and he played it for the students at the agricultural school.

He stayed on at Nahalal for several days, and for the first time he worked the land and saw the richness of the soil of Palestine as he hoed the long furrows where tomatoes and marrows would be planted. He scrambled up a fig tree, and fingers of sunlight stroked his upturned face. He sucked the pink heart of the green fruit that broke at his touch from the forked branch.

He played yet another concert at the agricultural school, and a girl whose curls clustered about her head in coal-colored ringlets and whose green eyes sparkled with laughter ran up to him afterward and demanded that he play a hora on his violin.

"I would rather dance one," he said and seized her hands.

They danced in a whirling circle, and then they walked through the silent fields, now talking breathlessly, now falling into a comfortable silence. Her name was Balfouria, she told him. She played the flute. She played for him that night, but he did not hear her music. He only saw her sea-green eyes reflected in the silver instrument. They kissed as the milky light of dawn crept across the fields of Nahalal, and they believed then that they had known each other always and would know each other forever.

He returned to Jerusalem and told his parents that he was resigning from the symphony and planned to join a group from Nahalal in the founding of a new kibbutz on the northern border.

The physics professor was aghast. His theorem had not provided for such a development. He was not unfamiliar with the rigors and deprivations of farm life. He had visited his grandparents' farm in the Carpathian mountainside. It was inconceivable that Daniel would sacrifice his musical gift to work in rock-filled fields, dragging irrigation pipes through dank swamps. Didn't he know that the settlers in the Jezreel valley battled malaria and typhus? How could he abandon his music?

Daniel was adamant. He was not abandoning his music. A kibbutz was a collective enterprise, and individual members could use their free time as they liked. He would always play his music, and there would always be an audience for it. Other members of their group played instruments. Perhaps one day there would be a kibbutz orchestra. His friend Balfouria was a talented flutist.

His mother stared at him as he voiced the girl's name. She saw the softness in his dark eyes, the curl of a smile. She understood. Balfouria. He loved the Galilee and he loved the strangely named girl who played a silver flute. He would not return to Jerusalem. She packed his warmest clothing and promised that she and his father would journey north when his settlement was established.

"We shall call it Hanita," Daniel told them. "Balfouria loves the name."

The dry log he had added now to the fire ignited suddenly, and tongues of orange flame sparked and sputtered against the dim light of dawn. Daniel's eyes squinted shut, and when he opened them he saw Balfouria.

"Good morning," she said, and he bent to kiss her.

She smiled. His lips were soft against her own and the long sweep of his dark hair waved in silken fold against her forehead.

"Today is our beginning," she said.

"Today."

Chapter 19

YIGAL ALLON, a tall, fair-haired young man whose carbine jangled against a bandolier of bullets, glanced impatiently at his watch. Yaakov Dori, the commander of ''Hanita Settlement Day,'' curled his fingers about a tin mug of ersatz coffee and studied the map with thin-lipped Moshe Dayan. He was glad that Moshe and Ruth Dayan were with them. Moshe had grown up on Kibbutz Degania. He knew the countryside well, and he understood both Arabic and the Arabs. It had been Moshe's idea that the settlers and the Haganah force that would help them occupy Hanita make camp on a distant coastal kibbutz so that neither English nor Arab suspicion would be aroused. It had been a good tactic, Yaakov Dori decided.

The camp area swarmed with men dressed in the field clothing of farm workers, baggy cambric pants and loose faded shirts. In contrast, the young women wore brightly patterned skirts and freshly laundered white blouses. Some even had woven long ribbons through their hair as though they had dressed for a festive occasion.

The largest contingent of men wore the field khaki of the ghaffirs, the Jewish Settlement Police Force organized by the British. The ghaffirs grinned hugely at each other and tossed mock salutes at the air. The morning adventure and their own duplicity pleased them. They wore uniforms issued by the British and carried British weapons to protect Jewish settlers who were founding a kibbutz in defiance of British policy. By nightfall many of them would have returned to their guard posts, where they submitted cheerfully to the orders of oddly accented Yorkshire Fusilier drill sergeants.

They drove northward in lorries and private cars, in the produce trucks of Nahalal and the poultry wagons of neighboring kibbutzim. At the incline that led to Hanita, they left the vehicles and ascended the rocky slope by foot. Yaakov Dori split them into two divisions. The first hacked out a track up the hillside, laboring with pickaxes and shovels, heaving aside massive boulders with catapults improvised from planks of wood and lengths of rope. Despite the chill of the morning, blots of perspiration circled their work shirts in damp patterns; when they paused, they shivered against the cold wetness of their own sweat.

The second group followed after them, laden with supplies and equipment. Balfouria carried Daniel's violin, her own flute, and a sack of bread. Occasionally, during the arduous climb, a tall, auburn-haired youth from Shimron relieved her of the instruments and added them to his own burdens. He, too, was a violinist, he told her, but of course, not as accomplished as Daniel Alkilai. Still, perhaps one day they would play a duet on Hanita. Perhaps, Balfouria agreed. Now she could see the crest of the hill crowned by an aureole of sunlight. She heaved her sack to her other shoulder and increased her pace.

By high noon, faint with exhaustion, pale with hunger, they reached the hilltop. But they did not pause to rest. Hurriedly, they bit into chunks of cheese, tore the bread apart, and swallowed lukewarm cups of tea before rushing off to help with the erection of a wooden watchtower. Balfouria and Liesel worked on the perimeter fence which would ring and shield the settlement. Their bright skirts grew matted with earth, and thistle burrs clung to their sweaters and blouses as they bent and rose and bent and rose again, reinforcing the double wall of wood with earth and boulders.

"Hurry!" Yaakov Dori's commands were brisk. "We must be finished by nightfall."

It was not unusual for the stockade and tower of a new settlement to be constructed in a single day to forestall the Arab attacks that came at nightfall. But the perimeters of Hanita were unusually wide, and Balfouria looked with despair at the area they would have to cover.

Briefly, she left her post to drink some water. Daniel was at the trough, and he filled the aluminum dipper for her. Her heart turned when she saw the blisters newly formed on his white musician's hands; his fingernails, always so finely shaped, were cracked now and circled with crescents of dirt. He followed her eyes, laughed, and kissed her neck.

"This comes first," he said. "Only live musicians can make music."

They worked fiercely through the afternoon and into the evening, but by nightfall they were not finished. Huge gaps remained in the perimeter fence, and those who still had strength continued to work. Balfouria slept briefly atop a sleeping bag in the hastily erected dormer tent. Her dreams were colorful, fragmented, laced with sound.

She and Daniel sat together in the plum tree at Sadot Shalom. He played his violin—the melancholy finale to his "Harvest" étude. She answered him with her flute. The instruments flirted with each other in melodic duet. Silver teased wood. Throbbing strings hurried after breeze-borne theme. Below them, in the orchard, her brother Amnon pounded his leather-covered drum. How loud his pounding grew. Too loud. It drowned their gentle music. She frowned and wakened. It was not the drum beat of a dream she had heard but the harsh ricocheting repeats of real bullets, flashing in rapid streaks from the nearby hills. The unfinished, unfortified settlement of Hanita was under attack.

The small handgun Amos had given her was in her knapsack, and she reached for it.

"It was Achmed's," Amos had told her. "A gift from Uncle David. He had it with him during the Hebron riots. I had it in Berlin. Take it with you to Hanita."

Swiftly, she stole to the perimeter fence where the ghaffirs were firing toward two distant hills. Now and again they spied a sudden movement in the moonlight as an Arab gunman dashed from one dun-colored breast of earth to another, but they could not fix exact locations.

"You don't have enough range with that pistol," Moshe Dayan hissed impatiently at her. "Are you a good shot?"

She nodded. He reached down and handed her a carbine, prying it loose from the fingers of a slumped and lifeless figure. Balfouria gasped. The fallen fighter was auburn-haired, and a ribbon of blood streaked his face and ran down his freckled neck. The bullet had hit him in the center of his broad forehead. His mouth gaped open as though death had caught him in midsentence, and there were unfinished phrases which he would never utter. Balfouria recognized him at once and thought, with an almost abstract sadness, that now he would never play a duet with Daniel at Hanita.

Daniel! Where was he? She looked frantically about but did not see him.

"We can't fix their location. Goddamn them," Moshe Dayan said bitterly. "Just shoot."

For the next hour and a half bullets flew in frenzied fusillade from the dun-colored hills to the unfinished barricade. At last Yaakov Dori raised his hand, and they held their fire. One minute of silence passed and then another. Still, they held their guns poised until a wild roar invaded the quiet. A young lion stood poised on the distant hillside, and his amber eyes glinted in the darkness.

"Behold the victor," Moshe Dayan said bitterly. "To him belong the spoils. Tonight he will eat the flesh and drink the blood, and tomorrow the Jews and Arabs will fight again and he will return for his victory dinner. We will not let him grow hungry."

"But will we always fight?" Balfouria asked.

He shrugged and wearily removed his field jacket, placing it gently over the dead youth's face.

"He was only nineteen," he said. "He was very brave."

"He played the violin," Balfouria added. They spoke his eulogy, but they did not know his name. If Daniel had fallen, would his comrades at arms know who he was—would they seek her out? The terror she had not felt during the fighting seized her now, and she trembled and felt the terrible cold of the night air.

"Balfouria!" Daniel raced toward her across rocks and boulders. "Are you all right?"

"I'm fine," she said and fell into his arms. But when he kissed her, the small handgun which she had thrust into her blouse bruised her breasts, and she wept. Daniel held her close. Behind them Moshe Dayan opened the bullet chamber of his rifle and filled it slowly with the cartridges he plucked from his bandolier.

They worked steadily for the next three days, crawling out of their tents at the break of dawn and flinging themselves down on blankets and sleeping bags when they could work no more. Often they slept in the work clothes they had worn throughout the day. The stockade was finished, and Daniel and Balfouria climbed the watchtower together and wove a web of chicken wire about the lookout deck.

Arm in arm then, they looked down at the huddle of tents and small cook fires. They watched their friends hurry from place to place. Ruth Dayan, Moshe's wife, six months pregnant, balanced a long strip of lumber on her shoulder which she passed to her husband. They were reinforcing the western rise of the stockade. Moshe took the wood from her, then bent and kissed the rise of her abdomen. Balfouria and Daniel turned away.

From the height of the tower they could see the northern road where a Hanita construction team was building an approach to the settlement. The narrow stretch ribboned its way through the newly green fields, which soon would be carpeted with cyclamen and buttercups. They had already seen patches of ivory-hearted carmelites, which always bloomed too early and vanished with melancholy swiftness. The farm truck which Yaakov Dori had covered with steel plate rolled up carrying workers from Nahariya who would help lay the pipes for the Hanita water system. They saw Liam Halloran descend from the truck.

Liesel Konigsfeld ran to greet him. He touched her hair, a swift and tentative gesture. She plucked a burr from the sleeve of his jacket. They walked together up a sloping hill and then, as they descended, his hand found hers.

"Do they love each other?" Daniel asked.

He felt a strange omnipotence. Here on their watchtower aerie, they spied on other lovers, glimpsed mysterious intimacies, and spoke with the contemplative slowness of those who have seen death and love compressed.

Balfouria shrugged.

"He's married, I know. And much older than she is. I think that they are both very lonely."

Her heart swelled with luxuriant sorrow for the lonely. She herself was loved. She would never be lonely. Daniel held his arms open and she glided into them. The platform of the watchtower was their own skybound nest, their refuge wrought of rough-hewn plank and wire mesh. Below them meadow flowers bloomed, a man's lips pressed against the movement of his unborn child, a young woman held a dipper of water out to a tall man. Above them clouds drifted in mounds of snowy softness, and the birds of spring winged their way home from the southland.

Daniel's hands moved across her body. He kissed her hair, her nut-brown neck, her mouth. Her fingers grasped his arms, newly muscular from the long days of labor. She touched his hands. Calluses grew at his fingertips, cushioned his palms. His new strength startled and excited her.

"When will we be married?" he asked.

Theirs would be Hanita's first wedding. They would stand beneath a marriage canopy woven of wildflowers, and she would walk toward him from the northern foothill where the mountains of Lebanon were shrouded in violet mist.

"Come with me from Lebanon—oh come, my bride, with me." He would play Solomon's song on his violin, and she would come with him, to him.

"In the late spring," she replied, "after the plowing and the sowing is done." She was a farmer's daughter and knew that their lives must follow the rhythm of the seasons.

"All right." He was bending to kiss her yet again when he noticed unusual activity on the northern road. He lifted his binoculars and through the powerful lenses discerned a task force of Arabs, some on horseback, some on motorcycles, moving southward toward Hanita.

"Moshe!" he shouted. "Arabs on the road north and east!"

Moshe Dayan and his men tossed their pickaxes to the ground and seized their rifles. They were at the perimeter fence and ready when the Arabs reached it. Yigal Allon tossed a grenade. A motorcycle overturned, and its fuel tank exploded in a pillar of whirling flame. The rider was thrown clear, and he ran toward the border. The other Arabs broke formation and retreated, firing random shots which the Hanita settlers did not bother to return.

The brief skirmish was over. The sky darkened. A group of men tossed buckets of earth at the smoldering flames. Liam Halloran left, and Liesel Konigsfeld stood at the gate and watched the armored truck disappear.

Slowly, Balfouria and Daniel climbed down the wooden ladder. They had planned their future. Within months they would become bridegroom and bride, but they would not forget that even as they made their plans, the fragility and vulnerability of their present had been exposed. They held hands in the gentle dimness of eventide and moved to join their friends around the reassuring blaze of the campfire.

They roasted small potatoes in the fire that night, drank the jugs of wine from the Rishon vineyard, and danced about the leaping flames. They had reached a milestone. The watchtower and the perimeter fence were built, and for now, the enemy was vanquished. The access road was cleared, and at last they would lay the foundation for the communal dining hall.

Daniel played his violin and Balfouria played her flute. The young people linked arms in a rhythmic circle dance; they rushed toward the flames, swayed together, and withdrew. They sang of the future, of years to come, when they would recall the days and nights of their youth, the adventures of days gone by.

"Then we will remember," they sang. "The hora—the hora that we danced together in the hills of the Galilee."

By the first week in June a roof had been raised on the prefabricated communal dining hall, and the fields in the north and south of the settlement had been plowed, furrowed, and sown with corn and durra wheat. Mazal Maimon arrived with lengths of white linen especially woven for Balfouria's wedding dress by the Druse women of Isfiya. The young women of Hanita, in their mud-caked boots and sweat-stained work clothes, watched wistfully as she molded the fabric to Balfouria's body. The dress would be a simple one, and many Hanita brides would wear it. Mazal's thoughts danced backward as she worked. Only yesterday, it seemed, she had been a

bride dressed in gold, circling Ezra beneath the marriage canopy on Sadot Shalom.

Balfouria's aunts, Mirra and Chania, arrived from Gan Noar
to cook the wedding feast. They brought with them enormous
cook pots borrowed from their own prosperous kibbutz
kitchen. The settlers invented excuses to visit the kitchen and
inhale the aroma of roasting chickens, simmering soups, and
sweetened carrots piled into soft golden mounds. Mirra and
Chania chattered rapidly as they stirred and chopped and sea-
soned. Their memories were myriad, their recollections vivid.

"You are lucky here at Hanita. The Jewish Agency gives
you equipment. The men of Gan Noar worked on road gangs to
buy hoes and rakes," Mirra said.

"And you have the Haganah to defend you. We worked the
fields all day and stood guard at night," Chania added.

Mazal listened to them as she sewed, and smiled. Every
generation in this land felt it necessary to impress the next with
tales of the dangers and privations it had weathered.

Balfouria's Yemenite aunts and uncle arrived with huge
sacks of condiments for the humus and the taboulliah as well as
the large leather-covered drums for the nuptial dances and the
fragrant herb bushes which would guarantee the young couple
a life of sweetness and renewed growth.

But when Ezra and Amos Maimon drove into the settlement
with Orde Wingate and Liam Halloran, Mazal felt a shiver of
apprehension. Orde Wingate's uniform was rumpled, the hem
of his khaki shorts was ragged, and his high socks sagged. He
wore clumsy combat boots and the battered pith helmet he
wore into battle. A heavy revolver hung from his holster, and
he carried a small worn, leather-covered Bible.

Mazal liked the intense, slender Englishman whose dark
eyes burned with intensity. Always, Orde Wingate looked directly into the eyes of the person to whom he was talking, as
though he would, by strength of gaze, inject each listener, each
interlocutor, with his dream, his vision. And his vision was
clear and openly stated. He had given Ezra a copy of his paper,
"The Jewish State: Internal Security and Frontier Defense.
Transition Period." Ezra had read it with surprise and growing
absorption.

"Ben Gurion or Weizmann might have written this," he had told Mazal.

The British captain was a Zionist who envisioned the establishment of a Jewish state equipped for heavy industry with a British-subsidized standing army. Such a state, he argued, would make Britain's position in the Middle East impregnable and satisfy Jewish demands.

He had urged his commanding officer, Sir Archibald Wavell, to establish Special Constables, Jewish police officers trained in techniques of anticipating and controlling Arab terrorism. He organized Special Night Squads, armed units who surprised the Arabs before they could attack. He trained his units fiercely, extracting military discipline, demanding precision and dedication.

"You are the future Jewish army," he told the units of young men who assembled at Ein Harod, Ayelet HaShachar, and Hanita for training. He outfitted them with special uniforms, blue police shirts and linen trousers and the broad-brimmed hats of the Australian army.

The Jews were impressed with the contacts Orde Wingate had made in the Arab community. His informants were diligent. Cryptic notes were left for him in the mailbox of his Talbiyeh flat in Jerusalem, in dispatch boxes, at mysterious safe houses in small settlements. Twice Moshe Dayan's crack squadron had been able to deflect attacks on the Iraq Petroleum Company pipeline because Wingate had obtained advance warning from an Arab.

"Will you have some tea?" Mazal asked, but Wingate shook his head, and both Ezra and Amos avoided her eyes.

"No time just now. We must have a meeting."

The leaders of Hanita hurried into the newly built dining hall. They sat about the plank table across which Wingate had spread a map of the area. The Arab village of Jurdeih was circled with a heavy red grease pencil. Wingate pointed to it.

"We have information from a very reliable source," he said, "that a raiding party is due to set out from Jurdeih and attack during the wedding celebration. There's been a lot of activity in the village for the past several weeks. Fawzi Kawakji's gangsters have been coming down from Syria. A lot of feed and flower wagons have been rolling in. We're pretty sure that under the sacks of oats and alfalfa and the daffodils we'll find German rifles, but we don't want to rouse their suspicions by stopping them for inspection.''

"If we know they plan to attack during the wedding, we'll be prepared for them," Daniel Alkilai said. He was the bridegroom, and he had thought to take up his violin and play the sonata he had written in celebration of his marriage, but if need be he would shoulder his rifle instead. Was a groom allowed to stand armed beneath the marriage canopy? he wondered.

"Naturally, we'll have a lookout on the watchtower—men posted all around the stockade," Moshe Dayan said. He was glad now that he had sent his wife to Haifa to await the birth of their child.

"That's not enough," Wingate said sharply. "You don't combat guerilla warfare by sitting in a barricaded encampment waiting for an attack. That's not what I did in the Sudan, and that's not what you are going to do here. We will make a preemptive attack on Jurdeih, cut off the exit, lay ambush for them, and confiscate their weapons."

He spoke in strained and stilted Hebrew, and for a brief moment the men of Hanita thought they had misunderstood him. Always before, they had set their ambushes near the approach to Jewish settlements; never had they ventured to close off access from the Arab villages that served as terrorist bases. Still, they recognized the military logic of the English captain's proposal, and they bent to study the field map.

Jurdeih was relatively isolated from other Arab settlements. If they could move in swiftly, strike, and withdraw, the terrorist operation would be thwarted, and for a time there would be peace in the area.

Joseph Fein, the chairman of the Hanita settlers, looked around the table and read approval in every face.

"When do you propose we set out?" he asked Wingate.

"Tonight. I'll want three patrols of Jewish squadmen. Halloran will command the Royal West Kents. They're encamped below. They'll cover you if they have to, but I want this to be a Jewish operation as much as possible."

"So do we," Fein muttered. "We can defend ourselves. We don't want any Brits to die for us."

"Three patrols mean every trained man on Hanita now," Amos said.

"Every man," Moshe Dayan agreed. "No exceptions."

Every man. The bridegroom and his friends. The brother of the bride and her father. A brief silence fell, pierced by the gay voices of the women in the kitchen, the clatter of cooking utensils. A spicy aroma filled the room. Mazal was preparing lamb with cumin for the wedding feast. A metal mortar danced noisily against a pestle as newly cooked chickpeas were pounded to a fine paste. Moshe Dayan opened and closed the cartridge chamber of his revolver. Yitzchak Sadeh ran his field knife against the splintered edge of the plank table. In the kitchen a girl laughed, a china plate crashed to the floor, and there were laughing cries of *"Mazal tov!"*

Orde Wingate flicked the leather cover off his watch.

"It is agreed, then?"

They nodded.

"We meet beneath the watchtower at midnight."

Daniel Alkilai left the dining hall. His palms were damp, and he was conscious of the hammering beats of his heart. Was it excitement or fear? he wondered and wished that he had a friend with whom he could discuss his deepest thoughts. In Prague he had had such a friend. He and Jan had pondered the mysteries of courage, the dilemma of martyrdom.

"Could you believe deeply enough in an idea to die for it?" Jan had asked. But then Jan had joined the Sudeten Nazi party, and such discussions had ended forever.

Now Balfouria, his love, his bride, was his closest friend, but he could not ask her such a question. It would both frighten and astonish her. The members of her family, during their long years in Palestine, had repeatedly demonstrated their readiness to die for Zion. He did not want to die. He wanted to live and plant the fields of Hanita and play music beneath its stars.

"Daniel!" Balfouria was running toward him, a wreath of snowy asphodel in her black hair, a white linen dress suspended on her outstretched arm. "My wedding dress is finished."

He smiled, touched the flowers in her hair, stroked the snowy linen of the dress.

"Try it on for me," he said.

"No. It's bad luck to see the bride in her dress before the wedding." She shook her head playfully, and her wreath fell askew, became entangled in a cluster of black ringlets.

"Try it on for me." His voice throbbed with urgency.

She looked gravely at him.

"All right," she said. "Let us go to our cave, then."

They had, weeks before, discovered a small cave just north of the settlement, and they wandered there sometimes, in the early evening, carrying their instruments, or simply walking hand in hand toward the shadowed enclave of privacy. They had covered the ground with a blanket and occasionally, at the hour of sunset, they stretched out on it, arms entwined, and watched the fading of sunlight and the bloodied birth of the mountain twilight.

They did not speak now, as they walked across the hilly terrain. In the shadowed cave, he watched as she peeled off her work clothes. Even in the dimness her skin was the color of firelight, and the rose-gold hearts of her breasts were dying candle flames. If he kissed them, they would sear his lips. She slipped the white linen dress over her golden body and fastened the long row of tiny pearls that buttoned the bodice. Her mother had designed the dress to caress each curve of her body. It hugged her waist and thrust her breasts upward, full and firm. The skirt flared about her calves, and he gasped at the beauty of her legs, so strong and shapely. It was strange, he thought, that he had never noticed before how beautiful her legs were. But then everything about Balfouria was beautiful. She was his golden girl, his laughing bride, dressed in white linen with asphodel in her hair.

"I love you," he said and took her hand.

"And I love you."

He straightened her wreath, touched her cheek, kissed her eyes, the curve of her neck, and at last her lips. His gentleness filled her with longing and, inexplicably, she began to cry.

The three Hanita patrols assembled a few minutes before midnight and descended the curving slopes to the rendezvous point. Orde Wingate, Liam Halloran, and a unit of the Royal West Kents waited in readiness. The British soldiers carried bayonets, and the sharpened lengths of steel shimmered in the mountain darkness. Wingate frowned.

"Get some charcoal and blur that steel," he ordered.

The English soldiers looked sullenly at each other, but they obeyed the command. They were not overly fond of this commanding officer. A Jew lover, that was for sure, and some said he was a faggot as well. His own batman reported that he was in the habit of lying about his tent naked, reading the Bible and scratching himself with a brush or a loofa sponge. A corporal cursed briefly as a charcoal smudge soiled his fresh khaki shorts. He couldn't wait to get out of this godforsaken land where Arabs and Jews killed each other over scraps of sand. He'd rather fight the Jerries, who at least were civilized Europeans. Damn Palestine and damn Wingate and his fool Special Night Squads. These Hebes couldn't fight.

"Are you listening, Corporal?" Wingate asked sharply.

"Sir!" The corporal sprang to attention.

Wingate's commands were delivered in a clipped, brusque tone. The Jewish patrols were to move slowly along the ridges of the hills and avoid the paths. The advance force was equipped with torches of Wingate's own design, electric flares affixed to long poles which made the signal visible above the scrub. As they cleared each hill, they were to signal to the Kent back-up forces, which would then move in behind them, offering close cover.

"Understood?" Wingate snapped.

"Understood," Joseph Fein and the Kent lieutenant answered, the one in Hebrew, the other in English.

They moved stealthily toward the east, and Daniel Alkilai realized that his fear and apprehension had vanished, and in their place he felt a strange excitement and exhilaration. Stars sequined the thick velvet darkness of the June night. There had been a light rain earlier, and the sweet, moist air was tinged with the lingering fragrance of wildflower. Wild orchids bloomed within the glades of these rock-bound hills, and as they marched they glimpsed the secret white hearts of the deep purple blossoms.

Like lovers in the silence of the night, the men were acutely conscious of one another, mindful of each stertorous breath, attentive to each twig that crackled beneath rubber-soled canvas shoes. They did not march in formation, yet instinctively, they matched their steps to one another's pace. Daniel knew with absolute certainty that any of his comrades would die for him and that he would die for them. His unarticulated question of the afternoon had been answered.

"Halt!"

Joseph Fein's voice was the sheerest whisper, but it reverberated in the nocturnal silence. "Look."

He stood on a promontory and pointed eastward. A small Arab hamlet nestled against the side of a hill. They discerned the squat stone house, pearl-colored in the darkness, and the embers of a dying cooking fire. Daniel breathed in sharply. Wingate's map had not been accurate. That hamlet had not been charted, and its presence raised the possibility that there were other unknown villages scattered near Jurdeih which might offer refuge to the Syrian infiltrators.

"We'll move on westward," Joseph Fein decided.

They walked more swiftly now, picking their way across the ridges until at last it was safe enough to fire a flare and alert the other units as to the change in direction. In the brief rocket of light Daniel saw the outline of a black goatskin tent; he heard a man's shallow breath. Instinctively, he reached down. His hand enclosed a man's neck, and he pulled the shivering creature to his feet. A wild-eyed Bedouin stared at him, his keffiyah askew, his grease-stained brown abayah matted with thorns and mud.

"Do not hurt me. I am a friend of the Jews, cousin to the children of Abraham," the man babbled hoarsely. The spittle of fear foamed at the corners of his toothless mouth, and he held his hands clasped together in urgent petition. Daniel winced at the fetid odor of his breath.

Joseph Fein strode toward them, his revolver outstretched. He held the weapon to the Bedouin's head.

"If you are indeed a friend of the children of Abraham, then tell us where the Syrians hide."

"I have seen no Syrian," the Bedouin whimpered. "I am here with my wife. Our best she-goat went astray, and we left our tribe to search for her. We have seen no one."

Joseph Fein released the safety catch on his revolver.

''Why should you protect the Syrians? Will they care that you die for them? Tell me what you have seen this night or I will kill you. And I mean what I say. The children of Abraham do not lie to their cousins, the tribes of Ishmael. This you know.''

The Bedouin fell to his knees and pressed his face against Fein's feet.

''You are right. Why should I protect the Syrians? They steal our animals. They steal our women. I will tell you, and Allah will forgive me. The Syrians are in Jurdeih. They are in the old khan where the village leads to the mountains. They mean to hide there until the morning of the wedding. But Allah does not smile on them.'' His words tumbled over each other and were lost in sobs. He wiped Fein's shoes with the edge of his abayah.

''All right,'' Fein sat at last. ''Go back to your tent. If you hold your tongue and remain there tomorrow, I will bring you three goats, one of them a female.''

''I will say nothing. Nothing. You are my brother. You are my brother,'' the Bedouin bleated, and he walked backward to his tent, his face turned plaintively toward them. If he turned his back they might kill him, but he knew that only a special breed of murderer kills a man whose eyes can be seen.

''You should have shot him,'' one of the younger men said bitterly to Fein.

The Hanita leader shrugged.

''There was a woman in the tent. If I had shot him, she surely would have given the alarm. This way we have a chance. Three goats are a fortune to him, and the Bedouins do hate the Syrians. So we gamble. It is not the first time.''

''You should have shot them both.'' The younger man was insistent. He had arrived from Germany only months before. His younger brother had been shot during *Kristallnacht*.

''I do not shoot women who sit in tents,'' Fein replied harshly. ''Perhaps they can betray and murder us, but they will not turn *us* into murderers.''

He stared hard at his men.

''All right, then. Enough philosophy. Fire the damn flare again.''

The orange flash of light streaked skyward, and they moved

swiftly on. Jurdeih was only kilometers away, and Fein knew the exact location of the old khan. He had met there only weeks before with the sheik of the Arb Rashmi tribe, who had promised never to give shelter to Syrian terrorists.

"Here. Surround the khan. Block the exits."

They ran to take up positions, but before they could achieve them a scream came from the Lebanese border.

Daniel recognized the voice of the Bedouin they had released. He had scrambled to refuge and now was sounding the alarm.

"My Arab brothers," he shouted. "The murdering sons of the Jews are upon us!"

A woman wailed, and the Syrians rushed from the khan, tossing grenades, firing wildly. They ran in every direction, but Wingate's back-up troops and the other units cut them off. Fire signals from the Lebanon blazed, and the Syrians retreated toward them, shooting wildly as they fled. Shouts and curses in Hebrew, English, and Arabic filled the air. The children of Jurdeih, wakened from sleep, screamed with terror.

A grenade fell into a wooden animal pen, igniting dried grass. Spikes of flame leaped skyward. Animals trumpeted wildly, and the stench of searing flesh filled the air. The men and women of Jurdeih ran through the village with buckets of water, shouting and crying. But northward, where the shadows of the Lebanon fell, darkness and quiet again ruled the night.

The battle was over. They pushed their way into the khan, flashing their torches about the barren room. A small armory filled the stone shelter. German rifles and grenades, cartridge boxes emblazoned with the seal of Krupp, and even a small cannon were ranged on the floor, which was littered with the remains of a hasty meal. A copper *feenjan* stood on an up-turned carton, and when Amos Maimon touched it, he felt the heat of the coffee within. Yet there was no fire in the khan. Clearly, the Arabs of Jurdeih had given shelter to the marauders.

Orde Wingate studied the weapons with a professional interest.

"Not a bad haul," he said. "The mufti's German connection is lucrative for him. Liam, are you all right?" He noticed for the first time that the Irishman was clutching his shoulders and his lips were clenched in silent acknowledgment of pain.

"A flesh wound," Liam Halloran said. "Nothing to worry about." But his voice was weak, and Ezra Maimon moved swiftly to his side. He had saved Liam Halloran's life on Gallipoli, and he felt a special responsibility to him.

"Is everyone accounted for?" Wingate asked.

"No," Joseph Fein said quietly. "Daniel Alkilai is missing. I have not seen him since the fighting began."

"He was with me when we fired from the thorn bush, but then he moved up," Amos said.

"He was next to me during the assault," Moshe Dayan added. "I saw him move toward the khan."

Ezra left Liam and stood at the entryway.

"Daniel!" he shouted. His voice trumpeted and drifted into echo. "Daniel!" The veins of his throat formed tight blue cords, and his scream rose in shrill command again and again. "Daniel Alkilai!"

There was no answer.

They searched the area. A puddle of blood moistened the dry earth at the eastern wall of the khan where Moshe Dayan had last seen Daniel. Droplets of the same ruby color formed a trail which they followed northward. They saw where the blood had begun to flow more freely, and followed the snaking trail around crushed bushes and broken underbrush. They found a bit of blue cloth, torn from Daniel's shirt by the branch of a thorn bush. Spots of blood glinted like crimson dewdrops on the newly green leaves of a terebinth. A blossom of gore trembled on a low-hung branch. Then there was a puddle of vomit, a few more drops of blood, and a white collar button of the kind used by the women of Hanita in their mending room. The trail ended at the Lebanese border.

Orde Wingate read the plea in Ezra Maimon's eyes.

"It would be suicide for us to cross the border. I'm sorry, but he's probably dead."

"They wouldn't have bothered to carry a dead Jew across the border," Ezra said. "He's alive. They took him prisoner to get information."

"We cannot go after him," Wingate said firmly. "I'm

sorry, Ezra, but I cannot risk the men's lives. They would have no chance.''

Ezra stared into the darkness and felt the chill of the northern wind. It was said that lionesses suckled their whelps in this tangled underbrush and that covens of jackals hid in its shadows awaiting the scent of blood.

''You are right,'' he said sadly.

Wearily, they turned southward. Amos and Ezra linked arms. United in loss, they silently comforted each other and searched for words to offer Balfouria, the unwed bride deprived even of her widowhood.

Chapter 20

"ANOTHER GLASS OF grapefruit juice, Sammy?" Mazal asked.

The tall young man wearing a newly pressed RAF uniform shook his head.

"It's very good. Delicious," he said hastily. "It's just that I'm not much of a juice drinker. You wouldn't have a Coca-Cola, would you?"

Mazal laughed.

"I wouldn't even know what it is. I've never been to America. Ezra was sent there before we met, during the First World War."

"Yeah. I know. I mean, I've heard my parents talk about him a lot," Sammy said and shifted uncomfortably in his seat.

That, of course, was not precisely true. His father, Alex Wade, occasionally referred to his first cousin in Palestine, usually when their guests were wealthy people interested in Zionist causes. Sammy had observed that his father selected his references to suit his company, much as a woman selects an outfit to suit a social occasion. If their guests were interested in sports, he displayed Sammy's tennis trophies. A conversation about the West meant a display of the photographs of Sonia Wade's former home in Arizona. Such observations about his father filled Sammy with discomfort. They implied disloyalty, he knew, but still he could not deny them. It occurred to him now that Sonia, his mother, rarely mentioned the Maimon family, although Sammy knew that it was Ezra Maimon who had introduced his parents to each other.

"And of course I remember Amos," he continued hastily.

"He visited us a lot when he was teaching at Columbia. People used to say we looked alike."

"You do look very much alike," Mazal said thoughtfully.

Indeed, when she had seen Sammy walking up the ashlar-lined path that led to the Sadot Shalom farmhouse, she had thought for a moment that he was Amos—the youthful, unbearded Amos with whom she had walked through silent Jerusalem nights before she had met and loved his father, Ezra. Sammy Wade had Amos Maimon's thick golden hair, as well as the beautiful sea-green eyes that ignited Amos's face and were still so startling in Ezra's lined and weather-worn visage. Amos's daughter, Miriam, and his baby son, Asaph, had also inherited those eyes, and Mazal suspected that in the distant Argentine and in Poland, other members of the dispersed family watched the world through those sea-colored orbs. A strong gene transmitted from generation to generation, heredity negating geography.

But the resemblance between Amos and Sammy went beyond their similar coloring. When Sammy laughed, he tossed his head backward, as both Ezra and Amos did, and he walked with the loose, loping gait of his Palestinian cousins. Even the timbre of his deep voice was reminiscent of theirs.

"I wonder," she asked, "would your mother have any pictures of my husband taken during his visit to the States?"

She had, in recent months, felt an odd and fleeting sense of loss because she had not known Ezra in his youth, because he had lived so much of his life before she met him. She could perhaps mitigate that loss by creating a construct of that unknown life, and she had already collected some photographs and pasted them into a black-paged album. There were sepia-toned prints of Ezra and his family during their first years on the Rishon farm. There was an especially sharp photograph of Ezra as a boy standing with his sister Sara, who looked so much like Elana.

Mazal shivered. They had not heard from Sara for over a year. Her last letter had arrived only months after the German invasion of Poland. It had been terse but not unduly pessimistic. The Germans were relocating many Poles, but Sara and her family had encountered no difficulty, although some of their Oscwiecim neighbors were disturbed because the Germans had hung a sign on the town gates calling the ancient city by its German equivalent, Auschwitz. There was construction under way at a huge military barracks in the town, but Casimir thought that a factory of some kind was being built there. Casimir was confident that all would be well. He had added a postscript to the letter in his cautious spidery script: "May the new year be happier than the one past," he had written. The letter had been posted from Switzerland by a friend of Casimir's and date-marked Christmas 1939.

Any year would be happier than 1939, Mazal had thought bitterly. The months of that year were marked in her mind like black squares in a board game of disaster, peopled by powerless pawns who could not gain reprieve with even the most fortunate toss of the dice.

In March, Czechoslovakia had been invaded. In the spring, when they had thought to dance with joy at Balfouria's wedding, Daniel Alkilai had vanished beyond the Lebanese border, and their laughing, gay Balfouria had abandoned all gaiety and laughter. But she had not abandoned her belief that Daniel was alive.

"They took him prisoner. He'll get away," she maintained. "He'll come back."

Her father and her brother looked away. They would rather have Daniel dead than a prisoner of the Syrians. They knew what the Syrians did to their prisoners. Ezra had seen the mutilated body of a nineteen-year-old Degania boy who had been held by Al-Futuwah. A Haganah patrol had found the corpse on the border. The boy had been castrated, his fingers were bloodied and scarred where the nails had been plied off, and milky white maggots writhed in the empty sockets where his eyes had been.

"He's gone, Balfouria. You must make a new life," he had told his daughter.

"I'll wait for him."

She had remained at Hanita. The white linen wedding dress, wrapped in tissue paper, was neatly folded in her foot locker. The wreath of dried asphodel nestled in its folds, emitting a dusky fragrance.

The dread months rolled on. Their hearts sank as they listened to newscasts. Through the long, terrible summer as Britain and France prepared for war, as Hitler and Stalin signed a pact of nonaggression, as Poland, too, submitted to the swastika, the Jews of Palestine became obsessed with events in Europe. They had families and friends in every country under siege. The battlefields of the vast continent were the streets and meadowlands of their childhood. The dead and the wounded, the missing and the imprisoned, were friends and cousins, siblings and parents. There was no laughter in the cafés of Tel Aviv, and the Haifa quays were haunted by men and women who besieged the trickle of legal immigrants for news. The Haganah redoubled its efforts to smuggle Jews into the country. In Palestine, at least, a Jew was guaranteed concealment if not physical safety.

Arab terrorism had intensified, spurred on by the mufti's impassioned broadcasts from Berlin. He had fled the country because of his Nazi sympathies, but his photograph appeared regularly in Arab newspapers, where he was seen reviewing SS troops in Germany, pro-Nazi Masbin soldiers in Yugoslavia. The Maimon family had listened attentively to his 1939 Ramadan message: "Rise as one man and fight for your sacred rights," the oily voice of the exiled leader cajoled his followers.

Elana, who was visiting her father's farm, remembered Achmed's description of the mufti, so deceptively soft-spoken, so outwardly cordial. He had given Achmed a scabbard, offered him sweetmeats, and ordered him killed. Elana pulled Shlomo closer to her, buried her face in her son's dark hair, and listened to the voice of the man who was responsible for the death of his father:

"Kill the Jews wherever you find them. This pleases God, history and religion. God is with you. Germany fights against the Jews. Arabs, we are about to win this war. We are now reaching the crossroads. Distinguish between your friends and your enemies. The German soldier is your protector and defender."

"Why do the Arabs hate the Jews?" Shlomo asked.

"Not all Arabs hate the Jews," Elana replied softly. "There are many good Arabs."

Across the room, Nadav, who held small Aliza on his lap, glanced at her, his eyes filled with familiar pain.

Now Mazal automatically switched off the wireless when she heard the mufti's voice. Depressed by the present, fearful of the future, she turned her thoughts backward to the past. She kept files of old letters, tattered concert programs, swift pen-and-ink drawings. She had found sketches of Ezra from the days of their courtship, and she was intent on searching out other mementos of her husband's life.

"I'm afraid my mother would not have kept any snapshots," Sammy Wade said regretfully. "She's a doctor, you know, and she's a fanatic about getting rid of clutter. She likes everything in its place."

He looked appreciatively at the Sadot Shalom living room with its burnished-copper vases and bowls and its woven rugs and pillows. Here color and comfort took precedence over order. His family's apartment on New York's Central Park West was comfortably but austerely furnished.

"I should like to meet your mother," Mazal said.

"I'm afraid you'll have to come to America, then. My mother hardly ever leaves the United States."

Sammy did not add that Sonia Wade had a particular aversion to Palestine. Only a few years earlier, Alex Wade had presented a paper at a medical conference in Athens and suggested that they visit his family in Palestine. Sonia had adamantly refused, and the Wades had spent a desultory week in the deserted Paris of August before sailing for New York. Yet Sammy had noticed the eagerness with which his mother opened all letters from the Maimon family and the careful scrutiny she gave to the photographs which Amos occasionally enclosed with his letters.

Once a year a carton of citrus fruits from the Rishon orchards arrived at the Wades' Central Park West apartment, and then Sonia touched the smooth-skinned fruit with tentative fingers and stared at it with a wistful gaze. Always, she selected a citron which she placed in a drawer among her handkerchiefs, and the small squares of linen with which she had wiped the young Sammy's tears carried the fragrance of the distant land where his father's cousin lived on a farm called Sadot Shalom—Fields of Peace.

His mother's ambivalence about Palestine confused Sammy, but then a great deal about his parents mystified him. He had visited his friends' homes, heard shouting and laughter, witnessed joy and anger, but his own household was quiet, orderly, well run and skillfully managed. It occasionally seemed to him that his parents were more professional associates than husband and wife and that he himself was simply another of their professional involvements, not unlike their clinic on the Lower East Side or the consulting rooms that adjoined their apartment. Just as a medical receptionist handled the details of their practice, so a succession of nursemaids and baby-sitters handled the details of his upbringing.

He had never doubted his parents' concern for his welfare, but he neither anticipated nor received their intimacy. He was a competent child who performed well in school and caused few difficulties. At thirteen his Jewishness was affirmed in an austere service held at the Temple Emanuel on West Sixty-eighth Street. Rabbi Stephen Wise spoke eloquently of his parents' wonderful work among the Jewish immigrants of the Lower East Side. Sammy sweated profusely in the gray serge suit from Bendel's but read the Hebrew prophetic selection with fluency and passion. It was taken from the Book of Zechariah, and for years afterward, the verses came flooding back to him.

Thus saith the Lord of Hosts: Behold I will save my people from the east country and from the west country. . . .

He remembered the verse yet again when his friends at Harvard persuaded him to attend a meeting at the Harvard Hillel House, where Dr. Abram Sachar, a professor of Jewish history, described the Nazi program against the Jews. "The president of the United States pretends not to believe it but he knows as I know and as you must know—Hitler's war is a war against the Jews," the impassioned white-haired scholar had told the students.

He documented his claim with photographs of camps that had been established in Germany, in Czechoslovakia, in Russia. There were rumors about those camps, Dr. Sachar told his audience. Unsubstantiated as yet, but threatening. Hitler spoke openly of a final solution to the Jewish problem. What, after all, was the final solution? The Harvard students looked at one another uncomfortably, and few of them asked questions about the rumors, perhaps because they feared the answers.

Sammy Wade studied the relief map that stood on an easel.

The Germans had moved into Poland. They might, despite the Hitler-Stalin pact, penetrate Russia. If Mendel Wasserman, Sammy's grandfather, had not left Russia, he himself would be vulnerable. He himself might be herded into one of those camps. He was in this Cambridge meeting room because of geographic accident, and he had an obligation to those left behind, unprotected, despite Zechariah's promise that "the people from the east country and from the west country" would be saved.

The next day he requested a leave of absence from Harvard, and with three other Jewish friends, he traveled to Montreal and volunteered for the British army.

Alex Wade had been appalled.

"It's not our war. It's Europe's war," he said harshly.

"It is our war. We are Jews," Sammy replied.

"Sammy must do what he thinks is right," Sonia Wade had said quietly, but her hands trembled and her fingers dug sharply into her son's shoulders when she embraced him at the LaGuardia Airport departure gate. In his British uniform, sun-bronzed from his training, he looked as Ezra Maimon had looked on that distant morning when he, too, had left her to fight a distant war.

"Be careful," she whispered, and her voice broke at the acknowledged impotence of her plea.

Sammy had been sent to England for training and then to Egypt to join a British force under the command of Major Orde Wingate. The Gideon Force, it was called, and it was said that eventually it would spearhead a campaign against the Italians in Ethiopia. After three months of training, Sammy Wade had won a sharpshooter's medal and a two-week leave. He hitched a ride to Lydda Air Base in Palestine, and from there he had made his way north to Sadot Shalom.

"I have family in Palestine. Cousins," he told the lorry driver who gave him a lift on the Haifa road, and for the first time since his arrival in the Middle East, he did not feel alone.

He had not written the Maimon family to tell them of his arrival, and only Mazal and the younger children were at Sadot Shalom when the lorry dropped him at the gate. Ezra, Mazal told him, had driven to Hanita to bring Balfouria, their eldest daughter, home for a visit. But they would be back by evening.

It would be good for Balfouria, Mazal thought, to have this handsome young cousin for company during her holiday. Perhaps he could sever the net of melancholy that had entrapped her since Daniel's disappearance—no, since Daniel's death. She, at least, would not play Balfouria's game of pretending that Daniel had survived capture and imprisonment.

Sammy was content to spend the afternoon with the tiny Yemenite woman who, by mystery of kinship, was his cousin. His young cousins sat on the flagstone terrace and listened to a story which Amnon, the oldest, told to the accompaniment of sweeping gestures and graceful movement.

"Amnon will be our writer, I think," Mazal said. "All the children have such different talents. The twins love to draw, and Rivka is a wonderful little dancer."

"And Balfouria? What is her talent?" Sammy asked. He was curious about this cousin, only a few years his junior, who had gone off to help found a kibbutz on a hostile border.

Mazal sighed. "She plays the flute, but she has not played for months now. You see, she was to have been married to a young violinist. But only days before the wedding there was a battle, and he was taken prisoner by the Arabs. We know only that he was taken across the border. That was months ago, and we have had no word from him. Balfouria is only now beginning to recover, and perhaps soon she will accept the truth."

"The truth?" Sammy asked.

"Daniel Alkilai is dead. He must be dead." Grief and acceptance commingled in her voice. Briefly, Sammy was reminded of his mother, who daily reconciled herself to death.

They heard the sound of a motor car then, and the children sprang forward, laughing and shouting.

"Abba's home. And Balfouria. Shalom, Abba. Shalom, Balfouria. What did you bring us? We have company—a cousin from America!"

Mazal rose, patted a vagrant hair into place, smoothed her skirt. An anticipatory smile curled her lips, and her eyes were soft. Almost two decades had passed since their marriage, yet Ezra's arrival, even after the briefest absence, filled her with a shy pleasure, a liquid weakness.

Sammy watched Ezra Maimon swing out of the car. His cousin was a tall, thick-bodied man, his hair and beard attractively tangled masses of iron gray, but his sea-green eyes matched Sammy's own. The young American's presence startled Ezra Maimon, strangled the greeting he had ready for Mazal, paralyzed the arms he had held outstretched for his younger children.

"A surprise, Ezra," Mazal said, lightly kissing his cheek. "This is Sammy Wade, the son of your cousins Alex and Sonia."

The two men, the aging farmer and the young soldier, faced each other, their features startlingly matched. Broad brow twinned broad brow, delicate clefts were carved into their chins, and their strong-boned cheeks were brushed by extravagantly long lashes. Only the lines of age in Ezra's face violated the mirror image.

Mazal stared at them, entranced; she saw Sammy smile and blink suddenly, and she recognized Ezra in both the smile and the blink—his spontaneous openness, so often followed by swift shyness. She observed the spread of his fingers as he held his hand out. Like Ezra's, his middle finger bent forward.

She knew then, with calm certainty, that the young American in the uniform of the British army was her husband's son, half brother to the children who gathered excitedly about him and to Balfouria who came forward to greet him now. Balfouria's black hair fell in a thicket of ringlets about her shoulders and her skin, braised by wind and sun, glowed golden against the pale blue of her simple cotton dress.

Mazal had always known that there had been another woman in Ezra's life—someone he had met during his travels after the death of Nechama, his first wife, and before he and Mazal had come together. She was strangely relieved now to know at last that the young woman had been Sonia Wade. She watched, with an odd dispassion, as Sammy smiled pleasantly at Balfouria.

"Please think of Sadot Shalom as your home," Ezra said to Sammy. "Balfouria, why don't you show your cousin the orchards?"

He and Mazal slid into the cool of the house.

"You saw?" he asked hoarsely.

She nodded. "It could not be missed. He is more like you than Amos. You didn't know?"

He shook his head. "It was all so long ago. A strange time. We cared for each other, but our lives were so different. She would not leave her work in America. I was a soldier in the Jewish Brigade, and I would not stay there. We were fighting in Gaza when I received a letter from her telling me only that she had married my first cousin, Alex Wade. I did not know about the child until years later. I had suspicions then, but it seemed pointless to follow them through. She had made her choice and I mine. You and I found each other. We married. Those months in America became a fantasy, a dream. Sometimes I cannot remember her face, the sound of her voice."

"Are you glad that we married?" Mazal asked. Her voice was small, almost childlike. For the first time she felt a twist of jealousy, a tremor of anger at the woman whose love for Ezra had preceded her own.

He put his hands on her shoulders, looked hard at her.

"When I found you, my life began. And every morning, since that day, it has begun again."

He held her close, his lips tender against her own; his long lashes, moist with sudden tears, brushed her cheeks.

The younger children burst into the kitchen and laughed to find their parents in close embrace. Sammy and Balfouria, who stood just behind them, blushed and turned away.

Sammy Wade spent the days of his leave on Sadot Shalom. It was the season of furrowing, and he and Balfouria rode the tractor out to the newly cleared western fields. The powerful engine throbbed as the machine's metal teeth tore dark gashes into the earth which it lifted and turned. Trenches for growth were carved into the soil which Saleem and his workers seeded.

"This is wheat," Balfouria told her cousin. "Alfalfa."

She held up pearly kernels of grain, and he split them as though to crack their mystery. He was a child of the city, the son of physicians who worked always indoors. He had never before been close to the earth, although he still remembered a bicycle trip he had taken through New England during which he had slept with a Radcliffe coed in a Cape Cod hayloft. She had been a pale girl, and her body had been alabaster-white against the fragrant hay. His cousin Balfouria's golden skin would blend with the sun-dried grass, he thought and smiled.

"What's the joke?" she asked.

"No joke. Just evil sensual thoughts. Don't pioneers ever have evil sensual thoughts? You're very beautiful, my cousin."

She turned her head. Pain flecked her eyes. She felt ashamed. She was Daniel Alkilai's bride (he *was* alive and he *would* return to her), and yet the words of her American cousin caused her heart to turn and mysterious moisture to form in the secret places of her body.

Still, she asked him to join her the following evening, when she visited a coastal kibbutz, although she warned him, before they left Sadot Shalom, that they would be participating in an Aliyah Beth operation—illegal immigration in defiance of the British White Paper which restricted Jewish immigration into Palestine.

"Don't wear your uniform," she told him. "We are performing treason against the king."

Her Haganah comrades glanced curiously at Sammy Wade, but she felt no qualms about including him, despite his British commission. She trusted him no less than she trusted Amos, her brother, or Daniel Alkilai, her lover.

A shipload of illegal immigrants was scheduled to dock off the kibbutz waters in the dead of night. Balfouria was assigned to a group that would flash signals to the long boat that rowed out to carry the refugees to shore. Sammy sat beside her, bundled into the same blanket. Together they studied the ink-dark sea for a flicker of light, a sign of movement.

At last they saw a pinpoint of brilliance, and they ignited their own flares. The rowers, wearing dark clothing, their long boats painted the color of night, launched themselves out to sea. The small craft, laden with heavy blankets, life jackets, and flasks of hot drinks, bobbed like flimsy toys on the gentle waves.

Balfouria taught Sammy to work the lantern flare that would serve as a directional to the returning craft. She herself pulled on rubber pants, long boots, a waterproof jacket. When the long boat came into sight, she waded out to meet it and returned, wading through the foaming water, with a small baby in her arms. The child's open hand formed a pale flower against the rough gold of Balfouria's neck, and she whispered softly to it as she walked.

"You're home now, little one. Don't cry. There's nothing to be afraid of. You're in *HaAretz*—the Land."

Spangles of sea spray dotted her black curls, and her lips were moist and berry-red. If he kissed them, Sammy thought, they would taste of salt, and he trembled with excitement and tenderness. He watched as she kissed the child and passed it over to the mother, an exhausted young woman whose skin was the color of ashes. Seventy-three German and Czech Jews had sailed on the ship that was briefly anchored off the coast of Palestine and would be gone by morning if their luck held. Sixty-two had disembarked.

"A coffin ship," the baby's mother said sadly.

Eleven passengers had died, and they had sailed for three days with the stink of putrefying corpses in their nostrils. Still, they thought themselves lucky. They at least had arrived in Palestine. They knew of other vessels that had not found refuge anywhere.

The last two long boats carried in the corpses, and Sammy was grateful that the surviving immigrants had been taken up to the kibbutz and were not on the beach to see the blanket-wrapped bodies which they now loaded on to a waiting truck. He helped to carry one and was surprised by the lightness of the corpse. A child, he thought, or an aged man. He was glad that he would never know, and he thought briefly of his parents, who confronted death each day. He had never before admired them.

At last the task was completed, and he and Balfouria crossed the beach to the Sadot Shalom truck. She had taken off her soaked boots, and she walked barefoot across the sand. They had parked beside a shoal of rocks, and he lifted her so that she would not cut her feet. In his arms, she was as light as the unknown corpse, but he felt her breath, swift and sweet in his ear, the pressure of her breasts against his chest, the steady beat of her heart keeping rhythm with his own. She was alive and young, as he was alive and young, although they lived in a time of war and death, danger shadowing their golden days, their starlit nights.

They reached the truck but he held her still, his lips light against her cheek.

"No, Sammy. No."

She slid to the ground, her face set in a small, stern mask.

"He's dead," Sammy said. "They all think he's dead."

His voice was calm, but his fists curled and uncurled in the darkness. He was angry with Daniel Alkilai for not dispelling the mystery of his fate.

They drove back to the farm in silence, but when they reached Sadot Shalom, she held her hand out to him in mute forgiveness. Fingers interlocked, they walked wearily up the ashlar-lined path. They did not speak, but their faces were turned to each other, as though secrets could be read in the line of brow, the curve of cheeks. Ezra and Mazal watched them from their bedroom window.

"They will have to be told," Mazal said.

"Yes."

There could be no argument, no rationalization. Already there had been too many secrets.

"It will be all right," Mazal said, but she twisted her wedding ring about her finger and wondered that her voice did not break against the lie.

But Ezra did not tell Sammy the truth the next morning, although he lay awake through the night, forming phrases, anticipating the boy's *(his son's)* questions, his own answers. ("Many years ago, during the first war, when I was in America . . ." "Your mother and I loved each other but . . ." "I did not know of your birth until years later, and even then I never knew . . ." "I am proud that you are my son—that you are brother to my children, *to Balfouria* . . .")

An Agency messenger from Jerusalem arrived at first light, summoning him to an urgent meeting. Plans were under way to parachute units of Palestinian Jews into eastern Europe to work with British intelligence units. Sir Archibald Wavell had sent his adjutant from Cairo to explore the possibilities. The prime minister, Winston Churchill, had remembered his old friend Ezra Maimon and had specified that he be consulted.

"You Palestinian Jews are in a unique position," the British officer told the group of Jewish leaders. "So many of your settlers are from eastern Europe. They know the terrain, the dialects. They could easily establish contact with resistance leaders, do undercover work.''

''And make Mother England's job much easier,'' Joshua Maimon said, his voice bitter.

''The war is our shared effort,'' the British officer replied stiffly.

''Only when it suits you,'' David Ben Gurion said bluntly. ''However, we have grown used to that. We will fight Hitler with you as though there were no White Paper, and we will fight the White Paper as though there were no Hitler.''

''Look,'' Nadav Langerfeld, the trained diplomat, said, ''let us be explicit. We will help you. Our people stand ready to do anything to assure the Nazi defeat. But even as we help you, the mufti of Jerusalem makes his headquarters in Berlin and aligns himself with the Nazis. Yet your government neither disavows him nor does it rescind the White Paper. In your communiqué to London, be certain that you express both our committed cooperation and our deep disappointment.''

''His Majesty's government is bound by the report of the Passfield Commission,'' the British officer replied, but the explanation sounded weak to his own ears. ''But I will relay your answer. I leave for Cairo at once. All leaves have been canceled and all British personnel have been recalled to base.''

''Ah. The Ethiopian campaign will be launched this week,'' Nadav said softly.

The officer stared at him, flushed and disconcerted. Where did these Jews get their information? They knew everything, anticipated everything. A foxy lot, with contacts everywhere. Wingate and his Gideon Force were welcome to them.

''I know nothing about Ethiopia,'' he replied brusquely. ''We will be in contact.''

They watched him leave. He turned at the door, hesitated for a moment, and then saluted. Pains in the ass, the Hebes were, but brave, goddamn it, brave and smart.

The group of Jewish leaders studied the maps and papers he had left them. David Ben Gurion hummed as he read, pulled a tuft of hair from his head and twirled it between his fingers.

''Not a bad plan,'' he said at last. ''And we will have more than enough volunteers.'' His desk was piled with letters and messages from Palestinian Jews eager to strike a blow against Hitler, to do something to rescue family and friends. "Come, let's have some schnapps."

They smiled thinly and filled their glasses. They were not drinking men, and none of them had ever tasted liquor before at such an hour, but the amber liquid burned pleasantly in their stomachs and briefly dulled the fear they carried with them everywhere.

Sammy Wade was not at Sadot Shalom when Ezra arrived home. He had received a telegram summoning him to Cairo. Balfouria was packing to return to Hanita.

"Sammy will be back on his next leave," she told them. She did not add that he had written his address on a piece of paper which she had slipped into her blouse.

That night, for the first time since Daniel Alkilai's disappearance, she played her flute. There was color in her cheeks and new warmth in her eyes. Mazal and Ezra watched her in silence as she set down the silver instrument and, still humming the graceful Rossetti tune, danced across the floor with the twins.

"It is good to see Balfouria happy again," Amnon said, looking up from his book. He was fifteen now, and the poetry of Yehuda HaLevi ignited his imagination, filled his sleep with restless mystic dreams: "Consider the glory of a precious stone . . . How it is red, how it is white . . ."

Mazal and Ezra could not meet each other's eyes.

"You must tell her," Mazal whispered fiercely that night.

"Not yet," Ezra replied. "Not yet."

In the darkness, the secrets of his past fluttered by, and conspired, like whispering demons, against his children. Briefly, desperately, he relied on the unknown future to sort out the tangled strands. He would have to write Sonia. He was not the sole guardian of the secret. Did Alex know, he wondered, that the splendid young man who carried his name was the son of Ezra Maimon? Ezra felt a surge of paternal pride in the son whose very existence had been unknown to him, and impatiently, he chided himself for it. He fell back against the pillows then, exhausted suddenly by the complexity of his life, of all their lives. In the next room Amnon, his youthful voice emboldened by the silent house, read HaLevi aloud.

"We know thee, O separation, from the days of youth
And the river of weeping—that ancient river."

A dream of his boyhood returned to Ezra that night. He saw
himself imprisoned by green waters on a deserted shore. But
now he stood, in mist-wrapped dream, at the water's edge,
with golden-haired Sammy Wade at his side. Daniel Alkilai,
his violin tucked beneath his chin, stood on the opposite shore.
He moved the bow in rhythmic sequence, but the strings made
no sound. Yet, on a flowered island, centered in the water,
Balfouria danced to the silent music. A wreath of asphodel was
in her hair, and her arms were outstretched, now yearning
toward one shore line, now toward another.

"My children," Ezra called in broken voice and he wept;
his tears seared Mazal's breast, and she held him close as night
drifted into morning.

Chapter 21

AT A GENERAL meeting of the Hanita collective, it was decided that the kibbutz would raise goats. Balfouria Maimon, who was familiar with the nimble-footed animals, was placed in charge of the project, and during the early winter months, she herded them northward, glad of the solitude and the freedom from the confines of the kibbutz.

The days of winter were slow-paced and wearying. The dun-colored fields of Hanita lay fallow, and often in the morning, glints of frost sparkled like bits of misplaced starlight on the hard earth. The settlers wore heavy jackets over layers of sweaters and blew on their reddened fingers as they worked on the construction of the communal buildings. They warmed themselves each hour at the kerosene heater in the dining hall and listened to the news on the wireless. They cheered at the report of Wingate's success against the Italians in Ethiopia. They grew somber at the thought of Syria in Vichy hands. Nazism was no longer isolated in Europe. It menaced the northern border of Palestine. Silence prevailed when the activities of Rommel's Panzerarmee were cited. Rommel was mobilizing for action across the Western Desert. Europe's war had become their own.

In the tent that she shared with Liesel Konigsfeld, Balfouria read and reread the few letters she had received from Sammy. Liesel was sad-eyed and silent. Liam Halloran, wounded during the last raid, had returned to Ireland.

"It seems I am always saying goodbye," Liesel told Balfouria in a small voice.

She had waved, unseen, to her father, forced to do penance

on a Berlin street corner for the crime of being Jewish. She had waved to Liam, who had looked at her sadly through the window of a British army ambulance.

"I know," Balfouria said sadly.

"Goodbye," she had whispered to Daniel Alkilai, standing before him in her wedding dress, a wreath of asphodel in her hair.

"Goodbye, be careful," she had said to her bright-haired American cousin. She had not whispered words of caution to Daniel Alkilai. Then, she had thought herself and those she loved immune to danger. She had mocked her sister Elana, who fought life with a tenacious vigilance. She understood Elana now, although Elana's way was not her own. It was good then, during the sad wintry months, to wander the mountains with her mischievous herd of goats. She carried a book, but she seldom read. Occasionally, she played the small recorder she carried, but more often than not she simply trailed after the lithe young animals, glad of the silence and the aimlessness. She welcomed even the roughest winds and the ominous clouds that sailed slowly northward to the skies of the Lebanon.

One chill afternoon, she paced herself to the vagaries of a skittish black kid, which danced in and out of hillside clefts and climbed steadily northward. Balfouria allowed the flock to follow.

She played her recorder and realized that she was playing the theme of the composition Daniel had called "Harvest." The mischievous goat danced across a patch of marjoram. The herb's tiny flowers were frozen into azure-colored teardrops that emitted a bosky fragrance. Balfouria pocketed her recorder and followed, moving more swiftly now.

"Come back," she called threateningly, but the goat scampered on.

"Enough!" Balfouria shouted. The foolish animal was at the border. She would have to grab it and carry it down. She reached into her pocket for the rope leash she always carried but seldom used, and a bit of milk-moistened sugar, always a certain lure.

"Come here," she called, holding the sugar out, but the

animal ignored her. Instead it lowered its sleek head and made small mewling noises as though calling for help.

"Damn. It's probably hurt itself," Balfouria thought.

She glanced down at the rest of the flock, placidly chomping the sweet herbal grass. Clouds were gathering in a huge purple mass, and the mountain reeds swayed against the sudden wind. At the kibbutz that morning, there had been a discussion of the likelihood of rain, and a vehement argument had broken out. It was, after all, safer to argue over the rain than over who was winning the war and whether the tactics of Jabotinsky would be more efficacious than those of Ben Gurion and Ben Zvi. Balfouria had taken no position, but she decided now that those who had predicted rain that day were right. Determinedly, she advanced toward the goat.

"Here, little one."

She stretched her hand out and crept through the grass. A sudden movement would startle and provoke the animal. She inched forward, her hands sliding across the thorn-encrusted earth, unprepared for their sudden contact with an alien smoothness—a rise of fabric covering a softness of flesh. The goat made sucking noises and groped for the sugar, but Balfouria ignored it.

A man lay outstretched on the ground, his face covered by a keffiyah but his breath coming in steady rhythm. Slowly, cautiously, Balfouria knelt beside him. His hands were motionless, his body still. She reached for her small revolver and held it in one hand. With her other, she reached up and touched the soft gauze head covering. The goat, having finished the sugar, moaned piteously and rubbed its head against her body, but Balfouria was intent on her task. Delicately she lifted the keffiyah and looked down at the peaceful sleeping face of Daniel Alkilai.

"I am dreaming," she told herself, but joy surged within her, and she bent and touched his cheek with her own. He opened his eyes and looked at her.

"Balfouria?" Her name was a wondering question. "Balfouria!" Her name was a shout of triumph, a proclamation of gladness, of love. "Balfouria!"

She was in his arms, their faces were pressed together, and their tears commingled and were washed away by the rain that came with fierce and cleansing suddenness. Soaked to the skin, driving the goats ahead of them, laughing and crying, they stumbled into Hanita. Daniel and Balfouria, bride and bridegroom, together again as one.

PART FOUR

The Years of Closing Doors

1941–1942

Chapter 22

"YOU ARE NOT standing at attention! Hold your rifle properly.
Don't look away, Tamar. When you are at attention you must
face your commanding officer. Eyes front!'' Nachum
Maimon's voice was strident, impatient as he gave orders to
his twin. He thrust his narrow shoulders back as he paced the
play area behind the Sadot Shalom farmhouse. Here, long ago,
Ezra Maimon had fashioned a slide for young Amos and suspended a wooden swing from a wide-branched eucalyptus tree.
The weathered wooden seat, still sturdy, had faded to a smoky
gray, and the ropes had been replaced many times as Elana and
Balfouria in turn had soared skyward on the swing, singing and
laughing, celebrating the freedom of childhood.

But the younger Maimon children and their cousins had
almost stopped using the slide and swing, the play implements
of peacetime. Their games reflected the war that dominated
their childhood, despite all their parents' efforts to shield them
from it. Ezra and Mazal spoke in hushed voices of the German
sweep across Europe, of Pearl Harbor and Tobruk. They listened to news reports late at night, lest the children be frightened. But fear did not touch Nachum, Tamar, and Rivka. The
danger and excitement of the war ignited their imaginations.

They plotted campaigns, improvised maneuvers, brandished
rifles carved of olive branches, and tossed unripened plums as
grenades. They organized Saleem's younger children and
grandchildren into opposing armies and stalked them across
wheat field and fruit orchard. They took prisoners and conducted interrogations. Occasionally Nachum was a Haganah
field officer, but more often he wore Ezra's field helmet and

pretended to be Orde Wingate. Their choice of enemies was
diverse. The children battled Germans, Arabs, and Vichy Syrians. They staged illegal entries into the country and avoided
British patrols. They were Italians battling the Free French and
Americans pursuing the Japanese. The enemies of freedom
were manifold. The meadows rang with their battle cries, the
fields hummed with their secret attacks, their intricate forays.

But today Tamar did not want to play. It was hot and her
blouse stuck to her skin. She wished fervently that she was
little again and could run about dressed only in rompers. But at
fourteen her body was changing, and the small buds of her
breasts were tender and oddly painful. She disregarded her
brother's orders, tossed her olivewood stick away, and began
to plait her long, dark hair into a single braid.

"Come on, Tamar," Nachum cajoled, "you're ruining the
game. We were supposed to drill today."

"I don't want to drill. Drill with Shlomo and Rivka." She
plucked a long blade of grass and used the pale green strip as a
ribbon. "Shlomo will do anything you ask him to do. Do you
want to play zoo, Shlomo? How about circus?"

She picked up the olivewood stick and prodded the small
boy with it.

"Here, Shlomo, I'm the animal trainer and you're the lion
cub. Jump over my stick."

Shlomo's face contorted into a knot of misery. Tears flooded
his blue eyes, and he retreated to the farmhouse, where his
mother and grandmother sat on the verandah.

"Now look what you've done, Tamar," Rivka said petu-
lantly. "Elana will begin shouting that we're picking on her
darling Shlomo. I wish she'd go back to Tel Aviv. I'm tired of
her chasing after us all day. What does she think—that if she
doesn't see us for a few minutes we'll disappear?"

"Imma says we must be patient with Elana," Tamar said
piously.

She was troubled now by her cruelty to Shlomo, ashamed of
the small thrill of pleasure she felt at the boy's tears. If Elana
was angry she would not invite Tamar to travel back to Tel
Aviv with her, an excursion she had looked forward to for
weeks. The cities of Palestine hummed with excitement. British soldiers arrived on leave from Cairo and Alexandria, and

the Palestine Buffs and Pioneers left to join British regiments in Europe and North Africa. Military bands played and flags waved. Young girls dashed after strolling soldiers on Dizengoff Square and offered them bouquets of flowers and bags of sun-dried dates and figs. But on Sadot Shalom the days were maddeningly similar—endless chores sandwiched in between Nachum's war games. Tamar glanced yearningly toward the road that led from the farm and was startled to see two figures approaching.

"Who can that be?" she asked, shielding her eyes with her hand and staring hard down the slight incline rimmed by the rows of ashlars.

"Where?" Rivka asked. "Oh, I see someone—no, there are two of them."

"You're just making it up because you don't want to play," Nachum said scornfully.

He, too, had given up on the game. Now he picked at a scab on his knee and scowled at the bloody crescent it left. He was too old for short pants. The boys of his age on Gan Noar, his cousins' kibbutz, were already wearing trousers. Some of them, he knew, even went along on Haganah drills. It was not fair that his brother, Amnon, who was only two years his senior, was already training with the Haganah, while he still had to play war games with girls and babies. He could fight as well as Amnon and was taller than his older brother. Only Nachum, of the five children of Ezra Maimon's second marriage, had inherited his father's height.

"No one is coming to visit," he added without getting up to look.

Few visitors came to Sadot Shalom now. When Rommel's armored division had advanced to Tripolitania, the British had rationed petrol, fearful that the German Panzerarmee might cut off their fuel supplies. It was said that Montgomery had Rommel on the run now, but there was still great uncertainty. Besides, even if fuel were easily available, there was uneasiness about traveling in the Galilee since Arab terrorism had increased. Even Elana and Amos visited rarely, and Daniel would let Balfouria come only when a group of Haganah members traveled with her. Only the week before, two Jewish girls hiking through the northern Galilee had been murdered and their bodies tossed into a dry wadi.

"But there are people coming, Nachum," Rivka insisted, and reluctantly the boy rose and stood beside his sisters.

"You're right," he said. "Two women. But they're not Jewish women. They're probably looking for Saleem's house."

Afterward, he would wonder what had made him decide that they were not Jewish. Even from the distance he had seen that their faces were not veiled and that they wore Western dress. He concluded at last that it was their posture and their gait that had deceived him.

His mother and his sisters, his aunts and cousins, moved with purpose and energy. Even when they were tired and their pace slowed, they moved with a confident thrust of their shoulders, and always, their faces were turned upward.

The women who approached Sadot Shalom walked as though they were burdened by invisible laden baskets, so precariously balanced on their bent heads that they dared not lift their eyes. They trudged up the shaded incline with painful slowness, invisible chains of fatigue braceleting their ankles. Each step was an effort, a straining against a stultifying fatigue which might at any moment strike them down on the ashlar-lined path. Their progress hypnotized the three Maimon children, who stared at them as they sometimes stared at the Bedouin women they passed as they traveled southward.

These veiled, black-robed women, burdened with infants and mysterious burlap parcels, spent their lives moving endlessly across a sea of sand with the sun in their faces and the wind at their backs, each of their days so like the one that had preceded it that they knew there was no need to hurry, to move with swiftness and determination. The sand and the wind, the endless work and wandering, all would wait for them.

"Look, one of them has a baby," Rivka said, and they saw that the taller of the two women cradled a bundle wrapped in a pink flannel blanket. She paused briefly, shifted its weight, straightened a blanket fold, and seemed to speak to it. Her companion waited patiently but made no offer to help or to move closer. As they drew nearer, the children discerned their features and gasped to see facial bones sharply etched against

the chalklike pallor of their skins, so oddly reminiscent of the
skull that Amos had brought home from the Tel Gezira dig.
But that skull had stared at them through empty eye sockets,
and these women had large dark eyes, stuck like anthracitic
lumps into their death-mask faces. Although it was a hot day,
they wore dark serge dresses, and one of them had wrapped a
threadbare crimson wool shawl about her shoulders. She held it
tight, as though imprisoning the vagrant warmth it held.

"They'll want water for the baby," Tamar said, but even as
she spoke she saw that no life was contained within that frayed
parcel of flannel. It was as empty as the eyes of the woman
who stood before her at last, holding out an envelope so mud-
spattered and creased that Tamar could barely read the address
scrawled across it. But when she looked closely and recognized the handwriting, her heart beat faster and her palms grew
moist. As a small girl she had delighted to run and meet the
mail cart, and always she had been elated when a letter in that
hand arrived, the envelope neatly decorated with the flowered
stamps of Poland.

"A letter from Aunt Sara!" she would shout as she hurried
up to the house, for she knew that her father always had an
embrace and a sweet for the bearer of such a letter. But there
had been no letter from Sara for almost two years, and now
suddenly, she read her father's name in that familiar spidery
script.

"Where did you get this?" she asked.

The woman looked at her blankly, held her hands open and
asked, in a hesitant voice, "Yiddish? Polish? *Deutsch?*"

"Hebrew, only Hebrew," Tamar replied despairingly and
wished now that she had not laughed at her father's efforts to
teach her Yiddish. The Maimon children were disdainful of the
language of the ghetto, of the Diaspora. It was, in fact, no
language at all, they claimed, ony a hybrid mixture of German
and Hebrew with a smattering of Slovak. Tamar cringed at its
guttural sounds, mocked its syntax, and giggled in the kitchen
with her sisters and brothers as the strange tongue was mouthed
by visitors. Her father and her uncles spoke it, of course. It
was the language of their childhood. Amos and Elana could
understand it and in turn could manage a few sentences, but
Mazal's children were proud to be free of the tongue fashioned

in ghetto warrens where Jews spoke in whispers and lived in
fear. Hebrew was their language, and they had not thought to
need another.

"Come. I'll take you to the house," she said and motioned
to the women who stared at her uncomprehendingly.

She pointed to the farmhouse, and Rivka sidled up to the
woman who held the pink blanket; she gently touched the
fabric, as though to stroke a sleeping infant, and then took the
tall woman by the hand and led her to the verandah where
Mazal and Elana stood. It was strange, Tamar thought, that
Elana's hands should shake, that fear should shadow her eyes.

Still, it was Elana who spoke with the two strangers in her
fragmented Yiddish. She led them into the living room and
settled them in the most comfortable chairs, drawing the shutters closed as though she had sensed at once that what they
would tell her must be whispered into the shadows. She sent
the children to the plum orchard to fetch Ezra and coaxed the
women to drink the tall glasses of orange juice which Mazal
brought them. She set plates of fruits and cheese before them
and nodded gravely as they introduced themselves. The
woman in the crimson shawl was Clara Straus. She extended
her hand with gentle gesture, as though used to greeting casual
acquaintances at afternoon tea parties.

The other woman nodded her head and announced her name.

"Hinda Klugstein," she said.

She picked up the pink flannel cocoon, smiled into its empty
folds, and added, "Fruma. Fruma Shifra." She sat down then
and gently rocked her ghostly burden while her companion
implored them, with wide-eyed gaze, to say nothing.

They said nothing but refilled the pitcher with newly
squeezed juice and made sandwiches because the two women
had slowly and methodically finished each sliver of cheese,
each slice of fruit, and had at last even eaten the orange peels.

At last Ezra burst into the room. He had run all the way;
beads of sweat sparkled in his gray beard, and his heavy field
boots spattered Mazal's shining wooden floor with mud. But
she said nothing, and he sat down opposite the two strangers
and spoke softly to them in that shared language of Europe that
excluded her. Ezra's eyes were riveted to the crimson shawl.
He reached out at last to touch it, his voice trembling in

puzzled query. Clara Straus answered his question and sat quite still as he fingered the fine cashmere, removing the shawl at last, and handing it to him. The children watched as Ezra buried his head in the soft folds of the strange woman's shawl. They huddled together, frightened by their father's grief.

It was Tamar who understood at last that children had no place in the room. She lifted small Aliza from Elana's lap, took Shlomo's hand, and motioned to Nachum and Rivka to follow her outside. They sat patiently beneath the avocado tree while Nachum told them one of Amnon's stories. They drew pictures with a long branch in the dry earth, and they helped Aliza fashion a house of pebbles. But all the while they listened to the soft voices of the strange women speaking the sorrowful language of a vanished world.

Ezra drew the curtains, barring the last shards of sunlight from the shadowed room, and Elana was reminded of the covered mirrors and darkened windows of a house of mourning. Her father was preparing himself for grief, she knew, bracing himself for loss. She recognized the set of his chin, the rigid posture of his shoulders. As the women spoke, Elana was relieved that she had to whisper rapid translations of their words to Mazal. The task shielded her briefly from the full impact of their story.

Hinda Klugstein and Clara Straus had arrived in Palestine only the week before. They belonged to a contingent of Polish Jewish women whom the Germans had released from concentration camps in exchange for German prisoners of war held by the British. Clara had slept beside Sara in the camp and had undertaken to carry her letter to Ezra, promising to deliver it herself.

"She gave me this shawl. She said that you would recognize it."

The frayed and faded length of crimson cashmere was draped now about his arm.

"I recognize it," he said softly. It had been a leavetaking gift to Sara from Chaim, he remembered, and he recalled, with startling clarity, the morning of their arrival in Jaffa over a half-century ago. Sara, wearing that shawl, had stood beside a rusted railing of the *Vittoria,* poised perilously close to the water. He realized now, what surely he had known then, had

secretly known all these many years, that she had searched for
death that day, in the clear green waters of Jaffa port. But she
had endured then, surviving whatever grief it was that had led
her to despair. He had been too young to even guess at the
source of her obscure misery, but even then he had recognized
his sister's strength, her talent for endurance.

And she had endured the death of Avremel, her first husband, although that loss had spurred her to flee Palestine and
its dangers. Later, after the pogroms at Kishinev, she had fled
Judaism itself, seeking refuge in a false apostasy. But he knew,
as he held her letter in his hand and fondled the shawl, worn to
a gossamer thinness, that she had at last encountered a peril she
could not escape, an attack on life which she could not endure.

"Read the letter, Ezra," Mazal said, and again he turned the
envelope in his hand, noting that the violet ink was so pale it
appeared to fade from the paper even as he studied it: the
spidery script blurred in a mist, and he realized then that he
was crying. His wife and daughter stared at him helplessly,
their faces taut with pain, suffering because he suffered. He
was at once grateful to them and impatient with them. This was
his private sorrow. Sara had been his sister. They had never
known her. Their pain was irrelevant.

"All right, I'll read it."

The Polish women retreated to a corner of the room. They
were merely messengers, strangers to this family and isolated
from its sorrow. Hinda Klugstein sang softly to the pink flannel
blanket she called by an infant's name. Elana recognized a
Yiddish melody which Rivka Maimon had often sung in her
frail and wistful voice.

> "Night falls so slowly, my darling, my dear.
> Sleep, my angel, as shadows draw near."

Ezra read the letter aloud. He paused after each Yiddish
sentence, as though searching for the strength to continue, and
at each pause Elana translated Sara's Yiddish into Hebrew, her
voice faltering and her hands tightly clasped, as though in
prayer.

Dear Brother—dear little Ezra, no longer so little,
Shalom.

We are old now, you and I. There is so little to do in this place that I count back across the years, and always it comes to me as a shock that you, my dear little brother, have passed your sixtieth birthday and I am an old woman, so much older than my seventy years and anxious now for my life to end. I think I fought to stay alive only so that I might write you this letter which Clara Straus, who is being released tomorrow, will bring to you. Please be good to Clara and to the young woman, Hinda Klugstein, with whom she travels.

Poor Hinda suffers the sickness of terrible grief. She carried an infant girl with her into this hell called Auschwitz—Fruma Shifra, a large-eyed baby with cheeks the same color as her pink blanket. A bit of life and color in this camp of darkness and death. But one morning at *Appell*, roll call, a Ukranian woman officer seized the baby from her and tossed it to another guard, as though the infant were a ball. Other guards held the mother, and still they threw the child back and forth, laughing at its screams, at its trembling wails of terror. It fell at last, that small pink bundle, landing oh so softly on the cobbled courtyard. Then they laughed again and told Hinda to clean up the mess that her baby had made. Blood and bone and spattered bits of brain. Fruma Shifra, who had had such a wondrous laugh. Hinda kept the blanket, the poor pink bunting. Her baby's shadow clings to it, she told me, and she whispers to that shadow and comforts it and tells it that soon the war will be over and they will pick flowers together in the meadowlands. Poor Hinda. Flowers will never bloom here again. And if they do, no one behind these walls and wire will survive to see their color or sniff their fragrance. We shall all be dead. I am already dead, my brother, even as you read these words. I am marked for a "disinfection procedure" tomorrow, and I pray that my name will not be removed from the list, that my invitation to death will not be withdrawn. I am ready. But first there are things that I must tell you.

My son is dead. He died during the typhus epidemic in 1941. Shimon was one of the few doctors in Warsaw, and he would not leave his hospital. His wife and two of his three children also died, but his youngest son, Yehuda, may have survived. Yes, Shimon named the boy for our father—you know that Shimon married a Jewish woman and blamed me always for leaving Palestine, for abandoning Judaism. "We cannot abandon our faith," he would say. Perhaps he was right. I know he was right. But of what use is the foolish wisdom of an old woman on the eve of her death? Would Shimon be alive if I had stayed in Palestine? *If? Perhaps? Maybe?* What does it matter? The time for questions is past, and there will be no time for answers. But it is because of Yehuda, the child, that I write to you, my brother. Please. Try to find my grandson, our father's great-grandson, his namesake, and bring him to safety, to Palestine.

My daughter Sophia and all my other grandchildren, too, are dead. Sophia poisoned her children's milk and watched them drink it before bedtime. Then she covered them with our mother's eiderdown and took poison herself. Her husband, a Polish banker, divorced her when he learned we were Jewish and denounced his own children to the Gestapo in exchange for a safe conduct pass.

I grieved when I learned of their deaths. Now I rejoice. I, a mother and grandmother, rejoice that my child and her children are dead, that they will not have to endure the misery of this camp, this city of slaughter. You see, my brother, I have not forgotten the Bialik we read together. Perhaps I will recite his verses tomorrow when I enter the showers. Certainly I will recite no prayers.

Chaim (why should I call him Casimir—that masquerade is over, and after all, we fooled no one all those years—our gentile neighbors rushed to the Gestapo to inform on us) died of a heart attack. I once read that despair can cause a heart to stop, and so I think that my Chaim died of despair. He lived as long as he thought there was some hope. Every day he went to the different consulates to check our position on the visa lists. He had applied early and he thought that surely, somehow, we would manage. All the world would not turn away from the Jews of Poland. Our names were near the head of the list at the Argentine consulate, and there were letters of invitation and affidavits from our aunt Haline. Chaim's sister in Cuba was working to obtain a visa for us. We paid out bribes and lived on hope until this cursed year—the year of closing doors. Argentina, Bolivia, Chile, Paraguay, and Panama—all said, No more Jews. No room in the United States. Do you remember, my brother, that you wrote to me from America, about the beauty of the great Southwest—I wonder, are all those deserts so full that there is no room for a few tent cities of Jewish refugees? Our children are so very small—Sophia's dead babies did not fill even half her bed—they would not take up much room in the vastness of the new world. They would be content to hide in mountain caves.

One morning Chaim read me an item in the newspaper. The British Colonial Office had said that Jews would no longer be admitted to Rhodesia because of that country's "limited capacity." Rhodesia. Shimon went to a medical conference there some years ago. He had done much research in oncology, and he thought that he was drawing close to an important clue in the mystery of cancer—now, of course, we will never know. (I wonder how many discoveries, how many cures, drift heavenward in the smoke of these chimneys. Doctors burn here, and scientists, and researchers. But you do not know yet about the burnings and about the chimneys. Brace yourself, my brother, because I must write to you about the chimneys.) Shimon told us that in Rhodesia, a man could travel for hours without seeing a settlement, a house, another person. The land is empty—only its capacity for Jews is "limited."

Rhodesia had been Chaim's last hope. He had been in correspondence with a cousin there. He carried the newspaper upstairs and stretched out on our bed. An hour later, when I went to him, he was dead. Now I am jealous of that death. He died on a bed, stretched out on blankets, fully clothed. I shall die naked, standing until I fall with other naked women and small girls beside me, strangers to me in life, perhaps, but my sisters in death.

But let me tell you, quickly, more about Yehuda. My

strength fails and I have only a few more sheets of paper.
I bought this paper from a Ukrainian guard. I gave her the
diamond ring that had belonged to Avremel's mother, and
she gave me this pad and pen and a tiny vial of this ink—
the color of the wild orchids that grew in our citrus grove
in Rishon. Avremel will forgive me for bartering his
mother's ring for the life of our grandson. Our Yehuda.

After Shimon and his wife died, a neighbor brought
Yehuda to us. He alone had survived the typhus but he
was terribly weak. Lenka, our Polish serving girl whose
family was in the underground, somehow managed to get
milk and eggs for him and we nursed him back to health.

When Chaim died, Lenka's brother came at night with
his cart and took the body. We did not report his death but
kept his ration card for Yehuda. I could not bury my
husband. I had to save my grandson.

No one knew he was in our house. We hid him from
our neighbors, from the Polish police, from the Germans.
Somehow, Lenka's brother learned that a Palestinian Jew
was gathering together Jewish children from every part of
Poland. He had no visa for them, but he was leading them
across the frontier into Russia and then to the port of
Pahlavia on the Caspian Sea. It was our only hope for
Yehuda. Lenka took him in the night. He could carry
nothing, but we piled sweaters and jackets on him, and
sewed your address into the hem of his coat and put the
wooden gazelle that had belonged to Shimon in the pocket
of his breeches. How could I send that last child of mine
away without a toy to comfort him? Such a sweet child.
Seven years old. His hair as golden as the wheat in the
fields of Rishon during the days of high summer. His eyes
the color of the waters of Jaffa Bay.

"Why are you crying, Grandma?" he asked me.
"We'll be together soon."

"Yes. Soon," I lied.

And I stopped crying and even felt some gladness because he had boots. Not new ones, but still they were
sturdy. Lenka had managed to buy them by selling my
candlesticks. Each Friday, during all these years that I
lived as a Gentile, I crept into the basement as evening fell

and lit those candles. Now my Sabbaths are over, but at least my grandchild will not walk barefoot across the Russian steppes. What strange exchanges we make—a diamond ring buys ink and writing paper, and Sabbath candlesticks buy a child's boots.

Ezra, this Palestinian Jew was called Moshe. That was all Lenka could tell me. But surely you will seek him out, and when you find him he will give you news of our Yehuda.

The day after Yehuda left I received the summons to report to the town square, and from there I and the other unfortunates were taken to this place, this camp, named for our town, for Oswiecem. Will our town be cursed forever because the Germans have called it Auschwitz and built chambers of death? There were lovely parks in our town, a small museum, and on Thursdays the farmers came to sell their produce in our square.

We were told to take only one suitcase, and I had no wish to take more than that. An old woman on her way to die needs very little. And I knew that I would die. You see, I had seen the chimneys and the smoke. The others said that they needed the chimneys for the factories in the camp. They were soldering metal, perhaps, or steaming chemicals. But I knew. The smoke told me. The smoke— that steady gray vapor rising from caldrons of tears, darkened by the calcium of bone, tinged with the aroma of roasting flesh. Yes, that was what we smelled when we passed through those gates and stood obediently on line while the silver-haired doctor with his sharp blue eyes strutted up and down, pointing his baton now to the left and now to the right—now to death and now to life. I was spared that day, I think, because of my age. They were doing medical experiments on the elderly, but now the rumor is that they no longer need us—they have enough human guinea pigs.

As I sniffed that almost forgotten odor of roasting meat, I remembered suddenly my wedding feast when I married Avremel, and how our father sent newly slaughtered lambs to the Arab workers. They roasted the meat over open fires, and Avremel and I, in our marriage bed,

smiled at the fragrance of that slowly cooking meat. Who
would have thought that incinerating human flesh had the
same aroma as that of roasting lamb? So the scent of my
marriage night mingles with odors in this barrack of
death.

Ezra, my brother, this is the second thing I must tell
you. *They are burning Jews in Auschwitz.* They are killing them as I will be killed tomorrow. They take them to
showers where no water issues from the spigots, only
clouds of gas. I shall breathe deeply when my turn comes.
I will hurry death and make certain of it because Clara's
son, who is a *Sonderkommando,* one who pulls the bodies
out of the gas chamber and shoves them into the ovens—
after removing the gold from the teeth, of course—has
told us that not all who are burned are already dead. The
Sonderkommandos have heard small moans from the
ovens. I do not want to be burned while I am still alive.

I charge you with these two tasks, my brother. You
must try to find my grandson, Yehuda. And you must tell
the world that they are burning Jews in Auschwitz.

I send you my love and ask your forgiveness. I was
wrong to think I could escape my destiny. Do not grieve
for my death. I am glad of it.

But take care of my grandson. Yehuda Schoenbaum.
Seven years old. His eyes are the color of the sea.

Ezra's voice grew fainter and fainter as he read until at last it
broke, fragmented into small sobs. His shoulders quaked and
the children paused in their play, bewildered by the fearful
sounds of their father's grief.

"What will you do, Ezra?" Mazal asked quietly.

"I must go to Jerusalem. I will show this letter to Shertok,
to Sir Harold MacMichael. My God, I'll go to London and
show it to Churchill. They are burning Jews in Auschwitz!"
Anger had replaced grief. Rage had suspended sorrow. His
sobs had become a shout. The weakness of grief had passed
and had been replaced with a swiftly formed determination.
The Polish women stared at him in terror, and Hinda Klugstein
clutched the blanket that sheltered her infant daughter's
shadow and whispered soothing words into its empty folds.

"Abba." Elana rose and moved toward her father. "Please. To you all this is new, but Sara's letter will be only one more confirmation of what they already know or have long suspected. Nadav told me that last week there was a cablegram from Geneva. Gerhart Riegner, the representative of the World Jewish Congress, confirmed that the Nazis are practicing what they call the 'final solution.' They are gassing Jews and burning the corpses. Thomas Mann has made broadcasts on the BBC reporting the mass killings. At first he was not believed, but now there is Riegner's memo and other letters and communications like Aunt Sara's confirming it. Last week, for instance, a man in Hadera received a post card from his father in Dachau. 'Uncle Mavet visits us daily,' the post card read. *Mavet*—death.''

"How many are they killing?" Mazal asked. Her own voice startled her. How did one ask such a question in an ordinary conversational tone? "Thousands? Hundreds of thousands?" Perhaps the finality of a single number would make her understand the inexplicable.

"How many Jews are there in Eastern Europe?" Elana replied.

The Polish women stood at the window. The hour of sunset had come, and the purple-and-gold radiance of approaching twilight veiled the fields and orchards of Sadot Shalom. Hinda Klugstein held the pink blanket toward the wondrous light, and for a brief and terrible moment it seemed to Elana that the poor bunting breathed, moved, and that the shadow of the child, smashed to death on the cobblestones of Auschwitz, writhed within its flannel folds and looked at the rainbowed prisms tossed by the dying sun.

"The boy, Yehuda. We must find him if he is alive. Amos will consult with Hans Beyth, with Henrietta Szold. Oh, Sara, my sister. Oh, my God." He sat down and rested his head against his folded arms. The sleeves of his pale blue work shirt turned dark beneath the steady flow of tears he could not suppress.

But an hour later he was dressed and ready for the journey to Jerusalem. The younger children embraced him timidly. Their father's savage sorrow frightened them, and they writhed within the strange urgency of his embrace.

"Do you want to play soldier, Nachum?" Tamar asked in a conciliatory tone, as the car pulled away.

"No. Let's pick some flowers and give them to the company." Rivka decided.

The children dashed across the meadow toward the thicket of wild grassland where daffodils shone golden in the last strips of daylight and daisies littered the greenery with snow-colored petals shaped like small teardrops.

Chapter 23

IN THE JERUSALEM office of the Jewish Agency Executive, Moshe Shertok sat behind his bare wooden desk, sipped tea from a glass, and slowly turned the pages of Sara's letter.

"She was a remarkable woman, your sister, to write such a letter only hours before her death. My clerk will make a copy of this letter."

"And then?" Ezra asked impatiently. This Shertok had always loved talk and argument. He confused the weaving of sentences, the compiling of files, with decision and action. It was too bad that Ezra's old friend Ben Gurion was not in Jerusalem, but he had been sent to London to muster support for a Jewish Legion.

"And then we will do what Jews have always done," Shertok said with a bitter half-smile. "We will wait."

"There is no time to wait," Ezra replied. "You've read my sister's letter. And my son-in-law, Nadav Langerfeld, tells me you have other evidence. What are you waiting for?"

Moshe Shertok stroked his pomaded mustache and loudly sucked the cube of sugar that remained undissolved at the bottom of his glass.

"What can we do, my friend? Do we have an air force? Can we bomb the railroad tracks that lead to the death camps? Can we organize an overthrow of the Gestapo? Can we smuggle arms to the prisoners or arrange their escape? We can only argue for all these things with the great powers. One day we will control our own destiny. One day there will be a Jewish air force to rescue Jews in trouble anywhere in the world. But for now we can only try to smuggle those who do manage to escape into Palestine. And with the British blockade, that grows more difficult every day.''

"I know. My daughter and son-in-law at Hanita work with Aliyah Beth—the illegal immigration. They have told us.''

"Ah, yes, your son-in-law. Daniel Alkilai, the violinist. I heard him play at a kibbutz recital last week. A remarkable young man. A hero among our young.''

"Yes," Ezra said and helped himself to a cigarette from the olivewood box on Shertok's desk.

Daniel's escape from the Arabs who had captured him three years before, on the eve of his marriage, had traveled the length and breadth of Palestine. Schoolchildren knew the story of the young violinist who had been taken prisoner after suffering a severe shoulder wound. His Arab captors had nursed him back to health, hoping that he would be a source of information for them. He had recovered and fashioned a reed pipe for himself, which he played in his compound prison cell between interrogations.

The commandant of the prison compound had an ailing wife, and Daniel's music soothed her. Daniel was provided with a recorder and then a flute. He played more intricate melodies. The sick woman had difficulty sleeping, but when the Jewish prisoner played for her she relaxed and closed her eyes. Sometimes, after such a rest, she felt strong enough to accept the thrust of her husband's love.

Daniel asked for a violin, and the commandant sent to Beirut and obtained an instrument for him. He played for her beneath her window and in her garden and as she fed the rainbow colored birds that hung in straw cages on her balcony.

"Your gift comes from Allah," she told him. "Allah sent you to me so that you might cure me. *Insh'Allah.*''

He smiled and played a new piece for her, but when she asked him to play the next movement, he shook his head and promised to play it the next day. Like Scheherazade, he schemed for his survival, teasing with music rather than with tale. But he knew that his days were numbered. The commandant was growing impatient, even jealous. The Arab guards looked at him angrily. Daniel had been able to tell them nothing about the strength and strategy of the Haganah, and they believed at last that he knew nothing. There was talk of moving the camp northward. The two other prisoners, a Circassian and a Palestinian Arab suspected of collaborating with the Jews, were taken out one morning, and Daniel heard the rapid repeat of gunfire and knew that they had been executed.

"*Sh'ma Yisrael,*" he said, "Hear, O Israel, the Lord is God, the Lord is one."

He thought of Balfouria, standing before him in her white wedding dress, the asphodel wreathing her dark hair. And he played his violin so that its mournful tones wept prayerfully on the mountain breezes. They did not come for him, and the day passed and evening came, and she sent again for him. That night she told him her name and allowed her veil to drop. Her features were delicate, carved out of the topaz contours of her face.

"Rabi. I am called Rabi," she said.

"Rabi," he repeated, and he considered that knowledge his death warrant. She had allowed him to look at her and told him her name because he was destined to die. He played a fragment of the Berlioz Requiem for her and was startled to see that tears glazed her almond-shaped eyes.

That night as he lay on his pallet, he heard the scraping of a key in the padlock and he jerked awake, determined to fight. He would not go quiescently to his death. He would be like the men of Balfouria's family.

"Shh." Her whisper brushed in silken sound across the darkness. She wore a long black abayah. He followed her, walking barefoot across the compound where the guards slept at their posts. She led him out through a concealed door.

"To the south," she said, pointing. "And to the east. Palestine."

He had not paused to thank her but had run then, stumbling over vines and roots, circling through windbreaks and crawling desperately through the underbrush, never knowing if he was headed in the right direction. When the sun rose he became desperate. They would see him and pursue him, capture and kill him. And he did not want to die.

"*Sh'ma Yisrael.* . . . Balfouria."

Prayer and memory spurred him. He ran, stuffing berries into his mouth, eating leaves and spitting them out because they were so bitter. And at last, after hours and hours, he had fallen on the ground in exhaustion and thought himself dreaming (or perhaps already dead) when he awakened with Balfouria's lips upon his cheek.

They were married two weeks later, and a poet in Tel Aviv wrote a ballad about their love, about Daniel's escape and Balfouria's fidelity, which was sung throughout the country. The younger Maimon children added rude verses to the song which angered Ezra but did not disturb Balfouria and Daniel. They were together at last in Hanita.

Moshe Shertok stared at Daniel Alkilai's father-in-law and shook his head ruefully. There would be no romantic escape for the Jews of Europe, no nocturnal flights across field and meadow. He had lived for weeks with the terrible knowledge that had brought Ezra Maimon to Jerusalem. "They are burning Jews at Auschwitz," the woman called Sara had written, her script a spidery scrawl across the cheap frayed paper. And they were burning Jews at Matthausen, at Dachau, at Bergen Belsen. The certainty of it was reinforced daily by letters like the one Ezra Maimon had brought him, and yet the British continued to enforce the White Paper, which all but invalidated the Balfour Declaration. It was ludicrous. The British now advocated the organization of a Palestinian state within ten years, and in the interim a quota of ten thousand Jewish immigrants per year for the next five years, plus another twenty-five thousand refugees, would be admitted. After these seventy-five thousand were granted entry, there would be no further Jewish immigration without Arab acquiescence, and the sale of land to Jews was prohibited. All over the world doors were being closed to the Jews, but the harshest slam came from the British at the gateway to Palestine.

"What can we do?" Ezra Maimon asked harshly.

Shertok shrugged. "Fight the White Paper."

"That's an answer?"

There was not a Jew in the country who did not actively fight the White Paper. Balfouria and Daniel gleefully told the story of the refugees they had brought to the shore of Ashkelon. It had been a sunny beach day, and the refugees had been instructed to mingle with the sunbathers. When the British arrived in search of the "illegals," every man and woman on the Ashkelon beach claimed to be a new arrival. Small sunburned boys and girls speaking perfect Hebrew had dashed after the British police shouting, "Arrest me, arrest me. I am an illegal immigrant."

But not all the stories of the clandestine ships had happy endings. Many sank at sea. The *Sandu*. The *Assioni*. The *Astir*. The *Liesel*. All rusted, unseaworthy vessels, crammed with tender cargo—with frightened men, women, and children, fleeing Hitler's hatred and turned away from the shores of Palestine by the British, Hitler's enemy. An unprecedented historic irony, Ezra thought, and he concentrated on the abstract because he could not bear to visualize the reality—the drowning, bewildered children gasping for air, the anguished screaming of their parents, the relentless crashing waves.

Joshua, David Maimon's eldest son, had been in Haifa harbor when the *Patria* sank. He had told Ezra of the explosion in the engine room that turned the waters of the bay into a phosphorescent caldron. Parents tossed their children overboard, into the glowing waters, aiming them like rockets at the rescue ships that bobbed frantically about. Joshua and other Palestinian Jews had dived again and again, pulling survivors out of the swirling waters, but in the end two hundred and forty refugees were drowned.

"I was baptized that day," Joshua said afterward. "I found a new faith."

"Terrorism is not new and it is not a faith," Ezra had replied.

But Joshua had not abandoned his credo. He was a leader of Lechi, the organization led by the wild-eyed poet Avraham Stern, who also called himself "Meir"—the Enlightener. Meir's followers had declared every British installation and soldier a target of terror and retribution.

Ezra disagreed with Joshua, but today, in Shertok's office, he understood the depth of the younger man's desperation. *They were burning Jews in Auschwitz.* They had burned his sister—Sara, his beautiful, gentle sister. The scent of death and ashes clung to the crimson scarf she had sent him, the scarf which Mazal had folded carefully and placed in a cupboard.

"We will give it to Yehuda, her grandson, one day," she had said.

She, at least, did not doubt that they would find Sara's grandson, and he loved her for her faith, her hope.

"Moshe," Ezra said now, "surely we can do more than accumulate files. I would be glad to offer my services if they could be useful."

"I hesitated to ask," Moshe Shertok replied, "because years ago you said that you were done with politics."

"That was then. Now it is different." There was no time for the luxury of personal choice while they were burning Jews at Auschwitz. "I will do anything that could help."

"Your name came up at an Agency Executive meeting last week. You knew Churchill years ago. As prime minister he has so many demands on his time that our people have difficulty getting appointments. But we think that he would find time for his old friend Ezra Maimon. Your sister's letter, the Riegner cable, some of our other material would have more immediacy if you brought them to him. Winston Churchill is the most powerful man in the free world. If he undertook the cause of the Jews, he could turn British policy around. And then we would ask you to accompany Chaim Weizmann from England to the United States. Rabbi Stephen Wise is working to arrange an appointment with President Roosevelt. Afterward we would want you to address a special Zionist conference we are convening at the Biltmore Hotel in New York. You would be a most effective speaker. You are the brother of a victim—the father of young people involved in rescue operations. . . ." Shertok held his hands out, palms upward, in the ancient gesture of the Jew, seeking to pluck answers and solutions from the air. Ezra noticed that his nails were exquisitely shaped and lightly coated with a transparent polish.

"Yes," Ezra said, and there was a glimmer of hope in his voice. "If Roosevelt knew what was happening at Auschwitz—"

"He knows," Shertok said dryly. "Henry Morganthau, his own treasury secretary, brought the Riegner memo to him weeks ago. But still, if you confronted him with your personal story, it might have some special impact—who knows?"

"I will go—of course I will go," Ezra said.

He was not a young man. Arthritis knotted his fingers, and although he still worked a full day in his orchards, an almost palpable fatigue weighted his chest, and he awakened often in the night, stiff-limbed and gasping. Long ago, he had thought his days of travel and supplication over. He had been a young man when he first traveled to England and America to muster men and money for the Jewish Brigade in World War I. But now he would go again, an aged man with a new plea. This time he would not wear a uniform nor would he make speeches in union halls and on boardwalks. This time he would wear the double-breasted suit of the politician and walk the thickly carpeted corridors of power, leaving his calling card at the prime minister's residence in London, at the president's office in Washington. "I would seek audience with your excellency on urgent business. My kinfolk are being burned in the caldrons of Europe. They are being drowned in the waters of the Mediterranean."

"Good," Shertok said. "And we will make inquiries about the boy, Yehuda. Your son Amos will consult with Hans Beyth, with Henrietta Szold. If the boy is alive, they will find him. Good luck, Ezra Maimon." He held his hand out and Ezra grasped it. He felt the fragile bones beneath the finger flesh. Shertok had lost a great deal of weight. Perhaps, like Ezra, he had lost his interest in food. Ezra had eaten little since the arrival of the Polish women at Sadot Shalom. With each bit of food he lifted to his mouth he tasted cinders and ashes.

It rained the morning Ezra and Mazal sailed for Constantinople. They stood aboard the *Caledonia,* a small British frigate, and waved at their family assembled on the dock to see them off. The gray drizzle, so unusual for Palestine in February, formed a watery curtain, and they huddled beneath a black umbrella and watched their children's and grandchildren's faces as the ship plowed toward the open sea.

Elana and Nadav stood side by side without touching (how seldom they touched, Mazal thought, and pressed her own body closer to Ezra's rigid torso, felt his arm come gently down upon her shoulder), but Elana held small Shlomo by the hand, and Nadav lifted Aliza so that they could see the dark-haired child's brilliant smile. Always, Aliza was as joyous as her name. Mazal was pleased that Elana and her children would stay at Sadot Shalom while she and Ezra were in America. Nadav would come from Tel Aviv on weekends, and Ruth and Amos would visit, although Amos could not leave Jerusalem easily.

"I must be immediately available," he had said obliquely, and Ezra refrained from asking questions. It was best to have as little information as possible. What was not known could not be divulged.

"Wherever you go, ask about the boy, Yehuda," Ezra told his son, and Amos nodded.

"We know who Moshe is. A Youth Aliyah emissary sent to Poland. We have no news of him—which is in its way encouraging."

Amos did not add that his carefully chosen words meant only that they had not yet received news of Moshe's failure and the children's deaths. His fingers curled about a decoded telegram informing the Youth Aliyah Jerusalem office that the frozen corpses of a dozen unidentified children had been found in a Carpathian mountain pass. Was one of the nameless children his aunt's grandson, Yehuda? he wondered and held his own son more tightly.

Balfouria and Daniel stood with arms linked as though they could not bear even the briefest separation. Often in the night, in their Hanita cabin, Balfouria would awaken suddenly and light the small brass lamp beside their bed. In the dim golden glow, she would study Daniel's face, committing it to memory as though fearful that he might disappear again, leaving her without even the solace of his remembered visage.

"What did Daniel look like?" her American cousin, Sammy Wade, had asked her, and she had struggled to remember and hesitantly described the swath of dark hair that swept across Daniel's forehead as he played.

The lamp had been a wedding gift from Sammy, brought to her from Cairo by an Australian soldier on leave in Palestine. Sammy had found the lamp in the Cairene brass bazaar and thought she and her new husband might like it. He had little news except that it was rumored that his unit would join a larger contingent somewhere in North Africa. He would write when he had more exact information. But months had passed, and she had not heard again from Sammy Wade.

Amnon, holding Rivka's hand, stood beside Tamar and

Nachum. The twins were taller than their older brother, who was lithe and small-boned, like the men in Mazal's family. Yet Amnon, at sixteen, was the youngest officer in the Haganah. "A born soldier," Moshe Dayan had told them. "He has the instinct, the organization, the courage."

Mazal listened bitterly to Dayan's praise. She had not thought to raise her first-born son for war. She thrilled with pride, not at his military prowess, but at the intricate stories he wrote. His skillful, clever drawings caused her eyes to fill inexplicably with tears. Only that week the literary supplement of *HaAretz* had published Amnon's long poem, "Sadot Shalom at Twilight." Ezra had read it aloud to the family, and they had marveled at the images Amnon had beaded together on the fragile thread of his poem to describe his father's fields at that magic hour when they were drenched with the luminous rays of the dying sun. When would she see their fields again at such an hour? Mazal wondered, and she turned her head so that Ezra would not see her face.

But he was not deceived. The shoreline of Palestine slowly vanished, and he held his wife close.

"Don't be sad," he said softly. "We will return, and at least our children are safe. We know where they are."

He was thinking, she knew, of the boy Yehuda wandering across the mountains of eastern Europe, of his son Sammy somewhere on a mysterious North African battlefield, of all the nameless and faceless children of their people lost on a continent transformed into a madhouse, illuminated by ghostly fires that emitted evil and mysterious odors.

"Yes. We know where they are. At least they are safe in Palestine."

It was an odd historic irony, he thought then, that Palestine, which so many European Jews had feared because of its mountain fastnesses, its barren deserts, had become a last refuge, a desperate haven. His grandmother, his mother's mother, had whispered fearfully about the Arabs, only to be killed by a Ukranian peasant. His sister, Sara, had fled the land, but she had died praying that her only surviving grandson would find deliverance there.

"Come," he said softly to Mazal, and led her, as though she

were a child, to the narrow white-walled cabin that smelled of damp wool and lemon-scented disinfectant.

The brief crossing was uneasy and difficult. Ezra and Mazal slept in their life jackets, and like the crew and the other passengers, they patrolled the deck with their binoculars trained on the open sea. German submarines and U-boats had been spotted in these waters, and British ships had suffered casualties as they followed the routes that carried them from Palestine to Cyprus and Rhodes, Greece and Turkey. Mazal trembled at each shadow that drifted across the foam-topped waves. She lay awake in her narrow bunk, listening to unfamiliar sounds and clutching her thin coverlet as though it might provide ballast against the tossing of the sea. She was a daughter of the desert. What was she doing, sailing these war-bound waters? She was ashamed then, and reminded herself that she was there because she could not bear to be separated from Ezra, because it was easier to face the harshness of reality than the shadows of fearful supposition.

She and Ezra stood together on the deck as the *Caledonia* glided through the Dardanelles. The narrow waterway was wine-colored that day, and Ezra's face paled as he looked up at the mountains of Gallipoli, stripped now of all their verdure and starkly outlined against the pale wintry sky. Did anyone remember now that only a war ago men had fought over these barren mountain passes and their blood had flowed in tender scarlet ribbons, across craggy rocks and untilled fields? Perhaps not. Gallipoli was no longer important. New wars brought new battlefields. In this war, other mountains and meadowlands would become the burial grounds of other mother's sons. A new generation of orphans would stare at framed photographs of uniformed men, seeking out the fathers they would never know. Would the cycle ever end? Ezra wondered. Would there ever be an end to war? Would his grandchildren one day walk his fields secure in the peace for which he had named his farm?

High above the place they had called Anzac Cove, a shepherd stood and watched the *Caledonia* sail through the once-embittered straits. Ezra saw him kneel and gather a black kid in his arms before he walked slowly on, a snow-colored sheep and a speckled goat trailing behind him.

The bright Mediterranean sunlight deceived them the morning they sailed into the harbor at Constantinople. The day was bitterly cold, and the wind that lashed their faces was fierce with the icy tenacity of a lingering winter. Mischievous islands of foam flecked the Sea of Marmora and danced their way across to the Bay of the Bosporus.

Mazal leaned over the rail and gasped at the beauty of the harbor of the Golden Horn, sorry now that she did not have her sketch book and her drawing pencils. She listened intently as Ezra pointed out the Dome of Saint Sophia, the Column of Constantine, the Mosque of Suleiman.

"And what's that?" she asked, pointing to the golden dome that she would later learn was the Seraglio, but Ezra did not reply. He stared instead at the milling crowds on the dock and at a neighboring pier, where a battered rusting ship listed restlessly in its narrow cove. It swayed as it lay at anchor, heaving about like an enormous wounded fish, writhing in discomfort. Mazal read the name that streaked its hull in peeling faded letters. It was the *S.S. Struma* out of the Rumanian port of Constanta.

"The *Struma*. I thought surely everything would be settled now," Ezra muttered.

"I remember the name," Mazal said. "You spoke with Nadav and Amos about it."

"Yes. The *Struma*'s been a problem for months now. Since the day the Jewish Agency leased it, in fact. We knew when we contracted to lease it that the damn tub probably wasn't seaworthy, but we had no choice. We had seven hundred and sixty-nine Balkan Jews, and we had to get them out somehow. The *Struma* was a cattle boat. It had leaks in its hull. Out-of-date steering equipment with space for about two hundred passengers. But it was all that was available. It floated, and we took it and crammed it with our Balkans—seventy kids among them, I think. The agency thought that with a little luck it might run the British blockade. But it was disabled and had to come into harbor at Constantinople. Our old friends, the Turks, wouldn't let the refugees land. We asked the British to bring the refugees into Palestine, and we even promised that we wouldn't oppose their deportation to Mauritius. I thought everything was resolved. Shertok told me that they were optimistic about negotiations, and Amos was promised visas for the children. He met with MacMichael—had his word on it. But damn it, the *Struma* is still here, and there are children on board.''

He stared through his binoculars, shook his head wearily, and passed the glasses to Mazal, who stared through them and gasped, seizing the ship's rail for balance.

Her sights had found a young woman whose wearied, unseeing dark eyes stared back at her. The woman was skeletally thin, and a small boy dressed in layers of clothing held her hand. In her other arm she cradled a small girl dressed only in a pale pink nightgown. Briefly, almost angrily, Mazal wondered why the sleeping child was so lightly clothed against the winter morning. Why hadn't the children's mother distributed the clothing more equitably? And then she realized that the small girl so tenderly held did not stir and that her limbs were not limp and malleable in sleep; they were rigid, frozen into lifelessness. She thought then of Hinda Klugstein, who had whispered to the tattered empty blanket that contained her daughter's shadow. Was the world haunted now by Jewish women who pressed dead children to their breasts and sang lullabies to bits of faded flannel?

Swiftly she turned her head, moved the binoculars from place to place on the cluttered deck. She held in focus two old men who sat on upturned crates, their heads bent over a tractate of the Talmud. Their feet were wrapped in rags, and their bodies quivered with the cold as they studied. They did not look up at the tall young woman who wheeled an aluminum tureen and spooned liquid into tin cups that were stretched toward her.

Mazal saw a crew member lowering buckets on a reel over the side of the ship. She gagged and choked down the sour phlegm of her own vomit. The *Struma*'s plumbing had failed midway through the Black Sea, and the excrement of its passengers now had to be rowed ashore to the specially constructed latrines at the mouth of the harbor.

At last, she trained her glasses on a group of children playing a circle game. They held hands and moved slowly through the ancient ritual of childhood, shielding themselves from the incomprehensible adult world in an enchanted circle. "All fall down,'' they would sing and sink to the ground, pleased that for once *they* made the rules and *they* predicted the ending. One small girl wore a bright blue sweater. Rivka had a sweater that almost matched it. She had worn it on the journey to Haifa Harbor. Mazal lowered the binoculars. Her tears obscured the sights, and briefly, terribly, she saw her youngest daughter's face float across the oil-scarred waters.

"Let's hope it's not a repeat of the *Salvador*," Ezra muttered.

The *Salvador*, too, had been an unseaworthy ship that had sailed to the Bosporus from Bulgaria. Its passengers had also been forbidden to land in Turkey. Finally, despite its disability, it had set sail for Palestine but was wrecked in a storm. More than half of the refugees were drowned, and the Turks sent fifty-nine of the survivors back to Bulgaria. The British allowed the remaining seventy to enter Palestine. Perhaps seventy was a talismanic figure for the English, Mazal thought bitterly. They had, after all, agreed to allow the seventy children aboard the *Struma* to enter Palestine.

"Can you find out? At least about the children?" she asked Ezra.

"Yes. I'll go ashore. I know our Jewish Agency official here. Surely, something can be done."

Already he was formulating his telegraphic appeal to the high commissioner's office in Jerusalem, composing a cable to Churchill, wondering if there was some way the *Struma* passengers could be dispersed among the Jews of Turkey. He lifted his binoculars again, and they focused on a thin blond boy who leaned wistfully against a railing. Could the boy be Yehuda? he wondered, and cursed himself for a fool. Thousands of fair-haired Jewish boys were wandering the cities of Europe, haunting its forests, sailing its seas on coffin ships. He could not will each such child to be his sister's grandson, the lone survivor of his European family. *Yehuda may be dead*, he reminded himself sternly, yet he repeated the boy's name aloud. Yehuda—named for the first Maimon.

At last they received permission to disembark, and on the dock he recognized a tall, bespectacled man, a Jewish Agency official who worked with Nadav.

"Hanoch!" he called, and the man turned.

Ezra saw the lines of fatigue etched in his face. Hanoch was a young man, a contemporary of Nadav's, but he walked with the stoop of the aged, and his face was frozen in the mask of disbelief peculiar to the newly bereaved.

"What's happened, Hanoch?" Ezra asked, seizing the younger man by the shoulders.

"Ezra Maimon, you will not believe this. We are waiting for the British to issue transit visas so that our people can disembark and board other ships. We have given up bargaining for entry to Palestine. The adults will be sent to Mauritius, but we have seventy children between the ages of eleven and sixteen, and the British have promised visas for them. The papers are in transit, expected today or tomorrow, but the Turks want the *Struma* to leave now. They will not allow us to wait for the documents. Ezra, that ship is not seaworthy. They are sending our people to their deaths, may they rot in hell!" His voice rose now in a shrill wail, and the folders he held in his hands trembled. Sheets of paper fluttered to the ground, but he made no move to retrieve them. The bureaucratic battle was over.

"Hanoch. Calm yourself. No one would send that ship out into open sea," Ezra said, but even as he spoke he heard Mazal gasp.

The *Struma* was moving. Agonized shrieks rose from the deck. One woman fell across the railing and would have jumped, but a ship's officer pulled her back. A small pink form was hurled through the air—a minuscule human torpedo.

"Save my child," a woman shouted in anguished Yiddish.

The body hit the water, floated briefly on the oil-stained debris of the bay, and slowly sank. Mazal turned away. She had recognized the child as the lifeless form so gently cradled by its mother that morning.

Two small tugs, snorting angry black clouds of smoke from their dirt-encrusted stacks, continued to tow the *Struma* out to sea. Suddenly the cries from the deck were stilled and a mighty chorus broke forth. The voices of men, women, and children met in a single prayer. "*Sh'ma Yisrael*, the Lord is God, the Lord is one."

"*Sh'ma Yisrael,*" Mazal whispered as a small Turkish craft dropped a net over the spot where the body of the child had disappeared.

Hypnotized by terror, they stood on the dock and watched as the clumsy vessel was towed out of the territorial waters of Turkey. The small tugs disengaged themselves and sailed back to the harbor, plunging through thickets of foam. Abandoned, the *Struma* rested briefly on the strangely tranquil sea. It listed slightly—a weary, graceless leviathan changing position. With increased tempo, it lurched from side to side, foundering now in the deep waters of the open sea. Still they watched, paralyzed by fear and uncertainty. At last it shuddered mightily and emitted a thunderous blast. The water about it blazed red as fire spurted from the ship's body. The rusting hulk hemorrhaged in a rush of flame; gusts of smoke spewed out, blackening the sky. Again an explosion rocketed the ship, and now they saw dark shadows in the molten waters—frantic, anguished swimmers. Mazal covered her ears against the shrieks of terror until her throat felt strained and sore, and she realized that she herself was screaming and Ezra was clutching her, tears streaking his face.

And then, too late, the rescue craft were launched, and Mazal and Ezra watched helplessly as they arrived back in the harbor with their deadly cargo of the drowned. Mounds of bodies stretched on lengths of tarpaulin. Nets, laden with corpses, were lowered on the rotting wooden piers. A child's shoe, scuffed at the toes, skittered across the dock, and Ezra plucked a water-logged, black-bound volume of the Talmud from between the corpses of two old men. The rags in which their feet had been wrapped had unraveled, and the exposed flesh of their bare soles glowed wet and pink in the wintry sunlight.

Chapter 24

EZRA SAT IN Winston Churchill's wide-windowed office on Downing Street, his feet plunged deep into the sculptured carpet which Clementine Churchill had sent down from Chartwell, and told the story of the sinking of the *Struma*. He related it in a monotone because he feared that if he altered the cadence of his voice, he might lose control of it, and he did not want to weep before this assemblage of men—Winston Churchill (grown so rotund now, his jowls drooping to his childlike chin, the ever-present cigar clenched between his teeth), Lord Lloyd, the colonial secretary, Anthony Eden of the War Office, and the Archbishop of Canterbury. Chaim Weizmann sat beside him, his hands clasped as though in prayer.

"There was only one survivor, Mr. Prime Minister. Four hundred and twenty-eight men, two hundred and sixty-nine women, and seventy children died," Ezra said tonelessly. It was simpler to quote statistics than to remember the bloated bodies of the children, the lengths of glistening seaweed caught in the hair of young women, the entangled bodies of a man and his small son, buried together at last because the burial society could not bear to separate them.

He paused, and the silver-haired archbishop buried his face in his hands.

"We must offer asylum to these Jews in Britain," the old man said, and he crossed himself and turned to the window. An early spring was stealing into London, and tiny white buds glinted on the branches of the chestnut trees. The constancy of nature, at least, defied the vagaries of men and their wars.

"A noble sentiment, Archbishop," Anthony Eden said

dryly. "But even if such a proposal were at all practical, what safety could we offer the Jews? We are evacuating our own children from London. Indeed, the Queen thinks of sending Princess Elizabeth and Princess Margaret Rose to Balmoral for the duration. My nephews are in Dorset, and we think of sending them to Canada." He smiled politely, as though satisfied that he had solved the problem.

Chaim Weizmann cleared his throat and allowed his hands to rest on his knees.

"It would not be necessary to bring our people to Britain," he said, "although, of course, we appreciate the generosity of the Archbishop's sentiments. All we ask is that your government relax the immigration quota and allow refugee Jews to enter Palestine."

"Impossible," Lord Lloyd said sharply. "We have difficulty enough with the Arabs. God knows what would happen if we allowed open Jewish immigration."

"I find it interesting that you are so deeply concerned with the sensibilities of the Arabs," Ezra replied. "The last radio broadcast I listened to before leaving Palestine was a plea from the mufti of Jerusalem urging the Arabs of Palestine to ally themselves with the Germans. Is this the man you would count as your ally—a man whom you fear to offend?" He coughed and continued. "Rashid Ali in Iraq is openly for the Nazis. In Egypt good King Farouk speaks of his good friend Adolf Hitler. And I know, Mr. Prime Minister, that I do not have to remind you of the incident involving General Aziz Ali al-Misri."

Churchill grimaced and bit down on his cigar. Damn good thing the RAF had intercepted the former inspector general of the Egyptian army before he could reveal British troop strength to the Nazis. Almost as bad as that bastard Farouk, whose ambassador in Teheran had offered to come to the aid of Axis troops at the decisive moment. It was a good thing Maimon didn't know about that.

"And of course," Ezra continued, "all of us here know that Vichy Syria airlifted weapons to Rommel."

He ignored Weizmann's disapproving frown. The truth had to be told. Once before he had sat with Weizmann in this beautifully paneled room, sipped lukewarm tea from Stafford-

shire cups, studied the portraits of Gladstone and Disraeli, and
pleaded the Jewish cause. That had been in 1929, after the
Hebron riots, when Beatrice Webb had stared at him with those
pale, cold eyes and wondered at his concern. As many Jews as
had been killed in Palestine were killed daily in traffic accidents in Britain, she had said in her impeccably accented
voice. But now the ante had risen. The British could not claim
daily vehicular accidents in the tens of thousands, but the latest
estimates from Riegner in Switzerland indicated that at least
that many Jews were being rounded up for the death camps
each day. In 1929 he had maintained an artificial calm, but
now the time for restraint had passed.

"The entire world is at war, Mr. Maimon. It is not only the
Jews who are threatened," Anthony Eden said coldly. "The
daily death count of British troops is not inconsiderable."

"I am aware of that," Chaim Weizmann said, and there was
a new hardness in his voice. "It may interest you to know that
my son, Michael, who served in the Royal Air Force, was
killed in action."

"You have our deepest sympathy, Dr. Weizmann," Winston Churchill said. He lit a fresh cigar as though the cloud of
smoke might absorb the sorrow and tension, the pleas and
recriminations that filled the room. He liked Maimon. He liked
Weizmann. But Eden and Lloyd knew what they were talking
about. Goddamn it, there was no easy answer. They needed the
bloody Arabs for their damn oil, and everyone in the room
knew it. The mufti meant nothing, but the other Arabs would
erupt if they allowed open Jewish immigration. And they
couldn't risk that—not with Montgomery jammed up in North
Africa. He'd have a time chasing Rommel without fuel.

"I wish that Britain could absorb these refugees," he said,
lowering his wonderfully reverberant voice to a tone of implied
wistfulness.

"My people would rather take their chances against random
bombs in London than walk into gas chambers in Poland,"
Ezra countered, but he knew that the battle was lost. There
would be neither asylum in England nor open immigration to
Palestine. But he had another cause to press, and he leaned
forward now in his deep leather chair and stared hard at the
Prime Minister.

"We hope, then, that at the very least, you will consider the formation of a Jewish Legion. The Jews of Palestine have been asking for their own military unit since the onset of the war."

"You have the Palestine Buffs," Lord Lloyd said. "And the Pioneers."

Ezra laughed harshly.

"With all due respect, Lord Lloyd, as colonial secretary, you know that the Palestine Buffs were designed to be joint companies of Palestinian Jews and Arabs. But the Arabs, whom you so fear to offend, have been unable to fill their quota of recruits, and the Buffs are largely Jewish companies without the dignity of fighting under a Jewish flag. As for the Pioneers—that's a fancy enough title for men assigned to digging ditches and maintaining latrines. That is the job you offered the Jews of Palestine, and because we would do anything to fight Hitler, we accepted your offer, just as we shepherded your mules in the first war. And so you have crack intelligence officers and sharpshooters shoveling manure when they could be more effectively used. Pardon my language, gentlemen, but I am not a diplomat. I am only a farmer and the father of sons who are prepared to fight for their people."

"We ask only for the elementary right of the Jew to go down fighting," Chaim Weizmann said softly. At least his poor young Michael had been granted that. He had not died in a gas chamber but in a Royal Air Force Spitfire.

"I agree," Winston Churchill said in that decisive tone which Ezra remembered from across the vanished years. "A Jewish Legion will be formed. And I will talk to Roosevelt about some solution for the refugees. As for Palestine—well, we can't reverse our policy now, but remember this, my old friend Maimon. I carved Palestine up once—I can unite it or carve it up a second time. Who knows?" He laughed and rose slowly to his feet. Winston Churchill had always been a clumsy man, but now his increasing girth impeded every movement.

Chaim Weizmann and Ezra Maimon read the note of dismissal in his voice. Gravely they shook hands with him and with the other cabinet ministers and the Archbishop. As they left the room, they heard the clergyman again plead for the admission of at least some Jews.

"Think of the security," they heard Anthony Eden say just before the heavy oak doors closed behind them. "Hitler would be sure to sneak agents in among them."

Ezra smiled bitterly.

"Well, at least we have the Legion. And Churchill's promise," Weizmann said sadly.

"We have the Legion," Ezra retorted, "and that is all we have."

Churchill's promises were as ephemeral as the wisps of smoke that drifted from the glowing tip of his cigar.

That night, he rested his head on Mazal's breast and allowed her long fingers to stroke the delayed tears from his eyes. They had knocked on their last door in England. The British would not help them. Jews would continue to burn in Auschwitz; Jews would continue to drown in the peaceful waters of Europe's seas. Not since the distant night of Nechama's death had he felt himself so alone and so hopeless. He had done all that he could do, but in the end there was nothing to be done.

In Washington, the graceful cherry trees which the government of Japan had given to the American capital in happier times were aglow with tender blossoms of pink and white. Young men in uniforms walked beneath them with girls who seemed oddly vulnerable in their light spring dresses and spike-heeled pumps. Once, Ezra remembered, he, too, had worn a uniform and strolled with Sonia beneath these same trees. They had stolen a secret Washington weekend from the urgent demands of another war.

He wondered suddenly where Sammy was. Balfouria had not mentioned him in her last letter. Somewhere with Montgomery's forces, he supposed, or perhaps with Wingate, in Burma. He hoped that the latter was true. If a son of his had to fight a war, he would want Orde Wingate to be his commander. How natural it was, he realized, for him to think of Sammy Wade as his son. He had felt an instant connection to him, and he was strangely content now to be a secret father to the fair-haired young man born of a distant love.

"What are you thinking about, Ezra?" Mazal asked. "Aren't these flowers marvelous? Tomorrow, while you are at the White House, I will come here and draw them."

"I was thinking just that—that they are beautiful. I wonder if they would grow in Palestine."

And then, because he had lied, and because he felt ashamed to be thinking about Sonia and their son while he walked beside Mazal, he drew her toward him and kissed her. She had tucked a pink-hearted flower behind her ear, and its fragrance teased his memory.

He went with Chaim Weizmann the next day to meet with President Roosevelt. It was a ten-minute appointment, they were told severely by the tall, middle-aged woman who stared at them accusingly from across her impeccably ordered desk.

"Secretary Morganthau insisted that the President see you, but he is a very busy man." She pointed to the crowded pages of the leatherbound appointment book where each minute of the chief executive's day was accounted for in graceful inked notation. "He has matters of great importance on his mind," she added.

"And we have matters of great importance to discuss with him," Ezra said quietly. It was, after all, a matter of great importance that they were burning Jews at Auschwitz, that Jews were drowning in the oil-stained waters of the Black Sea, in the viridian depths of the Mediterranean. Surely, Franklin Roosevelt would hear him out in sympathy. He knew that the American Jews adored this aristocratic Democrat who had restored economic stability to their country. Robert Szold had told him that they hung the president's photograph in their living rooms and that they joked about the three great *velt*s— *dies velt, yenner velt,* and *Roosevelt.* Surely, such a man would intervene on behalf of the Jews of Europe, if he had all the facts.

Ezra was optimistic then, as he sat beside Chaim Weizmann on the small green velvet couch and awaited the presidential summons. He noticed that the beige rug beneath his feet was not as thick as the sculptured carpet in Churchill's office and mocked himself for the observation. That was what happened when a farmer from the Galilee was sent to haunt the corridors of power.

But his optimisim faded when he overheard the conversation of two men who paused briefly at the secretary's desk and glanced curiously at himself and Weizmann. The elderly

chemist did not notice them. He was lost in one of the reveries
that came upon him increasingly since he had learned of his
son's death. Ezra wished suddenly that David Ben Gurion had
accompanied him. Ben Gurion had the force and vigor of a
man who has not yet lost a son to war. Sorrow, not passion,
motivated the elderly Weizmann, who did not even glance up
at the two Americans.

Ezra recognized the men from their newspaper photographs—Cordell Hull, the secretary of state, and Joseph Kennedy, ambassador to the Court of Saint James. The previous
day's edition of the *Washington Post* had carried a picture of
the ambassador embracing his young son, John Kennedy, who
was being shipped to the South Pacific. Mazal had looked at
the photograph and commented on the younger son's broad
smile, emanating vigorous optimism.

"He looks," she had said, "as though he believes that he
will live forever," and he had covered her hand with his own,
knowing that she was thinking of their own sons, of Amnon
who wrote too often of the rending beauty of dying light, of
Amos who commuted between the death lands of Europe and
the troubled shores of his own country.

Ezra watched the two men glance at himself and Weizmann;
they held a brief conversation with the president's secretary,
who showed them the appointment book. They muttered over
the entry and he heard fragments of their exchange. Like small
pellets, isolated bits of their conversation stung him.

"Jews," he heard, and "Palestine." "Refugees," he
heard, and "Jewish pressure—the damn *Times*," and then, in
a tone so loud that he was certain he had been meant to hear the
exchange, he heard the portly Kennedy say, "We ought not to
overestimate the Jewish influence in this country. I said as
much to Lord Halifax when I was in London. Why does the
president allow the Jews to waste his time?"

They left the antechamber then, walking briskly past the two
Jewish emissaries as though they were invisible, as though by
ignoring them they could wish them into nonexistence.

Ezra sighed heavily, and the secretary looked up from her
papers and smiled sympathetically at him.

"The president will not be long now," she said. Her voice

was gentle, soothing, reminiscent of the cadence used by hospital nurses in the dark hours of the night.

A light flashed on her desk, and she lifted her phone.

"Yes, Mr. President. At once." She smiled self-consciously as she spoke and smoothed her hair, as though the caller could see her.

"Mr. Roosevelt will see you in the Green Room," she said.

They followed the marine guard through wide, thickly carpeted corridors; the wainscoted walls were hung with portraits of presidents in ruffled shirts and somber suits, of first ladies with jewels at their throats and flowers in their hair. The faces comforted Ezra. These men and women had believed in human dignity, in the sanctity of human life, and Franklin Roosevelt was heir to their tradition.

They paused before an oak door guarded by a Marine who saluted their escort, knocked lightly at the door, opened it to allow them to enter, and then closed it very softly behind them. It was said that the American president suffered from migraines and could not tolerate unnecessary noise.

Franklin Roosevelt smiled thinly at them from a small white sofa beside a fireplace. The May afternoon was warm but a fire had been lit, and the low-burning logs spat out small blue flames. Sunlight flooded the room, yet the crystal candelabrum was aglow and the small brass lamp at the president's side splayed incandescent rays across his long-fingered, oddly hirsute hands.

Ezra recognized, then, that no room would ever be warm enough or light enough for Franklin Roosevelt. He was a man who had felt the chill of death, struggled through the dark shadows of pain, and always, now, he would strive for brightness, yearn for heat.

"Gentlemen, please be seated."

He motioned them toward the white sofa that matched his own on the opposite side of the fireplace. A welcoming smile played across his face, and Ezra noted the president's chiseled aristocratic features, his fine-textured silver hair, thinning now about his temples and artfully combed to conceal the pinkness of his scalp, peppered with the dark liver blotches of age. He wore a well-tailored pin-striped suit, a gleaming white shirt, and a narrow green tie that exactly matched the watered-silk walls of the room. If they had met in the Blue Room, would the president's tie have been blue? Ezra wondered and chastised himself for allowing the thought. Franklin Roosevelt's legs were encased in trousers so impeccably pressed, and his black shoes were so highly polished that it almost seemed he chose to remain seated, not because he was crippled but because he did not want his perfect toilette to suffer any disarray.

"I like this room," he said in the cultivated, sonorous voice that Ezra had listened to so often in radio broadcasts. He motioned to the portrait of George Washington that hung above the fireplace and to the gilt-framed Remington and Turnbull landscapes, illuminated by narrow fluorescent bands of light. "But of course you did not come here to discuss the decor of the White House with me."

"I wish we could have that luxury," Chaim Weizmann said. "But the times do not allow it."

"These are difficult times for my country," Roosevelt said, and the famous voice was tinged with sadness. Only a few days had passed since Japan's invasion of the Solomon Islands. The American casualty count in the South Pacific was mounting. Only that morning, on a quiet Georgetown Street, Ezra had seen a young woman hang a white satin banner embossed with a single gold star in her window.

"These are difficult times for my people as well," Ezra said, and he was startled suddenly by the difference between his choice of words and the president's. If his people only *had* a country. . . . Briefly, he envied Roosevelt, whose nation was at war but who, after all, had a nation.

"Mr. President," he continued, "it is my sad duty to tell you that Jews are being systematically destroyed in Europe. There are death camps in operation. Jews are being killed in gas chambers, their bodies are being burned in crematoria. My own sister . . ." His words came quickly. He had only ten minutes in which to plead his case. His fingers fumbled with the lock of his portfolio, where Sara's frayed letter nestled amid memorandums and statistics, but Roosevelt raised a hand to stop him.

"I know, my friend, I know. My own secretary of the treasury, Henry Morganthau, and my old friend Rabbi Stephen

Wise have made me aware of these barbarous undertakings. I share your sorrow."

"But Mr. President, surely something can be done. Surely you can arrange for additional refugees to be admitted to the United States, or perhaps other havens can be found," Chaim Weizmann said. "Could you not influence Great Britain to rescind the White Paper and allow free immigration into Palestine?"

The elderly scientist spoke very softly. There was no hope in his plea. He was exhausted. He had spent a lifetime seeking audiences with the powerful and those who one day might be powerful. His words had echoed through auditoriums in London and Ottawa. He had sought help in Zurich and in Lisbon. Everywhere, he had encountered the same reply. Always he was offered sympathy. Never was he offered assistance. No one wanted the Jews to burn, but no one would help them escape the encroaching holocaust.

"We have a firm immigration policy in this country," Roosevelt explained with exquisite patience. "If we made an exception for one ethnic group, we would be confronted with demands for other exceptions. And we have, naturally, made certain allowances. After the conference at Evian we did allow the Austrian quota to be added to the German quota, and we did say that special preference would be given to political refugees."

"We understand that, Mr. President," Ezra said dryly. "But even that combined quota allowed for the absorption of some twenty-seven thousand Jews, and there are millions to be saved. If the British would allow free immigration into Palestine, the Jews of Europe would have a chance. Mr. President, I was in Constantinople when the *Struma* exploded and sank—"

"Please!" Roosevelt's voice was clipped now. Impatience had taken sway over courtesy. "I know about the *Struma*. And you know of the ships my nation lost at Pearl Harbor. We each have our national tragedies. Let us not compete. I am certain that when you saw Mr. Churchill in London you raised the question of free immigration into Palestine, and he surely told you that the entire free world cannot be endangered to save Jewish lives. Without Arab cooperation our access to oil on the North African front may be destroyed. And if there is free

immigration into Palestine, there will be no Arab cooperation.
But do not think that Mr. Churchill and I are unconcerned
about the Jews. The British contemplate opening British
Guiana to Jewish refugees. And after the war we will all recon-
sider the Palestine problem. Jewish interests will not be disregarded. I have promised Dr. Wise as much.''

''British Guiana is tropical, all but inaccessible, and totally
uncultivated,'' Chaim Weizmann said in the toneless voice of
defeat. ''This is the opinion of your own commission, Mr.
President. It is, at best, a sop to the British conscience. It is not
an alternative for endangered Jews. Still, we thank you for
your concern.''

''No!''

Anger hardened Ezra's voice now, and he felt his heart beat
faster; new energy rippled through him, as though he might
subdue this elegant American president through sheer force. He
rose from his seat and strode about the room, checking his
wrist watch against the intricately fashioned gold clock that
stood on the fireplace, passing his hand across the straight-
backed chair covered in green-and-ivory brocade that stood
beside a polished rosewood table. Even the use of this pleasant
room, furnished in the style of a more peaceful century, had
been meant to deceive and disarm them. The fires of Auschwitz were obscured by the gently burning logs; the patina of
civilization defied tales of naked women herded into metal
enclosures to inhale their deaths.

''Your concern is not enough,'' he said, wheeling about to
face Franklin Roosevelt, who carefully, deliberately inserted a
cigarette into an ebony holder. ''We require your action. If you
will not admit our refugees, you must save the lives of those to
whom you refuse refuge.''

''And how can I do that?'' the president asked. He lit his
cigarette, blew a perfect smoke ring, and smiled modestly, like
a magician seeking the approval of small children at a birthday
celebration. The gesture was meant to seduce them. Were they
not, after all, like-minded civilized men who enjoyed slight
tricks and appreciated the beauty of a lovely room, the warmth
of a blazing fire?

''You can promise that when the United States has air supe-
riority in Europe, you will bomb the rail lines that lead to the

death camps. If the Jews cannot be transported to extermination centers, then they will not be exterminated. As simple as that, Mr. President."

Ezra leaned back and lit one of the cigars which Winston Churchill had pressed upon him as he left Downing Street, and he, too, blew a small but perfect cylinder of smoke.

"When and *if* we have aerial supremacy over eastern Europe," the president corrected him. "We may be years away from that, Mr. Maimon. This will be a long war. And even if we do achieve that kind of air power, I cannot tell you that it will be feasible to bomb the railway lines. Indeed, such an action may be against the best interests of the interned Jews. At least that is the opinion of the assistant secretary of the army, John McCloy. He recently sent me a memo about it, and although it is privileged information, I will share it with you, Mr. Maimon, so that you will know that we in America are not indifferent to the situation of the Jews."

FOR YOUR EYES ONLY was slashed across the tissue-thin memorandum which Franklin Roosevelt passed to Ezra. Odd that he should have had it so close at hand, Ezra thought, and he sat down at the round table to read it. "Such an operation," McCloy had written, "could be executed only by diversion of considerable air support. . . . There has been considerable opinion to the effect that such an effort, even if practicable, might provoke more vindictive action by the Germans."

"Forgive me, Mr. President," Ezra said very softly, "but I cannot imagine what action could be more vindictive than Auschwitz."

"You are very subjective, Mr. Maimon," the president said.

"My only sister was burned at Auschwitz. Perhaps that engenders subjectivity," Ezra replied.

There was a tentative knock, and the oak door swung open. They had exceeded their ten minutes, and the Marine escort looked at them reprovingly.

"We thank you for your time. Good afternoon, Mr. President," Chaim Weizmann said politely.

"Good afternoon, gentlemen."

Franklin Roosevelt avoided Ezra's eyes, but once again his strong voice was cordial, vaguely tinged with relief. The difficult interview was over. He straightened the neat crease in his trousers, and for the first time Ezra noticed the steel half-crutches neatly tucked between the sofa and table. As the door closed behind them, they heard the telephone ring, harshly, insistently.

"We tried," Weizmann said wearily.

"And now we know," Ezra said. "Help will not come from others. Jews must help themselves." His words echoed in the cavernous White House corridor.

Mazal waited for them outside the iron gates that surrounded the presidential mansion. She had plaited a sprig of cherry blossoms through her neatly coiled chignon. The delicate florets matched the wave of white that rippled through her dark hair. He held her close and inhaled the wistful fragrance of the flowers whose brief season of bloom was so swiftly ending.

A blue-and-white Jewish flag draped the platform of the makeshift dais that had been erected in the Grand Ballroom of the Biltmore Hotel in New York. Ezra noticed that its edges were frayed and a yellowing stain crept across it. The imperfections irritated and saddened him. Impatiently, he read the mimeographed program and counted seven misspellings. He looked up and studied the men and women who milled about the large room, conferring earnestly in a dozen languages, rushing toward each other and forming small groups which melded briefly and then dispersed. A feverish unrest haunted the room, and the delegates whirled about in a frenzied search for information, for reassurance, for verbal panaceas against encroaching despair. It was rumored that Hitler had cancer, that the United States was developing an awesome secret weapon. There were shortages in Berlin. The British were reconsidering the White Paper. Morale was high in Berlin. The British had strengthened the sea blockade. Rumors collided with each other, and men who had not seen each other for years embraced with mysterious passion, shared fragments of knowledge.

Relatives and friends of the absent and missing prowled the colonnaded ballroom, ferreting out bits of information, scavenging scraps of hope. Had there been any news of the Greenbaums of Lodz? When had Spiegel, the Zionist leader of

Munich, last been heard from? What of Menachem Begin's family?

Mazal stood beneath a crystal chandelier with David Ben Gurion, who maintained daily phone contact with Jerusalem. She was desperate for news. Five months had passed since the *Caledonia* had sailed from Haifa, the longest period of time Mazal had ever been away from her family. The Maimon children wrote regularly, but the British censored all letters and their references were often oblique.

Balfouria wrote that she and Daniel were spending a great deal of time at the shore, and Ezra understood that they had increased their efforts on behalf of the illegal immigrants. She added that Liesel was no longer at Hanita but was visiting relatives in her native city; Ezra surmised then that Liesel had returned to Europe as part of an intelligence operation. Amnon was traveling about the country a great deal. Amnon, then, was organizing Haganah units in various settlements. They read each letter carefully, as though decoding secret messages, and scoured the newspapers for references to Palestine. Spring had moved across their land, they knew, and they stared out the window of their Biltmore Hotel room at the briskly moving traffic on Forty-third Street and imagined the quiet fields of their farm, shimmering in moist verdancy.

Ezra watched Emanuel Neumann, Robert Szold, Israel Goldstein, and Louis Leventhal enter together. Once Louis Brandeis would have been in their midst, dominating the conversation, but Brandeis was six months dead, and his disciple, Felix Frankfurter, now sat on the Supreme Court and was no longer actively involved in Zionist affairs.

The huge room filled rapidly now. The Mizrachi delegation, the men wearing traditional skullcaps and the women with their kerchiefed heads—reminding him with sudden, unexpected poignance of Nechama and her family—took their seats beside the avowedly atheistic delegates of the Shomer HaTzair. There was no time now for ideological differences. *They were burning Jews in Auschwitz.* Rose Halprin of Hadassah wore one of her famous hats, a peacock-blue straw boater, but her eyes were red with sleeplessness. She had spent hours with the executive committee planning the agenda.

Youth group representatives, carrying the banners of their

movements, filed in, strangely shy and vulnerable in their blue-
and-white uniforms. They averted their eyes as the older delegates greeted each other in German and Russian, Yiddish and
Hungarian, speaking in the hushed voices of mourners at a
funeral, recalling the names of the absent and the missing. Men
and women clutched each other's hands, studied each other's
faces, as they separated to find their assigned seats. It was
almost as though this convocation of the Biltmore Emergency
Committee might be their last encounter.

Ezra sat back in his seat as Rabbi Stephen Wise gaveled the
conference to order and called on Chaim Weizmann. Stooped
with grief and disappointment, the elderly chemist, who had
for decades implored them to follow Britain's lead, admitted at
last that the British had betrayed them. The White Paper violated the Mandate, nullified the Balfour Declaration. Because
of it thousands of Jewish lives had been lost. No. Not thousands. Tens of thousands.

Tens of thousands. The audience sighed, stirred in restless
sorrow, and Ezra restrained himself from compounding their
grief with the truth. Not tens of thousands but hundreds of
thousands. Perhaps a million. Perhaps two million. Would the
bodies of two million Jewish children, piled one upon the
other, reach to the heavens? He struggled to recall the parable
about the laughter of children shattering celestial silence.
There was a traffic jam on Forty-third Street. They listened to
Chaim Weizmann and heard the bleating of automobile horns,
the shriek of an angry siren.

And then it was his turn to speak. Stephen Wise's introduction spared no detail. The audience would be addressed by a
pioneer, a hero of the Jewish Brigade, a veteran settler of the
Galilee whose family was involved in rescue and defense . . .
Ezra Maimon of Sadot Shalom, Palestine.

He frowned at their applause, commanded their silence with
his own, and began to speak, pleased that the secrets of oratory
had not deserted him after all these years.

"It was your voice I fell in love with first," Sonia had told
him so many years ago. But he had been a young man then,
and his voice had had the strength and intensity of youth. He
was an old man now, white-haired and white-bearded, and

sadness muted his words. Yet his audience listened, and he felt that sadness move from his heart to theirs.

He told them of the sinking of the *Struma*, of the woman who had come to his home in the Galilee carrying the shadow of her baby wrapped in a pale pink blanket. His voice trembled then, and to gain control he gripped the podium and stared for a moment into the audience. His eyes rested on a diminutive woman, her hair peppered with gray, her body slight within a dark suit and a white blouse. A schoolgirl's blouse, really. His heart beat faster and his throat constricted. Sonia, he thought. That is Sonia I am looking at. Sonia, who had fallen in love with the sound of his voice. A quarter of a century had passed since he had last seen her, but he knew that he was not mistaken. His hands trembled and the sheets of white paper fluttered dangerously, but he grasped control and continued.

"I have met with the prime minister of England, and he will not help our people. I have met with the president of the United States, and he will not help our people. No one will help the Jews. Therefore, we must help ourselves. We must redeem our children, where we can, and we must control our own destiny. We will no longer plead for a homeland. We will demand a sovereign state. We call for a Jewish nation—an independent state for the remnant that will survive!"

His speech did not evoke applause. The six hundred Zionist leaders acknowledged his truth with the weight of their silence. Someone rose and drew open the heavy red velvet drapes as though the introduction of sunlight into the Biltmore Ballroom would somehow dilute the darkness of Ezra's words. Mazal sat near the window, and a narrow golden ray splayed her cheek and turned her golden skin the color of amber. But Sonia's upturned face, even in the sunlight, retained the milky luminescence of a seed pearl. Ezra glanced down from his wife to the woman he had loved so many years before and felt a strange commingling of memory and desire.

Now David Ben Gurion ascended to the podium. His bristly hair stood out in tufts about his head, and he thrust his powerful chest forward as he spoke. Chaim Weizmann had spoken with sorrow and Ezra with solemnity, but Ben Gurion's voice burned with passion and rang with conviction. He pounded his fists as he spoke, and Ezra studied his old friend's hands, callused by hard labor on the highways and farms of Palestine, the skin broken by scythe and rifle. He thought of the American president's long, restless fingers, of Winston Churchill's plump, pudgy palms. Ben Gurion's voice rose to a powerful tremolo.

"A Jewish Palestine will arise. It will redeem forever our sufferings. . . . It will be the pride of every Jew and command the respect of every people on earth. . . ."

Now the audience applauded wildly and shouted affirmation. The delegates stood and embraced each other. There was a spontaneous burst of song from the young leaders of the Shomer HaTzair, and the older delegates joined them. They linked their arms and their voices rose as they sang the Jewish national anthem, "HaTikvah."

"We have not yet abandoned the hope of two thousand years
To be a free nation in our own land . . ."

They had been abandoned, but they had remained constant. Their people had been enslaved, but they would struggle toward freedom. They had been patient, but they could be patient no longer.

They remained standing, some still humming softly as Abba Hillel Silver shouted a valedictory. There could be only one solution to the Jewish problem—a Jewish state in Palestine!

Then the conference was over, and they dispersed in small groups that milled about the ballroom and overflowed into the lobby of the Biltmore Hotel. Mazal was swept up by a group of women who were curious about Chemed Handicrafts. Ezra heard her discuss sheltered workshops and cottage industries, and moved through the crowd, certain that Sonia was still in the room, that she would not have left without seeing him. Once before, so many years ago, he had searched for her through a crowded room. Distractedly, he signed the petitions that were thrust at him—a protest to Roosevelt about rigidity in immigration, a call for the formation of a refugee relief organization, an open letter to Winston Churchill calling for an end to the White Paper. He signed although he knew that the petitions would end up in wastepaper baskets or, at best, neatly filed in a bureaucrat's drawer. Petitions were the last resort of the impotent, but soon his people would no longer be impotent. Today, in this New York hotel, they had declared themselves ready for statehood. No longer would they beseech and plead. Now they would act and demand.

"Will you sign this one as well, Ezra?"

Twenty-five years had passed, but her voice was as soft as ever he had remembered it, as he had heard it in dream and reverie, before the battles in Gaza, in the hills of Judea and at the gateway to Damascus.

"Sonia!"

His hands formed an envelope for hers. He had forgotten how small they were, how delicate her fingers, how soft her flesh. He kissed her on the cheek. She wore the same scent. The vaguest violet. Absurdly, he remembered the shape of her atomizer and its whispered hiss as she sprayed it behind her ears each morning. But when he stepped back and looked at her, he saw that she was greatly changed. Lines of loss and sorrow had etched their way about her eyes and mouth, and sadness dimmed her eyes.

"What is it a petition for?" he asked, because he could not ask what her life had been like during all the long years since he had left her. Questions seared his mind, thrust their way forward. Had she been happy with his cousin Alex? Had the clinic, after all, brought her fulfillment, satisfaction? Had Sammy brought her joy, nourished pride? (Surely, that answer, at least, he knew. He had spent enough time with Sammy to know that he would be a source of joy, of pride.) Had she missed him? Had she regretted her decision? Unaskable questions. A diamond wedding band sparkled on her thin finger. He saw Mazal across the room, walking arm in arm with Ben Gurion. Would he, could he, introduce Sonia to his wife?

"It's a petition for the formation of a Jewish Legion," she replied. "It's ironic, isn't it, that I should be asking you to sign such a petition?" She smiled ruefully.

He had been a Jewish Legionnaire when they met, sent to the United States on Legion business. He had worn his uniform at their leavetaking. Glinting menorahs had sparkled in his epaulets and lightly grazed her cheeks when he held her close. His embrace had been a final plea which she had rejected with

tears that formed searing rivulets on his palms when he stroked
her cheeks. She had wept then because he was leaving her and
she would not go with him. There was no need for him to go to
war, to fight for Palestine. She could not comprehend why he
would not stay in America with her, how he could choose Zion
over all that they shared. She had not known, then, that she
was pregnant with their son, and later she had decided that if
she had known, she would not have told him. When he left her
he had forfeited all claims on her life and on their love.

"What made you change your mind?" he asked.

"I changed my mind because of Sammy," she said softly.

"Why because of Sammy?" His mouth was dry and he saw,
in his mind's eye, the golden-haired young man whose sea-
green eyes matched his own. He heard Sammy's laughter and
remembered how he had romped about the Sadot Shalom farmhouse carrying the younger children on his back. Gentle
Sammy, so tall and brave—his secret son, his disinherited
heir.

"He wrote that he had visited you in Palestine, that he had a
wonderful time with your family."

"Yes. We enjoyed him very much." He would say as little
as possible. They had kept silence these many years and built
their separate lives. He would not threaten their fragile peace
with revelations best left unrevealed.

"Sammy is dead." Her voice was toneless. "You could not
have known. He was killed in the battle at Gazala."

"How?"

She shrugged.

"We don't know. We received a telegram and then, later, a
letter from General Ritchie, telling us that Sammy had died a
hero."

She fumbled in her purse and held the letter out to him. The
British War Office used heavy cream-colored paper embossed
with the royal seal. He read it and returned it to her, grateful
that this, at least, she had shared with him.

"Do they send letters like that to everyone?" she asked.
"Do they, Ezra?"

He took her hand and led her to a seat. He felt weak, like a
man who has sustained a sudden and unexpected blow. He
could not remain standing. They sat, facing each other, on the

small velvet chairs of the Biltmore Hotel Grand Ballroom, and she did not pull her hand away. They were locked together in shared grief, and all that they had feared to say to each other was revealed in their silence.

"No," he said at last. "They only write such letters when a man dies bravely." *As our son died,* he thought and knew that she heard the words unspoken. His shoulders sagged. He felt weighted by the compounded losses he had suffered in this war. Sammy, Sara, her children and grandchildren. All except Yehuda. *Let Yehuda be alive,* he prayed. *Let the life of the wandering European child somehow counterpoise the death of the brave American youth.*

"Yes, he died bravely." Sonia's voice trembled now. "But he died wearing a uniform that was not his own. He died for the English, but he went to war for the Jews. You were right, Ezra, and I was wrong. We must have a Jewish state, a Jewish army."

"We will," he said.

"But too late for us. Too late for Sammy." Her tears flowed freely now, and spots of color blazed on her pale cheeks. He had forgotten how her blood rose when she wept.

"Sonia." His heart turned with pity for this woman he had once loved, this gray-haired, bereaved mother of the son he had so briefly known and whom he could not openly mourn. "I'm so sorry."

"I know."

He stood then, bent, and kissed her forehead. She remained seated and did not look up as he crossed the ballroom, moving rapidly to the high-arched doorway where Mazal waited for him, draped in a capelet of sunlight, her golden eyes soft with comprehension.

PART FIVE

Rescue and Escape

1944

Chapter 25

THE ENGINE OF the aircraft emitted a soothing hum, and Liesel Konigsfeld was reminded of the muted buzzing of the bees in the apiary of her parents' summer home in the Frisian Islands. She shifted her weight uncomfortably on the hard metal bench, toyed with the straps of her parachute, and tried to remember the name of the rare species of bees her father had cultivated. But she could recall only the pale, sweet honey they yielded, which her father had removed ceremoniously from the hive and spread across their brown breakfast bread. It had tasted of clover and lily and of the sun's own warmth. What happened to bees in wartime? Liesel wondered as the British transport plane soared above the billowing white clouds of the Mediterranean sky. Did they fashion their hives in the skeletal wastes of woodland battlefields and buzz futilely about meadows flooded crimson with blood, searching for flowers unspoiled by death? They were sensitive creatures, her father had said. She wondered now if the scent of death soured their honey.

Amos would know, she thought. Amos Maimon knew everything. She touched his shoulder lightly and saw that he was sleeping. He was, she knew, an expert sleeper. He had taught himself to snatch any opportunity for rest; he slept standing up or sitting down, and on even the briefest of journeys, he closed his eyes and allowed a heaviness to drift over his body, substituting Lethean lethargy for actual repose.

"A wartime trick, I suppose," he had told her, laughing apologetically. "I expect to put it to good use when the war is over. When I lead seminars at the Hebrew University, my students will never know that I am actually sleeping on my feet as they debate.''

He held his radio kit tightly now, as he slept, and Liesel gently loosened his grasp. The metal handle left an imprint on his palm and weighted his arm. There would be time enough for him to pick it up before they jumped. She also loosened the top button of his tunic. The bars of a brigadier glinted on Amos's epaulets, and she had sewn the stripes of a junior-grade lieutenant onto her own field jacket. The uniforms were essential to their plan. If they were captured, they were to represent themselves as Palestinian members of the British Air Force.

''And will anyone believe us?'' Enzo Sereni, the unofficial leader of the Jewish parachutists, had asked a British officer during a training session. Handsome, dark-haired Enzo was the oldest of the volunteers whom the British were training in Egypt. He was a founding member of Kibbutz Givat Brenner, and his father had been personal physician to the king of Italy. (''Too bad he wasn't personal physician to Mussolini,'' Enzo had said laughingly. ''One hypodermic needle would have accomplished more than all our parachutes and codes.'')

''Probably not,'' the British officer had replied coldly. ''But please bear in mind that you volunteered for this mission. If you feel it is too dangerous, you are free to resign.'' He turned back to his charts and maps and continued the briefing. He had little patience with these Jewish Palestinians who never polished their boots and belt buckles or wore their caps at the proper angle. They ignored rank, called each other by their first names, and laughed at the most inappropriate times. They would never make proper soldiers. Still, one had to admire their pluck. They were willing to parachute into Nazi-occupied Europe—into Rumania, Hungary, Bulgaria, Italy, Slovakia, Yugoslavia, and even Russia. And all of them knew the fate of Jews who fell into the hands of the Nazis. Of course, most of them were trained intelligence agents, but there were others, like Amos Maimon and Liesel Konigsfeld, who had volunteered to organize some sort of children's rescue operation.

''I didn't volunteer,'' Liesel had thought then. ''I just said yes to Amos because I would always say yes to Amos.''

Across the years she remembered, with detailed accuracy,

the afternoon she had first seen him. She had been a schoolgirl then and had arrived home to find her parents serving the tall Palestinian tea in the conservatory of their home in Donhoffplatz. Her class had been studying the Greek myths, and it seemed to her that the golden-haired man who set down his cup to take her hand in his own had leaped from the pages of her textbook. He was Adonis, descended not from Olympus but from the mountains of Judea, and he spoke to her not of the isle of Delphi or the hill country of Athens but of the fields of the Galilee and the mysterious changing sands of the Negev desert. When he looked at her she turned away, fearful that she might be dangerously seared by the febrility of his sea-green eyes. The next morning she had awakened and found flecks of menstrual blood on her bedsheet. She held it as a special sign that she had become a woman on the night that she first saw Amos Maimon.

He had been a guest in their home for several weeks, and when the archaeological conference that had brought him to Berlin concluded and he left, her life was forever changed: she was a Zionist, and her days now were consumed by meetings of the Blau-Weiss, HeChalutz seminars, and Hebrew lessons.

"You must study agriculture," he had told her, and so she had spent her summers on the Hachshara training farm of the HeChalutz movement, arriving at her parents' island summer home at odd hours for brief stays. She gave up her preparations for matriculation examinations.

"I am a Zionist, and I am going to Palestine," she told her parents.

"Zionism is a dream," her father, the banker, said. "The future is here in Germany. This Hitler will be finished in months, in a year. We will wait him out."

He did not play the radio in his summer house. Here, where bees swarmed and clover grew in sweet, thick patches, the voice of Adolf Hitler was briefly silenced.

Liesel had dreamed of Amos Maimon during those years. In nighttime reverie, she whirled in wild hora dances, and he pulled her into the center of an enchanted circle and held her in a quiet embrace. She sat alone on the shores of the Sea of Galilee while he called to her softly from a drifting boat. The family received occasional letters from him, cards at the Jewish New Year, Passover greetings. Boxes of lemons and oranges arrived from his family's citrus orchards in Rishon LeZion. The Konigsfelds ate the oranges as they listened to Adolf Hitler's messages of hatred on the radio. Her mother sliced the lemons for tea as they listened to the thunderous steps of the Hitler Jugend patrolling the streets of Berlin. Liesel had one last orange in her purse the day she saw her father for the last time, taken prisoner and humiliated in front of the bank his family had founded.

And then, suddenly, Amos Maimon was back in her life, shepherding her to freedom in the train that carried fugitive young Jews across Germany and through the Hagenau Forest. But he was a different Amos—older and sadder and in love with lovely Ruth Niemoeller. Liesel stood outside the Marseilles synagogue as Amos and Ruth were married, and she had been the first to hold their newborn son. The lover of her girlhood fantasies had become the friend and brother of her young womanhood, and his family had become her own.

Liesel had seen his concern over her love affair with Liam Halloran, but she could not give Liam up. The Irish officer had been so wise, so strong, so protective, and she had been so alone in this new land. Liam, too, was a stranger, and like her, he had turned to the Maimon family for warmth, for support, for connection. They had been thrust together on the Sadot Shalom farm. His family was in distant Ireland, and hers was lost forever in a Germany she no longer recognized as the land of her childhood. He was a soldier, often poised on the edge of death, and she was youth and life; she had lost her father, his protection and his wisdom, and the middle-aged Irishman held his strong arms out to her and spoke softly and gently into the night, comforting and cosseting her. But at last, that too had ended. Liam had been wounded at Hanita, and once again she was alone. It had rained lightly the afternoon the British ambulance carried Liam away, just as it had rained lightly in Marseilles on Amos Maimon's wedding day. And this morning too, on the concealed airstrip just outside of Cairo, a sudden shower had startled them just before they boarded the plane.

Lightly falling rain and unshed tears marked the journeys she shared with Amos Maimon, and she strained now to recall

whether or not it had rained the afternoon he had come to
Hanita to ask her to participate in this mission.

"It is very risky," he had said then. "We have a list of
Verschwindungsplätze—hiding places all over eastern Europe
where groups of Jewish children are being concealed. We want
to contact them and get them to the port of Pahlevi on the
Caspian Sea. From there we can transport them to Teheran and
then to Palestine."

"What is our cover?"

"We will be Scandinavian representatives of an international refugee organization. We are both blond, fair-skinned—
quintessential Aryans. Our English and German are excellent,
and with any luck we'll never meet a Swede. But it will be
difficult and dangerous. I'll understand if you cannot accept the
assignment."

"And what has not been difficult and dangerous?" she
asked wearily.

Danger and difficulty haunted her life on Hanita where they
were constantly vigilant against Arab marauders. Loneliness
and longing filled her nights. Alone she watched Balfouria and
Daniel walk the perimeter path, their arms entwined. Alone
she greeted Moshe and Ruth Dayan when they brought their
baby, Yaël, to visit the settlement. By the light of the paraffin
lamp she wrote long letters to Liam, which she did not mail.
On Friday evenings she joined the whirling circle of dancers
who celebrated the day of rest, but no strong arms reached out
to pull her into its center. At least, during this undertaking, for
all its danger, she would not be alone. Amos would be at her
side—Amos, her friend and brother.

"I'll go. Of course, I'll go."

Her family had been abandoned, but she would not abandon
the hidden children.

"Thank you." His voice had been grave. "This mission is
special to our family. We are hoping that one of the children
will be my aunt Sara's grandson, Yehuda Schoenbaum."

"It is possible," she said hesitantly and hoped he did not
discern the doubt in her voice.

The missing child had become at once symbol and legend
for the family. He was a grim legacy of responsibility for Ezra

Maimon. Yehuda was his beloved sister's grandchild; his survival meant affirmation, hope. Painstakingly he made inquiries, interviewed the weary illegal immigrants, urging them to remember a child, a golden-haired boy with eyes the color of the sea. One woman had seen such a boy in the forests that skirted a blazing ghetto.

"What happened to him?" Ezra had pressed the question urgently, and she had stretched her hands upward as though in prayer.

"He flew away," she had said. "Like my own children. Like Peshi and Mendy. God sent angels and they flew away to a place where there were no fires. No bullets."

Her own children had been shot in an action. Her son had died in her arms.

"They flew away," she repeated, and he turned sadly from the madness that glinted in her eyes, but he did not abandon his search. Avidly, he read reports from every agent in Europe. Twice he had hastened to Jerusalem because boys who resembled Yehuda had arrived in Youth Aliyah contingents. Each time he had returned to Sadot Shalom, weighted with new disappointment but never with despair.

But now there had been no word of the child for almost two years. Balfouria had confided to Liesel that she thought the child dead, and Elana, who saw shadows even when the sun blazed the brightest, avoided her father's eyes when he spoke of the boy. Yet Ezra Maimon continued to believe that the child named for his father had survived.

"I would know if he were dead," he insisted to Mazal, who remained silent, never reminding him that he had not known when his own son Sammy Wade had died.

"It would be a miracle if one of the children should be Yehuda," Liesel had told Amos, and then swiftly, deftly, she had put the child out of her mind. She had become quite expert at putting people out of her mind. She seldom thought of her father, of her mother, of Liam Halloran, or even of herself as a young girl, her head awhirl with the glory of Greek mythology. She thought now only of surviving from one day to the next. Somehow, her survival and the survival of others was linked to her presence in this broad-bellied troop transport plane that hummed like a giant malevolent bee as it stole its way across Europe's war-darkened skies.

"Maimon, wake up!" The British navigator stood before them and gently nudged his shoulder.

"What is it?" He was instantly awake, completely aware, a trick of his talent for spontaneous sleep. The transition into wakefulness was barely perceptible.

"There's been a hitch. We've had to switch course. We're not going into Slovakia. The word is that the Germans somehow got wind of this operation and they're waiting for us. They've already picked up one group of Jewish parachutists. It's too dangerous to go any farther west. Within the hour we'll be at the Russian border, and with any luck we'll drop you somewhere between the Black Sea and the Caspian. You have a list of contacts in both places, but we can't set up a rendezvous with partisans. You'll have to make your own contacts. And if we go any farther, we'll be in the Ukraine."

"Not the Ukraine," Amos said grimly. "In the Ukraine they eat Jews for breakfast."

He studied the charts and maps which the navigator stretched out before them.

"Here—not far from Kiev—there's a flat strip of meadowland," Amos said. "I don't want to risk the chutes getting caught up in trees in the forests. When you see the woodlands clear, circle over, give us a countdown and we'll be on our own. Right, Liesel?"

She smiled thinly, startled that her hands and feet were icy-cold yet her body was awash with perspiration; a streak of wetness inched down the leg of her trousers, glued her shirt to her armpits. She was frightened, she realized, and her fear shamed and surprised her. She had, after all, not been frightened when she dashed to freedom through the Forest of Hagenau. She had not been frightened when she fired at marauding Arabs from the perimeter fence of Hanita. She had trained for this mission almost with insouciance, jumping easily and gracefully, welcoming the onslaught of wind that struck her at the open door of the plane, the slow unfurling of the chute, the surrender of her body on the descent.

"I've never seen anything like it," the British training officer had said of her. "The damn girl jumps as though she doesn't realize she could die." His own wife back home in Leeds was afraid to drive a motor car and rode her bicycle only when the roads were clear. Liesel heard him and shrugged. He did not know that she had died the afternoon she saw her father last and that she had died again the day Amos Maimon took a wife and yet again when Liam Halloran had smiled wanly at her from his stretcher.

"I'm going home," he had said softly, and she knew he meant that he would not return. She was alone, adrift in Zion.

Clenching and unclenching her fingers, she fought to control the strange terror she felt now.

"You can call it off," the British navigator said. "Abort the mission. No one could blame you. You can come back to base with us."

"No," Amos said firmly. "But Liesel—if you want to go back . . ."

"No." Warmth stole back into her fingers. She stood and swerved in rhythm to the motion of the plane. "Of course, I'm going with you." She smiled at the navigator. "After all, I've never been to Russia, have you?"

He shrugged. All these damn Jews were crazy.

"All right, then. You've got the drill. Here's a new set of radio frequencies. There are partisans in the area, and our people have told them to listen for you. You've got the incendiary bomb. If the Germans approach you when you land, set it off—throw the radio, maps, lists, everything into it. You've each got another set of false documents. Keep your British uniforms on and maintain that you're Palestinian members of the British Air Force. Understood?"

"Understood," Amos said and smiled. "Here, Liesel, take this." He handed her the small revolver which she recognized at once as the one Balfouria had carried on the ascent to Hanita. Wordlessly, she pocketed it.

"Good luck." The navigator saluted, and Amos and Liesel saluted back. The plane hit an air pocket, and they fell, hands still outstretched, into each other's arms. They laughed, and the navigator held his hand out. Amos shook it.

"Come visit me in Jerusalem when this is over," Amos said.

"I'll do that," the British officer replied, although he knew it was more probable that it would be Amos Maimon's widow he would see and that he would sit across a room from her and tell how brave her husband had been in those last moments before he jumped.

"Crazy bastards. Crazy brave bastards," the navigator muttered to the pilot when he reached the cockpit. His eyes were moist and he wiped them impatiently. The damn war was getting on his nerves, softening him.

Amos and Liesel stood beside the hatch door, watched it slide silently open. The half-light of dawn shone out at them—it was the perfect hour for jumping. The white of their parachutes would be masked by the smoky clouds, their bodies veiled by rising mists. They held on to the sliding rope and braced themselves against the impact of the wind. The plane slowly descended and the count began.

Ten, nine, eight, seven, six . . . ("Amos, are you all right?" "I'm fine. You're a wonderful girl—a brave girl.")

Five. ("Amos, am I pretty?" "You're very pretty, Liesel.")

Four. ("You'll go to see Ruth if I don't come back?")

Three. ("Of course. But you'll come back. We'll both come back.")

Two. ("Of course we will.")

One.

He went first, and she counted the requisite ten seconds and followed him. Now there was no fear, no excitement, only a wondrous calm. She was free, afloat amid sky and cloud, caught between worlds, counting calmly—she had always been a diligent student, following her instructions to the letter, to the number. One hundred ninety-nine. Two hundred. Two hundred and one. Pull the cords. Now the chute opened and she was suspended from the straps, falling steadily, triumphantly, and she saw the giant white flower of Amos's chute burst slowly into blossom.

Airborne, they floated groundward, slowly, slowly, swerving away from leafy treetops, in view now of sere stretches of earth through which blood-colored blossoms thrust their heads. They missed a break of conifers, a scrub of fire-eaten birch. Bushes trailed at their legs. Her body thrust forward; she heard a thud, felt a sudden shock. She was no longer skyborne but had touched earth. The flowering chute withered now, drained of air. She felt her legs, brought her hands up to her breasts. She was whole and alive, grounded somewhere in Russia between the Caspian and Black seas. And only yards from her, Amos, too, had landed and was crawling out of his chute. She hurried to follow his example, loosening her kit bag and dragging the chute behind a gray field boulder. She covered it over with bracken and leaves, intent on concealing it, as she had been taught. Absorbed in her task, she did not hear the crush of twigs or notice the shadow of the tall man who stood suddenly before her, training a pistol on her kneeling form.

"What are you hiding there?" He spoke German, and his voice was harsh and very loud in the stillness of the dawn.

She wheeled about and faced him, reminding herself yet again that she must maintain that she was a British soldier in British uniform, protected by the rules of war. Still, her hands trembled and she clasped them tightly so that he would not discern her fear.

He was a tall man and she saw, with surprise, that he was not in uniform but wore the thick quilted jacket and pantalooned trousers of a farm worker. Yet his German was correct, although oddly accented, and his revolver was standard-issue Mauser. He might be an officer on leave, wearing civilian clothing. He might be a Russian who knew German and had become a confederate of the occupying army. In Lithuania and in the Ukraine, scores of residents had volunteered their services to the Germans. Indeed, Nadav Langerfeld had told them that without the cooperation and acquiescence of the resident population, it would be impossible for the Germans to administer the death camps.

He kept his eyes trained on her, and she realized that he had not yet noticed Amos, who was concealed in a thicket only meters away. And Amos, absorbed in setting up the radio equipment, was unaware of danger. He had to be warned so that he could ignite the incendiary bomb and destroy any incriminating evidence.

She rose slowly, carefully, and he watched her through strangely vacant gray eyes. She noticed that his thick hair was iron-gray and stood about his head in grizzled masses, although his face was unlined and his body had a youthful resilience. His hands were very large, and despite the chill of the spring morning, he wore no gloves. He flexed his leathery fingers with arrogant cruelty, shifting his gun suddenly from one hand to the other, teasing her with the ease of his mastery, his control.

"Well, what do you hide there?" he repeated.

"Are you a military officer?" she asked and noticed the surprise on his face. Her voice had betrayed her. An officer's cap concealed her fair hair, and until she spoke he had not realized that she was a woman.

There was a click as he released the safety catch.

"It is I who ask the questions," he said. "What are you doing here? Are you alone?"

He was impatient now. His eyes shifted from her face, raked the landscape. Amos was too far away to be seen, but the smallest movement might reveal his presence. She had to warn him. Her hand darted into the pocket of her field jacket, her finger's curled about the small revolver. She lunged at her interrogator, her finger straining toward the trigger.

"Tod am Faschismus! Freiheit am Volk!" she shouted. Death to fascism! Freedom to the people! She would die with her convictions on her lips.

And then her body was caught up in the soft quilting of his jacket and her weapon was wrenched from her hand. Metal scraped her cheek, and his fingers clawed her hair, thrust her head back. His body smells assaulted her. She inhaled the commingling of sweat, gunpowder, and tobacco as his arm covered her face, and she bit at his flesh and heard his laughter even as he struggled with her, clamping one hand across her mouth, twisting her wrist with the other until she whimpered with pain, acknowledged defeat. Then he thrust her away, disarmed and helpless. She knelt before him on the ground, waiting for him to kill her with her own gun, but instead he bent, held out a hand to her.

"Tod am Faschismus. Freiheit am Volk," he repeated softly and helped her to her feet. "I am Dmitri of the Red Star Freedom Fighters."

Bewilderment struggled with calm. She waited for her

breath to come more evenly, for her heart to stop pounding in fierce tympany.

"Shalom, Dmitri," she said at last. "If this is the way you treat your friends, then I am glad I am not your enemy."

"I am sorry," he said, and his regretful smile was almost shy. "But I had to be careful."

"Yes, of course."

He helped her then to conceal her chute, and they dashed across the field to Amos.

"Liesel?"

He held his pistol cocked and stood between two slender birches.

"It's all right, Amos," she said. "He is a partisan."

She ran to Amos's side and slid into the comforting circle of his arms, startled by her own tears. He held her close and patted her gently while Dmitri, the Russian, watched them and wondered if they were lovers. Brother and sister, he decided at last. There was no passion in their embrace.

They followed him then into the forest, to a hut concealed among the giant firs whose feathery branches arched skyward. There a half-dozen partisans had gathered. They were gaunt and bearded men who walked softly and spoke in hushed voices. They had been moving furtively across the heartland of Russia since the Nazi invasion.

"We cross the borders into Poland and Slovakia," their leader told Amos. "We have a two-target operation—*relsovya, voina*—we destroy telegraph wires and dynamite railroad tracks."

"And wherever we can, we kill Germans," Dmitri added harshly.

"Exactly where are we now?" Amos asked.

"A few kilometers from Kharkov."

"Kharkov." He repeated the name as though it had a magic incantation. "Kharkov. My father was born in Kharkov. He spent his childhood there."

The tales Ezra had told him of his Russian boyhood whirled through his memory. His father had told him of games played in sunny meadows where scarlet-tinged flowers called the Blood of Russia grew. And today, in the thin light of dawn, Amos had descended onto those same meadows and crushed the bright flowers with his body. Ezra had spoken often of the river near Kharkov where the twins Saul and David had fished when they played truant from the yeshiva. Amos and Liesel had walked along the banks of that river to reach this woodland hut. He had arrived, after a long and hazardous journey, at the exact spot where his family's journey to Zion had begun. It was a good omen, he thought.

"Are there still Jews in Kharkov?" he asked. There were no hiding places for Jewish children in Kharkov on the coded lists he carried.

The partisans looked at one another, and they all stared at Dmitri. Their leader filled a tumbler with whiskey, drank deeply, and then spat on the dirt floor.

"Dmitri will tell you about the Jews of Kharkov," he said. "He was married to a Jewish woman."

Dmitri went to the window and stared out at the barren landscape. Two sea gulls flew in tandem through the cloud-dark skies, calling mournfully to each other.

"They fly to the Sea of Azov," Dmitri said softly. "We went there on our marriage night—to a boarding house where they served fish stew for breakfast. When the Germans came, I wanted my wife to go back there, to hide. But she said there was no need to hide. She was a Russian woman, married to a Russian man. And so the German army came, and then the *Einsatzgruppen*. They rounded up the Jews and they told my wife, the Russian woman, that she, too, was a Jew. There is a lime pit outside of Kharkov. The Jews were herded there. We partisans watched through field glasses. We could do nothing. A dozen of us with hand guns and supplies for Molotov cocktails. Hundreds of them with tanks and automatic weapons. A bad joke that history played on us. And so we watched as the Jews disrobed. My wife wore a blue dress, and she took it off and folded it so neatly. She stood with the others, naked. It was cool, but they did not shiver. I do not remember them shivering. And then the shooting began, and when it was over the lime pit was full of bodies. Small naked children with their arms about their mother's necks. Some still wore their eyeglasses. Naked and dead, but their eyeglasses neatly in place. Of course the Germans took the glasses—those that were rimmed with gold. The *Einsatzgruppen* made the Russians cover the pit with earth and lime. They worked in shifts for two days until not one pink limb, not one baby, could be seen. The German soldiers fought over the Jews' clothing. Especially the women's dresses. They wanted to send the best to Germany, to their wives and mothers. But I watched through the glasses, and I knew where my wife had put her blue dress. I went there in the night and took it. I have it still. I could not save her. How could I save her?''

Dmitri's question was a statement, repeated in the same lilting, singsong voice he had used throughout his narrative, and Amos recognized the cadence. It was a rhythm used by small children to soothe themselves to sleep as they repeated familiar tales, masking horror with melody. ''And then the evil giant ate the beautiful princess,'' his small brothers and sisters had intoned in the darkness of the Sadot Shalom farm-house. . . . ''And then the evil Germans killed my beautiful wife,'' Dmitri had chanted in his own litany against the terror that had drained the color from his hair and left his eyes vacant and staring.

Dmitri's voice drifted into silence, but he did not turn from the window.

''Did any Jews survive?'' Amos asked.

The leader nodded.

''There was one group of Jews in Kharkov that the Germans did not know about because they were strangers in the town and not listed in any synagogue registry or town census. The townspeople themselves knew nothing of them. Only we partisans knew about them, and so they were not rounded up.''

''Who were they?'' Amos asked.

''Polish Jews mostly. Children. They crossed the border at Brest into Pinsk and made their way through the forests. The underground hid them in the caves outside of Zhitomir and Kiev. It was our job to get them to the Sea of Azov and from there to the Black Sea, where a ship was waiting. But when we heard about the *Einsatzgruppen,* we suspended our operation. Instead we hid the children in different places in Kharkov. An empty tannery. The basement of a saloon. Even a brothel. Some of them were lost—rounded up in random raids, betrayed by neighbors. But those children who were captured never revealed that they were part of a larger group. When the

Einsatzgruppen left, and it was safer, we gathered the children together and hid them in one place. Their leader told us that somehow contact would be established with the Jewish underground. And so we have waited, and they are still here in Kharkov."

"It seems that by a combination of accident and miracle, Liesel and I are that contact," Amos said. "Do you know the name of their leader?"

"He is a Palestinian Jew—like yourselves. A strong man named Mendel. In Palestine he lives on a *kolkhoz*."

"A kibbutz," Liesel said. She saw the disappointment flash across Amos's face and touched his arm gently. "Amos, you could not have thought that their leader would be named Moshe. To find Yehuda here would be stretching the long arm of coincidence too far. He will be in another group."

Amos shrugged.

"I am an archaeologist," he said. "We rely on accident, on coincidence, on finding improbable clues in impossible places. And you are right—always there is the next time, the next excavation, the next mission. But for now, we can help these children. Where are they hidden?" he asked the partisan leader, who smiled craftily at him.

"We have found the best hiding place of all. The most obvious. The one place in an occupied town where Germans would never look for Jews. Especially in a town where the *Einsatzgruppen* have already done their filthy work."

"You talk in riddles," Amos said. "I am too tired for riddles."

His own fatigue weighted him down; his eyelids were heavy, his limbs torpid. He yearned to close his eyes and drift into sleep. The pallet of pine branches covered with a coarse blanket in the corner of the hut seemed a heavenly bower to him. Liesel, too, moved slowly, and her cheeks were flushed, as though her own blood raced to defend her against an overwhelming weariness.

"Where are the children?" he asked again, and his words were slurred.

"We have hidden them in the Jews' own place—in the synagogue of Kharkov. Each day the Germans pass it, and they may spit or throw a stone to break yet another window, but they don't go in. After all, it was the first place they looted. They have all the ornaments—the lamp which your people always kept burning over the ark, the velvet coverings, the Torah crowns. They did not find the holy scrolls. The rabbi had buried them in the forest weeks ago, and they did not search for them. Parchment has no value to them, although we have heard that sometimes they have cut the Torah scrolls up and used them to patch their shoes and line their uniforms. Still, they know that the synagogue of Kharkov is emptied and looted, and so that is where we have hidden the children. They are in the dirt basement, beneath the ark.'' The Russian stroked his mustache, pleased at his own cleverness.

"A master stroke," Amos said in congratulation. "How many children are there?"

"Forty."

"Forty," Amos repeated. "An important number."

His grandfather, Reb Shimon of Kharkov, had believed in *gematria*, the mystic theory of the symbolism of numbers, of their magical repetition and confluence. In his own weariness now, the image of ten quadrupled whirled and eddied. The children of Israel had wandered through the desert for forty years; Noah had drifted in his ark for forty days, waiting for the flood waters to recede. Forty children awaited an end to the flood waters of hatred. He and Liesel would bring forty children across treacherous borders into the land of promise. Soon. Soon. When darkness came. Now darkness brought safety in a world where all tradition had been reversed.

He struggled across the room and stretched out on the pallet, tumbling into a sleep so sound that he did not hear the partisans slowly leave the hut, nor was he aware of Liesel, who came to lie beside him, her long hair caping both his shoulders and her own.

"Ruth," he murmured and awakened, startled to find his fingers smoothing Liesel's thick golden hair when he had thought to touch his wife's silken moon-silver locks.

Chapter 26

THE DISTANT CONCERTINA music trickled in musical stream through the nocturnal silence. Liesel recognized the tune—a Bavarian jig to which she had often danced at weddings and during village fests. Even the words drifted back to her: "My Fräulein has lips of strawberry, my maiden has hair of gold." There was a party in the village. A German quartermaster had discovered the hiding place of three kegs of strong vodka. The tavernkeeper had been punished for concealing them by having his tongue and lips brushed with coarse salt, after which he was bound hand and foot and forced to stand on the gleaming wood of his own bar, parched with thirst, while he watched the soldiers drink. Dmitri, who had visited the tavern, reported without sympathy that the man had wept, and when his tears were noticed an SS officer punished him further by spraying the bar with bullets; he was forced to dance about like a clumsy wounded animal constrained by his bonds, blinded by his tears.

"Still, it is good for us," Dmitri had said thoughtfully. "Most of the Germans will be drunk. The brothel is already full and the guards on duty are angry and careless because they are missing all the fun. We must make our move tonight."

Swiftly then, they had made their plans. The mustachioed leader had scoured the village for food and produced hardened lengths of sausage, tiny bitter dried apples, and thick-skinned cucumbers, important because they contained moisture and assuaged thirst. A medical kit was assembled. A precious phial of morphine. A small cache of belladonna. Disinfectant. Their parachutes had been retrieved, and the white nylon was sliced into strips for bandages.

"We can only give you ten cyanide tablets," the leader said regretfully, and Liesel and Amos smiled bitterly at each other. A good host should certainly be able to supply poison for all his guests.

Amos had studied his maps, struggling to commit them to memory. They would make their way along the Donets River, traveling at night. The river would serve as a natural trail. They had only to follow its meanderings and they would not get lost. Its rich banks were responsible for a thick overgrowth which would conceal them and provide natural hiding places in thickets and glades. Partisans along the way would supply them with food wherever possible. Then they would follow the Volga to the Port of Astrakhan on the Caspian Sea.

"And from there?" Dmitri asked.

Amos shook his head.

"Perhaps to Iran. Perhaps to Iraq. We have Haganah contacts in both Teheran and Baghdad. We will have to see."

"Yes. Of course."

The Russians glanced uneasily at each other. The Palestinian Jew, with his maps and his compass, his small radio and his secret lists in code, made it all seem comprehensible and possible. But they were Russians and they knew the forests; the mysterious woodland terrain was dangerous and deceptive even in daylight. Yet these Jews planned to negotiate it in darkness. Animals hovered in hidden warrens, their covens concealed in thickets of vines. Wolves howled ominously as night fell, and their voices ripped through the darkness as they bayed at the moon, which shot long fingers of frail silvery light across the quivering branches. The rivers, too, were treacherous. Pools of quicksand bubbled along the banks of the Volga. Those who drank the brackish water of the Donets fell ill with the river fever that bloated their stomachs and closed their throats. And the forests were the last refuge of criminals who allied themselves to neither the Germans nor the partisans but lived beyond the restraint of all laws.

"Why do you not stay in Russia until the war is over?" Dmitri asked hesitantly. "It cannot be long now." The bulletins from the various battlefronts cheered the partisans, gave them reason to hope. The Germans had recaptured Kharkov, but Marshal Paulus's Sixth German Army, one hundred thousand strong, had surrendered at Stalingrad. And the United

States had begun an offensive in Tunisia. It was rumored that within the year Allied forces would cross the channel and launch a second front. The Jews had waited so long to find these children—could they not wait a little longer? Surely, by summer, Kharkov would be free.

"We must get the children to Palestine," Amos said.

"But they will be safe here."

"I have my orders."

This reply, Amos knew would be understood. He could not tell them that he would no longer count a Jew safe anywhere except in a place where protection was guaranteed by other Jews. Russian partisans offered them safety now, but his father and his grandfather, both Kharkov-born, had told him other tales of this woodland. Here, Jews had hidden during pogroms initiated not by Germans but by Russians, and he had a suspicion that this very hut might have been a hiding place constructed by Jews during the days and nights of terror when they fled the Cossacks' horses. He could not trust the children to the descendants of those who had been responsible for the deaths of his ancestors.

The partisan leader looked at Dmitri and shrugged. These Jews were stubborn, crazy. But they might yet surprise everyone and survive. One never knew with Jews. They had secrets, mysterious connections. They traveled from country to country and always some coreligionist emerged from sheltering shadows to help them. Perhaps this Amos Maimon had information he was not sharing with them, contacts he had not told them about.

"Go, then. Dmitri will take Liesel to the synagogue. But you, Amos Maimon, must wait for her and for the children in the forest."

"Why?" At once Amos was wary. He did not want to be separated from Liesel.

"One of our village boys works as a boot boy in the German barracks. He overheard two officers talking about an intelligence report which indicated that someone had sighted two parachutes. They had instructed their patrols to be on the lookout for strangers, especially for two strangers traveling together. One person, particularly a woman, will not arouse their suspicions."

"What do you think, Liesel?" Amos had asked worriedly.

"We must do anything we can to reduce the risk," she had replied and hoped that her voice did not tremble with the fear that invaded her entire being. She struggled against nausea and alternately shivered with the cold and grew inexplicably hot. And yet she continued to slice the nylon of the parachute and roll it into neat cylindrical bandages, and she gravely studied the maps and asked questions about the plant life in the forest. Were the berries now in bloom edible? How did one know if the water was safe to drink?

And so now she was alone in the forest, silently following Dmitri along the secret path which led to the old synagogue, listening to the distant concertina and the sudden chorus of night birds that shrilled high above them and slashed the tender-leafed trees with scissoring wings.

"There. You can see it just below us," Dmitri whispered.

From their perch on a bracken-covered ledge, she saw a small gray building, its darkened windows covered with boards. A Jewish star, carved of dark balsam wood, dominated the front door, and shards of colored glass clung to the splintered window frames. This, then, was where Yehuda Maimon, Amos's grandfather, had stood with his aged father, Reb Shimon, and told him of his decision to leave Russia for Palestine. Liesel, during her stays in the Sadot Shalom farmhouse, was a faithful listener to the stories Ezra Maimon told his children—the tales of his boyhood in Russia, of his irrepressible twin brothers, his beautiful lost sister, Sara. Her own childhood had been stolen from her, and so she was an eavesdropper now, jealously scavenging scraps of another family's past, remembering their names in odd and soothing litany.

It had been late afternoon, according to the story, and the stained-glass windows must have been aglow with the jeweled light of sunset. The old man had cursed his son then, for betraying his faith, for abandoning the messianic dream and striving to create his own destiny. God controlled history, not man, Reb Shimon had shouted. Reb Shimon had died in Russia, but they had saved his name and given it to Sara's son, born in Palestine but taken back to Russia and then to Poland by his mother. Shimon. Who in turn became father of a boy named Yehuda. The cycle of names danced in rhythmic sequence through the history of their people. Men died, but their names were reclaimed and bestowed on infants of their blood.

Continuity was preserved, remembrance assured. Reb Shimon of Kharkov, who had studied the tomes of the law in this synagogue, was long since dead, but somewhere in this besieged land his great grandson, Yehuda, the son of yet another Shimon, wandered.

"Here, I leave you," Dmitri said. "From here you must proceed alone. You know where to meet Amos?"

She nodded.

"Dmitri—why did you help us?"

"Because," he said, "every child we rescue is a victory over the Germans, and we have had too many defeats. My wife was pregnant when they killed her. When I save a child, it is my own murdered child that I save."

"Dmitri, I want to thank you," she said. Her voice broke. She remembered how she had thought him the enemy, how she had struggled against him, biting at his fingers, clawing at his neck—this tall, burly partisan whose eyes were dead and whose hair had been shocked into the color of grief because he had watched his wife fold her blue dress, oh so neatly, and stand with her arms covering her exposed breasts while bullets tore holes in her naked flesh. Had a bullet pierced her womb and killed the tiny fetus nestling there? Did unborn children feel pain? Had there been weeping within the dead woman's womb, soft, bewildered whimpers that would surely reach celestial ears?

"I wish you success," Dmitri said. "And remember us—your non-Jewish comrades."

"I will remember. I could never forget."

He turned back then, scrambling with startling nimbleness down crag and precipice. As agreed, she waited a full ten minutes, the steady tick of her watch thunderous in the nocturnal stillness. Even the concertina was stilled. The tavern party was over and the Germans had scattered to barracks and brothel. The night birds perched in silent vigilance on barren branches. Slowly, carefully, she began her brief descent.

Twigs snapped beneath her feet and she paused, startled by the sharpness of their sound. A chipmunk darted out of the hollow of a tree. She stumbled, reached for her revolver, and then, seeing the tiny animal, laughed at her own fear. She and Amos had practiced shooting that morning. At Hanita she was known as a good rifle shot and often stood guard at the perimeter fence, but in the Russian forest her hand trembled, her eye was unsteady, and she tasted her own fear, vile and sour, in the back of her throat.

The Arabs attacked because they feared the Jews would disrupt the rhythm of their lives, because they felt their lands were threatened. Their assaults were terrifying, yet they did not unnerve her because she understood them. But the Germans were obsessed with an irrational hatred. They were defending neither their lands nor their lives. They were merchants of death who worshiped dark, necromantic gods. The Arabs were frightened, but the Germans inflicted fear. The Arabs fought with saber, dagger, and rifle. They hurled rocks and lurked in mountain passes. But the Germans devised spigots that breathed poisonous gases, truncheons of leather, and double-edged serrated blades that slowly severed arteries and ripped through flesh. They shot naked, defenseless men, women, and children beside open pits and in village squares. She fought them both, but it was the Germans, lords of the land of her birth, who terrified her. They spoke the language she had once called her own and filled the silent night with concertina melodies that caused her feet to twitch in remembered rhythm. She could not forgive them for betraying the illusions of her childhood.

A low-hanging vine tickled her face, and she risked shining her tiny torch. The needle of light sliced the darkness, and she saw that she was halfway down the hillside, within meters of the Kharkov synagogue. A small stream gurgled nearby, and she remembered Ezra Maimon telling them that he had accompanied his grandfather, Shimon, to that stream each New Year's day, so that they might toss pebbles into its flowing waters and symbolically divest themselves of their sins. With any luck, she and Amos and the children would pass the brook that night. Perhaps they, too, would drop small stones into its swirling depths. But what sins would they expunge? The sin of being Jewish? The travesty of being small and vulnerable in dangerous, violent times? The impertinence of staying alive against all odds?

Impatiently, she extinguished her light and proceeded down. Almost there. Almost safe. Her breath came more evenly now, and her steps were longer and more confident. She whispered aloud the code name she would give to the children's guide,

Mendel. "I am Ruhama Maher," she was to say. Swift Mercy. Now the ground was soft beneath her feet. She was traversing a bed of forest gorse. It grew in thick profusion in the woodlands of Bavaria, and once, on a Zionist camping trip, she had stretched supine on it and a dark-eyed medical student from Heidelberg had pressed his body against her own, threaded her hair with garlands of the purple-flowered foliage, and whispered to her tenderly, urgently. She had kissed him and allowed his hands to move across her body, teasing her into a sweet, responsive moistness, but in the end she had pushed him away and danced free of him, scurrying down the mountainside through the thickly growing forest cover. Only months ago she had learned that he had been killed at Dachau, and she had been regretful then that she had resisted him, denied him.

Even now, her body tingled as she remembered that long-ago flight. She slid between two giant elms. Only a few more steps and she would be at the rear door of the synagogue, her fingers on the latch. A cornucopia of light splashed suddenly across the darkness. She froze. Her heart stopped, and the scream that gathered at the back of her throat was stilled only by the shrilling of a night bird in the stark silence. Someone had stolen up behind her, she knew without turning. A hand clamped across her mouth, and strong arms wrestled her to the sweet-smelling earth. Insistent fingers manipulated the buttons of her jacket, probed her breasts. Her legs were free and she kicked wildly, but her attacker turned her easily onto her back and stretched astride her, paralyzing her with his bulk, his weight. His hand still across her mouth, he bent close to her. She stared up at him, her eyes glazed with fear. He was full-bearded, and the coarse facial hair bruised her cheeks as his mouth traveled upward to meet her ear.

"Ruhama Maher," he whispered, and abruptly released his hand from her mouth, emitted a deep playful laugh, put a gorse blossom behind her ear, and sat up as branches crackled and a bright circle of light blazed down on them.

A German guard stood over them, his service revolver in one hand and the illuminating search light in the other. He trained its brightness on Liesel's exposed breasts, which she covered swiftly, fumbling with the buttons of her jacket.

"What are you doing here?" the German asked. "Where are your papers?"

"We were only having a bit of fun," the bearded man said in broken German. He squeezed Liesel's hand and she remained silent. Her own cultivated German would at once betray her. No Russian country girl would speak in her accent. "There's no place else to go. German soldiers are quartered in both our houses. Not that we aren't glad to have them. Oh yes. They are welcome. My mother gives them the best of everything. But where can I go to be alone with my girl? You know how it is. You have a girl back home, don't you? Here, have some vodka."

He pulled a flask from his belt and passed it to the German, who looked at it suspiciously and then took a swallow.

"It's cold out here," the German said with the tinge of a whine in his voice. Liesel recognized the accent of Westphalia. He was a boy, still in his middle teens. It was true, then, the rumors that the Germans were low on manpower, that they were conscripting troops in the secondary schools. He drank uneasily and licked at the line of moisture on his upper lip. He shivered as the liquor coursed through him and then took another swallow.

"That really warms you up," he said as though something he had long suspected were at last proven true. "All night long they were drinking in the tavern while I patrolled this damn forest. The music is playing and they are drinking and screwing, and I'm shining my light on trees because some damn peasant thought he saw two parachutes going down. They'll say anything to earn a couple of rubles. There were no parachutes. Who the hell would have the guts to parachute into Russia now? No one will go against the Fatherland. Rommel showed them a thing or two in the Kasserine Pass. Paulus's army will be replaced. Didn't we retake Kharkov? No one is going to parachute. But still, if they say so, we have to stand guard. Just my luck I have to pull sentry duty on a night when the vodka is flowing."

"This vodka is better than the rotgut the tavernkeeper hid," Liesel's companion said. "Her father has his own still—his own still and his own potato field. Not a bad combination, eh?" He squeezed Liesel's shoulder and kissed her on the cheek. In return, she smiled playfully. His lips were strangely smooth against her skin.

"You can't make love in a still, though," the German said

and laughed uproariously as though he had said something very clever. The liquor had changed his mood, altered his perception. They were all comrades now, all boisterous young people chasing after drink and sex in field and forest. They were united in the conspiracy of youth, the lust for privacy and excitement.

"I made love outside once," the German confided. "It was too cold. Froze my balls off. My apologies, Fräulein." He swept his helmet off, and Liesel tittered appreciatively. She doubted that he had ever slept with anyone, inside or out, this schoolboy in uniform. His hair was as thin as that of an infant, and it was cut close about his skull, exposing its pinkness, its network of thin blue veins.

"I've got an idea," he said. "Why don't you go into that synagogue? You'll have some shelter at least."

"There's a thought," Liesel's companion said enthusiastically. "We'll do that. Here, you take the flask. I've got what I need to keep me warm."

His hands traveled across her breasts. Playfully, she slapped him away and laughed flirtatiously at the German, who choked as he took another swallow of the vodka. She was beginning to enjoy the charade, and she found the touch of his hands on her body oddly comforting.

"Good. *Danke*. Go, then, and have fun."

He waved them away, his helmet still dangling from his wrist as he accommodatingly trained his searchlight on the synagogue. At the doorway they waved to him, and he lifted his flask in a toast. He did not see the bullet that ripped through the air as he drank. The pellet of steel penetrated his forehead. A ribbon of blood trailed down his cheek, but he made no sound as he fell to the ground. Mendel and Liesel waited briefly before they dashed up to him. He was dead, his face frozen into a mask of disbelief, like that of a child who has been startled at the discovery of a favorite playmate cheating at a game. They dragged the body into the synagogue and slammed the heavy wooden door behind them.

"I had to do it," he said. "He might have gone back to the tavern and described us. This beard is rather distinctive, but shaving has been difficult on this journey." He laughed and held his hand out.

"What is your real name, Ruhama Maher?"

"Liesel Konigsfeld. And you are the famous Mendel."

"No. Mendel is not my name, but it was easier for the partisans to remember than my real name and so I took pity on them and told them Mendel."

"Then what is your real name?"

"I am called Moshe, Moshe Aharoni," he said, and her heart soared.

"Is it possible," she asked, her voice very quiet, very steady, betraying no optimism because they had learned in this war that hope was more treacherous than hopelessness, "that the child Yehuda Schoenbaum is in your group?"

"He is with us," Moshe replied. "A farmer from Oswiecem brought him to us. Come, you will meet him—you will meet all my children."

The interior of the synagogue was pitch-dark and dank. Moshe did not light his torch, but he moved skillfully through the empty room, taking her hand to guide her past the stumps of pews that had been wrenched from their posts and the splintered study stands where holy books had rested while scholars argued vagrant points of law. Once this silent, fetid room had been filled with the cadences of study, the rhythms of prayerful song. Memorial tablets that attested to life and death had been affixed to these walls, encrusted now with the verdigris of mildew. Children had skittered through these doors, convulsed with mischievous laughter, absorbed in intellectual debate. Brides and grooms had celebrated their nuptials here, and learned rabbis had delivered sermons and eulogies. But now the room was bare, stripped of its furnishings, cloaked in the silence of death and decay.

"The winter was bitterly cold," Moshe said. "The Germans and the townspeople took whatever they could for firewood. We heard them, and we only feared that they would rip up the floorboards and discover us. But that they were afraid to do. In Kharkov they have long believed that the Jews bury their holy men in the basements of the synagogue and that if they are disturbed, their spirits will come to life and strangle those who disturb them."

"Too bad it's not true," Liesel said bitterly. How wonderful it would be, to be protected by an army of bearded ghosts, by saintly wraiths who breathed death through quivering nostrils, stifled life with fleshless fingers. Moshe Aharoni glanced at her knowingly.

"You are very tired," he said softly.

She did not reply. The gentleness of his tone brought tears to her eyes, and she had not cried since that day in Berlin when she caught her last glimpse of her father.

He was in the front of the synagogue now, on the small platform which had housed the ark, struggling to raise the floorboards that concealed the trap door.

"They built these things well," he muttered.

"They had to."

The Jews of eastern Europe built trap doors beneath the arks of the Law so that when pogroms threatened, the scrolls could be swiftly concealed. In some synagogues the entire cellar had been hollowed out to provide a hiding place for refugees from the rampaging mobs. The Jews themselves had cultivated the myth of holy men being buried beneath the floorboards, a tale derived from the legends of Babi Yaga, who buried living children beneath forest huts. The stories were flimsy and desperate insurance policies, but the peasants, who lived in fear of summer thunder and winter lightning, believed them.

Moshe lifted the trap door and whispered softly into the darkness below.

"It's all right, children. All is well."

Liesel heard no sound, discerned no movement. The hidden children were skilled in the tricks of immobility, the habits of silence. She followed Moshe down the rope ladder, thinking that Amos's Kharkov ancestors must have scrambled down these same clandestine steps of hemp. The stench of the underground area was noxious, and she reeled beneath its fetid breath. The stink of human waste mingled with the odors of unwashed bodies, of vegetal decay, of soiled clothing. Odors became discrete. Sour menstrual blood and stale vomit were overlaid with the vagrant sweetness of forest greens. Attempts had been made to obscure the odor, to mask it. The children had placed sweet herbs and foliage about their hideaway. Such an effort at such a time seemed a triumph to her. She descended the last step, and a small boy, a ghostly welcomer, drifted out of the darkness and handed her an evergreen branch. Gravely she accepted it, pressed it against her cheek.

"Shalom," she told the children. "I have come to take you home. To *Eretz Yisrael,* our promised land."

Still, they said nothing. Moshe lit a candle, and she saw them illuminated by the flickering flame. Skeletal creatures, wearied by their wanderings, wide-eyed and shy of glance, open-mouthed and impish-faced, they looked up at her, and suddenly a small girl who had hidden herself in the shadow of a tall boy, began to sing in a high frail voice.

> "There in the land of Israel
> There in the village of Ezekiel
> We will find life, we will endure. . . ."

It was an old song, sung in Jewish nursery schools, danced to at Jewish weddings. The small girl had dredged it up from earliest memories, but the other children knew it, too, and slowly, softly, their voices joined her in tentative but hopeful chorus. "We will find life, we will endure," they sang into the darkness, lit by a single candle.

"Are you from Palestine?" a small boy asked her.

She nodded, and he touched her hand as though her skin were possessed of some chimerical property which she might pass on to him.

"My father was born in Palestine," he said. "This is from Palestine." He held out a small gazelle, carved of olivewood, worn to satin smoothness by the hands of many children.

She looked closely at him. His hair was so matted with dirt that she could not discern its color, and his pale face was grimy, the cheekbones jutting out starkly, and above them his large eyes glowed—green eyes the color of the sea.

"Yehuda? Are you Yehuda?"

"That is my name," he said and looked at her in surprise.

"Yehuda." The name seemed a prayer now, and she pressed his thin body to her own, felt the birdlike wings of his shoulder blades quiver beneath her touch. "I know your uncle, Ezra Maimon," she said and tasted the salt of her own tears.

A miracle had happened in the fetid darkness of the secret basement. Against all odds they had found the boy, the last remnant of the Maimon family in Europe—Sara's grandson reclaimed for the land where his father, Shimon, had been born.

"My uncle," the child repeated as though it were a miracle that he had a relative, someone of his bloodline who had not been shot or gassed or left to die of typhus.

Moshe looked at her questioningly, but there was no time for explanations. The children gathered their things together in pathetic small packs, and slowly, one by one, they ascended the rope ladder, never looking back at the basement where they had cowered in darkness through so many days and nights. As they emerged from the synagogue, the fresh night air kissed their faces, and they gasped with delight, held their hands out, lifted their faces to the gentle wind, to the sweet odors of earth and trees, to the promise of freedom.

"It is over," the child Yehuda said.

"No." Liesel put her arm about his quivering shoulders. "It is just beginning."

They walked silently then, through the dark forest, to the grove where Amos waited for them. Moshe Aharoni's eyes narrowed when he saw Liesel rush toward Amos Maimon. Her eyes burned with excitement and her arms reached up to embrace him.

"Amos," she called, and Moshe heard the febrile intensity of her voice.

He turned away then, remembering the softness of her flesh beneath his hand, the sweetness of her lips upon his own. He had felt the tremor of her body, the swift intake of her breath. Briefly, on the parapet above the synagogue, danger and excitement had united them. But it was to Amos Maimon that she had rushed.

Wearily, Moshe turned back to his children, organizing them into twin columns for the long march, adjuring them to empty their bladders and bowels now, before they set out again on their journey.

Chapter 27

THE STREETS OF Baghdad swarmed with merchants who impatiently shoved beggar children out of their way as they wheeled their laden carts across the half-paved roads. They had heard of the arrival of a new contingent of British troops and had abandoned the bazaar in search of prospective customers. The war had taught the Iraqi vendors that the young British soldiers, who did not know when they would next see their homes in Shropshire and Surrey, were eager to send talismans of the Middle East to the thatched cottages and row houses of their boyhood. The most enterprising of the hawkers squatted in front of the Hotel Umayyad and plucked at the tunics of the officers who hurried through the gilt framed front doors.

"A bargain. Special for you," they bleated in imploring chorus and held up pots of hammered copper, mysteriously shaped amulets, lengths of shimmering fabric shot through with metallic thread.

Moshe Aharoni, outfitted in a well-cut white linen suit, paused beside the makeshift stand of an itinerant goldsmith and contemplated a length of gold chain.

"For you a special price," the craftsman cajoled, and Moshe was briefly arrested by his entreaty.

"Do you have a special price for Moledetski?" he asked hopefully.

"A special price for the English raj," the merchant replied and twirled the metal length like a lasso. "Heavy gold. I can make it longer. I can make it shorter."

But Moshe, his shoulders sagging in disappointment, had already entered the Umayyad lobby. The heavy leather furnishings and marble counters and tables were swallowed by the enormous room. British officers lounged against the pale pink marble columns and laconically made plans for the day. It was rumored that there were fish to be caught in the Tigris. An excursion was being organized to the meeting point of the Tigris and the Euphrates.

"It's a mud hole really," the colonel who was organizing the boat trip said, "but it will be something to write home about. You know—the aquatic crown of the fertile crescent and all that."

"Mesopotamia's a stink hole," his adjutant replied, but he continued to circulate the lobby, signing men up for the river outing. He glanced curiously at Moshe, who stood at the reception desk.

"Any messages for Moledetski?" Moshe asked the clerk, ignoring the officer.

"None. But you have guests. Mr. and Mrs. Nordstrom are in your room."

"Thank you," Moshe said, and he smiled, in passing, to the British adjutant, who nodded briskly.

"Who's that chap?" the colonel asked when his adjutant circled back, morosely displaying his registry of five names. They would need at least ten men to make the cost of chartering the river craft viable.

"I think he's something to do with an international refugee agency," the adjutant replied indifferently. "We could make up the party if we took some of the Gurkha officers. Do you think anyone would mind having the wogs along?"

"I personally don't give a damn if monkeys come along," the colonel said irritably. "It's just something to do, after all, isn't it? Something to fill up the bloody day."

Boredom was the perennial enemy of the British forces in Baghdad. The drab, ancient city, with its low dun-colored brick buildings offered few diversions. Clouds of golden dust hovered in the heat-laden air, and the British soldiers kept their lips tightly pressed together, lest the grit slip into their mouths and coat their tongues. Often they changed their shirts several times a day, wringing the fabric saturated with their sweat. They sought out squares of shade in sun-drenched street cafés and sat beneath slowly revolving propeller fans, but there was

no relief from the oppressive heat. Doggedly, they brushed
their uniforms and shined their boots, but they could not win
the struggle against the encroaching silt. Loneliness drove
them from their quarters, but the covered bazaar was only
briefly interesting and the race track provided minimal excitement.

Most of the British troops were temporarily stationed in
Baghdad, awaiting transit from one theater of operations to
another. Others had been in the Iraqi capital since the spring of
1941, when Whitehall had requested emergency reinforcements from India and Palestine to crush Rashid Ali's pro-
German regime. Some had heard the Arab leader declare war
on Great Britain, and others had seen the swastika banner
hoisted over the caliphate palace.

The fighting then had been fierce but swift, most of it concentrated at the aerodrome at Hinaidi. The British, of course,
had prevailed, but they had not left even after Rashid Ali's
deposal. A weary Winston Churchill read the communiqués
and acknowledged that there was too much instability in Iraq,
and, as always, the Jews were the barometer of that instability.
Only days after the military victory, Nazi Arabs had attacked
the Jewish quarter and massacred four hundred Jews. Defeated
by soldiers on the battlefield, they took their vengeance on
civilians in the marketplace.

The pragmatic British quite understood that they could not
leave. The problem was that there was little to do while they
stayed. Their presence was necessary, but Baghdad's only stra-
tegic function now was as a transit point, dispersing troops to
Palestine, to Basra, to Cairo. The contingent of Gurkhas,
whose officers might be persuaded to join the river excursion,
were awaiting transport to the Galilee.

"If we don't go out on the boat trip," the adjutant said, "we
could organize a tour of the museum."

"If I see those damn Hammurabi inscriptions one more
time, I shall be sick," the colonel said. "If we don't go out on
the boat, I shall stay right here in this disgusting lobby and get
sozzled."

That was not such a bad idea, he decided. Perhaps that
Scandinavian woman who was also somehow involved in refugee relief would come down to the lobby and join him in a

drink. She was a damn good-looking woman, and her husband didn't seem all that attentive. So busy reading his mail that he hardly spoke to her. Small things like that gave one a clue. The colonel was the veteran of a dozen brief liaisons, most of which initiated in the lobbies of hotels not too dissimilar from the Umayyad. He was, after all, only human, and it was not his fault that his wife was clipping roses in Surrey while he sat out the war in this dust-covered city. If that leggy blonde came down to the lobby alone, he would simply go up to her, introduce himself, and tell her how deeply concerned he was about the refugees. That was the ticket. Satisfied, he went into the paneled bar, and even though it was too early for serious drinking, he ordered a sloe gin fizz and reflected that it was damn decent of the Scandinavians to involve themselves in refugee relief work.

In the opulently furnished Umayyad room that a Haganah agent had rented in the name of the Scandinavian Friendship League, Liesel Konigsfeld, Amos Maimon, and Moshe Aharoni disconsolately studied a large map stretched across the pink satin spread that covered the double bed.

"It's no good," Moshe said. "There is no way to cross the desert. I wouldn't risk it."

"You risked the forests of Europe," Amos said.

He turned away from the map and reread the letter from Ruth he had received that morning.

"I cannot believe that you have escaped from Europe and are almost home," she had written. He imagined her seated in the shade of the olive tree that grew in their Jerusalem garden. At this season its graceful leaves would match her silver-blond hair.

Ruth, he thought. *My Ruth.*

He himself could not believe the miracle of their safe passage and the reality of their arrival in the Middle East. Still, in the night, he awakened in the luxurious hotel suite, startled to find himself in a bed and not on a forest floor.

They had led the children along the banks of the Donets River, concealing themselves in the woodlands during the day and walking through the night. When the younger children whimpered with fatigue, the older ones carried them, stagger-

ing over exposed roots and fallen branches. Amos had carried
the boy Yehuda. The child was frightened, his body board-stiff
against Amos's back, his fingers clenched about the tiny
carved wooden gazelle; to calm him, Amos told him stories of
Yehuda Maimon.

"My great-grandfather planted orange trees in the desert,"
Yehuda told the other children, who looked at him in disbelief.
Some struggled to recall what an orange had looked like,
whether the juice had been sweet or tart.

At the Volga River, Moshe made contact with a boatman
who was a loyal partisan, and he took them to the Port of
Astrakhan on the Caspian Sea. They slept through most of the
journey and awakened to stare up at the black night sky sequined with frost-colored stars. Because the craft was an open
fishing skiff, Liesel had blanketed the two smallest children
with her overcoat. She shivered violently, and Moshe moved
toward her, but Amos Maimon already held her close, shielding her with the warmth of his own body. She nestled naturally
into his embrace and slept again. Moshe lay awake, weighted
by a familiar and terrible loneliness.

Almost three years had passed since the Haganah had re-
cruited Moshe Aharoni for the rescue missions in Europe. He
had been a natural choice. He had been born in Petach Tikveh,
and his Russian father, one of the early *Shomrim,* had trained
him from boyhood to be comfortable with rifles and unafraid of
danger and solitude. His mother was from Germany, a rec-
titudinous woman who saw Zionism as more than an ideology.
Love of Zion was a *mitzvah,* a commandment, divinely inspired, to be dutifully obeyed. God had given Moshe the privilege of being born in Zion. He would share this privilege with
others. Her voice was very soft when she said this.

Moshe was multilingual from childhood, switching easily
from Polish to German to Hebrew, occasionally dreaming in
Arabic and thinking in English. He was a skilled marksman, a
natural horseman. He had trained with Orde Wingate in an
early ghaffir unit and had moved up easily through the ranks of
the Haganah when the secret Jewish army was formed. He
achieved a small fame in the country for his ability to travel the
most difficult terrain alone. He had even traveled twice to

Petra, the ancient Nabatean capital of rose-red stone on the eastern slope of the Wadi el-Araba.

"If he can make it back and forth from Petra, he'll make it across Europe," Yehuda Arazi, the Haganah leader in charge of rescue operations, had said when Moshe's name was put forth.

Moshe shared his leader's confidence. He had not been confounded by either danger or privation. He knew which forest herbs were edible, which berries could be squeezed for juice, and how to skin squirrels and chipmunks and roast them over open fires. (During his desert wanderings he had skewered jackals, eaten snake meat.) The children in his charge had sometimes been hungry, but they had never been in danger of starvation. He had taught them the secrets of silence, and his easy command of Polish and German had saved them during dangerous confrontations. Once he had told suspicious Polish villagers that he was a counselor at an orphanage, charged with transferring the children to a distant location. Another time he had informed German interrogators that he had been commissioned by Heydrich's second-in-command to bring the children to an industrial location. A rocket site, he had confided, where their small sizes would be useful. The Germans had been impressed by both the mention of Heydrich and the rockets and had allowed him to proceed, Moshe's certainty overcoming their doubts.

He carried with him a bewildering assortment of documents and identity papers and always magically managed to produce one that would, however briefly, establish credence. But the pain of his solitude was overwhelming, and often when the children in his charge slept, he held monologues, declaiming aloud biblical passages, poems by Bialik, Agnon stories, even singing Guri's hymns. He imagined conversations with friends left behind in Palestine and invented mysterious trysts with Chana, the dark-eyed daughter of a Petach Tikveh shopkeeper who had long since married a kibbutznik from Givat Brenner.

"I'm crazy," he would tell himself angrily, but he knew that in truth he was only lonely. The camaraderie between Amos and Liesel intensified his feeling of aloneness, and he schooled himself to maintain a careful distance. He knew that

Amos was married, but he knew, too, that in time of war marriages were fragile and often irrelevant. He asked no questions, and they offered him no answers. If, occasionally, he caught Liesel gazing at him in invitation or in puzzlement, he shrugged and turned away. But he was powerless to fend her off in dreams when she invaded his sleep and, drifting and weightless, took his hand.

Liesel sat beside him as they crossed the Caspian Sea on a small steamer to Pahlevi. They had thought to travel from there to Palestine, but the Haganah agent who met them insisted that they journey on at once to Baghdad. Iran was no longer a reliable way station. Only recently a group of children had been diverted from Pahlevi, forced to travel all the way to Karachi and then to Port Suez before finally reaching Palestine.

"We don't want to repeat the experience of the Teheran children," the agent said. "It will be safest to proceed directly to Baghdad. We can hide the children in the Jewish quarter, and you can assume your original cover. Amos and Liesel will be Mr. and Mrs. Nordstrom, Scandinavian angels of mercy. Moshe will be Mr. Moledetski, debonair but incompetent refugee agency bureaucrat. We'll make transport arrangements to Palestine and get word to you."

"How?" Moshe's voice rasped with impatience.

The others looked at him curiously. After all their wanderings, the dangers and discomforts, the caves and the forests, the dank basements and the boats that reeked of fish and sweat, did it matter if they spent an extra week in Baghdad as opposed to being caught and sent to the other side of Asia?

"Our agent will contact you," the Haganah representative said briskly. "You will check into the Hotel Umayyad. The code will be a special price or a special message for Moledetski."

They had been given clothing to befit their status in Baghdad, a sheath of currency, and an address in the Jewish quarter where the children would be safe.

Moshe was troubled at parting from his youngsters. He knew the pattern of their moods, the rhythms of their fears. He knew how to comfort Genia when she cried in the night and how Reuven grew calm when he slept beside tall Shaia, and how Lara needed only the lightest pat on the head, a small murmur of reassurance when she awakened from sleep. He instructed the Iraqi Jews on each child's needs, and Liesel was moved by his tenderness, his concern. She looked at him, but when his eyes met her gaze, he turned away, his lips set in a thin line. He did not like her, she knew. He avoided her and answered her questions curtly. His dislike pained her, festered poisonously, like an open sore about her heart, and she wondered that she cared so much. But it did not really matter. Back in Palestine she would return to Hanita and he would rejoin his Haganah unit. They might never see each other again. And she was growing accustomed to never again seeing those with whom she had shared the greatest intimacy—her father, Liam, even the young medical student who had stretched out beside her in the tall grass of the Bavarian forest so long ago. Soon, she and Moshe would part.

But they had been in Baghdad for almost a week now, and still there had been no message for Moledetski.

"We can last another week—perhaps," Moshe said now, loosening his collar against the sweltering heat of the hotel room. "And then we will begin to arouse curiosity. The British haven't much to do here. There are too few brothels and not enough bars. It is difficult to go to war in a Moslem country. Already, their colonel has been looking too hard at our Liesel. They will grow restless and begin to ask questions. Our travel documents won't survive careful scrutiny."

"What do they say in the Jewish quarter?" Amos asked.

"The Haganah cell there is edgy, I can tell, but they continue to insist that they expect word from Jerusalem any day. I hope they are right."

"Look!" Liesel said suddenly. She had wandered over to the window as he spoke, and now she stood rigid with excitement, her eyes riveted to the scene below.

"What is it?"

They rushed toward her, and Moshe noticed with annoyance that Amos almost automatically put his hand on her shoulder. He himself stared down at the murky waters of the Tigris but noticed only a white-turbaned Iraqi desolately paddling his *gufa* downstream. The rounded wickerworked boat bobbed on the rippling waters like a child's toy. Wildly, it occurred to him that, viewed from a height, they might all seem to be

diminutive playthings, involved in a complicated game of
chutes and ladders, rescue and escape. Perhaps God was an
oversized, self-absorbed child busily moving his pawns about
on the great gameboard of the earth. Here, the capricious celestial being might invent a game of war, and there, in a moment
of contentment, he might create a landscape of peace. Moshe
sighed deeply, disturbed at the imagery that teased and diverted him.

"I don't see anything," he said flatly.

"No. Not toward the river. Look there, in the hotel courtyard."

He shifted his gaze and gasped with surprise. A passenger
bus stood beneath the hotel portico, coated with the heavy
white dust of the desert journey. But beneath the film of silt
and sand the vehicle's blue-and-white markings could be discerned. The bus was the property of the Egged Cooperative
Transport Company of Tel Aviv, Palestine.

"What the hell," Amos wondered softly, "is an Egged bus
doing in Baghdad?"

The phone rang then, a small shrill sound that briefly bewildered them. They stared at it without moving, and then it
jangled again, imperiously. Moshe lifted it and heard a hoarse
voice say, "I have a message for Moledetski. We have a
special price for him. Is he there?"

"This is Moledetski," he replied. "Come right up."

They stared at each other and then, as if by agreement, they
swiftly checked their weapons. Liesel's small revolver was
thrust into the pocket of her skirt, and she kept her hand on the
cold metal as the door slowly swung open.

Nadav Langerfeld stood in the doorway, his clothing covered with dust, his bald head glinting with sweat. He held a
sack of oranges and a pile of Hebrew language newspapers.

"Shalom," he said. "Elana thought you might want an
orange, and Ruth thought you might want something to read.
It's hot in Baghdad, isn't it? And the waters of Babylon stink.
The psalmists didn't mention that."

He grinned happily at them as Amos pounded his back and
Liesel kissed him and embraced him. Moshe Aharoni, suddenly shy, shook hands with him. Nadav Langerfeld. Who was
married to Amos Maimon's sister, Elana. Another tentacle of

the huge and variegated Maimon family. He himself was an only child, the son of only children. Again, his solitude and isolation weighted his heart, and he was curt in his acknowledgment of Nadav Langerfeld's compliments on the success of his mission.

"The Jewish Agency is amazed at your success in getting the children out of Europe," Nadav said.

"That's all very well," Moshe replied. "But now, how do we get them out of Iraq and into Palestine?"

Nadav settled himself into a wicker chair and slowly peeled one of his oranges.

"The British have tightened their restrictions on Jewish immigration. And we, in turn, have given up any pretense that we are adhering to the White Paper. The Irgun, you know, has issued a manifesto stating that there is no longer an armistice between the Jewish people and the British administration which hands our brothers over to Hitler. I think that is an exact quote. But that, of course, is more Jabotinsky's style than Ben Gurion's. At the Jewish Agency we still strive to keep up appearances. We attempt subterfuge—nocturnal landings, clandestine border crossings."

"And you have such a plan for my children?" Moshe asked.

He stroked his dark beard, carefully shaped now to follow the strong curve of his chin, and Liesel noticed, for the first time, the astonishing length of his eyelashes. They swept his cheekbones and flashed upward to almost touch the thick brows above his gray-blue eyes. In visage and in temperament, Moshe Aharoni combined a fierce strength and a natural tenderness.

"We do have a plan," Nadav said. "Audacious. Ambitious. But workable. As you see, I arrived in Baghdad in an Egged bus. The British, in their wisdom, chartered a convoy of our buses to bring a Fusilier's unit from the Galilee to Baghdad on furlough. The passengers on the return journey are an Indian battalion, the Gurkhas, scheduled to take up positions on the Carmel. A colorful lot. You may have seen them in the city."

"I've noticed them," Liesel said.

The turbaned Indian soldiers stood out among the regular British units in their dull regimental khaki. The Indians laughed a great deal, their very white teeth flashing against dusky skin. Of all the British troops, only they were comfortable in the fierce heat of Baghdad, and they strolled through the deserted bazaar in the blaze of the noonday sun, comfortable in their soft blue silken shirts and pantalooned trousers, their long fingers fondling the soft leather wallets and purses which they purchased in extraordinary quantity.

"They are not very tall, are they—these Indian allies of ours?" Nadav observed, and a mischievous smile played about his lips. "In fact, many of them are the same height as our youngsters. Am I not right?"

"You are right," Moshe said, and he too smiled, in admiration. In a flash he had perceived Langerfeld's plan. He whistled softly. "You plan to dress the children in Gurkha uniforms and take them into Palestine as part of a British unit?"

"Why not?" Nadav asked. "Why shouldn't His Majesty's government provide safe conduct for at least some Jewish children?"

"But how will you get the uniforms?" Amos asked.

"We already have them. The British quartermaster at the Latrun base is notoriously careless with his keys. He also has a very low threshold for liquor. Your brother, Amnon, was by way of being a favorite ghaffir of his. And one night Amnon brought him a newly bottled flask of brandy from the Rishon distillery. The Tommy took the brandy, and Amnon took the keys only an hour later. The new Rishon brandy is one hundred proof. Amnon managed to get enough Gurkha uniforms to outfit a small orphanage, and they are now in the boot of the autobus." Nadav laughed with the delight of a small boy who has outwitted stronger playmates.

"Amnon did that?" Amos asked in surprise. The war, it seemed, had revealed hidden talents, had transformed gentle dreamers into daring partisans. Nadav Langerfeld, once immersed in the abstract philosophy of statecraft, was now a daring ambassador of intrigue. He himself had abandoned the lecture hall and excavation site for the dangers of strange forests and mysterious mountain passes.

"Can it work?" Moshe asked, but he knew his question to be rhetorical. It had to work. They had no choice, and of all the risks he had taken during the long years of wandering with his children, this was not the most hazardous. "When do we leave?"

"Tomorrow at dawn. The convoy will leave before daybreak, and your bus will join the others at Bab el-Wastani, the city gate. There will be four buses—the first two will carry the Gurkhas and so will the last one. You and the children will be in the third bus. The driver and his mate are both Haganah men. They will cover for you, if necessary. The important thing is to keep the children away from the windows and to make sure their heads are averted."

"We can darken their faces with charcoal," Liesel said. "The British won't notice them."

"It's not the British I'm worried about," Amos said. "It's the damn Iraqi fascists, the remnants of Rashid Ali's men. The merchants in the Jewish quarter say that they've formed guerilla forces and boast of their success in attacking British troop convoys."

"We'll have to take our chances," Moshe said. "Tomorrow morning then, at Bab el-Wastani."

Amos and Liesel were pressing Nadav now for news of home, and Moshe turned away from their eager talk and looked down at the blue-and-white bus that would carry his children home at last, to the land of Israel.

Chapter 28

THEY ASSEMBLED AT the appointed hour, and the heavy-lidded children shivered in the chill of the predawn air. They sat nervously erect on the battered vinyl seats of the bus and held their small heads very still beneath the unfamiliar weight of the blue satin turbans. Now and again, however, they stole a glance through the window, where a dull amber light stole across the dimness of the sky. An ox cart lumbered past them, laden with freshly baked pita, and the aroma of the bread made the children dizzy, but Moshe held a finger to his lips and they said nothing. They were well schooled in the habits of hunger, the discipline of silence and stealth.

Amos sat next to small Yehuda, who whispered softly to the carved gazelle. How long would it take his young cousin to relearn the small secrets of childhood, the ease of laughter, the thrill of wild play? He thought, with the comfortable longing that knows imminent appeasement, of his own children in Jerusalem.

"Soon we will be at home in Palestine. With our family," he told Yehuda. The green eyes that exactly matched his own stared up at him.

"Yes, Amos. Soon we will be in Palestine," the child replied. Home and family were enigmas to him. His home had been destroyed. His family was dead.

At last the rest of the convoy arrived, and their bus fell in line. They moved southward in ponderous procession. The ancient black iron filigreed gate to the city vanished into a silhouette behind them. Almost without warning, the dawn exploded into day, and they were assaulted by the brightness and heat of the Mesopotamian southland. By the time they reached the open, almost trackless desert of El-Hamad, rivulets of sweat coursed down their cheeks, washing away the layers of charcoal which Liesel had so diligently applied that morning. They yearned for the slightest breeze, but Moshe cautioned them to stay away from the windows. They were still not far enough away from the city. It was improbable that Rashid Ali's men had traveled this distance but certainly not impossible.

Then, at last, the children were free to move about the bus, to talk freely and to eat and drink. The British hard tack was consumed with relish, and they drank water from canteens that carried the insignia of the Royal Quartermaster Corps.

"Only fitting that the British should offer some assistance," Moshe said, and Liesel laughed.

How beautiful she was when she laughed, he thought. Her full mouth was relaxed and her hazel eyes glinted with merriment. But minutes later she was asleep, her bright head resting quite naturally on Amos Maimon's shoulder. Moshe turned away.

He stared out the window and felt the familiar peace which the desert vista always brought him. The endless waves of sand, the clear sky, the sudden mysterious formations of rock and basalt that erupted out of the barren landscape, invariably filled him with awe. Briefly, then, he glimpsed infinity and knew how it was that the world's religions had emerged from the deserts of his land.

He loved the harsh, unrelenting heat, the wild abandoned terrain. During his journeys to Petra, he had reveled in the depth of desert silence and still held close the memory of an ibex that had appeared quite suddenly on a hillock of sand, and the taste of manna licked from tamarisk reeds that grew within the shadows of the dunes.

The face of the Jordanian desert changed from meter to meter, and the same was true of the Mesopotamian desert through which their bus trundled now so laboriously. The waves of sand drifted from mauve to gold; dun-colored craters stood sentinel over wadis brushed with amber. Flame-hued blossoms blazed on cactus plants, so draped in verdigris that they seemed to melt into the sand. A desert jackal, coal-black and fleet, danced out of a hidden warren. Moshe pressed his face against the window, intrigued by the small beast, forgetting the warning he had given the children. He was so intent upon the animal that he did not notice a sudden movement behind a boulder. A man's hand jerked out, gripping a long-nosed pistol, and Moshe watched, as though hypnotized, as a phallic silver cylinder whirred through the bright desert air, pierced the window of the bus, and ignited a fire in his own flesh.

"No!" he shouted in fear and anger.

He had come too far and he was too close to die now. He could not surrender on the sands of the desert when he had cheated death in the caves of Carpathia, in the forests of Bessarabia. His hand leaped up and was soaked by the hot flow of his own blood.

"Oh no." Now his voice was foreign to him. Was it he who had uttered that whimper, that low moan of despair? His eyes closed and he heard the heavy dull thud that was the impact of his body as it slid from the seat to the floor of the bus.

"Moshe!"

Liesel hovered over him. Tears glazed her eyes. He raised a hand and touched her face. Her skin was velvet-smooth beneath his bloodstained fingers. He was in heaven then, dreaming the sleep of the dead. In that dream, she returned his touch, wept for him, told him that she loved him. As he had loved her. Too late. It had all come too late.

"I should have told you," he muttered. "I should have told you when there was time. That I loved you."

"Shsh." Her voice was the sheerest whisper in his ear. Her bright hair brushed his face. "Lie still." Her hands were cool. Now she passed a wet cloth across his brow. "You're all right. The bullet only grazed your shoulder. You're all right. And there is time."

"Time for what?"

He felt the pain now in searing thrusts, and he rejoiced in the anguish. The dead felt no pain. He was alive—alive and vulnerable—alive and loved.

"Time for what?" he asked again.

"For this."

Her face met his, and her lips were as light as the petals of a newly blossoming flower against his own.

"But Amos and you . . ."

His voice faltered, and he saw the surprise in her eyes.

"But he is like a brother to me—a brotherly comrade. I thought you understood that."

He leaned back. He had understood so little.

And then carefully, competently, she dressed his wound as the children watched. Their eyes were bright with relief that he had not died, that he would complete their long journey with them. He thought them very beautiful in their satin turbans that exactly matched the desert sky. He smiled benignly as Amos Maimon filled a hypodermic needle with morphine and gently pressed it into a bulging vein, freeing him of pain, releasing him into sleep.

Days later, the clumsy Egged bus, caked with mud and streaked with sand, which had been indifferently waved through British checkpoints in the Beth Shaan valley, lumbered up the ashlar-lined pathway that led to Sadot Shalom. It was an hour past midnight. A storm threatened and the velvet black sky was starless. Ezra Maimon, who had heard the vehicle because he slept only lightly and fitfully now, carried a torch as he walked through the darkness. His gait was slow, as though he labored always beneath a heavy burden that could not be set down. There had been no swiftness in his step since the day the Polish women had brought his sister Sara's letter to the house. The trip to the United States had both aged and saddened him, and since his return he had napped each afternoon, retreating into a desperate fatigue that frightened Mazal and the children.

He reached the bus at last and stood in the circle of light cast by his torch. The door opened, and Liesel Konigsfeld and a dark, bearded man descended first. Liesel supported her companion, who seemed to be in pain, and stared concernedly up at him. Behind them, came Amos, carrying a sleeping child.

"Abba."

Amos moved forward so that the light of the torch flared on the child in his arms, illuminating the ringlets of gold that encircled the finely molded head. The sleeping boy awakened then and opened his eyes, green eyes, the color of the sea. And Ezra stretched his hand forth to touch first his eldest son, and then the small boy who carried the name of the first Maimon.

"Welcome home, Yehuda," Ezra whispered, and he took his sister's only surviving descendant in his arms. The child rubbed his eyes with a small fist, still clenched about the gazelle carved of olivewood and worn to a satin thinness through the years.

Mazal watched as her husband walked toward the house, carrying the child. There was a new strength to his step and, briefly, he lifted his eyes to the starless sky, through which an electric rib of lightning trembled. She went to meet him and stared down at the small boy who had arrived at last in the land that had been promised to him.

EPILOGUE

1945

THEY STREAMED INTO Tel Aviv from every part of Palestine that bright May morning, when at last official announcement confirmed that the guns of Fascism had been stilled. They waved their newspapers with the stark triumphant headlines. PEACE! SHALOM! SALAAM! Convoys of trucks rumbled southward from the kibbutzim of the Sharon and the Galilee. They were festooned with banners and bunting and packed with adults and children who jubilantly waved their flags and sang hymns of thanksgiving in all the languages of the victors. Horse-drawn wagons lumbered up the coastal road from the moshavim and villages of the southland. The horses were garlanded with wreaths of newly blooming orange blossom and flame-colored cactus flowers, their flanks draped with lengths of red, white, and blue fabric. The families within chattered and laughed, greeting each other exuberantly.

"It's over. It's really over."

"*Baruch HaShem*. Thank God."

"No more war."

"*Insh'Allah*. Let Allah will it."

The drivers of intercity buses refused to accept fares and made unauthorized stops wherever they spotted travelers. Huge families of Arabs lurched onto the vehicles. The Arab children sat on the laps of Jewish passengers while their mothers distributed bunches of grapes from their laden wicker baskets and accepted the honey cake and sweetened strips of apricot from the Jewish women.

A troupe of black-garbed Chassidim danced single-file down

the highway. Their white-bearded leader embraced a Torah scroll dressed in scarlet velvet, which passers-by kissed as they passed. The voices of the Chassidim were vibrant.

"This is the day which the Lord hath made," they sang. "We will rejoice and be glad in it."

The vintners of Rishon LeZion and Zichron Yaakov carried barrels of wine into the city and pressed glasses of the sparkling concord drink on the celebrants.

"L'Chaim!" they called. *"L'Shalom!"* "To life! To peace!"

The girls of Tel Aviv gaily toasted British soldiers. Jewish Agency officials and bureaucrats of the high commissioner's office gravely tipped their glasses toward each other.

"To Winston Churchill."

"To David Ben Gurion."

"To Joseph Stalin."

"To Franklin Roosevelt of blessed memory."

Ezra Maimon, wearied by the journey from Sadot Shalom, stood in the courtyard of Elana's Tel Aviv house and watched his children. Tamar carried a Union Jack, and Nachum, her twin, hoisted the French tricolor. Rivka, the youngest, proudly waved the American flag which Ezra had brought from New York to Palestine a war ago. The largest banner of all, the blue-and-white Jewish flag, which Mazal had stitched late into the night, was carried by the child Yehuda. Sara's grandson neither laughed nor sang, but stared at the excitement about him as though struggling to comprehend it. Slender Amnon, wearing the mufti dress uniform of the ghaffirs, urged the younger children to march in formation. Elana and Nadav Langerfeld distributed blue-and-white balloons, which inevitably were loosed into the clear sky, where they floated lazily out to sea.

Ezra noticed a new spontaneity between his oldest daughter and her husband. The war had altered Nadav. He had become a man of action, and a new confidence distinguished him, an assertiveness to which Elana responded with a loving softness. She had missed Nadav during his absences, and her heart beat faster when he returned.

"Tell your father . . . ask your father," she would advise Shlomo when he complained to her of a hurt real or imagined, another child's cruelty, a teacher's injustice. Nadav was in charge. He would cope. Once, when Nadav was in Baghdad, she had dreamed about him and awakened, remembering that in the dream his eyes had been as blue as Achmed's, as Shlomo's. She did not ponder it. She was pregnant again, and she carried this new child with gladness. A baby conceived in love, to be born during a time of peace.

Ruth and Amos chatted with Liesel and Moshe Aharoni. The newly married couple would soon take charge of a children's village on the outskirts of Jerusalem. Ruth and Mazal had promised that Chemed crafts would decorate the children's rooms.

"They must be homelike," Liesel said urgently. The children who lived in them would have to be taught again the intricacies of home life, the mysteries of soft cushions, of pictures hanging on freshly painted walls. Mazal had had to coax small Yehuda to sleep beneath the clean sheets of his bed, to eat his fresh breakfast roll rather than conceal it in his pocket.

The Gan Noar family carried in kegs of beer, brewed from the new crop of hops introduced by the newcomers from Germany.

"You must try it on Hanita," they told Balfouria and Daniel, who sipped the golden liquid and allowed mustaches of foam to form above their lips. Daniel licked hers away, and they lifted their instruments and played lively melodies for the dances of victory. The Maimon family and their friends linked arms and whirled about the ancient beach palm which Elana's grandfather had refused to cut down because it bore witness that a city had been built on the sands.

"We have come to the land," they sang, "to build and be built by her."

Ezra gripped Mazal's waist and danced her into the heart of the circle. Her gold-flecked eyes were moist, and waves of silver crested her jet-black hair. He held her even tighter, his tiny bride, the mother of his children, the sweet companion of his long and dangerous journeys.

Moshe and Liesel, Ruth and Amos, Elana and Nadav, Balfouria and Daniel dipped back and forth in a lilting debka while the children abandoned their flags and games and swept about in a wild dervish. Saul and David, the twins, danced the low *chazatski* of their birthland. Aging men, their bright hair faded to whiteness, they reclaimed their youth through the strength of music, the joy of victory.

"The nation of Israel lives. David the king endures." Their voices grew hoarse and their faces gleamed with sweat, but they danced on.

At dusk, they stood on the beach and watched the fireworks. Rockets of red, white, and blue splashed riotously across the soft evening light. Crimson stars danced in shimmering vortices and turned the Mediterranean the color of anemones. Blue-and-white arrows burst into flares of iridescent light while music blared from radios and loudspeakers. Anthems converged upon each other. The "Marseillaise" and "God Save the King," "The Star Spangled Banner" and "HaTikvah," the "Internationale" and the battle hymn which Chaim Guri had written for the clandestine Jewish army. There was a brief silence, then a young girl's sweet contralto rose in the hymn of the Partisans, the song sung by the fighters of the Warsaw Ghetto.

"You must not say that you now walk the final way
Because the darkened heavens hide the blue of day.
The time we've longed for will at last draw near
And our steps as drums will sound that we are here."

Other voices joined her, and the song of the fallen heroes swelled in a mighty chorus across the beach front and in the gardens and along the boulevards of the young city named for the sweet promise of springtime.

Later, when the younger children were at last asleep, Ezra and Mazal walked to the heart of the city. They made their way through the crowds of young people dancing frenzied horas about lampposts, to the brightly lit expanse of Mograbi Square. The arched windows of the Municipal Building were draped with an enormous Jewish flag, fringed with borders of black. On this day of victory, the countless dead were not forgotten.

Names and numbers swam in Ezra's memory. Millions had been lost in the death camps of Europe. Fruma Shifra, the tiny baby whose body had been shattered on the paving stones of a

...tz in Auschwitz, drifted through his thoughts. He seemed to feel again the fragile pages of Sara's last letter. But at least her legacy had been fulfilled and the child, Yehuda, had been found.

A cordon of boys and girls, hands on each other's shoulders, swept across the square in an intricate snake dance. He imagined shadows adhering to their graceful moving bodies, so lithe and spirited—the shadows of the dead who would never dance again. The two hundred thousand Jewish soldiers in Red army uniform lost on battlefields and in German prison camps. Scores of Jewish Brigadiers buried in Crete and Syria, Iraq and North Africa, Italy and Austria. Brave Orde Wingate lost in a plane crash over Burma. Sara. Shimon. Sara's daughter Sophia and her small children. The children of the *Struma*. Sammy Wade, whose eyes, like those of Yehuda Schoenbaum, were the color of the sea. Lives had been lost and lives had been reclaimed. His cheeks were wet. Startled, he realized that he was crying.

Slowly, hand in hand, he and Mazal walked on to the Grand Synagogue on Allenby Street, their children following them. Rabbi Yitzhak HaLevi Herzog, holding a braided candle whose leaping flame sent prisms of golden light across his white beard, stood on the steps of the building. Sonorously, he read from the Eighteenth Psalm: "They encompassed me about like bees; they are quenched as a fire of thorns."

Now crowds of young people surged through the streets, thousands strong, their voices raised as one in a thunderous plea.

"Open the gates of Palestine! The gates of Palestine must be open!"

Ezra sighed. The war was over and the war was begun. Hitler was defeated, but the British still ruled Palestine, and wide-eyed children still stared out at the world from behind gates of barbed wire, walls of brick. They had triumphed, but there was no quenching of a fire of thorns. Mazal's small body pressed against his own, and his children encircled him. Amos and Elana, Balfouria and Amnon, the children of his dreams, inheritors of his hopes. Their faces glowed golden in the light of the torches carried by the marchers. The next war would be theirs. The new griefs, the new joys of the land of their birth

belonged to them. His heart turned with fear and swelled
pride. They were singing now, and his own trembling voice
mingled with theirs.

"From lands all green with palms to lands all white
        with snow
We now arrive with all our pain and woe.
Where our blood sprayed out and came to touch the land
There our courage and our manhood rise and stand."